# ALWAYS

# TIME

# TO DIE

# ALWAYS TIME TO DIE

# ELIZABETH LOWELL

**HarperLargePrint**
*An Imprint of* HarperCollins*Publishers*

This book is a work of fiction. The characters, incidents, and dia-
logue are drawn from the author's imagination and are not to be
construed as real. Any resemblance to actual events or persons, living or dead, is entirely coincidental.

ALWAYS TIME TO DIE. Copyright © 2005 by Two of a Kind, Inc. All
rights reserved. Printed in the United States of America. No part
of this book may be used or reproduced in any manner whatsoever
without written permission except in the case of brief quotations
embodied in critical articles and reviews. For information address
HarperCollins Publishers, 10 East 53rd Street, New York, NY
10022.

HarperCollins books may be purchased for educational, business,
or sales promotional use. For information please write: Special
Markets Department, HarperCollins Publishers, 10 East 53rd
Street, New York, NY 10022.

FIRST HARPER LARGE PRINT EDITION

Printed on acid-free paper

---

Library of Congress Cataloging-in-Publication Data

Lowell, Elizabeth, 1944–
    Always time to die / by Elizabeth Lowell.—1st ed.
        p.   cm.
    ISBN 0-06-050415-3 (Hardcover)
    1. Women genealogists—Fiction. 2. Governors—Family
relationships—Fiction. 3. Millionaires—Fiction. 4. New
Mexico—Fiction. I. Title.

PS3562.O8847A79   2005
813'.54—dc22                                        2004065639

---

ISBN 0-06-078717-1 (Large Print)

05 06 07 08 09 WBC/RRD 10 9 8 7 6 5 4 3 2 1

**This Large Print Book carries the
Seal of Approval of N.A.V.H.**

# For
# Eric and Miranda

# The future is yours.

# QUINTRELL LINE
## MALE DESCENT

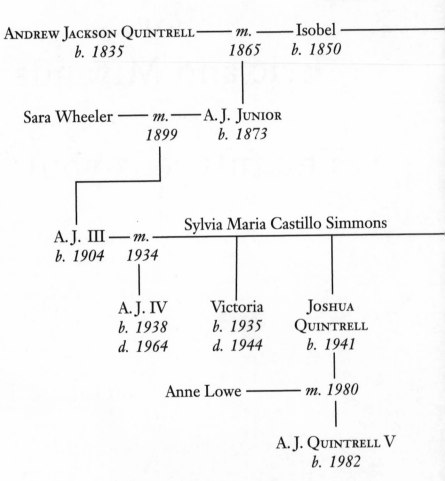

Castillo

Andrew Jackson Quintrell ——— *m.* ———Isobel ———————
b. 1835                        1865      b. 1850

Sara Wheeler ——— *m.* ———A. J. Junior
            1899          b. 1873

Sylvia Maria Castillo Simmons

A. J. III —— *m.* ———————————————————————
b. 1904    1934

A. J. IV      Victoria      Joshua
b. 1938      b. 1935      Quintrell
d. 1964      d. 1944      b. 1941

Anne Lowe ——————— *m.* 1980

A. J. Quintrell V
b. 1982

## Sisters

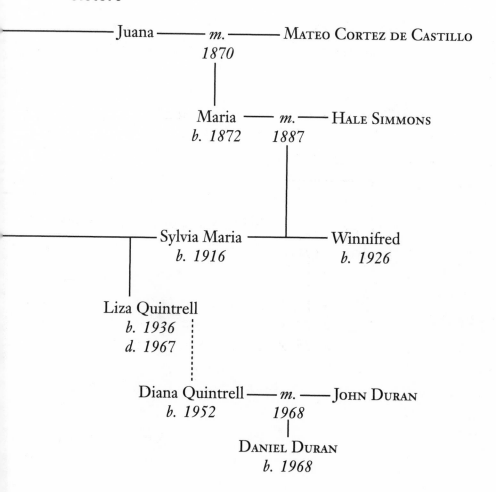

Juana —— *m.* —— Mateo Cortez de Castillo
*1870*

Maria —— *m.* —— Hale Simmons
*b. 1872*    *1887*

Sylvia Maria —————— Winnifred
*b. 1916*                      *b. 1926*

Liza Quintrell
*b. 1936*
*d. 1967*

Diana Quintrell —— *m.* —— John Duran
*b. 1952*              *1968*

Daniel Duran
*b. 1968*

# ALWAYS
# TIME
# TO DIE

# PROLOGUE

THE CUTTING EDGE OF A WINTER STORM MADE THE old house sigh and moan as if someone was dying.

**Someone is. Soon.**

The ghostly smile, the laughter, and the words were silent.

No one saw the intruder glide across the ancient Persian carpet on soundless feet. No one heard the door to the library open.

The hospital bed and oxygen bottle looked bizarre among the ranks of leather-bound books and gilt-framed portraits of Andrew Jackson Quintrell I and his wife, Isobel Mercedes Archuleta y Castillo. The ambition that had created one of New Mexico's biggest ranches and launched the national political careers of future Quintrells blazed out of A. J. Quintrell's Yankee blue eyes. The matching ambition of one of New Mexico's oldest families smoldered in Isobel's hazel green eyes.

The old man lying motionless on the hospital bed was their grandson. The fires of ambition had almost burned out in him. He would end his life as he had begun it, on the Quintrell ranch. No hospitals, no nurses, no doctors. No muttering and fussing and false smiles of hope.

There wasn't any hope.

For nearly a century the Senator had enjoyed the wealth and prestige and power of the Quintrell family. For eighty years he had run the family with the closed fist of absolute power. Now he was slowly succumbing to congestive heart failure. At the moment, oxygen made him rest easier. In time it wouldn't help. Then he would drown.

**Die, old man. Why can't you just die and save us all a lot of trouble?**

No answer came but the slow, shallow, damnably steady breathing of Andrew Jackson Quintrell III.

**You lived like a pagan king. Why couldn't you just die that way? But no, you had to have it all—pagan life and Christian afterlife.**

Father Roybal would be visiting again this morning, urging former Senator Quintrell to purge his soul of all evil and reach out for God's forgiveness. Forgiveness would be there, waiting for him.

It always was for prodigal sons.

**Confession might be good for the soul, but it's hell on the living. I don't want to live in hell, old man.**

**It's your turn to do that.**

**Finally.**

Gloved hands removed the oxygen tube from the Senator's nose. Gloved hands took a pillow from the bed and pressed it gently, firmly, relentlessly over the old man's face. Breathing slowed, then stopped. He stirred just a little at first and then urgently, almost violently, but he was no match for the deadly gentleness that shut off his air. A minute, two minutes, and it was over, breath and heart stopped, death where life had been.

It took less time than that for the murderer to tidy up the bed, reinsert the oxygen tube, replace the pillow, and walk out into the bitter caress of night.

# 1

TWO MEN SQUINTED AGAINST THE WIND AND stared down at the Quintrell family graveyard. It lay a few hundred yards below and six hundred feet away from the base of the long, ragged ridge where they stood. A white wrought-iron fence enclosed the graveyard, as though death could be kept away from the living by such a simple thing.

At the edge of the valley, piñons grew black against a thin veneer of snow. Cottonwood branches along the valley creek had been stripped by winter to their thin, pale skin. In the black-and-white landscape, a ragged rectangle and a nearby tarp-covered mound of loose red dirt looked out of place. Three ravens squatted on the tarp like guests waiting to be served. A polished casket hovered astride the newly dug grave, ready to be lowered at a signal from the minister.

The first of the funeral procession drove up and stopped outside the ornate white fence. There wouldn't be many cars, because the graveside service was limited to clergy and immediate members of the Senator's family. The public service had been yesterday, in Santa Fe, complete with a media circus where the famous and the merely notorious exchanged Cheshire cat grins and firm handshakes and careful lies while the smell of dying flowers overwhelmed the stately cathedral.

Automatically Daniel Duran looked over his shoulder, checking that his silhouette was still invisible from below, lost against a tall pine. It was. So was his father's.

He and John weren't famous or notorious. They hadn't been invited to either the memorial or funeral service for the dead man everyone called the Senator. The lack of invitations didn't matter to Dan. He wouldn't have gone anyway.

**So why am I here?**

It was a good question. He didn't have an answer. He wasn't even sure he wanted one.

The wind rushing down from the harsh peaks of the Sangre de Cristo Mountains tasted of snow and distance and the kind of time that made most people uncomfortable. Deep time. Unimaginable time. Time so great it reduced humanity to an amusing footnote in Earth's four-billion-year history.

Dan liked that kind of time. Humans **were** amusing. Laughable. It was the only way to stay sane.

And that was something he'd promised himself he wouldn't think about for a few months. Staying sane.

**If you can keep your head when all about you are losing theirs, chances are you don't understand the situation. Why else would ignorance be called bliss?**

With a grim smile he turned so that his injured leg didn't take the force of the brutal wind.

"You should have stayed home," John Duran said.

Dan gave his father a sidelong look. "The exercise is good for my leg."

"That old man never acknowledged you or your mother as kin. Hell, he barely acknowledged his own legitimate daughter."

Dan shrugged and let the wind comb dark hair he hadn't bothered to have cut in months. "I don't take it personally. He never acknowledged any of his bastards."

"So why bother hiking here for the Senator's funeral? And don't waste your breath on the exercise excuse. You could do laps around the Taos town square with a lot less trouble."

For a time there was only the sound of the ice-tipped wind scouring the ridge. Finally Dan said, "I don't know."

John grunted. He doubted that his fiercely bright son didn't know why they were freezing their nuts off on Castillo Ridge watching one of New Mexico's most famous womanizers get buried. Then again, maybe Dan truly didn't know.

"You sure?" John asked.

"Yeah."

"Well, that's the most hopeful thing that's happened since you turned up three months ago."

Once, Dan would have smiled, but that was before pain had etched his face and cynicism had eroded his soul. "How so?"

"You cared about something enough to walk three miles in the snow."

Dan's dark brown eyebrows lifted. "Have I been that bad?"

"No," his father said slowly. "But you're different. Much less smile. Too much steel. Less laughter. More silence. Too old to be thirty-four."

Dan didn't argue. It was the truth.

"It's more than the injury," John said, waving at his son's right leg, where metal and pain had exploded through flesh. "Muscle and bone heals. Emotions . . ." He sighed. "Well, they take longer. And sometimes they just don't heal at all."

"You're thinking of Mom and whatever happened with her mother."

John nodded. "She still doesn't talk about it."

"Good for her." **I hope.**

"You didn't feel that way a few years ago."

"A few years ago I didn't understand about sleeping dogs and land mines. Now I do."

And that's what was bothering Dan. The Senator's sister-in-law Winifred was running around kicking sleeping dogs right and left. Sooner or later she would step on a land mine and wake up something so brutal that his own mother had never once spoken of it, even to the man she loved.

Silently the two men watched the shiny white hearse wait next to the graveyard's wide gate. The couple in the rear seat, Josh Quintrell and his wife Anne, waited for the driver to open their doors. Their son, A.J. V, called Andy, got out and turned his back to the windblown snow. When his parents stepped into the gray daylight, their clothes were as black as the ravens perched on the graveside tarp.

A second car pulled up close to the hearse. As soon as it stopped, a tall, lanky woman emerged into the bitter wind with just enough hesitation to show her age. The iron gray of her hair beneath a black lace mantilla marked her as Winifred Simmons y Castillo, sister-in-law to the dead Senator, and a woman who in more than seven decades hadn't found a man—or anything else—she couldn't live without.

"Hell on wheels," John said almost admiringly.

"Is that what you call someone who looks for land mines by stomping and kicking everything in sight?"

John shook his head and shut up. He didn't know why Dan was upset by Winifred's quest for her family's past. When he'd asked what the problem was, Dan had shut down, all hard edges and silence. John hadn't asked again. When his son had worked for the federal government, he hadn't talked about his job. After he'd quit a few years ago to work for St. Kilda Consulting, he still didn't talk about his job.

Another figure got out of the car with the lithe energy of youth. Whatever the woman wore was concealed beneath an overcoat that went to her ankles. The loosely tied wool scarf around her head lifted in the wind. She snatched it with gloved hands and knotted it more securely. But for just a moment, rich auburn hair burned in the winter light with the vivid colors of life.

"That her?" John asked.

"The fool who's going to go stomping around in the Quintrell minefield? Yeah, that's her, one Carolina May, Carly to her friends."

"You check her out?"

"What do you think?"

"You did. And?"

"Sweet Carly hasn't a clue."

John grunted. "Too bad."

"Shit happens."

The gate clanged open and the ravens flew into the pale cottonwood branches to wait.

# 2

CARLY MAY HAD BEEN RAISED IN THE COLORADO Rockies, which meant that she was no stranger to the knife-dry cold of a mountain winter. Even so, her hands felt numb beneath the black gloves she'd hastily bought for the funeral. Part of Carly, the part that loved to discover and write family histories, was honored to be at the renowned Senator Quintrell's family funeral. The rest of her felt like the outsider she was. No news there. She'd been an outsider all her life.

Hoping she looked suitably attentive to the funeral of a man she'd never met, Carly mentally checked off a list of the electronics and clothes she'd crammed into her little SUV. After Winifred Simmons's demand that Carly come to the ranch four weeks early to work on the Castillo family history, she'd shipped some of her basic genealogical supplies by overnight air to the Quintrell ranch. They hadn't been waiting for her when she'd arrived last night, exhausted by the drive from her northern Colorado home.

She bit back a yawn and focused on the grave. This was what she had rushed here for, to witness and relate for future generations the funeral of a legendary man.

". . . not to mourn the passing of a great man," the minister said, "but to celebrate his transition from the bitter coils of . . ."

Carly kept a straight face while the minister sliced and diced Shakespeare to fit a former senator's graveside eulogy. She glanced sideways at another man of the cloth, a priest who had hoped to be celebrating the conversion of a dying celebrity to Catholicism. Father Roybal was here at the special invitation of Josh Quintrell, the Senator's only surviving child and the governor of the great state of New Mexico. Despite the honor, the good father looked like he would rather be saying mass than standing mute. Or perhaps he was simply unhappy over losing one of the best-known souls in the nation.

The wind flexed and raked icy nails over the land. Anne Quintrell pulled her mid-calf sable coat more closely around her and raised the wide hood over her head. Yesterday in Santa Fe, where cameras flashed and TV lights burned like wild stars, she'd worn a simple black wool coat. The fact that she'd been born to sable rather than wool was something that she and her husband were careful not to parade in front of voters. No matter how blue the blood, when cameras were present near a man who had presidential hopes, the man dressed like Abe Lincoln and made sure his wife did the same.

Carly noted Anne's rich sable coat with the same detachment that she'd noted Miss Winifred's occasional chesty cough and the lines of fatigue on Governor Josh Quintrell's face. Even when you were over sixty, losing your father was hard.

". . . with the blessed as they wend their solitary way . . ."

Now the minister was mining Milton. Carly ducked her head to hide a smile and wished she'd been brave enough to bring her recorder to the graveside. She didn't want to lose any of the small facts that would transform the Quintrell family history from a dry genealogy to a living story of hope and loss, hate and love, success and tears and laughter. But she'd only been here a few hours, and hadn't quite dared ask to be allowed to digitize the private service.

The minister kept talking despite the fact that his audience showed every sign of being cold and miserable. Even the relentless wind couldn't hurry the man along. He'd come with a feast of platitudes and intended to serve up every oily crumb.

Carly shut him out. Despite her work of researching and writing family histories, she hadn't

attended any funerals professionally until this one.
Usually she was called in before the fact of death,
when someone felt the chill whisper of mortality
and truly believed for the first time **I will die.** That
was when people wanted to fix their place not only
among the dead, but among the survivors.

**See me and know you will die, too.**

She wiggled her numb toes inside dress boots that
hadn't been designed for standing around on frozen
ground while a minister of very ordinary intellect
tried to encompass life's greatest mystery by pillag-
ing the work of dead poets.

". . . burning in the forest of the night . . ."

It was Blake's turn on the chopping block. Carly
glanced beneath her long dark lashes, trying to see
how the audience was responding to the lame
eulogy. Andrew Jackson Quintrell V looked green
around the edges, but that probably had more to do
with a pulsing hangover than the minister's words.
Anne Quintrell had no expression except occasional
wariness when she glanced at her twenty-three-
year-old son to see if he was still standing. Josh
looked worn and sad or maybe just cold and bored.
With a professional politician it was hard to tell. He
certainly was a good-looking man, standing tall and
straight in his sixties, with a mane of wind-tossed
silver hair and brilliant blue eyes.

Miss Winifred looked raven-eyed and bleak. She, too, stood tall and straight, but lacked her nephew's muscularity. She was as gaunt as the winter cottonwoods.

". . . held him green and dying . . ."

Another poet raped. Carly swallowed hard but still made a stifled sound. She sensed Miss Winifred looking at her and schooled her mouth into a flat line. Now was the wrong time to let her peculiar sense of humor off its leash.

**Think of something sad,** she told herself firmly. **Think of Dylan Thomas spinning in his grave.**

A raven made liquid noises as it talked to itself in the cottonwoods. The sounds were too much like laughter for Carly's comfort. She bit the inside of her lip—hard—and hid her emotions beneath a blank face. It was the same thing she'd done all through her school years, when assignments about searching out your parents were given out, or when questions were asked about her family history.

She was adopted. The file was sealed. End of assignment and casual conversation.

But not an end to feeling different, to being outside the vast mainstream of human experience, a nameless reject from someone's family tree.

**Stop with the pity party,** Carly told herself.

**Martha and Glenn raised me better than most kids are raised by their biological parents.**

She shifted, trying to bring her feet to life.

The minister was made of sterner stuff. Only his lips moved.

Andy glanced sideways at Carly and winked. She ignored him. Even without the green tinge to his skin, the scion of the Quintrell family didn't appeal to her. He was a little too in love with himself. All right, a lot too in love with himself. Unfortunately, other than the employees' kids, Carly was the only woman under forty on the whole ranch. Two seconds after Andy met her, he'd decided that she was going to take the curse off the boring rural nights.

Finally the minister ran out of poets and signaled for the casket to be lowered into the grave. The mechanism worked slowly and not quite silently. When it was finally still, Josh threw the obligatory handful of dirt on the casket.

"Ashes to ashes, dust to dust," he said quietly.

Winifred surprised everyone by dumping a double handful of soil onto the casket. Her expression said she'd like to shovel more in and be done with it—and the Senator.

Carly made a mental note of her employer's hard pleasure in the Senator's death. If any of the Quintrells were surprised by Winifred's actions, no one showed it. That, too, intrigued Carly. Emotions were the flesh and wine of family history.

As the governor and his wife withdrew from the graveside, Father Roybal went to Josh. "I'm sorry, my son. Although the Senator never confessed to me, I feel that God will welcome this good man's soul into His keeping."

Winifred made a sound rather like the raven's.

Josh ignored her. "Thank you, Father Roybal. You and your church have brought comfort to many of New Mexico's citizens. I'll be certain to express the Quintrell family's appreciation in a more tangible way in the years to come."

The other man nodded. Like Josh, the priest knew that many of the citizens in the state were Catholic. Any good deeds done for the Catholic church by the governor would please a lot of voters.

"May I come and talk with you as I did your father?" Roybal asked.

"Unlike the Senator, I'm content in my religion," Josh said easily. "If that changes, I'll seek your counsel."

Roybal was young and ambitious, but he wasn't stupid. He accepted the refusal with grace. "I will keep your family in my prayers."

"Thank you, Father." Josh took Anne's elbow to help her over the frozen earth toward the hearse. "Prayers are always welcome."

Carly watched the state's first couple head toward the relative warmth of the hearse, followed by the Protestant minister and the Catholic priest. Each man of God had his own modest car. Vehicle doors opened and closed in a series of sharp noises.

She glanced at Winifred hopefully. The old woman was looking into the grave with an odd expression on her face. It could have been regret or even pleasure. It could have been indigestion. Carly didn't know Winifred well enough to judge. But if Carly had to bet, she'd go with a grim kind of pleasure.

"Carly?" Andy said. "Why don't you ride back with us? There's plenty of room. We could talk about family and things."

Winifred shot him a black look. "I'm paying her, not you. When I want her to interview you, I'll tell you."

"Hey. Indentured servitude is passé," Andy said. "She's a fully grown woman. She can talk for herself."

"She certainly can," Carly said distinctly. "Thank you for the offer of a ride, but Miss Simmons y Castillo and I have a lot to discuss before I'll be ready to interview family members."

"I won't be here long," Andy warned.

**Thank God.** Carly managed a smile. "Telephones work for me."

"They aren't very personal."

"Handicaps just make a job more interesting."

Andy's blue eyes narrowed. He turned and stalked after his parents.

Winifred laughed, a sound almost as rusty as a raven's warning cry. "Just like the Senator. Doesn't think there's a female alive that won't spread her legs for him."

Carly hesitated, then decided that it had to be covered sometime, and now was as good as any. "My research hinted that the Senator was rumored to be very, um, sexually active when he was young."

"He lifted every skirt he could get his hands on, and he got his hands on most. When he was too old to perform, he got those erection pills and kept at it until he died."

Carly's eyebrows rose. "He managed to keep his romantic life out of the media."

"Romance had nothing to do with it." Winifred's thin upper lip curled. "Lust, that's all. The reporters always knew how he spent his nights and lunch breaks. But back then, a politician could fornicate with anything willing or unwilling and no one said a word. Then Clinton came along." Winifred made a dismissive gesture. "By that time the Senator was on his way out of elected public life. Stories about his shopgirls and prostitutes weren't news anymore."

Carly made her all-purpose sound that said she was listening. It was what she was best at: listening.

And remembering.

"Who are those people?" she asked, looking beyond the fence. "The ones who didn't come to the graveside."

Winifred looked at the couple waiting patiently just outside the gate. "Pete and Melissa Moore. Employees. He's the Senator's accountant. She's the housekeeper."

**The one who forgot I was coming?**

But Carly didn't say it aloud. The Senator's death must have thrown the household into turmoil. She would find out when she met Melissa if there was anything deliberate in the oversight. Carly hoped there wasn't and at the same time was prepared for the opposite. It wouldn't be the first time she hadn't been welcomed by some members of the household whose history she'd been hired to record. An important part of her job was to disarm hostile people, getting them to relax and open up to her.

"Well, no need to stand here freezing," Winifred said. "Leave the diggers to finish their work. Then I'm going to buy some shiny red shoes and dance on that philandering bastard's grave."

The old woman marched toward the waiting car with the stride of a woman decades younger than her nearly eighty years.

Carly glanced for the last time at the grave, memorizing small details of color and temperature, wind and scent. After a few moments she sensed a flicker of motion on the ridge that defined the other side of the valley. She looked up just in time to see two silhouettes drop down the far side and out of sight.

Someone hadn't even cared enough to stand outside the fence.

**When I get to know Miss Winifred better, I'll have to ask her who else wants to dance on the Senator's grave.**

The only tears cried at this funeral had been clawed out by the icy wind.

# 3

THE DURAN FAMILY LIVED ON THE OUTSKIRTS OF Taos, beyond the tourist area with its timeless adobe buildings and modern parking meters measuring out minutes in silver coins. The Durans inhabited a Taos few visitors saw, a place of modest houses crouched among winter-bare pastures, surrounded by willow-stick and barbwire fences.

John drove into a narrow adobe garage that had once been a tack room and turned off his truck. Though the building was more than two hundred years old, it had been wired in the twentieth century. Motion-sensing lights flashed to life, revealing every timeworn adobe brick. The space itself was clean. Neither of Dan's parents tolerated garbage, clutter, or worn-out machinery tossed around the property. Some of the neighbors felt that every man had a right to his own junkyard, but no one got upset about it either way. New Mexico had a long history of live and let live.

"You think Mom's back from the pueblo yet?" Dan asked.

John glanced at his watch. Two o'clock. "She should be. She teaches after the noon mass."

"Still doing English?"

"It's what the kids need most. She does some simple math, too."

Dan shook his head. "She never gives up, does she?"

"That's why I love her. Heart as big as the sky. You should get a good woman to make you happy."

"I'm already happy."

"Really? You better wear a sign. Otherwise your expression will scare small children."

"Yeah yeah yeah," Dan said without much heat. He knew his father was right, but that didn't change his memories of the past twelve years, the years when he'd experienced firsthand just how much of an animal man could be.

He shoved the memories away. They didn't have anything new to teach him. He didn't have anything new to bring to them. That was why he'd come home, hoping to find something new, something worth the pain of living for it.

John waited, hoped, but Dan didn't say another word. "You're like your mother. You keep it inside."

Dan didn't answer.

John didn't expect him to.

The back door opened before Dan put his foot on

the first step up to the narrow porch. Diana's hair was short and dark black except for a wide streak of white at her left temple, legacy of a nameless ancestor. Her eyes were as dark and clear as ever, and her smile just as unexpected in her serious face. Gently rounded and as determined as any man, Dan's mother was the light of many lives, including her son's.

"That was certainly a long walk," she said, watching him climb the stairs. Though she didn't say anything, concern for his injury was in her eyes and in the troubled line of her mouth. "You must be freezing."

Dan scooped her up in a hug and set her down gently. "I'm too big to freeze." He sniffed the air that was rushing out of the kitchen. "What's that?"

Diana gave John a worried look. He shook his head slightly.

"Posole soup and fresh tortillas," she said, frowning. "I've got the woodstove going. Come in and warm your— Get warm," she corrected quickly. Dan didn't like discussing, or even acknowledging, his injured leg. Despite that, she couldn't help wanting to ease the pain she saw occasionally in his face. "And carnitas. You didn't eat much breakfast before you left."

Dan's gentle smile was at odds with the grim lines

that usually bracketed his mouth. "I'm not a teenager anymore, **Mamacita**. I'm all grown up."

"But—" She bit back her worry. Her son wasn't a child to be fussed over, yet she had a lifetime of nurturing reflexes that made her want to coddle and cuddle him. "Coffee, too. Just the way you like it."

"Hot as hell and twice as bitter," John said unhappily. "Whoopee."

Diana stood on tiptoe and kissed her husband's mustache. "I made a second pot for you."

Dan heard his mother giggle like a teenager behind him and knew that his father was nibbling on her neck. Dan smiled slightly, almost sadly. The older he got, the more he wondered if he'd ever find a woman or if—as he suspected—he was better suited for living alone.

With a stifled groan, he eased himself into the chair that was pulled up close to the old woodburning stove. Piñon crackled and burned hotly, scenting the air almost as much as the food bubbling on the stove itself. He dragged off his coat and hung it over the back of the chair. The black turtleneck he wore under his denim shirt was made of a high-tech cloth that breathed when it was hot and held heat when it was cold. At least, that was the theory. There was always an uncomfortable time before the cloth decided what it should do.

Right now, he was hot enough to think about going back out to the garage.

"So, did you see Mrs. Rincon on your walk?" Diana asked John.

"Didn't go that way."

"Ah, then you saw Señor Montez. How is his gout?"

"Didn't go that way either," John said.

Diana paused in dishing up soup. "No? At least you saw the Millers. Is their newborn—"

"We didn't go there," John interrupted.

Dan waited tensely for his mother to ask where they had gone.

She didn't. Sometimes she could be just as tight-lipped with her family as she was with everyone else except children. She set the food out in front of her men and went to stir the fire.

Dan looked at the rigid line of his mother's back and sighed. She didn't have to ask where he'd been. She knew. He didn't understand how she knew, but he was used to that. He'd inherited her fey ability to take a few words here and an expression there and come up with a conclusion that left other people wondering how he'd seen what they hadn't. It was a gift associated with curandero blood, with natural healers, but Dan had never felt any call to herbs or potions.

"Mom," he began unhappily.

"No." Her voice was flat. She reached in her pocket for a tissue and held it to her nose. A spot of red appeared. Then another. The dry winter air always made her nose bleed. Not much, just enough to be annoying. She tipped her head back and pressed hard. "I will not hear the name of evil spoken in this house."

"He was just a—"

"He was evil," Diana cut in, crossing herself. "Do not say his name in my presence."

"He was your grandfather," Dan said.

She tilted her head forward, felt no more blood, and stuffed the tissue in her pocket. After she washed her hands, she picked up a plate of steaming tortillas and set them down in front of Dan with enough force to make them flutter.

Silence.

"Men do evil things," Dan said, "but they're still human."

Silence.

"He was my great-grandfather. I wanted to . . ." Dan's voice died. "I don't know what I wanted. I just knew I had to go."

"You did and it's done," Diana said. "Now eat."

Dan glanced at John. His father had a worn,

unhappy look on his face, the same look that came every time the subject of the Senator arose.

**How can Dad stand living with her pain, with the ingrained fear of the past that lives beneath her silence?**

For some people, time healed. For his mother, time made everything worse.

Abruptly Dan stood up, tired of dodging around family taboos and ignoring the dark, bitter currents that flowed deep beneath his mother's quiet surface. His leg protested the sudden change of position, but held with little more than a sharp reminder of injury. The high, clean air of Taos was doing more to heal him than all the hospitals, surgeries, and medications had.

"Silence won't make it go away," Dan said in a level voice. "If it did, you'd be free. Why let a cruel old man ruin the rest of your life the same way he must have ruined your mother's?"

"What happened to sleeping dogs and land mines?" John asked his son roughly. "Eat or take a walk."

"Shit," Dan said under his breath.

"You'll not swear in your mother's presence."

"Sorry, Mother," Dan said neutrally. "I keep forgetting that reality isn't welcome here."

"Daniel." John's voice was a warning.

Dan lifted his coat off the back of the chair and

said to his father, "Call me when you want to get that tractor running."

He closed the back door carefully and told himself he couldn't hear his mother weeping.

But he could.

# 4

ANDY QUINTRELL V REACHED FOR ANOTHER BEER, only to have his father take the can away.

"You need to sober up," Josh said.

"Why?" Andy waved his hand casually. "Not a camera in sight."

"Winifred's pet historian has cameras and her digital recorder is always on."

"Who cares?"

Anne Quintrell walked into the kitchen. "I do. Your father does. You **should**."

"Because you want me to be a senator when I'm thirty?" Andy belched richly, legacy of the two beers he'd drunk without a pause. "What about what **I** want, huh? What about that?"

Anne smoothed back hair that was already perfectly in place. "What do you want?"

"To get laid."

Disgust flickered over Anne's face.

Josh laughed roughly. "A real chip off the old block, aren't you?"

"Hey, Granddad humped everything he saw and he spent his whole life being reelected."

"That was then," Josh said. "Today that kind of womanizing won't fly at the polls."

"Fuck the polls."

"It's about the only thing you haven't jumped," Anne said tiredly. "Why can't you just keep it zipped?"

Andy rolled his eyes. "Spoken like a nun."

"Then get married," Anne said. "The Meriwether girl would be an excellent wife."

Andy made retching sounds. "I've seen better-looking dog butts. Just because her father's a senator doesn't make her hot."

"Hot?" Casually Josh reached out and jerked his son to his feet. "Listen to me, Andy, and listen good. I've had it with your hyperactive dick."

"Josh—" Anne began.

"Not now," Josh said without looking away from his son. "You have two choices. Grow up or sign up for the Marines. They've made men out of sorrier boys than you."

Andy closed his eyes. "Not another lecture on the value of serving your country."

"No lecture. Just fact. I'm through supporting you and I won't let your mother give you so much as a dime."

Andy's eyes snapped open. What he saw in his father's eyes made him cold.

Josh nodded. "That's right. This is the end of the line. The Senator kept seeing himself in you, kept smiling at the thought of you drinking and screwing your way through life."

"He understood me," Andy said.

"He's dead. Times change." Josh let go of his son. "Change with them or get your spoiled ass out of my life."

Andy looked at his mother.

"No," Josh said. "She can't help you. The Senator who understood you so well left everything to me."

"How will it look if you simply throw out your only child?" Anne asked quietly.

"I'll pay for rehab in Santa Fe. After that, he's on his own."

"Rehab?" Andy said. "You're crazy. I'm not an alcoholic or—"

"If you refuse rehab," Josh interrupted, "I'll give a more-in-sorrow-than-in-anger interview to Jeanette Dykstra for her sniggering TV show. There are more parents out there with screwups for kids than solid citizens. If anything, my standing in the polls will go up."

"That's all you care about!" Andy shouted. "That's all you've ever cared about!"

Josh shrugged. "And all you care about is getting laid. So what?"

A volatile mix of tears and rage shimmered in Andy's eyes. He pushed past Josh and slammed out the back door of the kitchen.

"He has an appointment in Santa Fe with the New Day Clinic on Monday at ten o'clock," Josh said to his wife. "If he doesn't keep it, he's on his own."

"But this is so . . . sudden," she said, shaking her head.

"Only for you. I've been ready to throw him out for ten years. But if I so much as lectured Andy, he'd go crying to you or the Senator."

"But Andy's so young," she whispered.

"Men his age have fought and killed and died."

"You say that like you approve."

Josh swore wearily. "We've had this conversation too many times. Andy either cleans up his act or I'll cut him loose. Conversation over."

"The king is dead, long live the king, is that it?"

"That's it."

Tears magnified her eyes. "I'll divorce you."

He smiled slightly. "No you won't. You want to be first lady as much as I want to be president. You've worked and sacrificed for that goal all our married life. You won't throw it away because a spoiled child pitches a fit."

Two tears slid down her cheeks. She didn't want to agree with him, and she knew that he was right. "You know me too well."

"That's what it's all about. Knowing people. When you know what they want, you have them by the short and curlies." He finished his coffee and set the cup aside. "I'll be in the Senator's study going through papers."

She sighed. "Need any help?"

"I'll let you know if I do."

But before he let anyone read over his shoulder, he'd be certain that the Senator had died without confessing his sins in a private journal.

# 5

CARLY WALKED DOWN A HALLWAY IN THE OLD Castillo home. With each step she murmured into her lapel, where she wore a nearly invisible microphone that was attached to a digital recorder at her waist.

"I wish the walls could talk," she said quietly.

The walls in question were adobe, more than two feet thick at the base, and older than the United States. At least, one of the walls was that old; it had once held up the front of the original Castillo ranch house. The other walls dated from the first quarter of the nineteenth century, when the Castillo in residence had been favored by the new nation of Mexico. With the new duties and authority came prosperity. The rectangular shape of a gracious Spanish-style home had been built around a courtyard alive with fruit trees and the silver dance of fountains.

From what Carly had discovered, the Castillos' enviable position had lasted only two decades, until

New Mexico was ceded by Mexico to the United States after the Treaty of Guadalupe Hidalgo. Then the customs of the Spanish, the Indians, and their culturally mixed children known as **genizaros** had bowed before the onslaught of Navajo raiders, Kit Carson, and land-hungry citizens from the eastern coast of the young, brawling United States.

"It seems so long ago to me," Carly said in a soft voice, running her fingertips over the much-plastered surface of the adobe wall. "But it isn't. Winifred's grandmother lived through it." **What would it be like to know who your grandparents and great-grandparents were, what they felt, how they'd lived?**

But that was one thought Carly didn't murmur into her microphone.

"The Castillo family, or some member of it, continuously occupied this house since it was built," she continued. "Then, after the new house was built by the Senator and his wife, the old house became basically a guest quarters. From the look of the furnishings—antique and in reasonably good condition except for the dust—the guest house hasn't been used very much."

She continued down the hall, then hesitated at the door leading to the central courtyard. "It's an odd feeling to see wooden doorsills worn concave by the passage of generations, doorways so small that I feel like ducking when I go through them, and I'm barely five foot four inches. Good food, good medicine, and suddenly bigger people are born to each generation."

With a hard tug, she opened, then pushed the door shut behind her. As she hurried across the courtyard, a few dead leaves lifted on the wind, curling around her ankles like a cold cat. She could have stayed warm by taking the longer route through the hallway-gallery that ran along the inner side of the rectangular house, but she felt the need for fresh air.

Winifred might have invited her to live in the old place while she worked on the Quintrell history, yet Carly had the uneasy feeling that everyone else would rather she went home.

When she'd arrived, the guest quarters weren't fit for a rat—which according to one of the maids, the ranch had plenty of. Winifred had been furious about the state of the guest quarters because "everyone knew" Carly was coming today. Rather than being apologetic about the oversight, the maids were surly, saying they hadn't been warned that the guest was coming a month early. Carly had overheard the maids talking flawless English with Winifred, but when it came to the forgotten guest, the language of the day was Spanish.

Carly had started to respond in kind, then decided

she could play the **yo no comprendo** game. So if
Carly lacked something in the guest quarters—
toilet paper for instance—she went to the main
house and got it or asked Winifred to tell the maids
what was needed. It was cumbersome, but worked
well enough once Carly understood the game. The
towels and sheets she'd requested were even clean,
if old enough to vote.

Besides, eavesdropping on the blond hispana maid
and her buddy was just another way to fill in the
gaps of the local story. At least Carly hoped it would
be. The tirades and weeping about Alma's no-good
ex-felon boyfriend were better suited to TV day-
time drama than the Quintrell family history.

The door leading into the entrance hall of the
guest house from the courtyard didn't respond to
Carly's key. She tried again, eyed the sagging doorframe, and gave the door a judicious thump just
below the lock. The door opened obediently.

**Wonder if the same trick would work on the
maids.**

Smiling slightly, Carly pulled the door shut
behind herself, discovered that the lock was broken,
not stubborn, and shrugged. The old house wasn't
exactly a magnet for visitors or thieves.

The front gallery was well rubbed and clean
beneath the dust, telling Carly that the neglect was
relatively recent.

"Wonder if the hired help used the Senator's illness to slack off," she said into the microphone. "I'm getting the feeling that Winifred doesn't have much clout around here. That could be a problem. If the living aren't willing to cooperate, I'll be stuck with photos and newspaper files and such. Oh well. Won't be the first time."

Unlike the other doors in the house, the openings leading into the outer world made a grand statement—huge double doors with a beautiful handmade wrought-iron bar thrown across the eight-foot width to secure the opening. The bar's grip was worn smooth by the countless times someone had grabbed it and moved it aside. The lock on the front doors was ancient and worked better than any modern lock in the house. The big skeleton key she'd been given turned easily and smoothly in the lock.

Carly hesitated, then shrugged and locked the door again behind her. Wind swept down from the cloud-shrouded peaks. She pulled her wool jacket more closely around her. The weaving was from the town of Chimayo, a place renowned for the quality of its wool garments. Bright, distinctive Southwest designs covered the jacket. The wool was thick and heavy, but no longer stiff. She'd worn the jacket for years and would wear it for years more. Chimayo weavings were made for the long run by people who understood the climate of northern New Mexico and southern Colorado.

The new house was a few hundred feet away. If dead or dormant plants were any indication, the pathway between the houses wound through a kitchen garden, a rose garden, and a family orchard. At the moment, everything that wasn't white with snow was brown and ragged.

"Note: Ask Winifred for photos and/or memories of the garden in spring and summer and fall. In the right seasons, it must have been a favorite place for parties and quiet breakfasts."

Carly ducked her head against the wind and moved as quickly as she dared with ice hiding under some patches of snow. Her shoes were sleek and leather and totally wrong for the outdoors at seven thousand feet in the winter. When she was more familiar with the intimidating Miss—**not Ms.**— Winifred, Carly would wear more casual shoes. Until then, it was leather shoes and wool slacks and cashmere turtlenecks under one of the three jackets she'd brought.

The new house had a sweeping modern design with a wall of triple-paned glass facing the Sangre de Cristo Mountains, which rose almost seven thousand feet above the Taos Valley floor. The layout of the house suggested a boomerang with the outer edge made of glass and the inner edge enclosing two sides of the patio with its zero-edge pool shimmering with concealed lights. Off to one side, connected by a glassed-in walkway, was an apartment once used by visiting dignitaries and now home to Pete and Melissa Moore.

"Interesting," Carly murmured into the microphone. "Most people cover their pools in winter. Wonder if there's a story behind that, or if it's just an oversight because of the Senator's long decline."

The shorter side of the boomerang enclosed Miss Winifred's suite and the specialized accommodations for her sister, Sylvia Quintrell, the Senator's widow. Not that Sylvia knew she was a widow. She hadn't spoken to anyone or otherwise acknowledged her surroundings since the 1960s.

"Note: See if there are any movies or videos of Mrs. Quintrell before her illness."

Carly crossed the patio, skirted the pool, and arrived at Winifred's door on a blast of wind that rocked her. She lifted the antique knocker—an upside-down horseshoe, to hold all the luck inside—and rapped three times.

No sound came from inside the house.

She waited, shivering in the wind. She'd decided to knock again, harder, when the door opened. Alma's angular, aloof face appeared in the narrow opening. The maid didn't say a word.

"Miss Winifred is expecting me," Carly said.

Alma hesitated just long enough to make Carly angry before she stepped out of the way and grudgingly allowed the guest inside. Alma looked mussed and irritated, as though she'd been interrupted in the middle of some important task.

"You'd be much more attractive if you'd smile," Carly said pleasantly in the language Alma acted as if she didn't understand. "Perhaps if you smiled more, you'd be married."

Alma's eyes narrowed slightly, telling Carly what she already knew: the maid understood English quite well.

"But not all women are suited for marriage, are they?" Carly continued in the same friendly voice. "Though it's a pity you don't have Miss Winifred's resources. Being a housemaid at seventy sounds quite bleak." Carly's sympathetic smile was all teeth.

Alma was forced to smile and nod in return, the timeless response of someone who didn't comprehend a language—or wanted to appear not to understand.

"Very good," Carly said. "You're quite pretty when you smile." **For a bitch.**

The maid turned abruptly and led the way through a living room, past a small kitchen-dining area, and through the double doors that combined Winifred's bedroom with her sister's rooms. With a curt gesture, Alma turned and walked away, her spine straight and her dark slacks rumpled.

Carly took in the room with a glance. Sylvia Quintrell was a slight, motionless mound beneath the blankets of a hospital bed. An IV dripped fluid and medicines into her body. A feeding tube lay concealed beneath the blankets. The bed was positioned so that its occupant could look out over the patio gardens and pool. The murmur of Jeanette Dykstra's muckraking talk show **Behind the Scenes** came from an old TV set.

The room was hot enough to grow orchids.

Winifred sat in a leather recliner next to the bed. She was wearing black—blouse, jacket, slacks, and shoes. It wasn't out of respect for the recently dead Senator. Black was simply her preferred color.

Her eyes were closed and her right hand was wrapped around her sister's slack fingers. An old, heavy Indian turquoise ring and matching cuff bracelet rested uneasily on her lean hand and wrist. The silver gleamed with the soft patina of constant use.

Slowly Winifred opened her eyes. They were dark, full of emotions. Carly wondered if the older woman would be willing to share those emotions with the family historian she'd hired, apparently over the protests of the rest of the Quintrells.

"Sit down," Winifred said, gesturing toward an

overstuffed chair. "Take off your jacket." She leaned forward and fed a chunk of piñon into the fire. "I keep the room warm for Sylvia."

Gratefully, Carly peeled off her jacket and hung it over the arm of the chair. "Thank you." She looked toward the bed. "How is she today?"

"Same as every day."

**Right,** Carly told herself. **For now, I'll shelve the topic of Sylvia Quintrell.**

Winifred shifted the recliner lever so that the chair supported her legs. The soles of her sturdy shoes were scuffed and worn. Her skin was pale beneath its normal olive color. She looked exhausted and determined in equal measure. Breathing seemed to be an effort.

"We could do this tomorrow," Carly said. "The funeral must have tired you."

Winifred waved a gaunt hand, dismissing the younger woman's concern. "I'm fine."

Carly twisted the microphone pickup so that the tiny head was pointed toward Winifred. The sound quality would be uneven, depending on who was speaking, but she was used to that. She opened her laptop, called up the Quintrell file, and prepared to type as needed.

"You're aware that my recorder is on?" she asked.

"You told me that whenever I saw you I should assume I'm being recorded," Winifred said. "I have a good memory, Miss May. I don't need any fancy gadgets to tell me what I heard a few hours ago."

Neither did Carly, but the recordings sure saved arguments over who said what and when.

"I envy your memory," Carly said, checking that the computer was ready to go. She had a digital camera, too, but didn't want to start taking pictures until everyone was more at ease with her.

"Where do you want to start?" Winifred asked.

"That depends on what you want to accomplish. How far do you want to trace the Quintrell history—"

"I don't give a tinker's damn about Quintrell history," Winifred cut in. "It's Sylvia's and my history I want preserved. We go back a lot farther than the Quintrells. I traced us back all the way to Ferdinand the Great."

"Fascinating," Carly said, trying not to sigh. Most connections to distant, famous ancestors were wishful thinking. Modern descendants weren't happy to hear that their illustrious family tree existed only in some dead grandparent's mind. "Do you have documentation?"

"My mother got it from her mother, who got it from her father's sister, who was told by her mother."

"I see. Anecdotal evidence is always a lively part of any family history," Carly said carefully. "Physical evidence, such as land grants, marriage and birth registers, military records, church—"

"I have them, too," Winifred interrupted curtly. The hand wearing the turquoise ring waved in the direction of a huge antique desk. "All the way back to the seventeenth century."

**Wonderful,** Carly thought with no enthusiasm at all. **That leaves a gap of six hundred years before we get to the eleventh century and Ferdinand the Great.**

Carly typed quickly on her laptop computer. "I'm eager to go through those papers, but I'm unclear as to what you want me to do. How far back in time do you want my narrative of your ancestors' lives to go?"

Something unpleasant flared in Winifred's black eyes. It was in her voice, too, rough and nearly savage.

Computer keys clicked softly as Carly's flying fingers took note of the dark emotion.

"The original land grant was given to the husband of Ignacia Isabel María Velásquez y Oñate before the Reconquista," Winifred said.

Carly flipped through her memory of early Spanish history in the area that became New Mexico, and pulled out the date. "Late in the seventeenth century."

"My ancestors held land in Taos before the Indians rebelled."

"That's what makes this so exciting for me." Carly leaned forward with an eagerness she couldn't hide. "I love working with a family line that has roots deep in a state's history. Do you know the name of the original holder of the ancestral land grant?"

"Juan de los Dios Oñate."

Carly wondered if the older woman knew that "de los Dios" most often meant a bastard child. De Jesús was another popular name for the fatherless. The custom came from centuries earlier when marriage was expected only of noblemen, but conception came to all classes of women. The luckiest of the noble bastards found favor with their aristocratic fathers. Apparently Juan de los Dios Oñate had been one of the lucky ones. Land grants hadn't been handed out to people who didn't have influence with the Spanish court.

"Do you—" began Carly.

A sharp gesture from Winifred cut off the words. She leaned toward the bed, staring intently. Sylvia's head turned slowly toward the room. Her dark eyes were open, and as vacant as the wind.

"What is it, **querida**?" Winifred said gently to her sister. "Did you hear the new voice? This is Miss

Carolina May. She has come to write **our** family history. All of it." Winifred's smile was as predatory as her voice was soothing. "There will be justice, dear sister. On the grave of our mother the curandera, I promise this."

# 6

DAN SHUT THE WEATHERED DOOR OF THE **TAOS Morning Record** behind him. he nodded to the receptionist-secretary whose improbable red hair defied the lines in her face. She'd worked for the **Record** longer than Dan had been alive and her hair color never changed.

"Those better not be doughnuts," she said, sniffing the air hopefully. "My doctor told me to watch the sugar."

"I never touch doughnuts," Dan lied, heading for the editor's door.

"Huh. There's powdered sugar on your lips."

"Oops. Snow. That's it—snow."

Smiling, shaking her head, the woman went back to typing.

Dan walked down the hallway. The uneven floor was the legacy of centuries of use and the random settling of the earth beneath the building. The door to the editor's office was ajar for the simple reason that the doorframe itself was warped.

Gus looked up. As usual, there was a telephone pressed to his ear. He held up two fingers.

Two minutes.

Dan set the box of doughnuts on the desk, poured himself a mug of the black sludge Gus called coffee, and looked over the framed front pages in the editor's office. Except for those chronicling the Senator's career, and that of his son the governor, most of the biggest headlines were more than a century old. In Taos, not much in the way of banner headlines happened from year to year.

The printing presses had arrived in the 1830s, and the Spanish newspaper that ultimately became known as the **Taos Morning Record** began. The Mexican governor made large land grants in 1842, with the major benefactors being Señor Baubien and Señor Miranda of Taos. Soon afterward, Lucien Maxwell married Baubien's daughter and set the stage for the Lincoln County War. Kit Carson and Lucien Maxwell, both of Taos, scouted for John Frémont in the 1840s. The Mexican-American War flared in 1846. The Civil War rated a passing mention because it kept the newly created Territory of New Mexico from becoming a state. Billy the Kid and Pat Garrett played out their violent destinies in the 1880s. Statehood in 1912 rated a headline as big as the paper.

After that, very little that was both local and

newsworthy happened until the 1960s, when a ski resort was opened, the Senator's oldest son was killed in Vietnam and his other son injured, the hippies invaded Taos County, and a triple murderer was caught with a bloody knife. The fact that one of the women murdered was the Senator's wild-child daughter—a clinically designated pathological liar and a famous druggie—was discreetly mentioned, but not emphasized. Just one of three female bodies.

Much more ink was given to the Senator's grief over the death of his oldest son and his dedication to discovering and celebrating the service history of every Taos County veteran of the Vietnam War. Instead of lobbying for a memorial just for his son, the Senator dug into his own pocket and commissioned a statue listing the names of each Taos County hero of an unpopular war.

Other important local news was the big bridge over the Rio Grande gorge outside of town, which saved the locals a long detour and increased tourism greatly. The most recent excitement was years ago, in 1998, the four hundredth birthday party of New Mexico, historic land of many nations.

**Is this why I came back?** Dan wondered. **To read about how men and women from a rural county had to go halfway around the world to die?**

**No matter who lives or dies, nothing really changes.**

Gus hung up and reached for the carton of pastries. "Thanks for the doughnuts. I'm starving. Marti was up all night with the youngest and my cooking is **caca**. Is Dad's back still bothering him?"

Dan turned and watched his foster brother take a huge bite out of a bear claw. "I'm starving, too, so save at least one for me. And if it's still bothering him, it didn't show. We hiked six miles yesterday."

"Yeah? Why?"

"I felt like it. He felt like coming along."

"Huh." Gus swallowed the last of one doughnut and reached for another. "Any coffee?"

"Besides the sewage you keep in that pot?"

Gus winced. "Yeah."

"Sorry." Dan saluted with the mug he'd barely sipped from. "This is as good as it gets."

"I keep thinking if it's bad enough I won't drink as much."

"Has it worked?"

Gus eyed the coffeepot warily. "Most of the time. But I didn't get much sleep last night, so . . ." He shrugged and refilled the stained mug that rarely left his desk. "How's the leg?"

"Better."

"That's what you always say."

"It's always true."

Gus sipped, grimaced, and hastily ate more pastry. "Considering that your leg wasn't worth much when you got here, I guess you're right." Covertly he looked at his older brother's posture. Erect and relaxed at the same time. Must be some trick they taught in Special Ops, because the regular army sure hadn't made a long-term dent in Gus's habitual slouch.

"Where'd you hike?" Gus asked.

"Castillo Ridge."

"Pretty. In the summer."

Dan shrugged and ignored the question implicit in his brother's words.

Gus went back to the sweets. He'd learned in the last few months that when Dan closed a subject, it stayed that way.

The phone rang.

Gus picked it up, listened, and automatically glanced through a window into the adjacent room to see if one of the paper's three part-time reporters was warming a chair. "Thanks. Someone will be there in ten minutes." He hung up, hit the intercom, and gave Mano his marching orders. The reporter slammed a hat over his red hair, grabbed his jacket and camera, and hurried out.

"Bar brawl?" Dan asked idly.

"Cockfight. The sheriff busted Armando again."

"Sandoval?"

"Yeah."

"I thought he was in the joint for running dope."

"That's his older brother. His mama assures everyone that Armando is a good boy, goes to mass every day and twice on Sundays, yada yada yada."

"Is he dirty?" Dan asked.

"Oh yeah. Never make it stick, though. The hispanos were here a long time before you Yankees, and the border is a joke played by mother nature on Uncle Sam. If the sheriff gets within ten miles of the Sandoval clan's dope operations, bells go off from here to the poppy fields of Mexico." Gus yawned and rubbed his face with one hand. "Every so often they throw the sheriff a bone and get caught with fighting cocks. Big honking deal."

"Sounds like the same old same old."

"Nothing changes but the names of the players." Gus grinned suddenly. "I love it."

Dan hesitated, then asked, "Don't you ever get tired?"

"Of what?"

"Crooks being crooks. Cops being cops. A big dumb mutt chasing its own dumb butt."

"Nope."

"But you don't print even half of what you know. Doesn't that get to you? Don't you want to grab people and shake them and say, '**Look around you, fool. Everything you think is true is a lie.**' "

Gus's dark eyes widened. "No, I can't say as I do."

Dan shook his head.

"Look," Gus said calmly. "There's print news about elections and drunks and governments and traffic lights and cockfights. Then there's what everybody knows about everybody else, the kind of stuff that's better kept out of print. And sometimes there are the kind of secrets that only one or two people know, the kind people kill over. I don't look for those kinds of secrets. Neither does anyone else with half a brain."

"What do you do when public and private knowledge intersect?"

"That's when I don't like my job, because that's when people I know are getting hurt."

Dan shook his head again. "The Sandoval clan is running drugs for one of Mexico's highest elected officials, pimping for underage Mexican prostitutes who may or may not have agreed to their new career, and selling babies as a sideline. The Quintrells have used public office to get rich at the cost of people who are poor or simply unaware—BLM land leases, national forest leases, land swaps with the government to make the family land more valuable, employing illegals, legislative favors for their—"

"Tell me something I don't know," Gus interrupted. "Hell, tell me something everybody doesn't know. Have you ever heard of a big politician who left office poorer than when he went in?"

"Why isn't that in your newspaper?"

"My newspaper? In my dreams. Guess who owns the newspaper now?"

"The Quintrells?"

"God, no. That would be too obvious. A good friend of a rich donor who—"

"Never mind," Dan said over his brother's words. "I can fill in the blanks. Only happy Quintrell news makes print."

Gus shrugged. "You think it's any different with any other paper anywhere in the world? All papers have an editorial page. Daily news stories that contradict that editorial view don't get published or else they're put way in the back with the personals." He yawned. "Stories that polish the editorial viewpoint get good play above the fold on the front page. Human nature, that's all. No conspiracy or secret handshakes necessary."

Dan grabbed a doughnut and bit into it like it was an enemy. He knew all about editorials and human nature and the denial of the elephant under the electoral rug.

"None of this is news to you," Gus said, "so why the snarl?"

Dan shrugged and chewed. "Sometimes I get a gutful, that's all."

"You came back from wherever you went with a permanent gutful."

"There was plenty to eat."

"And you still don't want to talk about it."

"Why bother? Nobody wants to know."

"I do."

Dan dusted off his hands. "No you don't. Not really. No one does. And I don't blame them. I wish I didn't know." He wiped his hands on his jeans. "So, does Lila have the flu?"

Gus swallowed the change of subject along with the bitter coffee. "Seems to. It's going through the kids one at a time."

"The joys of parenthood. Have you and Marti had the bug?"

"So far so good." He grinned slyly. "Want to come to dinner?"

"Sure. I'll cook."

"I was kidding. I don't want you to get sick."

"I won't. I've been inoculated against stuff you can't even dream of."

"You sure? I'm afraid Marti's coming down with it. She looked pale this morning."

"What do you want me to fix?"

"Garlic chicken," Gus said instantly.

"When do you want to eat?"

"Six. If I'm not there—"

"I'll leave it in the oven on warm," Dan said, "just like Mom used to."

"You don't have to. Really. I was just kidding."

The shadow of a smile flickered over Dan's mouth. "I want to. I can't stop or even slow down the train wreck of international politics, but I can see that my brother and his family get a warm meal when they're sick."

Gus didn't know whether to smile or cry. The buzz of his intercom kept him from having to decide. He cleared his throat and held down the button. "Yeah?"

"A Ms. Carolina May to see you."

"What does she want?"

"Miss Winifred Simmons y Castillo has hired her to research the Castillo family."

# 7

CARLY GLANCED AROUND THE CLEAN, WORN reception area of the **Taos Morning Record**. Two chairs that looked like they were left over from the Spanish Inquisition sat side by side to the left of the receptionist's desk. An unopened copy of today's newspaper lay on a low coffee table in front of the chairs. Through a glass door on the right she could see a narrow hallway that presumably led to the newsroom and/or the editor's office.

There was barely enough room to swing a cat. Like the old adobe ranch house, this space had been made for people who were smaller than the norm today.

"Ms. May?"

Carly turned from her appraisal of the old building to find a much more modern creation. She took him in with the speed of someone who makes a living out of summarizing people. Mid-thirties, maybe forty. Easily six feet tall, probably more. Good shoulders beneath a turtleneck and leather jacket, long legs in a pair of worn-soft Levi's and scuffed hiking boots, dark hair, the face of a fallen angel, and green eyes that had seen hell. Whatever his history was, it hadn't been written in smiles.

"Mr. Salvador?" She walked toward him, smiling, her hand extended. "It's good of you to—"

"I'm Dan Duran," he cut in, shaking her hand briskly and releasing it the same way. "Gus is on the phone. Follow me."

She noticed a very slight unevenness in the first few steps he took. His left leg was stiff.

"Are you a reporter?" she asked, catching up and walking alongside him in the narrow hallway.

"No."

She waited a few moments, then ignored the man's lack of invitation to chat. "Rancher? Artist? Skier? Cop?"

"No."

"Butcher, baker, candlestick maker?"

He glanced sideways at her. Something close to amusement changed the line of his mouth beneath at least a day's worth of dark stubble. "Nope."

"Wow, a whole four letters in a single word," Carly said. "Careful. You're going to talk my arm off."

He glanced at the arm in question, and then at the woman, and wondered how someone with as much life and sass in her as Carolina May had chosen to make a career digging up graves. The thought of her with the gaunt, dour Miss Winifred made him shake his head.

"What?" Carly asked.

"Just imagining you with that old curandera."

"Who?"

"Miss Winifred. She makes potions and lotions for half of Taos County." She was also reputed to make spells and poisons, but Dan didn't see any need to talk about it with a nosy outsider; his mother was often mentioned in the same breath with Winifred. Locally, both women were curanderas of great respect.

"I didn't know Winifred was a healer," Carly said.

"I didn't say she was."

With that, Dan opened the door to Gus's office and gestured Carly in.

Frowning, she asked, "What does that mean?"

He ignored her.

Gus held up one finger.

"He'll be done in a minute," Dan said. Then he gestured toward the wall of framed first pages. "Enjoy."

He turned to leave.

Carly put her hand on his sleeve. "Wait," she said in a low voice, not wanting to disturb the editor of the Taos newspaper. "Have you known Miss Winifred long?"

"Yes."

"Were you raised here?"

"Yes."

"I'd like to interview you on the subject of—"

"No."

"Don't leave yet," Gus said, pointing at Dan.

When Dan shrugged and leaned against the wall, Gus spoke quickly into the phone. Then he hung up and stood, holding out his hand across the desk with a warm smile that was meant to balance his brother's chill.

"Ms. May, I'm Gus Salvador. Don't mind Dan. He lost his sense of humor somewhere in Afghanistan or Africa or Colombia, along with his manners."

Carly looked from Gus to Dan and back again. "Pleased to meet you, Mr. Salvador."

"Gus."

She smiled. "Gus. Miss Winifred isn't feeling well today, so she sent me here to search through the morgue for clippings on the Quintrell and Castillo families. Is that all right?"

"Sure," Gus said.

"Are they computerized?" she asked.

Gus laughed. "Do we look computerized?"

"Um, microfilm?"

"It's our standard archive method. Actually, a lot of the info is in searchable computer files, thanks to

Dan. He made it a crusade, back when he was thirteen and a real computer geek."

She glanced warily at the man leaning against the wall. Although he appeared to be relaxed, she sensed he wasn't. What she didn't know was why.

**Maybe he hates women.**

"So, you're an archivist?" she asked Dan.

"No." He really didn't want to encourage the lithe young woman who was out stomping on everything in sight, looking for land mines.

"Yes, no, nope," she said. "You're the kind of interview that makes me want to kick something."

"Me, for instance?" Dan asked against his better judgment.

"Yeah." Then she smiled, pulled her scarf off her hair, and shook out a loose tumble of red-brown curls. "You spend words like hundred-dollar bills. Good thing you're not a Quintrell."

Gus started to say something. A look at his brother's face changed his mind.

"The newspaper archives are always available for research," Gus said after a moment. "Only rule is no smoking and no food or drink."

"I don't smoke and won't eat or drink in the archives."

Gus glanced at his watch. "I've got a paper to put together." He looked at Dan. "Take her to the archives and show her what she needs. You know more about it than anyone else."

Dan started to refuse, but didn't. Beneath his smile and warm manner, Gus was tired, over-worked, and worried about his family.

"Right," Dan said. "You keep the key in the same place?"

"Lost the key." The phone rang. "Broke the lock." He reached for the phone. "Never fixed it. Yeah?" he said into the phone. "Mano? Did you get the perp walk?"

Carly waited until they were out in the hall to ask, "What's the—"

"Perp walk?" Dan cut in.

She nodded.

"That's the photo op that comes when the cop slaps cuffs on the presumed bad guy and marches him in front of the media," Dan said.

Carly digested that while they walked down the hallway, away from the reception area. The back of the building opened out onto a small, deserted, and neglected courtyard. Maybe in summer it served as a retreat for workers in the surrounding buildings, but right now it looked as inviting as a meat locker.

"Perp walk," she said. "Got it. Who was it?"

"Armando Sandoval, cockfighter and drug smuggler."

"Drugs? He'll be going away for a long time."

Dan shook his head. "He was busted for the cocks. He'll pay a fine and be home for dinner."

She closed her eyes against the wind lifting grit and snow from the courtyard. Her ankles and fingers stung from the cold. She yanked her scarf over her head and held it in place. "Does this happen all the time?"

"The wind?"

"No. The perp walk and the arrest and the fine."

Dan shrugged. "As often as it has to."

"What does that mean?"

"You ask a lot of questions."

"I need a lot of answers," she said. "It's what I do. Like a reporter, except that a lot of my subjects aren't alive to speak for themselves."

"So you suck up hearsay, rumor, gossip, and innuendo."

"You can go back to one-word answers anytime."

"Okay."

He grabbed the handle on a door that sat crookedly in its frame and gave it a yank. Frozen wood scraped over icy stone. She stepped past him quickly, eager to be out of the wind.

"Wait."

She stopped when she felt the strength of his fingers gripping her arm. "What?" she said.

"Bad footing."

Instead of the uneven wooden floor nearly all the

old, single-story buildings had, this doorway opened abruptly onto a rickety cellar door set right in the floor. A tarp covered the door to keep in the heat of the room below. Dan flipped the tarp aside and turned on a switch.

Carly's eyes widened as she looked at the ancient door. The holes between the slats were big enough for her to step right through. Dan might not be the most outgoing man she'd ever met, but he'd kept her from a nasty fall.

"Used to be the town icehouse," he said, opening the cellar door. "During Prohibition it was the local speakeasy. Now it's the archive for the paper. They cut another entrance to the first floor around the corner, but this way is easier to get to the basement."

She looked up at him with hazel eyes that flashed gold in the unshielded overhead light. "Thank you."

His left eyebrow raised in silent question.

"For not letting me fall," she explained, waving at the unprotected gap in the floor. "I know you don't want me here."

He looked at the gold and smoke of her eyes, her lips full and slightly parted, and the shiny, lively curls falling over her cold-flushed cheeks. She was too intelligent, too attractive, too innocent, and way too alive. He didn't want to see her hurt as part of the collateral damage of asking questions that shouldn't be asked and finding answers that weren't worth the cost of getting them. He was an expert on those kinds of answers.

"You're right," Dan said, releasing her. "I don't want you here. But we don't always get what we want, do we? I'll go first."

"Why? Are there rats or snakes?" she asked jokingly.

"Snakes? Not in the winter. I go first so that if you trip, I can catch you before you break your nosy neck. Watch the fifth step. It's cracked."

**Nosy neck?** She would have smiled but she knew he hadn't been joking. She wondered if it was all outsiders he resented, or just women.

If there had ever been a handrail, it hadn't survived into the twenty-first century. Nor did the flooring right around the opening look very trustworthy.

"What's stored over there?" she asked, pointing toward the crates and boxes lining the walls of the first story.

"Supplies."

Dan was already halfway down the stairs to the basement, moving with an ease that surprised Carly. His leg might bother him from time to time, but it didn't affect his balance.

**Okay, I guess he could catch me if I tripped.**

But she wasn't interested in putting it to the test. She turned sideways and edged carefully down the ten cement steps, taking special care with the fifth one. The thought of staggering down the steps and rolling into Dan like a human bowling ball made her smile. At the very least, it would shake up his cool reserve. Or maybe it wouldn't. Either way, she'd learn something about him.

**Forget it. He's not part of my research.**

**Too bad. That's an interesting man. Really interesting.**

The thought surprised her so much she missed the last step. Before she could catch herself, Dan did. He was so quick that she found herself lifted, set on her feet, and released before she could do more than make a startled sound.

"My bad," she said. "I was thinking when I should have been looking." **And I was thinking stupid. The last thing I need right now is a big, moody male messing up my life.**

"No problem." He leaned past her and flipped a switch. Light flooded the basement. Stainless-steel cabinets and files gleamed.

"Wow," Carly said. "I was expecting piles of crumbling newsprint."

"We've got some of that, too."

"I'll save it for last."

Dan opened a cabinet and pointed to row after row of narrow trays. "Microfilm. Most recent at the top. Oldest at the bottom. I haven't scanned in anything for the last six years," he added, pointing to a computer terminal. "Quality isn't great on the photos but rats don't nest in the hard drive."

"And they do in the newspapers and microfilm files?"

"Every chance they get."

She glanced around at the shadowy corners and aisles between storage cabinets. "You need a big cat. Several of them."

"Too many coyotes."

"Even in town?"

"Especially in town. Nothing like a trapline of garbage cans to fill a lazy hunter's belly."

Dan went down an aisle and along the far wall. Twice he bent down, fiddled with something she couldn't see, and then stood up again.

"What are you doing?" Carly asked.

"Resetting traps."

When he came back, two big dead rats dangled by their naked tails from his left hand.

"Yuck," Carly said. "At least mice are cute. Does this happen all the time?"

"It's late to be catching rats. Usually they come in after the first hard freeze. They must have been chased out of their digs by the last storm." He glanced at the computer. "I'll get rid of these and show you how to use the archive program. Don't poke around while I'm gone. There are more traps. You could break a finger if you aren't careful."

"Is that why they use live traps at the Quintrell ranch house?"

"One of Sylvia's purse pets was maimed in a kill trap a long time ago. Ever since, they've used live traps only."

"Makes sense. Can I use the computer?"

"The program you'd be working with is a bitch to learn. Stick with microfilm until you know your way around."

She watched him climb easily up the treacherous steps. The dead rats swung in rhythm with his stride.

"Don't forget to wash your hands," she called after him.

Carly thought she heard him chuckle, then decided it must have been just his boots scuffing over cement. The outer door opened with a groan and a scrape and closed the same way, leaving her alone with the past and a roomful of rattraps.

**Now I know why newspapers call their archives the morgue.**

Rubbing at goose bumps that wouldn't stay away, she set her jaw and headed for the first cabinet.

# 8

THE WRITING WAS IN THE ERRATIC FAINT SCRAWL OF
a man at the end of his strength.

> **Blackmail, Josh.**
> **One of the charities has to be a front.**
> **Never found out who. Safer to pay.**

Josh Quintrell wondered who of all the many
people the Senator had screwed had finally found a
way to get even. Winifred, probably. She heard all
the gossip from the hispano community; they feared
her as much as they respected her. She'd hated the
Senator after she'd found out about his women, and
she hadn't known the half of it.

**Senator, you were a real piece of work. Which
of your secrets was it? You had almost as many of
them as women.**

Josh didn't want to read about any of it in the headlines. Not until after he was the surviving candidate
in the primaries. Not until after the election itself.

The Senator's secrets had been kept for almost a century. Surely Josh could keep them buried for eleven more months.

He closed the Senator's private safe without looking at the gun and the cash, but he did remove the kind of evidence of civic corruption that some cops would have loved to have. The dial spun with a vague humming sound. After a glance at the locked door, Josh stood and went to the corner fireplace. There were only a few small pieces of piñon burning, just enough to give the room a scent of resin. He dropped the Senator's note in, watched it burn, and ground the ash into a smear across the small hearth. He did the same with the other papers.

Obviously, someone knew too much, which meant he couldn't trust anyone local. At the same time, he couldn't afford to make local people suspicious. He'd act like it was business as usual and use an out-of-state accountant to track down the blackmailer.

Until that happened, he had other problems. Carly May was at the head of the list.

Josh unlocked the office door and strode quickly to the end of the house everyone called the Sisters' Suite. He knocked very softly before he opened the door to Sylvia's room. He didn't wait for permission to enter; it was his house now.

As always, Sylvia's body made a slight mound on

the hospital bed. As usual, Winifred's chair was drawn close and the piñon fire was blazing. Sylvia's empty black eyes stared into the room from beneath a carefully combed halo of white hair.

Nothing much changed from visit to visit except the seasons beyond the windows and Sylvia herself, becoming more and more ghostlike, translucent. Every week when the doctor visited, he told Josh that he expected Sylvia to be dead.

So far no one had been that lucky.

"Good morning, Aunt Winifred," he said quietly. "How is Mother today?"

"Alive."

Josh bit back a sigh and a curse. Neither would make a difference. Winifred had never liked him. She would go to her grave that way. "Alma said you weren't feeling well."

"I'll live."

"I'm sure you will. Nothing would be the same without you."

Winifred leaned forward, opened a rough pottery jar, and scooped out something that looked—and smelled—like it had been scraped off a barn floor and mixed with rotten fish. Gently she rubbed the greenish goo over Sylvia's withered torso, careful not to disturb the various tubes.

"Your love and devotion have kept her alive," Josh

said, trying not to gag on the smell of whatever Winifred had concocted. "We're all grateful for that."

The old woman didn't answer.

Slowly, like a leaf caught in an uncertain eddy, Sylvia's head turned toward the window. It was the only movement she ever made, gradually turning her head to one side or the other. Since her eyes never focused on anything, it was impossible to say why her body made the effort.

"Get out and leave her be," Winifred said, pulling up the blankets again. "She's got pain enough without you."

For a moment Josh's eyes narrowed and his hands flexed. Winifred's insistence that her sister had times of awareness was maddening. Every famous clinic in America—and more than a few overseas— had declared the opposite. The stroke that felled Sylvia had left her body alive and her mind forever beyond reach. The fact that she'd survived so long was a miracle.

"If you don't want her disturbed," Josh said evenly, "we should leave the room while we discuss this pseudo-historian you've hired."

"Nothing to discuss."

"I don't think this 'family history' is anything more than a scam."

"Doesn't matter what you think," Winifred said. "I hired her, it's my money, and that's that."

"That might have worked with the Senator, but it won't with me. As long as you're living on my ranch, you will at least be civil to me."

Winifred gave him a look from black eyes and touched Sylvia's hair gently. "It's not your ranch. It's **hers**."

Josh told himself not to lose his temper. He dealt with more difficult and more powerful people five times a day. And that's what he should be doing now—working as the governor of New Mexico, not dancing attendance on one madwoman and the ghostly remains of another woman who hadn't spoken in almost forty years. It was nearly impossible to think of that slack mass of skin and bones as alive, much less as his mother, but a politician didn't get anywhere speaking ill of a woman who hung on to life long past reason.

**So long, so damned long. When will it end for her?**

**For all of us.**

"I'm her guardian now," Josh said. "The ranch is part of my legal responsibility to her."

"Throwing me out won't win you any votes."

Wearily Josh shook his head and pulled at the tie he'd worn for a taped TV interview an hour ago. A

waste of time, but the reporter worked for a well-
known national paper and was solidly in the governor's camp for the coming election.

"Nobody said anything about throwing you out."
Josh sighed as his collar button gave way. "The
ranch has been your home for a long time. No matter what changes, I'll see that you're taken care of."

Winifred gave him a long, black look. It was the
kind of look that had the more superstitious—or
cautious—of the local people crossing themselves
when she walked by.

"I'll hold you to that," she said finally.

"I'm hardly likely to forget," he said impatiently.
"But there's a difference between having a roof
over your head and running the ranch and the house
according to your whim. Important people in my
party have decided that I'm first-class presidential
material. The primaries will be tough. The presidential campaign will be brutal. The last thing I
need is a bright-eyed little outsider mucking around
in the Quintrell past. Some things are better left
buried."

"It's the Castillo past she'll be researching."

"One way or another, the Quintrells and the
Castillos have been tangled up since before the Civil
War." Josh's voice, like his expression, was impatient. His blue eyes were icy. "At least have the
decency to wait until after the election in Novem-

ber. Then you can air the Senator's filthy laundry from hell to breakfast. But not now."

Handsome, angry, arrogant, he looked so much like the Senator that Winifred wanted to slap him. "I'm only interested in the Castillos. The Quintrells—all of them—can go straight to Satan where they belong."

"But until then, you don't mind living on the devil's generosity, do you?"

"It's the least you Quintrells owe me for taking care of Sylvia."

"Sylvia **is** a Quintrell."

"Not since that philandering son of a bitch broke her heart. Not since her first son died. Not since she went to make up with Liza and had a stroke. Not since you took over. She's Castillo now. **Mine**, not yours."

Josh shook his head and gave up. Winifred lived in the past. She always had. She always would. Nothing he said could change that. He turned and headed for the door. "If you don't keep a tight rein on your little historian, I will."

The door closed hard behind him.

# 9

CARLY MURMURED INTO HER COLLAR AS SHE BENT over the microfilm reader. Until Dan brought her up to speed on the computer program he'd used for archiving, she was stuck researching the old-fashioned way. Somehow she didn't think Dan was in any hurry to make her job easier.

Despite the rather primitive room with its cracked, uneven concrete floor, the microfilm was in good shape and the filing cabinets were kept warm enough that she didn't have to worry about condensation on the film when she took it from its canister and put it into the reader. For the moment, her biggest problem wasn't the equipment, it was translating the oldest documents. Her colloquial Spanish was good enough, but her historical Spanish was barely passable.

"Wonder if Winifred could translate these?" she muttered.

"Probably," Dan said from the bottom of the stairs. "She spends a lot of time with old books."

Carly jerked and barely managed to bite back a shriek. "Don't sneak up on me like that."

His left eyebrow lifted. He hadn't made any special effort to be quiet when he secured the cellar door and walked down the steps. "You asked a question. I assumed you knew I was here."

"I'm taking notes," she said, pointing to the tiny microphone along her jaw. "I thought I was alone."

He glanced at the microphone, then came in for a closer look. "Nice. Voice recognition or straight recording?"

"Both. Voice right now, record when I'm interviewing. They haven't come up with reliable multivoice recognition software yet."

Dan knew they had, and it was classified, so he just nodded. "How much longer will you be?"

She blinked. "Is there a time limit?"

"Usual business hours." He glanced at his watch. "You have until five."

She looked at her own watch. "Does someone have to be here with me all the time?"

"Yes."

Carly wasn't surprised, but she wasn't pleased that Dan had been assigned to babysit her. Something about him was distracting and she had a lot of work to do.

From beneath lowered lashes she watched while

he shrugged out of his jacket and denim shirt. Stripped down to a black turtleneck and faded jeans, he went to a storage cupboard at the back of the room. He pulled out some yellowed, fragile papers, and went to work with a piece of equipment she assumed was some kind of scanner. Despite the size of his fingers and a physical strength made clear by the fit of the turtleneck, he handled the papers with a delicate patience that intrigued her.

"You've done that a lot, haven't you?" she asked.

Dan nodded without looking up.

"But you're not an archivist?"

He nodded again.

She didn't take the hint. "Then why did you take on the job of translating microfilm into computer files?"

He looked up at her. In the stark light and shadows of the room, his green eyes had a catlike glow. "I wanted to."

"Why?"

"Why do you care?"

"I'm curious. And don't bother telling me about curiosity and the cat. Been there, heard that, wasn't impressed."

The line of his mouth shifted slightly. Almost a smile. But then, his face was in shadow so she couldn't be sure.

"Somehow I'm not surprised," Dan said.

"Somehow I don't think much could surprise you."

He looked at the smoky gold of her eyes and knew she was wrong. She surprised him. Everyone else walked on tiptoe around him, trying not to disturb whatever was brooding inside him. But did she tiptoe? Hell, no. She nudged and nipped and kicked.

"When I was thirteen, I chose to microfilm the computer files as a school project," he said, surprising himself again. "Back then, the newspaper wouldn't let me near the really old stuff, so there's a lot still to be done." He lifted and turned the sheet and hit the button again. "I modified a computer scanning program and kept working on it until I left for college when I was eighteen. No one else could figure out how to make my program work, so they just kept on with the microfilming and I'd do the 'translation' when I visited."

She looked at the power implicit in Dan's shoulders and shook her head.

"What?" he said.

"I'm trying to picture you as a pencil-necked geek teenager. Ain't happening."

"Muscles don't reduce your IQ."

"Maybe in your case." Carly shrugged.

"You have something against men who aren't nerds?"

"As long as they don't mistake brawn for the Second Coming of Christ, no."

"Somebody burned you good."

"No. Somebody bored me. Big difference. Then he couldn't believe I didn't want him. Finally had to serve the jerk with a court order not to be where I was, ever, under any circumstances."

"How long ago was that?" Dan asked.

A quality in his voice made her look at him again. Though he hadn't moved, there was a difference in him, more intense, more alert, all relaxation gone.

"Eight, nine years," she said. "A long time."

Whatever had tightened his body left as silently as it had come. He leaned back into his chair and said, "Not long enough, apparently."

"What do you mean?"

"You're still afraid of men."

Carly didn't like that description. Being careful wasn't the same as being afraid. "I don't like men who won't take no for an answer," she said. "The big boneheads are more intimidating than the smaller sizes of stupid. Must be something genetic in me that makes me avoid the big ones."

"Common sense?" he suggested dryly.

"Bingo. So what interested you about the past enough that you spent a lot of time down here scanning old newspapers and making high-tech computer files out of microfilmed data?"

For a while she thought he wasn't going to answer. So did he. Then he surprised both of them.

"I believed that the past explained the present," Dan said.

"It does."

He lifted one shoulder. "The recorded past? Not really. It's written by winners. That leaves at least one whole side unrecorded. Playing cards with half a deck is a sure way to lose the game."

While Carly thought about his words, she wound a curl around her index finger, a childhood habit she'd never been able to break. "That's an unusual insight," she said finally.

"If you're thirteen, maybe. After that you outgrow it." He went back to scanning in old papers.

She tried to decide if she'd just been personally insulted or if he was rude to everyone.

**Not my problem. I'm here on Winifred's nickel and his last name isn't Quintrell or Castillo.**

Having decided that, she heard herself asking, "Do you understand the old Spanish?"

"Yes." He brought down the scanner lid and hit a button.

"Good. The more I read about the original Oñate land grant, the less sense it makes. Since you have to be here anyway, would you help me with the translation?"

"There's a lot about the old land grants that no one understands, no matter what the language."

"Is that a yes or a no on the translation?"

He looked up. "It's a possible maybe. What's giving you the most trouble?"

She rolled her eyes. "Maybe it's more a cultural question than a translation issue. The original Oñate grant was passed along under the Spanish rules of inheritance, right?"

"Every son inherited equally, and under some circumstances, so did the daughters. Is that the sort of thing you mean?"

"Yes. It's confusing to me because the only family histories I've researched this far back have been under the British system where the oldest son inherits and the rest of the sons go into the military or priesthood or whatever, because in terms of any inheritance, they don't get much more than a few hundred dollars and a pat on the head."

"The British way is very effective for concentrating family wealth and power from generation to generation," Dan said as he removed the paper, turned it, and placed it on the scanner again. "The Spanish method was different. The grazing and woodcutting lands were held in common by all family members. Rights to the river and irrigated lands were divided so that each inheriting member of the family had a water source and fields for crops."

Carly hesitated. "Common lands? Like the Indians had?"

"Not quite." Dan hit the button on the scanner. "The Indians, whether they lived in pueblos or followed the old hunting, gathering, and raiding way of life, held all land in common—if they held any land at all." Carefully he set the paper aside and picked up another yellowed sheet. "The Spanish rules were more complex. They called for a combination of individual and common lands within the original grant. The common lands remained the same size. The individual lands got smaller and smaller with each generation. Big families dividing and subdividing the same land over and over again."

"Got it. But what happened to the land grants when political control passed from Spain to Mexico?"

Dan placed another fragile piece of paper on the scanner and carefully lowered the lid. "Mexican rules of inheritance were basically the same as Spanish, which meant that old land grants generally passed intact to the next generation despite the change in government. Other than the change from Spanish priests to Mexican priests and the resulting outlawry of the Penitente sect of Catholicism,

New Mexico hardly noticed the change from Spanish to Mexican governors. In any case, by the time Mexico kicked out the Spanish in 1821, New Mexico had been around long enough as a frontier to think of itself as a separate entity."

"So the effect through time was to have more and more New Mexican families owning smaller and smaller patches of the original grant?" Carly asked.

"Yes, while still holding the mass of the pasturage and woodlands in common. Big common lands. Tiny personal lands."

"What happened when New Mexico became a U.S. territory?"

"The shit hit the fan."

She smiled wryly. "I gathered that much from reading the microfilm. But why?"

"Lots of reasons." Dan kept working as he talked. It was easier than looking into her changing, intelligent hazel eyes or watching her pink mouth shape words or her tongue licking moisture over dry lips.

Apparently his body had just decided that it was one hundred percent healthy and ready to ride.

"Under Spanish and Mexican control, taxes were pretty much avoided," Dan said. "A tax collector who was too diligent ended up beaten, dead, or run out of town. The taxes that were collected mostly stayed in New Mexico. In fact, throughout its history, New Mexico has been a fiscal drain on whichever government claimed it, right into modern times. That's the thing about frontiers. They're expensive to try to control."

"So the Spanish and Mexican governments let New Mexicans get away with not paying taxes?"

"That's modern thinking."

She blinked. "Excuse me?"

"We live in a time when communication is immediate, every transaction is recorded, and the government gets its taxes at the same time a worker gets his paycheck."

"Sure," she said, "but governments throughout history have managed to collect taxes, no matter what the state of the communications."

"In towns and settled areas, yes. Frontiers? No. It's the nature of a frontier to be beyond the pale of society, of civilization, of control. Essentially, New Mexico spent more time after its 'discovery' as a frontier than any other piece of American real estate. New Mexico had three hundred years of being somebody's edge of the earth, somebody's dumping ground for outlaws, adventurers, city rejects, dreamers, and politicians." Dan's mouth turned in a wry downward curve. "While Oppenheimer and the boys were inventing the atomic age at Alamogordo, curanderos and **brujos** were still practicing their ancient trades in the rural areas, using natural drugs like morning glory, poppy, and mescaline, drugs that were outlawed by a culture that never understood them. Between formal wars there were still informal shoot-outs over land and water. Penitentes still carried heavy crosses and flogged themselves bloody following in the steps of Christ." He shrugged. "Some say they still do."

Fascinated by the light and shadow flowing across Dan's angular face, Carly watched his movements as he worked over the scanner. "What do you say?" she asked.

For several breaths the room was quiet. Then he looked up, pinning her with a glance. "I say it's better left alone. For every step you take away from a New Mexico city, you're going back in time. Frontiers are dangerous. Smart people leave dangerous things alone unless there's no other choice. You have a choice."

She tilted her head slightly. Light slid through her hair, picking out the gold among the shades of dark red and darker brown.

"Something wrong?" he asked, sensing her intensity.

"I think you believe a lot of things are better left alone."

"Sleeping dogs and land mines," he said under his breath.

"What?"

"Nothing. Family joke."

"You don't look like you're laughing."

Dan put another sheet in the scanner and touched the button. "Once you begin thinking of New Mexico as a long-lived frontier rather than a modern state, its history makes a lot more sense."

Carly wanted to protest the change of subject, but didn't. She was here to learn about a family history, not this man's personal history. If she'd rather pry into Dan's affairs than the Quintrells', that was her problem.

"How so?" she asked.

He shrugged. "The pueblos might be the longest continuously inhabited structures in America, but they aren't Anglo. Santa Fe has a history longer than that of the United States, but three-quarters of Santa Fe's history isn't Anglo. We've been a state for barely three generations. My mother's grandfather lived on a frontier where men carried guns because there was no other law." He pulled out a sheet, replaced it. "Outside of Santa Fe and Albuquerque, the people of New Mexico live a lot closer to the bone than most Americans do. Closer to the wild lands. Culturally separate from our neighbors."

"I thought this was the great state of cultural mixing."

He straightened and faced her again. Deliberately

he interlocked the fingers of his hands. "If you call this mixing, then we're mixed."

"So we're talking salad rather than melting pot?"

"Other than cuisine and art, the Indians, the hispanos, and the Anglos lead pretty separate lives. Side by side, but not together."

She frowned. "Is that good or bad?"

"It just is, Carolina May. It just is."

The sound of her name spoken in his husky, matter-of-fact voice raised gooseflesh on her arms.

**Uh-oh. Not good.**

She rubbed her skin briskly and told herself she was sitting in a draft.

But she knew she wasn't.

# 10

"THANK YOU, MISSY," JOSH SAID, REACHING FOR the sandwich Melissa Moore had put in front of him. "I didn't realize how late it was."

"Thanks, honey," Pete said as his wife put another plate in front of him. "I was getting hungry enough to start in on the leather-bound ledgers."

Melissa smiled at both men. "Beer, tea, coffee, soda, wine, whiskey, water?"

"Coffee," both men said instantly.

"Coming up."

Pete watched his trim, jeans-clad wife walk out of Josh's home office. Light gleamed in her fair hair and glanced off the colorful cowboy boots she wore. The Indian turquoise necklace shifted against her silk blouse and the full breasts beneath. The breasts, the tight butt, and the huge dark eyes were the legacy of her mother.

"Sometimes she's the image of Betty," Pete said.

Josh looked up from the ranch report, followed

Pete's glance, and said, "Thank the Lord she didn't inherit Betty's taste for booze and pills."

Pete's smile flashed against his narrow, almost ascetic face. "Not my Melissa. She's as smart as they come and twice as gutsy."

"If it weren't for her keeping a lid on stuff here, I'd have talked the Senator into selling the ranch and living full-time in Santa Fe long ago."

"Never happen. Quintrells have lived here for six generations."

Josh shook his head. "This place is a money sink and a pain in the ass. I love Santa Fe and Washington, D.C."

"But you look so fine on horseback or walking over the fields with your hunting dogs and shotgun. Not to mention the ranch's yearly Founders Barbecue with all the cultural mixing and fireworks, costumes and deal-making. The photographers go nuts and the voters can't get enough of it."

The governor gave a bark of laughter. "Maybe I should make you my campaign manager instead of Mark Rubin."

"No thanks," Pete said quickly. "I'm a small-town guy at heart. So is Melissa."

"Good thing, or she'd be running for my office. That is one organized female you married."

Pete grinned. "A real terror."

Melissa returned with coffee cups and pot on a

tray. She fixed each man's coffee the way he liked it, set the cup in front of him, and asked, "What else do you need?"

"More feed from less land, more rain on all the land, and peace on earth while you're at it," Josh said.

"Try church," she said.

"I do every Sunday."

"God has a lot to watch over." She pushed her long hair away from her cheek. "Maybe you should go twice a week."

Josh snorted. "You and Father Roybal."

Her eyes narrowed for an instant, then she smiled again. "He's not my Father Roybal. I'm a Methodist."

"Methodist, Catholic, New Age, they're all the same in one way," Josh said.

"Spiritual?" Pete suggested.

"No." Josh tapped a computer printout. "They all want my money."

Pete looked at the list of charities Josh had told him to prepare, along with the Senator's annual contribution to each. "Everybody wants money. Nothing new about that."

"Including me," Josh agreed. "Running for president is damned expensive, and neither one of you heard me say that, understand?"

Pete and Melissa exchanged fast glances.

"Of course," Pete said.

"Nothing you say ever goes beyond this house," she added, smiling. "Do you need anything else?"

"No," Josh said.

Melissa touched her husband's shoulder and walked quietly out of the room.

Josh was too busy reading the charity list to notice if Melissa left or stayed. When he was younger, her gently swaying breasts would have required that he get in her jeans. No more. He had more important things to worry about than casual sex. After he'd married Anne, he'd stayed monogamous. He hadn't enjoyed it, but he'd known it was necessary, like eating rubber chicken at a thousand fund-raising dinners. Today a politician couldn't set one foot toward the White House without having everything about his sex life vetted on the evening news. So, like Caesar's wife, a candidate was required to be purer than pure.

And eat rubber chicken with a smile.

"About these charities," Josh said, frowning at the list. "I think several million a year is way out of line. What was he trying to do, buy his way into heaven? Most of the biggest contributions began when he was in his eighties."

Pete hesitated, choosing his words carefully. "Considering the gross receipts of the Quintrell Corporation, the amount is generous but not excessive."

"Gross receipts be damned right along with generosity."

Pete started to object, swallowed, and thought better of it. "Whatever you say, sir. It's your money now."

Josh looked at Pete with the Senator's hard blue eyes. For a few moments he wondered if his accountant was the blackmailer, then decided it wasn't very likely. Pete was an outsider, and the only things worth paying blackmail for had taken place when Pete was in Florida discovering why girls had bouncy breasts. Melissa was an insider, of sorts. She also was the daughter and granddaughter of sluts and drunks who'd never thought further ahead than their next bottle. Hardly the stuff of blackmailers.

Winifred, however, was another matter. That old bitch was too smart and too mean. If anybody knew where the bodies were buried, she did. She also had plenty of reason to make the Senator and his son miserable.

All Josh had to do was prove it.

On the other hand, maybe the Senator was right to just pay. Even if every charity on the list was a blind for blackmail, it was only five million and change per year. A small price to pay for the presidency.

But first he'd make sure he had to pay it.

"I'm talking profit," Josh said. "The ranch is a

charity case all by itself. I don't need to give millions
to other fools who can't balance a budget."

"If you didn't make those contributions, you
would lose up to fifty percent of the total difference
to taxes of one kind or another."

"Which would still leave me with millions in cash
that I don't have now."

"Agreed. It would also leave a long list of charities
crying to various media about the Senator's stingy
son, the one who wants to be president."

"Blackmail."

Pete blew out a long breath. "What is public opin-
ion but a kind of blackmail? Your choice is whether
you pay it or not. Some do. Some don't. People who
want to be president—"

"Pay," Josh finished bitterly.

The accountant shrugged. His new employer
looked really pissed off. Not a good thing.

"Okay," Pete said after a moment, "which charities do you want to cancel? The one that provides
chickens and llamas to poor families in South America, or the one that opened a vaccination and pre-
natal care clinic in Africa, or the AIDs orphanage
that—"

"Shut up, Pete."

Pete shut up.

Josh sipped his coffee and thought about possibilities. Only one led to the White House.

"Keep paying," Josh said finally.

Pete nodded and made a note.

"But while you pay," Josh added, "I want you to investigate every charity the Senator contributed to since 1990."

The other man hesitated. "Investigate? Do you think something is wrong?"

"Charities have public records. See which ones have passed along the most money to the needy, as opposed to entertaining wealthy officers and contributors at luxury resorts."

Pete nodded. "Got it. Then if you cut some charities from the list, you'll have a reason to give to the press."

Josh smiled like the combat soldier he'd once been. "Something like that."

# 11

CARLY'S STOMACH GROWLED.

Twice.

Dan looked over at her. "Need a lunch break?"

She hoped she didn't blush, but she doubted it. "Considering that breakfast was a protein bar scrounged from the bottom of my purse six hours ago, yes, I need lunch."

Surprise came and went so quickly from his face that she couldn't be certain she'd seen it at all.

"Odd," Dan said, lifting a sheet out of the scanner. "The Senator is famous for his hospitality."

"The Senator is dead." Carly winced. She hadn't meant that the way it came out. "That is, there's so much going on with the funeral and, um, everything, that I . . ." She waved her hand and wished she'd just kept her mouth shut.

"I see."

And he did. Apparently he wasn't the only one in town who didn't want someone kicking around in the past. He wondered if that other person or persons was just being difficult, or if something darker was at work.

All things considered, Dan was betting on the dark side.

"Got any recommendations for a local lunch place?" she asked.

Before he could answer, someone knocked on the door and called down.

"Dan? You in there?"

"I'll be right up, Dad." Dan glanced at Carly. "Get your stuff. We can meet back here in an hour, okay?"

Her stomach growled.

"Was that a word?" he asked.

"Yes."

His mouth curved at one corner. The harder he tried not to like her, the more he knew he was kidding himself. Just by being herself, she seeped through his defenses. He still didn't know whether that made him glad or mad. It sure as hell made him uneasy.

While he shrugged into his shirt and jacket, she gathered up her coat and notebook, checked that her recorder didn't need a quick energy fix, and beat him to the bottom of the stairs.

"If you go up first, I can't catch you," she pointed out.

"I'll take my chances. The cellar door looks

ragged, but it's plenty heavy. You'd have a hard time lifting it."

"After you," she said, waving him ahead.

A few moments later Carly felt a cold current of wind. She went up the stairs in a rush, only to collide with a solid body. Hands came out to steady her.

"Yikers, Dan," she said into his jacket. "You startled me. I thought you were holding the door."

"He is," said a voice that wasn't quite as deep as Dan's.

She jerked her head back and looked up. The man's hair was brown and silver, the shape of the face was different, he was inches shorter, and had flashes of jungle green in his hazel eyes.

"You must be Dad," she said. "I'd call you Mr. Duran, but a lot of families don't have the same last name from generation to generation."

He smiled. "Duran is correct, but call me John. You must be the stranger whose hair was the only bit of true color at the Senator's graveside."

Carly swept back the wild curls that kept wanting to lift on the wind. "I hoped nobody noticed."

"I doubt that they did," Dan said. "Carolina May, meet my father."

"Better known as Dad," John said, deadpan.

"And I'm better known as Carly. I was just asking Dan about lunch places in town."

"And he was taking you to Chez Duran," John said.

Carly opened her mouth.

Dan beat her to it. "Actually, I was about to recommend Joseph's Table."

"Diana would have your butt for a football if you sent a pretty lady somewhere else to eat. Especially alone."

"Dad—"

The note in his voice gave wings to Carly's tongue. "Thank you but it's not necessary. Dan's been trapped in a basement babysitting me while I work with the newspaper archives. I wouldn't think of imposing on him anymore." She glanced at her watch and then at Dan. "Back here at two-fifteen, right?"

"Wrong," John said, holding her firmly in place. He gave Dan a cool look. "**Trapped** with a good-looking woman? **Imposing** on you?"

"Gus didn't have anyone to spare," Dan said.

"So you volunteered?"

"Not exactly."

John shook his head at his son, sad and irritated at the same time. "We can live without you smiling. But bad manners? Your mother and I won't have it." He turned and smiled gently at Carly. "Do you like New Mexican food?"

"Thanks, but I'm not hungry." Her stomach rumbled.

"Hell," Dan said, disgusted. "Take her home and

feed her. I've got some online work to do." He looked at Carly. "One hour."

"What work?" John said. "I thought you were on vacation."

Dan walked off without answering. The less his father knew about why he was here, the better. Nobody who worked for St. Kilda was ever truly on vacation.

Carly was still trying to find reasons why she shouldn't go to the Duran house with John when he opened the front door of his home and gently nudged her inside.

"Diana? I brought you a treat," he said.

Carly wanted to groan. No woman considered an unexpected, unknown guest to be a treat.

"Bring it back here," called a woman's voice.

John led Carly through a cozy living room. One room was brightened by the framed, smiling faces of children in school photos. Some baby and toddler pictures were clustered on a table. She looked for photos of the previous generations, but saw none.

**Odd. Most people keep all their family photos together, young and old and in between.**

The thought vanished as soon as Carly walked into the kitchen. It was alive with the kind of food smells that made her stomach want to howl. Several pots simmered on the back of a tiny woodburning stove that also served to heat the room. A vintage gas range stood opposite a refrigerator and big sink. If the tank visible in the backyard was any indication, the range had been converted to use propane. Heavy, well-used pots and pans hung from the ceiling within reach of a big butcher block that was so old its surface was gently dished. Ropes of dried peppers in many colors and sizes hung with the pans, interspersed with braids of onions. Smaller braids of garlic, an ingredient not often associated with traditional Southwest cuisine, peeked from behind a huge frying pan.

Carly took a deep breath and tried not to drool. "What a great kitchen."

"It's my favorite room in the house," John said. "Used to be Dan's, too, but nothing much pleases him now."

Before she could ask what had happened to Dan, John gestured her toward a small glassed-in room just off the kitchen. Inside, a nicely rounded woman wearing jeans and a man's shirt was tending to row after row of small plants. Her short hair was very dark, with a startling streak of silver at her left temple.

"Wash your hands, sweetheart," John said. "I want you to meet Carly May."

For an instant, Carly thought she saw tension stiffen the woman's body.

**"Momentito,"** Diana said, the word almost too

soft to hear. Deliberately she washed and dried her hands, keeping her back to the guest.

Carly wanted to sink between the cracks in the old wood floor.

Finally Diana turned around. The lines on her face said that she was old enough to be a grand-mother. The darkness in her eyes said that life's journey hadn't been an easy one. Then, after an uncomfortable moment while Diana assessed the stranger in her kitchen, she smiled. It transformed her from a dark, brooding presence to a beautiful woman.

**Well, no doubt where Dan got his looks,** Carly thought as she automatically held out her hand while John introduced them. **But, wow, that smile. You could light up winter with that.** She wondered if Dan had inherited the smile along with the coloring.

Then she wondered what it would take to find out.

"You have a fantastic kitchen," Carly said. "I've always wanted one like this, a place that's warm and welcoming."

"You're very kind," Diana said. Her voice was subdued, almost hesitant, and vibrant with leashed emotions.

**Dan's voice has Diana's intensity and their smiles are to die for.** Carly almost sighed. **It must**

**be nice to look at someone and see yourself reflected.**

The familiar sense of being somehow incomplete flickered through her. She shrugged it off, reminding herself that a lot of people didn't know who one or both parents were, and got along just fine anyway.

"I'm sorry to impose," Carly said. "Your husband, um, didn't listen to me."

Diana's eyes softened as she looked toward John. "He's a bulldozer, but a gentle one. I don't mind when he brings interesting people home."

Carly sighed. "I'm very ordinary."

Diana shook her head and said distinctly, "No, Ms. May. Nothing intelligent is ordinary."

Carly's stomach growled even as she said, "Please call me Carly."

"She's starving to death," John said, "and Dan was sending her to Joseph's Table."

"An excellent place," Diana said, "but my kitchen is less crowded. Sit down, Carly. How do you feel about carnitas and beans?"

"Predatory."

Diana's laugh was as incredible as her smile. She kissed her husband's cheek. "Thank you for bringing her. Now let's get the poor girl some food."

Grinning, John warmed a colorful plate, put carnitas and beans and steaming hot tortillas on it, and set it down on the table in front of Carly. Diana put a bowl of mixed salad greens next to their guest and sprinkled homemade herb dressing over it.

Carly looked at the fresh, fragrant food and almost drooled.

"Eat," Diana said. "There will be time enough for questions later."

Carly ate and listened to John and Diana talk about the Indian children in Taos Pueblo, which ones were learning well and which weren't, and how to reach the ones who didn't want to learn. The conversation was normal for a teacher's household, the camaraderie of husband and wife was unusually deep, and the food was incredible.

As the slow, sweet heat of New Mexican cuisine spread through Carly, she learned that Diana had been born and raised in Taos and John hadn't. Diana knew the parents and grandparents of the children she worked with. Sometimes even the great-grandparents. John was at home in the area, but not a lifelong resident. Both husband and wife shared the common concerns of parents for their grown children, and relished the chance to hold and love their grandchildren.

Several times Carly tried to get Diana to talk about the Taos of her childhood and of her parents' and grandparents' childhood. Each time, the conversation gently parted around Carly's words and flowed on, following its own course while she was urged to eat, there would be time for questions later.

She took a third tortilla from the warmer, told herself that she wasn't hungry, and filled it with carnitas anyway. If the first day had been any example, she'd be fending for herself when it came to mealtimes at the Quintrell ranch house. The only one who seemed pleased to have her around was Winifred, and she wasn't feeling very frisky at the moment.

So Carly enjoyed her late lunch, mentally compiled questions to ask Diana when there was a break in the conversation, and enjoyed the byplay of a man and a woman who were thoroughly pleased to be with each other.

Not until John gave Carly directions back to the building holding the newspaper archives did she realize that, despite the repeated promise of time for questions later, there hadn't been a real opportunity to ask Diana about the Taos of her childhood.

As she drove into town, Carly thought about all that had been said and not said during lunch. Most people were happy to talk about themselves. Diana Duran definitely wasn't, which made Carly curious.

**Was she an adoption, like me? Is that why she avoids talking about her parents?**

Carly parked in an alley and walked through the old building that housed the newspaper, still thinking about Diana. As she let herself out the back door, she wondered if Dan would talk about his mother's childhood, or if he would ignore Carly just like his mother. Frowning, she walked over the courtyard's weedy, frozen earth without noticing the man who stood across the courtyard, waiting for her.

Motionless, Dan watched her approach the old building. There was grace in her walk and worry in her expression. He wondered what had gone wrong during lunch.

**Damn it, Dad. Why'd you have to take a professional busybody home to Mom?**

Even under the best circumstances, his mother wasn't exactly outgoing with anyone other than family—unless they were under six. With young kids, she was another person entirely, laughing and giggling and transparent as sunshine.

"Indigestion?" Dan asked mildly.

"What?" Carly jumped, startled. She'd almost walked right into him. "No, the food was fabulous. I was just, um, thinking."

"And frowning."

"Talk about the pot and the kettle," she said, too low for him to hear.

He heard anyway. "You have salsa on your mouth."

Automatically she licked her lips. A spicy taste

rewarded her. "Mmm, your mother sure can cook. Did she learn it from her mother?"

"No."

To anyone with more sensitivity than a rock, the tone of Dan's voice closed off that avenue of conversation.

Irritation flared in Carly. She made her living asking questions about the past, and she was real tired of running up against roadblocks in the present. Especially with Daniel Duran.

"Did her father like to cook?" Carly asked.

"No."

"Grandmother? Grandfather? Aunts, uncles, elves?" she asked sarcastically.

Dan wondered if she'd somehow found out. "Why do you care? She's not part of Winifred's project."

Carly blew out a frustrated breath. "You're right. But your mother has the kind of kitchen that looks like it was handed down through generations, yet there weren't any pictures on the wall of parents or grandparents. Kids, yes, the living room was lined with their school photos. Some babies, too."

"She and Dad put the kitchen together themselves from swap meets and secondhand sales. He built the greenhouse in back and the two bedrooms where the girls and boys slept. It was crowded, but a lot better than where the kids who were placed with us came from. Nobody shouted, nobody raised a fist, and nobody did drugs or sexual brutality." The line of Dan's mouth twisted when she flinched. "You see, Ms. Nosy, not everyone has a family they want to remember and record."

"Are you saying your mother didn't?"

"Ask her."

"I wanted to."

"And?"

"Somehow I couldn't get a word in edgewise without being rude."

"That's your answer," he said.

"What?"

"A very polite way of saying 'None of your business.'"

# 12

AT THE BACK OF THE QUINTRELL HOUSE, DAN parked his truck, got out, and closed the metal door. The sound carried like a shot through the darkness. Dogs barked but didn't rush out. The air was clean, sharp, an icy knife blade against his nostrils. He breathed deeply, savoring the moment. Snow swirled around his head and gently bit his cheeks.

It was a far cry from the toy-cluttered intimacy of Gus's home, warm with love and the smell of the garlic chicken Dan had made for the Salvador family. The salad he'd carried in along with dinner was from Diana, as were the various herbal medicines she'd made to help them fight the flu.

Usually Diana made her own deliveries, or had John do it for her, but tonight Dan had volunteered— even though half of the packages had been destined for the Quintrell ranch. His willingness to drive miles over a rough road on a cold night had surprised everyone, including himself. Like attending the Senator's funeral, Dan didn't know why he'd acted on the push of his instincts and taken the herbs from his mother; he only knew that he had.

Maybe it was simply the full hunter's moon overhead that made him restless, unable to sit in the small adobe house he'd rented on the edge of town or in the warmth of his parents' kitchen or in the gentle chaos of Gus's home. Outside of the buildings there were pastures glistening with snow and moonlight, dark fences and tree shadows where hunters waited in ambush, the soundless flight of an owl seeking a warm mouse. Dan had needed the living night in a way he didn't question.

But even now, standing in the midst of it, he was still restless.

As he walked toward the kitchen entrance, scents from the packets of dried herbs he carried tickled his nose, bringing memories of hiking the valley and mountains with his mother during the snow-free months, gathering plants and seeds, shoots and roots and leaves. Some were used fresh, in teas and tinctures. Some were dried and pounded together with various fats to make salves, like the one weighing down his left jacket pocket right now. Others were tightly wrapped and stored for future use.

He'd never asked about the source of his mother's countless recipes for easing the pain of daily living among people who were too poor to be able to afford—or who didn't want to use—Anglo doctors and pills. Probably he hadn't questioned simply because he'd learned by the time he was six that his mother appreciated silence more than chatter. As for questions, they'd better be about the present, not the past.

A stranger opened the back door in answer to Dan's knock. The way the man moved and measured Dan told him that this was one of the unobtrusive bodyguards who kept the nutcases away from the governor of New Mexico. Just part of the price of being a public figure.

"I'm Dan Duran," he said. "Miss Winifred is expecting me."

"I'm new around here," the man said, "so if you don't mind, I'd like to see some photo ID."

The bodyguard's soft Georgia accent didn't fool Dan; he could show ID or he could stand outside until he froze solid. And if he wanted to make an argument out of it, there was another bodyguard just inside the door, watching.

"No problem," Dan said easily. He pulled out his wallet and showed his driver's license.

The guard compared Dan's face to the one on the license, nodded, and stepped aside. "Come in out of the cold. The cook left some coffee if you're interested."

The combination of no-nonsense bodyguard and

Southwest hospitality with a southern accent almost made Dan smile. "Thanks, but I want to catch Miss Winifred before she goes to bed. I hear she's feeling a little under the weather."

"You know the way?"

"Is she with her sister?"

"Yes."

"Then I know the way."

Dan went through a kitchen that could have been in a medium-size restaurant. The ranch had always been a popular place to host contributors, supporters, reporters, fellow politicians, and anyone being wooed for money or votes. The place went from nearly deserted to overflowing with little warning. Folks in town could always tell by the helicopter traffic when there was something going on at the Senator's—now the governor's—ranch.

Tonight the kitchen looked like it hadn't been used for much more than coffee and a light dinner for the family. Dan wondered if Carly had been included, or if she'd settled for a snack scrounged from the bottom of her big purse.

**Sooner or later she'll get the message that no one but Winifred wants her here.**

He hoped it would be sooner, before anyone got angry enough to hurt the pretty woman with light in her eyes and laughter in her voice.

Though it had been years since Dan had been

inside the ranch house, he hadn't forgotten the turns and hallways and doors separating the kitchen from Miss Winifred's suite. He didn't meet anyone along the way. Melissa and Pete had probably already retired to their apartment. The maids had gone home. During the summer, the hired hands lived in the bunkhouse or in one of the house trailers tucked back in the trees along a curve of the hill. In winter, the buildings were empty.

When Dan had been younger, he'd spent the summer tending sheep and cattle on the ranch and learning to hunt with the Snead brothers. They'd been barely a decade older than he was, yet they'd been great teachers. Like their mother and grandfather, they were "wolfers," hunters hired to keep predatory animals in check. Even as an adult, Jim managed to scratch out a living in the high country. Blaine had ended up in prison for armed robbery.

**Long ago, far away. But, damn, those men could shoot.**

At least, Dan had thought it was long ago and far away until he'd seen tracks on Castillo Ridge yesterday. A man's tracks, and a dog's. He couldn't be certain who else had hiked several miles to watch from afar while the Senator was buried, but Dan knew that only someone with Jim Snead's skill as a stalker could have gotten within fifty yards of Dan and not given himself away. Since Jim was the best man on the stalk in northern New Mexico, it figured that he was the one who left the tracks.

**Wonder why he didn't say hello.**

**Wonder why he was there, period.**

**Maybe that's why he didn't show himself. He didn't want to answer questions.**

Dan knocked lightly on the wide double doors that had been put in to accommodate a hospital bed. In the warm months, Winifred rolled her sister outside. If it made any difference to the patient, only Sylvia knew.

"Who is it?"

"The curandera's son."

The door opened slowly. Winifred's black eyes looked Dan over. "Heard you were back. And busted up."

"A little accident, that's all."

She made a sound that said she didn't believe him, but she stepped aside. "Well, come on in."

The heat of the room brought sweat out across Dan's back. His glance went around the room, missing nothing, including a surprised Carly sitting on the floor surrounded by photos of all ages and sizes. He nodded coolly to her.

He didn't like discovering that he'd driven forty minutes over frozen ruts because he hoped to catch a glimpse of a busybody's smoke-and-gold eyes.

"You're looking well, Miss Winifred," Dan said.

It was a lie; she looked tired, pale, and unusually gaunt.

"Wish I could say the same about you." Despite her curtness, Winifred smiled. "I was hoping you'd come around to see an old lady. About time you remembered your manners."

He shook his head. "You haven't changed a bit."

She gave a bark of laughter. "What did you expect, a miracle? God has better things to do than transform me. Give me a hug and I'll forgive you for waiting so long to see me."

Carefully Dan hugged the woman who was old enough to be his grandmother and tough enough to be Satan's sister. Winifred was all sinew and bones and attitude. The realization that he'd missed her amazed him. Like the Snead brothers and the warmth of his parents' kitchen, Winifred was part of a childhood that he only now was coming to value instead of simply accepting as a given.

"How is Mrs. Quintrell?" Dan asked.

"Winters are hard on her," Winifred said, looking toward the bed.

Dan nodded as if he thought Sylvia noticed the difference in the view out her windows from spring to summer, fall to winter. But the changing seasons mattered to Winifred, so they had to matter to Sylvia.

Sometimes he wasn't sure what Winifred believed

in the silence of her own mind, but he knew that those beliefs made it possible for the old woman to face another day of caring for a sister who would never care about anything in this life.

"Well, what did your mother send me?"

"I'm an errand boy, not an herbalist," Dan said. "All I know is the package with the red tape is for fever and cough. Mom said you'd probably be needing that if you have the flu that's been working its way through the valley."

"Let's see what you have," Winifred said, stifling a cough. "I can't afford to be sick. Sylvia needs me. Without me, she'd die."

Dan believed it. Certainly nothing else was keeping Sylvia alive.

He began pulling paper packets from his jacket pockets. Next came small baked-clay containers, plus one larger one, until finally his pockets were empty. He peeled off his jacket and hung it over his arm. The room was way too hot for anyone healthy.

Which explained why Carly was wearing a loose T-shirt and jeans, bare feet, and a sheen of sweat on her forehead. Her feet were narrow and high-arched. Bright purple toenails struck a note of rebellion. Something Celtic had been tattooed on the inside of her right ankle. He wondered what the design was, and if it would feel or taste different from the rest of her skin.

Deliberately he ignored that line of thought and looked back at Winifred. She picked up each package and container in turn, sniffed, and nodded approvingly.

"No one equals your mother," Winifred said, "except maybe my mother's grandmother, and there were whispers about the unfortunate state of her soul."

Dan saw that Carly had quietly come to her feet and was standing nearby, close enough to catch what he and Winifred said.

**Recording every word, I'll bet.**

He tried to be irritated, but whatever scent Carly was wearing smelled better than everything else in the room.

**Innocence and spice. Hell of a combination.**

"Don't let me interrupt," Dan said. "Like I said, I'm only a delivery boy."

Winifred laughed huskily. "You stay put and let me see you. Thought we'd lost you this time for sure."

"Just a climbing accident," he said. "Those volcanoes are tricky."

She snorted and gave him a look that told him she knew what had really happened. Somehow, someway, she knew.

**It has to be the Sandoval family,** Dan decided. **Smugglers' grapevine. Drug runners' grapevine. Curanderos' grapevine.**

**Shit. I'd really hoped it wasn't the Sandovals.**

And he'd known it was.

That was why he was on "vacation" leave in northern New Mexico, where Sandoval men had been devils and their women had been patient saints for three hundred years.

Winifred nodded once, abruptly, and turned back to Carly.

**Message delivered,** Dan thought. **Too bad I'm not sure which side of the law Winifred lives on.**

"We were talking about my childhood memories," Winifred said to Carly.

"Yes," Carly said eagerly.

"My grandfather and grandmother were both Castillos." As Winifred spoke, she sorted through the herbs and potions and salves Dan had brought. "They weren't close enough in blood to bother the church, and not distant enough to divide up the Oñate grant even more. My grandmother died giving birth to her first child, my mother María. María was fourteen when she married the son of a blue-eyed Anglo bandit. Not that we thought of our father that way, a bandit. Hale Simmons came from a long line of men who'd lost one war after another, either the Civil War or older wars in Scotland. Those men didn't have much use for governments and laws that took what a man earned."

Dan's mouth took on a sardonic curve. Nothing

much had changed. Nothing ever would. The law benefited those in power. Lawlessness benefited those without power. The good and the law-abiding got ground up between law and outlaw. People who tried to change that woke up with bullets in their body.

If they woke up at all.

"The Castillos didn't obey any laws they didn't have to. That was the way of New Mexico, where no government really got a grip on the rural people," Winifred said. "Everyone thinks it's different now. It isn't." She handed an envelope to Carly. "You asked for pictures of Sylvia. Here are some school photos, wedding photos, birthday and Christmas, that sort of thing. The last photos, the ones of me in the garden, were from 1964. I came back in to the ranch for good the following year, when Sylvia had her stroke. The Senator was going to put her in an institution, but I told him to forget it. He needed the Sandoval vote to get elected again, and I'd see that he lost it unless Sylvia stayed at the ranch."

Dan was glad that he'd learned to have a poker face at an early age. He'd always wondered why the Senator hadn't walked away from his hopelessly ill wife. Now he knew.

And now he wondered how deep Winifred's ties to the Sandovals really were.

"Could you have done that?" Carly asked.

"Yes." Winifred looked straight at Dan. "Castillos and Sandovals have intermarried for three hundred years. Two of my father's sisters married into the Sandoval family. One Sandoval in Mexico. Another in Colombia. They had no use for Yankee laws. Their sons and daughters and grandchildren feel the same. They remember a time when poppy and peyote, morning glory and cocoa leaf were legal, the medicines of the curanderos. They remember when they walked tall and Anglos were carpetbaggers."

"That was a long time ago," Dan said quietly.

"Not to those who lost. To them, it's new and bitter. It always will be until the wrongs of the past are righted."

"That will never happen," Dan said. "The remembered wrongs will always be bigger than anything the present can offer as payment."

"I don't believe that." Winifred's voice was thin, harsh.

Carly looked between the two of them, surprised by the undercurrents. She'd never been in a family where history ran so close and hard beneath the surface of today. It was exciting and . . . unsettling. She felt like she was walking through a minefield of past emotions that might explode at any instant.

Winifred let out a long breath and wiped her forehead on the back of her arm. Silver gleamed from the thick cuff bracelet she wore. She looked at the herbs spread across the coffee table and felt much older than her years. She felt ancient.

**He's wrong.**

**I will have my vengeance.**

Winifred picked up the small clay pot that was surrounded by herbs and went to Sylvia's bedside.

Silence grew until Carly was sure everyone could hear her breathe. She cleared her throat and tried to find a neutral topic. Her glance fell on the packages of herbs.

"Is that what your mother was growing in her greenhouse?" Carly asked Dan. "Herbs and such?"

"Herbs, pepper and tomato seedlings, garlic and onion starts, even some rare kinds of beans," he said. **And some other things best left unmentioned.** "At seven thousand feet, the growing season is short. Mom gives her garden a head start."

Carly opened her mouth to ask another question.

"Do you need anything else?" Dan asked Winifred quickly. "Mom will be happy to send whatever you want."

"All I need is luck and time." Then, to Carly, "Spit it out, girl. I don't have all night."

"I just wondered who taught Mrs. Duran about herbs and potions."

"I did, but she has her great-great-grandmother's uncanny way with plants."

"Is Mrs. Duran related to you?" Carly asked, startled. "She wasn't on the list of relatives you gave me."

"If your family has been here for more than three generations, everyone's related, one way or another," Dan said before Winifred could. "Like any other old village, you have all kinds and degrees of cousins under every bush."

Winifred's mouth thinned. "You wouldn't believe how close to the bone some of the old families bred."

Carly's eyes gleamed gold. "I'd love to do a DNA study of—"

"What's that?" Winifred cut in.

"You remember the Dillons of Phoenix? You mentioned them when you first called me."

Winifred nodded. "I heard about them on **Behind the Scenes.** When I called you and you sent me the article on the Dillons, I ordered your family history of them, and hired you on the spot. There was something about DNA in the article, and how it helped them to connect up parts of their family they didn't know about."

"Right," Carly said eagerly. "They were looking

for a lost great-grandfather, so they traced the Y-DNA, which is passed down through the male germ cell. Turns out that they were related to Thomas Jefferson through—"

"I should have figured the test would only be for men," Winifred cut in. "I'm interested in my family's women. Men get more than their share of everything just by being men."

"That's true," Dan said quickly, trying to cut Carly off.

It didn't work.

"If you're more concerned with female relatives," Carly said over his words, "you work with mtDNA, which comes down only from the female germ cell. Mothers pass it to daughters, who pass it to their own daughters, and so on. If a woman doesn't have any daughters, her mtDNA line dies out."

**Don't take the bait, Winifred,** Dan urged silently. **More people are hurt by having too much knowledge than by having too little.**

"Wait." Winifred frowned and tried to concentrate. The small fever she was running didn't help. "Are you telling me that you can know who is or isn't related to a woman by using special DNA tests? Does it work for men, too?"

"Yes."

"How?" Winifred asked, intrigued despite herself.

"The male's germ cell can't carry his mtDNA to the female germ cell, so the only way you get mtDNA—man or woman—is from the maternal line."

"Is the test expensive or painful?" Winifred asked.

"No pain at all," Carly reassured her. "There are several labs around the country that specialize in just such tests. It's not cheap, but if genetic certainty is important to you, then it's worth the cost."

For a moment, more than fever brightened Winifred's dark eyes. "What do you need for the test?"

"Almost anything will do. A swab from the inside of your cheek, a few drops of blood, the root of a hair. If you like, I'll order the test packet."

"Do that. Order a bunch."

"A bunch? Four? Six? More?"

"Ten. Ten should do it. Get them here quick. I'll pay for it."

**Ten?** Carly thought. **Is she going to test everyone in the household?** But all she said was, "They'll be here by Wednesday."

"Send them in my name."

"Of course."

Winifred nodded curtly and turned her attention

to the herbs Dan had brought. "Thank your mother for me."

"I will. She asked after Lucia's two youngest kids. They missed her weekend reading classes."

"Alma was complaining that Lucia didn't come in to work today. Bet the kids are sick." Winifred sighed. "I'll check on them first thing in the morning."

"I'll do it on my way home," Dan said. "You shouldn't be out in the wind until you're better."

Winifred looked like she was going to object, but didn't. "I don't like leaving Sylvia alone. I have a feeling . . ." Her voice died. She rubbed her gnarled hands together. "Saw a raven flying alone over the cemetery. Not a good sign." She glanced at Carly. "Go with Dan to the Sandovals. The men haven't been worth a damn, but the women have lived in the valley since the Rebellion. Maybe they'll be able to answer some of your local history questions."

"They might not want company right now," Dan said quickly.

"Why?"

"Armando just got busted for cockfighting."

Winifred said something in the old Spanish that Carly had been struggling with in the archives. Then Winifred sighed and went to a cupboard across the room. She opened a drawer and came back to Dan with some limp bills in her hands.

"Put this where Lucia will find it," Winifred said. "Those no-good brothers of hers never leave any cash in the house."

# 13

THE KITCHEN DOOR SHUT BEHIND CARLY, LEAVING her literally out in the cold. She shivered and clutched her computer closer as the night air bit through her thin clothes. Stars glittered thickly overhead.

"Is Lucia a Sandoval by birth or marriage?" Carly asked.

"Both. Third cousins, I think." He saw another shiver take Carly. Now that the storm had passed, it was much colder. "This is stupid," he said. "You don't have to come along with me. Winifred won't know. She just wanted a way to get rid of you without admitting how worn out she is."

"And you'll take any excuse handy to do the same," Carly said. "You lose. I'm coming. A family that's been living side by side with the Quintrells and Castillos for the last few hundred years, and marrying back and forth, is just what I need. Despite Winifred's bias, men and their personal histories are necessary to a family narration."

"Don't tell her that."

"Do I look stupid?" Then Carly thought of her wild curls and bare feet shoved into tennis shoes while she froze solid in the icy wind. "Never mind. I'm not. Besides, every time I bring up the necessity of men, she changes the subject."

Her teeth chattered.

"You wore sensible clothes to the funeral," Dan said impatiently. "Where are they?"

"In my room, and how do you know what I wore to the funeral?"

"Are you staying in the old house?"

"Y-yes."

He took her arm in a grip that was more impatient than polite. "Hurry up. You're freezing."

She didn't argue or try to pull away. The difference between the hothouse temperature of Sylvia's room and the frigid night was making Carly light-headed.

When they came to the big double doors of the old house, she took out the skeleton key. Her hand was shaking so much that Dan grabbed the key, stuck it in, and said, "It's unlocked."

"I locked it."

He didn't argue. He just shoved the key back into her hand, opened the door, and pushed her through to warmth. Without pausing he closed the door and automatically gave it just enough push so that the ancient lock mechanism settled into place.

"Do you live here?" Carly asked.

"No."

"Then how did you know the door is sticky?"

"Lucky guess."

Carly didn't believe it and was certain he wasn't going to talk about it. "You know," she said reasonably, "the more you don't answer questions, the more curious I get."

"The more questions I answer, the more you ask." He started down the hall toward the big guest room.

"Wrong way," she said. "I'm across the courtyard to the right."

His left eyebrow shot up. He wondered who had assigned Carly to what had once been the lowest housemaid's quarters.

"What?" she asked.

"Nothing." Dan realized that his breath was visible even in the entry hall. It was warmer than the outside, but hardly comfortable. "Somebody forgot to turn up the heat."

"Doesn't matter to me." Carly pulled a key out of her back pocket and unlocked the door leading to the courtyard. "My room never was modernized."

"Meaning?"

"No connection to central heating. I use the corner fireplace to warm up." She turned the handle and leaned in. The door didn't open.

"Why did you lock it?" Dan asked.

"I didn't. I unlocked it." She frowned and turned

the key the opposite way. The door opened. "At least I thought I did."

Dan looked at the deserted courtyard. Several sets of tracks crisscrossed the snow. Fresh tracks. He stopped being irritated at himself for being attracted to Carly and started thinking. Fast.

"Did you come back here after it stopped snowing?" he asked.

"If I had, I'd be wearing my coat. I just sprinted over there in light clothes so I wouldn't suffocate once I got there. It was snowing then, and about twenty degrees warmer. Why?"

Training that Dan had tried to leave behind clicked into focus. Adrenaline hummed, tuning his body for fight or flight. "Did someone come to clean your room while you were with Winifred?"

"I doubt it. Once I pried clean sheets and towels out of Alma, she vanished."

"You expecting company? A boyfriend?"

Carly put her hands on her hips. "You're real good at questions yourself."

"Be good at answers," he said, focusing on her.

The bleak intensity of his eyes chilled her as much as the night. "I'm not expecting company of any kind or maid service or Santa and his hustling elves. Does that cover it?"

"Wait here for me."

"Where are you going?"

"Your room."

"Then you'll need me. I know I locked my door."

Dan started to argue, then stopped. Unlike the people he was used to working with, Carly wasn't trained for self-defense or strategic offense. She'd probably faint at the sight of a gun.

He couldn't leave her alone.

**Damn.**

"Stay two steps behind me," he said in a low voice. "Don't talk. If I stop, you stop. If I say run, you run. If I say hit the floor, do it."

Her mouth opened, then shut without one word.

"No questions?" he said. "I'll savor the moment."

Before she could change her mind about questions, he turned and went down the long hallway. It would have been quicker to cross the frozen courtyard, but once outside, the bright moonlight made everything that moved into a target. He'd take the wide, shadowed gallery with its centuries-old Persian rugs, massive dark furniture, and gilt-framed paintings.

Carly stayed a precise two steps behind, hugging her computer close to her body. She couldn't believe how quiet Dan was. Her tennis shoes made more noise on the patches of bare tile than his boots did. He moved differently, now. No impatience. No vague limp. Just a kind of poised readiness that made the hair at her nape stir.

**What did he do before he came back home?**

The question was silent. The answer was equally silent, the noiseless stalk of a predator when prey is in sight.

He stopped.

She froze.

He gave a hand signal which meant **Don't move.**

At least she hoped that was what it meant, because she wasn't going to take one step closer to him while moonlight turned half his face to silver intensity and the other half to black mystery.

He flattened against the wall, took a quick look around the corner, and signaled for Carly to follow him again. She wondered if it was accident or intent that took his steps to every bit of shadow the hall offered. Then she all but laughed out loud. There was nothing accidental about the man right now. He was pure dark purpose.

At the next corner Dan repeated the stop, flatten, sneak a peek, and go on. As he moved from shadow to shadow, Carly started to tell him that her room was the next door on the right. Before she made a sound, she remembered how easily he'd closed the sticky outer door of the house. Obviously he was more familiar with the place than she was.

But he didn't know that she'd turned off the light in her room.

She touched his arm. He froze. She pointed to the ragged stripe of light showing around the warped door, then pointed to herself and shook her head.

He nodded. With a gentle, immovable grip he eased her down behind the only cover available, next to a thick mahogany buffet that was as old as the house itself. Scarred and scuffed, the buffet held old towels and cleaning rags these days rather than heavy silver and freshly pressed linen.

Dan turned Carly's chin up with his fingertip and looked at her, willing her to stay where he put her. She nodded slightly. He brushed his fingertip over her mouth, a warning, a caress, a plea, or all together. She was too shocked by the touch and his poised violence to do more than nod again. He moved away from her with a silent purpose that chilled her.

It also told her that he, too, had noticed the watery shine of fresh footprints on the tile in front of her doorway.

After a moment he was standing to the side of her bedroom door. It was ajar just enough that he knew it wasn't locked. Motionless, he listened for any sound.

All he heard was his own light breaths and a shifting of weight that told him Carly was getting uncomfortable huddled in the uncertain shelter of old mahogany furniture. His hand grasped the cold wrought-iron metal of the door handle. Since there was no way something that old and massive would give way silently, he made it part of his attack.

The door slammed back against the wall with enough noise to startle any intruder. Before the echo faded, Dan was inside, diving low and to the right, searching for a human figure even as he hit the floor and rolled.

He didn't see anyone. Even so, he waited, listening.

Silence.

The flow of adrenaline eased in his blood, letting him notice ordinary things once more—like the bitch-ache in his leg. He stood and went through the room's few hiding places with ruthless efficiency, finding exactly what he'd expected. Nothing dangerous.

It was ugly, though.

Somebody had gutted a rat and put it on Carly's pillow. The blood was fresh enough to shine. The rat was still warm.

"Sweet," he said under his breath. "Really sweet."

Before he could remove the rat, Carly was standing in the doorway, her eyes wide in her pale face. Freckles he hadn't noticed before stood out on her nose.

"You were supposed to stay put, remember?" he asked.

She just stared at the mess on her pillow.

He stepped between her and the bed. "Wait in the hall."

She blinked, then shook herself. "I'll take care of it."

He moved as she did, keeping between her and the ugliness. "You didn't do it, why should you clean it up?"

"Neither did you. Why should you?"

"I'm used to rats."

Slowly she focused on his eyes. "No one could get used to . . . that."

"You'd be surprised. Why don't you check and see if anything of yours is missing."

It wasn't a question.

"You're good at giving orders," she said.

"Too bad you're not good at taking them."

She gave him a wavering smile, then let out a long breath. "If you really don't mind handling that"— she gestured at the bed with her chin—"I'll check my stuff."

"I was raised hunting. We cleaned and ate whatever we shot. I don't mind dealing with this."

"Tell me you didn't eat rats."

"I didn't eat rats," he said. **Not as a kid, anyway.**

When he'd had advanced training in living off the land, rats were the least repellent thing he'd eaten. **If it moves, eat it. If it doesn't move, eat it before it moves.**

She headed for the old dark dresser that dominated one side of the room. Then she stopped, looking at the deep drawers almost warily.

"You're right," he said. "There could be more."

"No, I'll—"

He brushed aside her protests, opened each drawer in turn, and patted through the silky stuff, the sweaters, and the jeans. If he enjoyed handling lace thongs more than denim, it didn't show.

"All clear," he said.

She started through the drawers herself, carefully not watching when he carried the pillow and rat into the hall. A door opened and shut, letting in a rush of cold air. She bit the inside of her cheek and told herself to suck it up; the rat had taken the hit, not her. Better to think about where Dan had learned to be so quiet on his feet, so quick. So dangerous.

She shivered, hugged her computer close, and decided she should concentrate on finding out if something was missing.

After a few minutes, the courtyard door opened again and Dan walked into the room. Cold air clung to him like perfume.

"How does it look so far?" he asked.

"Nothing missing. I have some expensive electronics—scanner, special cameras, color printer, and other stuff, and they're still under the bed where I left them."

"So this was some sick bastard's idea of a joke rather than a robbery."

"I guess."

"You want to call the sheriff?"

Carly looked at Dan. "Would it do any good?"

"It would establish a pattern if this, or something like it, happens again."

She hesitated. "It would also give the media something to howl about. That wouldn't make Governor Quintrell happy."

"He's a big boy. He'll cope."

"If it happened to you, would you call the sheriff?" she asked.

"No."

"Why?"

"If it's a prank, it's not worth wasting the sheriff's time. Law enforcement is spread too thin out here."

"Exactly."

"If it's a threat," Dan continued, "it will be made again in some other way no matter how many reports the sheriff files."

Her mouth twisted down. "Well, thanks, that sure does makes me feel better."

"I'm not trying to make you feel better." His green eyes watched her intently. "Has anything like this happened to you before?"

"No."

"No recently pissed-off boyfriends, jealous lovers, angry clients?"

"No."

"Not even the guy you served with stay-away papers?"

"Last I heard he was married and living in Texas."

"So you believe this has something to do with your work in Taos," Dan said.

"I don't know what I believe."

"Then believe this. Whatever Miss Winifred is paying you isn't worth what it will cost you to earn it."

# 14

CARLY TRIED NOT TO THINK ABOUT ANYTHING ON the bumpy ride to Taos. She just pushed her little SUV to keep pace with Dan's truck ahead of her. But every time his brake lights flashed red, she saw the rat's blood smeared across her pillow.

**Whatever Miss Winifred is paying you isn't worth what it will cost you to earn it.**

With an involuntary shudder, Carly shoved the words and the images out of her mind.

"Just somebody's idea of a sick joke." She clenched her hands on the steering wheel. "That's all."

But no matter how many times she told herself that, she couldn't quite believe it. The idea that someone she didn't know hated her that much was frightening.

For an instant a small graveyard flared into life, pinned by the lights of Dan's truck while he turned left. The afterimage on Carly's eyes was a cascade of white crosses festooned with vivid plastic flowers, bound in ribbons and silence, standing vigil around a fresh mound of dirt and rocks. There was no tarp, no grave gouged out of frozen earth. This burial had been aboveground.

Brake lights burned in the silvery darkness ahead. Dan's truck turned right and parked under an old cottonwood. He got out, shut the truck's door, and waited for Carly's little white SUV to park nearby. When she got out, she looked doubtfully at the small adobe house. Only one light showed in the window.

"Did you call ahead?" Carly asked.

"Yes." He wondered if Winifred knew how worried Lucia's husband would be when he discovered Dan had visited his wife. Then Dan wondered if Winifred trusted him not to bug Lucia's house. After all, it had been Sandovals who ultimately took in his mother when her own mother was murdered.

"You're sure Lucia will see me?" Carly asked.

"She'll see you," Dan said neutrally. "She wants to please Miss Winifred."

Carly grimaced. "Great. Another reluctant interview."

"You don't have to do it. You could—"

"Get in my car and go back to where I belong," she cut in impatiently. She'd heard it all before from him. She didn't like hearing it any better now. "News bulletin, Mr. Duran. I belong right here, doing my job."

"News bulletin, Ms. May. People don't like outsiders poking into their private affairs."

"Oh, bull. People line up to tell me their stories."

The wind lifted, swirled. She shivered despite her jacket. At the corner of her eyes, just beyond her vision, she kept seeing reflections of blood gleaming. Yet when she turned quickly there was nothing to see but Dan, looming over her like a stone monument.

If he hadn't kept her from a nasty fall down the cellar stairs, she'd be wondering if he'd used one of the rats trapped in the archives to decorate her pillow.

She shuddered again.

Dan discovered he didn't have the heart to see the naïve little busybody shiver when he could make her comfortable. "Come on. Let's get inside before you freeze."

Lucia opened the door as soon as Dan knocked. If rumor was correct, she was some kind of cousin to his mother. Right or wrong, it didn't matter to him. He didn't want anything to do with the man who had fathered his mother and abandoned her before she was even born. Sperm donor. Nothing familial. Certainly nothing personal.

"Come in," Lucia said. She had the face of a woman whose life had never been easy. "I have coffee, if you like."

Dan thanked her and made introductions. He didn't miss the edgy speculation in Lucia's eyes when she met Carly.

"Miss Winifred asked me to talk to you," Lucia said, "but she didn't say what I was supposed to talk about."

"Your family has been in the valley as long as the Castillos and longer than the Quintrells," Carly said.

Lucia didn't say anything.

Carly searched the other woman's intent dark eyes and admired the single black braid that lay heavily over one shoulder. Her features were an intriguing mix of Old World Spanish and New World Native American. Her skin was luminous despite the wrinkles at the corner of her eyes and the brackets of unhappiness around her mouth.

"I'm interested in stories of the old days that were passed down to you by your parents and grandparents," Carly said, "or pictures you might have of the land and the people generations ago."

"Ah, the past," Lucia said, breathing out in relief. "**Sí**. Yes. I'm as close to a family historian as the Sandovals have."

"Wonderful!"

Carly's enthusiasm made Lucia smile for the first time.

"I'm not organized, you understand," Lucia said quickly. "I just kept the old pictures and mementos that other family members couldn't find room for."

A sleepy voice came from the back of the house. Lucia answered in Spanish that was as fluent as her English, telling the boy to go back to sleep, everything was fine, his aunt was here to take care of him.

"Where is his mother?" Dan asked. He didn't have to ask where the father was. A man who was caught with twenty pounds of Mexican brown heroin spent time in prison, no matter how good his lawyer was.

Lucia lifted one shoulder. "She went back to Mexico with the girls. The boys stayed. It was what Armando wanted. Perhaps when Eduardo is free again . . ."

Carly started to ask a question, caught the slight negative shake of Dan's head, and made a sound of frustration. She was tired of swallowing questions around him.

Pretending to search his pockets, Dan leaned down and said very softly in Carly's ear, "Later." Then he straightened and said to Lucia, "Miss Winifred asked me to give you this."

Lucia took the money. When she saw the size of some of the bills, her eyes widened.

So did Carly's. The money had multiplied many times over in Dan's pocket. There were several hundred dollars now.

Tears gleamed in Lucia's eyes for a moment. She

tucked the money out of sight, deep in the pocket of her worn jeans. "Miss Winifred is a saint," she said huskily.

Dan doubted that, but didn't say it aloud.

"Sit, sit," Lucia said, gesturing toward a clean threadbare couch covered by a colorful weaving. "I will bring the photos and coffee."

Carly sat down in the middle of the couch, rested her fingers on the recorder at her waist, and wondered if she should bring up the subject of recording the conversation. The couch cushion next to her sank beneath Dan's solid weight.

"Don't ask to record anything," he said quietly.

She jumped. "What are you, a mind reader?"

"Nothing that fancy. I saw you touching the recorder. And don't ask about the missing husband and his brother, Eduardo. The brother is doing hard time for selling Mexican brown. The husband, the husband's father, and his uncles on his father's side run the smuggling organization that gives Rio Arriba County the highest rate of heroin overdose deaths per capita in the United States."

Carly didn't know what to say. Dan's words were as disorienting as falling down stairs. Sure, she knew that drugs came up from Mexico into New Mexico, but it wasn't real to her. It wasn't something that ordinary people dealt with. She took a slow breath and looked around the room. Nothing showed the kind of wealth she expected from the wife of a man who had a successful heroin smuggling business.

"This isn't Armando's house," Dan said. "It's Lucia's."

"Now I know you're a mind reader."

"Just a trained observer with a working knowledge of human psychology," Dan said. "Drugs equal wealth if you're selling them, poverty if you're taking them. Lucia isn't taking them and doesn't want to know anything about the heroin business. She lives on her income from working for the Quintrells. Her husband, Armando, lives with her when he feels like it. Right now, he's probably in Las Trampas bragging to the homeboys over mugs of homemade pulque about how he outwitted the Anglos again."

"Armando, the cockfighter?"

"That's him. When he's not smuggling drugs."

"Right." She swallowed and hoped Armando didn't plan on visiting his wife tonight. "So what is it safe to ask about?"

"Anything that the statute of limitations has run out on."

At first she thought he was joking. Then she realized that he wasn't.

"That doesn't help me," she said. "I'm a personal historian, not a criminal lawyer."

"Thirty years in the past is okay, especially if your

recorder is off. Otherwise, I'd go for fifty years. The Sandovals make bad enemies."

Carly swallowed her response as Lucia came into the room with two mugs of coffee on a battered tray. She held a large worn manila envelope clamped between her right upper arm and her body.

"Milk? Sugar?" Lucia asked.

"Not for me," Dan said.

Carly thought about asking for something just to get Lucia out of the room long enough to ask Dan more questions, but didn't. She really hated sugary or milky coffee. If she asked for it, she'd have to drink it. "No thanks."

Lucia put the tray in front of her guests, sat down next to Carly, and grabbed the envelope. It was several inches thick and patched many times with various kinds of tape.

"It's been years since I looked at any of these." Lucia pulled out a sheaf of photos of all sizes. "None of the kids are interested yet. Maybe they'll never be." She shrugged. "What will be will be."

Carly looked at the weariness on Lucia's face, in the line of her shoulders. "I appreciate this, but I don't want to keep you from anything."

Sleep, for instance. The woman looked like she could use a few weeks of it, uninterrupted.

Lucia's smile was tired and real. "The children

are sick. It will pass. I wouldn't want to disappoint Miss Winifred."

"She would understand if—"

"No, no." Lucia waved off Carly's words and began spreading pictures on the coffee table.

Most of them were school photos, baptisms, marriages, engagements, Quinceaneras—a girl's coming-out party at fifteen—first babies, funerals, graduations, and formal celebrations. Since they weren't of members of the Quintrell or Castillo family line, the pictures weren't much use to Carly. She'd seen many like them; only the names attached to the smiling faces differed. That was one of the things that struck her each time she opened a family's photo collection—the sameness of the pictures, the singularity of the identities, and the subtle genetic threads weaving it all together. She'd become pretty good at picking out the shape of eyes, smiles, posture, hairlines, bone structure, and the like, as each appeared and reappeared from generation to generation.

So she smiled and commented on healthy babies, beautiful young girls, and handsome men as picture after picture drifted into her lap.

"Wait," Carly said, holding up a faded color photo. "Isn't that Senator Quintrell on the right?"

Dan went from half-asleep to full alert.

"**Sí,** yes," Lucia said. "He gave a big party on his ranch the first time he was elected from this district, and every year thereafter. Armando's grandfather, Mario, was always one of his biggest supporters. The Senator remembered friends." She flipped through a lapful of pictures. "See, here he is again, at the baptism of Armando's father, and at Easter mass in the San Geronimo chapel in Taos."

Carly looked at all the photos, but reserved special attention for the ones that had been taken at the yearly barbecue. Winifred hadn't showed her anything like these. From the clothes and hairdos on the women, the first barbecue had been held in the 1930s. Another photo displayed clothing from the 1970s, platform shoes and unlikely combinations of colors and fabrics. A third photo showed the full-circle skirts, stiff petticoats, and poodle appliqués of the 1950s.

One of the women—a teenager, actually—tickled Carly's sense of the familiar. She was certain she'd seen the woman before, or maybe her sister or mother or cousin or aunt or daughter. It was in the way the young woman held herself, the tilt of her chin, the shape of her eyes.

"Who is this?" Carly asked.

"The Senator's daughter, Liza." Lucia crossed herself. **"La pobrecita."**

Silently Dan willed Carly to put the photo down and keep going.

She didn't. She let other photos pile up in her lap while she memorized the young woman in the picture. This was one of the few pictures she'd seen of Senator Quintrell's second daughter. The wild child. Either the Quintrell collection had been purged after the family threw her out, or else there never had been many photos of the beautiful baby who grew up to be something ugly—clinically diagnosed as a pathological liar, arrested as an alcoholic, a junkie, and a whore.

Impassively Dan looked at the picture of his grandmother and said not one word.

# 15

CARLY STRUGGLED OUT OF A NIGHTMARE OF GUTTED rats and blood spurting in time to a ringing phone. The phone, at least, was real.

With a groan she sat up, shivering in the chill air, and tried to remember where she was so she would know where the phone was. The only light in the room came from the moon. Her breath hung in the air. Despite her best efforts, the fire in the little adobe hearth had gone out, leaving the room without heat.

And the phone was still ringing.

"Quintrell ranch house," she said, remembering. "Light switch by the door. Telephone in the hall. Incoming calls only. Wouldn't want the maids or guests to take advantage, would we?"

She kicked off the heavy covers and reached the door in two strides. The bare tile floor was icy against her feet. The light switch didn't work.

"Hell," she said, smacking the wall with her fist.

The light flickered on, all forty watts of it.

The phone kept ringing.

She dragged a chair away from the door—no lock, no key, and she was damned if she was going to sleep in an unlocked room after the rat. She yanked the door open and stumbled into the hall. Like everything else, the hall was cold. The phone was even colder.

"Hello?" Carly said automatically.

Silence.

Breathing.

A woman's scream that climbed and climbed, breaking into sobs, pleas, then a shriek driven by unimaginable pain.

Carly was too shocked to move. "Where are you? Who are you? Let me help!"

The scream fragmented into sobs.

Silence.

And a voice whispering, **"Get out of Taos or you'll be the one screaming."**

The receiver slid from Carly's numb fingers. Sickness turned in her stomach. She leaned against the wall and tried to slow the terrified beating of her heart.

# 16

JOSH QUINTRELL HUNG UP THE PHONE AND RUBBED his forehead.

"Headache, darling?" Anne asked.

He looked up from his desk. His wife, as always, was a walking definition of wealth and breeding. At the moment she was dressed "casually" in supple leather jeans and handmade Ruidoso boots, five-hundred-dollar designer shirt, and discreet Tiffany jewelry at ears and wrists and throat. A four-carat diamond flashed against her simple gold wedding band. If there had been a photographer around, the diamond would have been in a locked case and the gold band would have sent its own quiet message to the voters who cared enough to look: despite family wealth and the fame of high political office, Josh and Anne were real people.

"He wants me to step up the amount of time I'm on the road," Josh said.

Anne knew that "he" had to be Mark Rubin,

Josh's campaign manager and the one man Josh took orders from.

"Isn't it a bit soon after the funeral?" she asked.

"That's what I said. He said that voters have a short attention span. I've been out of circulation too much. I need to be on some front pages and be featured in some six o'clock news leads."

"We can be packed and gone by afternoon."

"What about Andy?"

She hesitated. A line of tension appeared between her beautifully shaped eyebrows. "He'll go with us. He thought about what you said and decided rehab was best for everyone."

"Translation: He put the bite on you and you turned him down."

She nodded jerkily. "I still think . . ."

He bit back a twist of anger and said, "Yes?"

"I . . ." Slowly she shook her head. "I wish there was another way."

"Can you think of anything we haven't tried?" His voice was patient despite the frustration that gnawed a hole in his gut every time he thought of his spoiled son screwing up a lifetime of work. Two lifetimes, if you counted the Senator. "We've done shrinks, meds, military schools, soft-love schools, tough-love schools, guilt trips, shouting matches, and New Age fuzzy-wuzzy. Nothing has done any good. The older he gets, the more he reminds me of Liza. Wild, careless, dangerous. Hell-bound and willing to take everyone along."

Tears glistened. Anne didn't argue.

"I know it's old-fashioned," Josh said slowly, "but I think there's some bad seed in the Quintrell line. Sure as hell there are some kinks. The Senator knew what he was doing when he cut Liza loose. She would have ruined his public life."

"Are you," she swallowed, "thinking of legally severing ties between us and our son? Of disowning him the way the Senator disowned Liza? At least he—he gave her money sometimes. Didn't he?"

Josh ignored the hopeful question. "I'm praying Andy will get his act together. I'm hoping you'll help him by letting him go. He'll never stand on his own as long as you're busy giving him money and propping him up behind my back."

Anne flushed. "I've only done that—"

"Every damn time he got close to hitting bottom," Josh cut in coldly. "Every damn time he would have had to suck it up and grow up."

"I couldn't see him go hungry!"

Josh snorted. "Fat chance of that and you know it. When he's sober, he can charm chrome off a trailer hitch."

Her fingers twisted together. "I know you're

right. It's just . . . he was such a beautiful little boy."

"Liza was a beautiful little girl. As an adult she was a liar, a whore, and a junkie." Josh stood and went to Anne. He needed her for the campaign to come, needed her as first lady if he won. And he had a very good chance of doing just that. The other candidates from his party would drop out after a few primaries. After that his only opposition was the aging vice president to a president nobody liked anymore. "I can't do this without you. Are you in or out?"

"In," she whispered.

He nodded. "You'll be the most beautiful first lady ever. Designers will stand in line to have you wear their creations. You'll be able to chair committees, lobby politicians at parties, and get the nation interested in your favorite charities."

She smiled. "I'm looking forward to that—the committees, fashion shows, charities. One of the first things we should do is cut the Senator's standing contributions so that we can make our own name on the charity circuit."

"I put Pete to work on it already."

"Perhaps a more high-powered accountant," she began. Then she saw Melissa out in the hallway. "I'm sure Pete will get the job done," Anne said loudly, telling Josh that they weren't alone anymore.

"He always has," Josh said, turning toward the doorway. "What is it, Melissa?"

"You asked me to tell you when Miss Winifred and her personal historian were together. They're working in the Sisters' Suite right now."

# 17

CARLY FLIPPED QUICKLY THROUGH PHOTOGRAPHS, placing them in a kind of rough generational order based on clothes, faces, or what she'd managed to get out of Winifred. The older woman had very definite feelings about what was important and what should be ignored. Carly had pointed out repeatedly that a family history that left out the men wasn't a "history" at all. Winifred had finally said she'd think about it, and while she did, Carly could work on the Castillo women.

So Carly set her teeth and looked at photos of women. It was better than thinking about the frightening call, the screams, the husky whisper threatening her.

**Get out of Taos or you'll be the one screaming.**

Carly told herself that the sweaty, clammy feeling she had was because of the hothouse temperature of the room. She'd dressed for it by cutting off a pair of jeans and knotting the tails of a blue work shirt below her breasts. Her feet were bare. Her boots, scarf, mittens, and winter coat were stacked to one side of the door. The heat of the sickroom was suffocating.

That's why she was sweating. The temperature, not the awful screams and ugly words.

"I understand that the Senator held yearly barbecues at the ranch," Carly said.

Winifred answered without stopping the repetitious exercises that, along with liberal amounts of herbal salve, were supposed to awaken or maintain nerve pathways in Sylvia's body. Or at least to keep the body as healthy as possible. "Yes." **Bend and two and three and four and hold.** "He loved playing **el patrón**."

The good news for Carly was that after the first fifteen minutes, her nose had stopped protesting the smell of the homemade salve Winifred rubbed into her sister's unresponsive body. The bad news was that Carly had to get used to it all over again every time she left the room.

She studied the picture she was holding. It showed a much younger Andrew Jackson Quintrell III, soon to be known as the Senator, standing near a young woman whose body was as lush as her smile. The sexual speculation in his expression was unmistakable, yet he was still dressed in his wedding suit and his beautiful bride was laughing on his arm.

"Do you recognize this girl?" Carly stretched to

show the photo but didn't stand. She'd been up and down with pictures so often this morning she felt like a yo-yo.

Winifred glanced over without breaking the exercise routine. "Guadalupe Mendoza y Escalante. One of Sylvia's bridesmaids."

"Did she know the Senator?"

Winifred made a rough sound. "She was female. He liked women. A lot of them."

"Then Guadalupe was his lover?"

Winifred flexed her hands, dipped some more reeking cream from a clay pot, and began the massaging motions that improved circulation to Sylvia's limbs.

"According to Sylvia, yes," Winifred said. "But she didn't know it when that picture was taken. It took her years to catch on to the philandering son of a bitch."

"Were there any children?"

"With Guadalupe?"

"Yes."

Winifred rubbed slowly, then briskly patted her hands over Sylvia's withered leg. "Not that I know of."

"Would you know?"

Winifred shrugged. "It was different seventy years ago. Unmarried girls who got pregnant took some herbs from a curandero or had the bastard and gave it up for adoption. Mostly the girls just had the bastards. Either way, it wasn't much talked about outside the family. People took care of their own."

Carly didn't say anything. She suspected that she herself was the unwanted result of a brief affair, something to be gotten rid of as soon as possible. Silently she flipped through more photos. It seemed that every time there was a picture of the Senator, he was eyeing one woman or another.

**Mostly the girls just had the bastards.**

"No wonder Dan said that in a village there are cousins under every bush," Carly said quietly into her microphone.

If Winifred heard, she didn't say anything.

"Did the Senator ever acknowledge any of his children outside of marriage?" Carly asked in a normal tone.

"His bastards?"

Carly winced. As far as she was concerned, the Senator was the real bastard. He had a choice. Any children born to his lovers didn't. "Yes."

"Never. He knew what was good for him." Winifred massaged in more cream.

"You mean he didn't want to ruin his reputation because of his political ambition?"

"No." Winifred's hands moved vigorously. "He kept it quiet because my mother and grandfather would have had his philandering balls, and I don't mean maybe."

"Are you saying they didn't approve of Sylvia's choice in husbands?"

Winifred straightened, stretched her back, and flexed her hands. "The family knew what she was getting into. She didn't. She was in love with him."

"Then why did your parents allow the marriage?" Carly asked, gesturing with one hand toward an old photo album of the wedding.

"Same reason a branch of the Castillos married off one of their daughters to the first Andrew Jackson Quintrell in 1865. Land, pure and simple. The Castillos held a big piece of the original Oñate land grant. They saw their cousins and friends having land seized because they didn't understand the Anglo system, where you pay property taxes or lose the land, where you're taxed individually on lands held in common. In any case, the Castillos didn't have money to pay taxes to their new government in Washington, D.C."

"So the Castillos arranged to marry an Anglo into the family, as a way to cope with the new rules?" Carly asked.

Winifred nodded and bent down to Sylvia again. "The Castillos had land, cattle, water, horses, and the certainty they'd lose all of it to the Anglos. A. J.

Quintrell had the connections to keep the Castillo land intact and a willingness to defend that land at gunpoint. He married Isobel Castillo and spent the rest of his life consolidating the Castillo grant."

"Was it a happy marriage?" Carly asked.

The old woman shrugged. "No one ever said anything about it one way or the other. Back then, you married for the family, not for yourself. Isobel gave the first Quintrell an heir and two girls. The girls were married off to Sandovals in Mexico. A. J. Junior grew up to be an even better manager than his daddy."

"So the Castillos got what they wanted."

"One side did. The other side got swindled out of their rightful heritage. **My** side."

"What do you mean, your side?" Carly frowned, wondering what she'd missed. Quickly she checked the charge on her recorder. Once Winifred started talking, names and memories and family anecdotes came tumbling out too quickly to sort through, much less understand.

"Isobel had a sister, Juana. She married a third cousin, another Castillo. They had one surviving child, María."

Carly wished she had the standard genealogical forms with her so she could begin filling in the blanks. Unfortunately she hadn't planned to get into preceding generations this morning. And that was why she always had the recorder on; no one could predict where a conversation would go.

"María," Winifred said, "married an Anglo, Hale Simmons, but it was too late. The shared land had been lost to Quintrells. But Simmons proved as adept in his own way as the first A. J. Quintrell. Using Castillo and Sandoval family connections, Hale set up a caravan trade down into Mexico. Since he never paid duty, he did pretty well for the family."

"Wait," Carly said. "Where did the Sandovals come from?"

"Spain and Mexico, just like the Castillos. They were here before the Rebellion." Winifred put Sylvia's leg beneath the blankets, pulled out one wasted limp arm, and began massaging it firmly. "Lots of marrying back and forth since then. The border doesn't mean spit to families."

Carly thought about the weary Sandoval woman she'd talked to last night and wondered if Lucia was somehow related to the Senator's spoiled grandson.

**Cousins under every bush.**

"So the Sandovals are part of your family," Carly said.

"Don't waste your time and my money on them.

I'm only interested in Castillos. María Simmons was my mother. Sylvia's mother."

Carly felt disoriented, like time was rushing around her, calling out names and memories. In one breath Winifred was talking about the settling of Mexico by Spain four centuries ago and the coming of the Anglos after the Civil War. In the next breath she was talking about her mother, as if history ran through her family as surely as genes.

"My mother, María, had two living children." Winifred bent Sylvia's frail arm to a four-count beat and held the position. "Sylvia was María's first child. I was her last. There were two miscarriages and a stillbirth between us."

Before Carly could ask a question, there was a knock on the door. Josh walked into the suite without waiting for permission to enter. The expression on his face reminded Carly of how she'd felt when Winifred had first opened the pot of vile-smelling cream and gone to work on her sister. Carly's nose had finally stopped noticing. Josh wasn't that lucky.

"God, what a stink," he said through his teeth.

Winifred ignored him.

"Good morning, Governor Quintrell," Carly said quickly, getting to her feet.

"Family photos?" Josh said, glancing at the various stacks.

"Yes. Miss Winifred has been—"

"Airing all the dirty laundry," he cut in. "It's what she does best."

"What do you want?" Winifred asked. "I'm busy."

Josh glanced at the pale, slack flesh held between her dark hands. "My wife, son, and I are leaving this afternoon."

Carly thought she heard Winifred say "Hallelujah" under her breath.

"I take it that you're going through with your so-called family history project," Josh said, gesturing to the photos.

Winifred focused on him with hard, dark eyes. "You take it right."

The skin on Josh's face tightened. "You can't delay even a few months?"

"I'm in my late seventies. The Senator's finally dead. I'm through waiting."

Carly eased toward the door. She'd write about the quarrels of the dead and the living, but she'd really rather not have a front-row seat to the harangue.

"Excuse me," she murmured.

"Stay where you are," Josh said.

Carly froze more at his curt tone than at the order itself.

"My aunt won't listen to reason," Josh said to Carly. "For your sake, I hope you will."

She looked up at Josh and saw the Senator all over

again in the ice blue of his son's eyes and the hard, impatient line of his mouth. This was a man accustomed to power. To getting his way.

"I don't know what you mean, sir," she said evenly.

"Turn off your recorder."

Her eyes widened and her hand went to her waist in a protective motion.

"Please," Josh said.

She prayed that the governor didn't know anything about her high-tech machine. Her thumb depressed the pause button. The status lights flickered and went on standby.

In five seconds the recorder would come back on.

"It will come as no news that I'm running for president," Josh said, "but until I make a public announcement, I don't want a recording of my intent."

Carly relaxed. "I understand. I won't say anything. And congratulations, sir. It's an honor to be chosen by your party for the highest office in the land."

He smiled automatically. "Thank you. I haven't been chosen yet, but I'm confident I will be."

Winifred dipped more salve and began working the smelly stuff into Sylvia's other arm. Despite the new voice in the room, she lay slack, unresponsive. Her blank eyes gazed out over the shimmering mystery of the swimming pool.

"The next months will be difficult for me and my family," Josh said, holding Carly's gaze. "The other side will be looking for every bit of dirt it can find to smear me with."

She nodded. Mudslinging was the least attractive part of running for public office.

"Once the primaries and the election are over, it won't matter," Josh said, "but I have too many people depending on me to throw it all away on the whim of a spiteful spinster."

With an effort Carly kept herself from looking at Winifred.

"My aunt refuses to delay publication of her so-called family history until after the election," Josh said.

This time Carly did glance at Winifred, who was working in salve without pause, as though the conversation had nothing to do with her.

"Isn't that correct, Aunt Winifred?" Josh asked.

"Yes." The old woman's voice was as curt as his. "Carly said it will be ready by April. There's nothing you can do to stop me." Winifred looked up. Shadows made her face more angular than usual, and her eyes very black. "I made a will and Carly's pay is in it. So even if I die before my next breath, the Castillo family history will be written and published."

Josh made an impatient gesture. "Dramatic as

always." He turned back to Carly. "If you use any-thing about the Senator, me, my wife, or my son that isn't available from public records or approved of in writing by me, my lawyers will make your life a living hell."

Shocked, Carly backed up a step.

"I see you understand," he said. "I can't stop you from writing a pack of lies, but I can stop you from making it available to my enemies. And I will."

Josh left as suddenly as he had come. The door closed firmly behind him.

Winifred capped the salve with a decisive motion. "You're right."

Carly blinked. "Excuse me?"

"We need more than Castillo women. I'll make up a list of names."

"Names?"

"Of the Senator's local women. Some of their kids might be the governor's kin. We couldn't leave them out of the family history, could we? Wouldn't be right." Winifred's eyes were as black and empty as the night.

Carly looked at her employer and wondered what she'd gotten herself into.

**Get out of Taos or you'll be the one screaming.**

# 18

DAN PUT ANOTHER SHEET ON THE GLASS BED OF the scanner, punched the button, and waited for the machine to do its magic. From overhead came the sounds of paper being delivered or supplies being moved. Cold air settled down the stairway; the cellar door had been opened to remind the employees working on the first floor that there was a big hole next to the door. The chill made his leg ache.

He knew he should just forget about getting anything useful done and go back to his rental to read the latest dispatches from the geopolitical train wreck. His body, not his brain, was on medical leave. His boss was waiting for an assessment on the political situation in Colombia, where drug money had transformed some warlords into politicians and financed private armies. Colombia wasn't the only nation lurching closer to becoming a failed state, which was a polite description of the kind of anarchy that meant rape, murder, disease, and ruin for anyone who couldn't get out.

It had happened before. It would happen again. Bang-bang and skeletal babies for the TV mini-cams, the roll call of global disasters that fed the public's "right to know."

**So what else is new?**

The scanner flashed and transformed another piece of the past into electrons sandwiched between microscopically thin slices of silicon.

**I really should get back to work.**

Yet the thought of the small adobe house, its leaky plumbing, and its relentless stream of documents to be digested, annotated, and directed to somebody who cared didn't appeal to Dan. But then, nothing did. He'd awakened restless, irritated, and out of sorts. An hour of rehab exercises hadn't made a dent in his bad temper. Neither had ten miles of jogging and walking.

He saw Carly in every bit of sunlight, heard her laughter in the breeze, and ached every step of the way. It pissed him off almost as much as it worried him.

"I'm too old for wet dreams," he muttered, turning the paper sideways.

"Excuse me?"

Dan whipped around, his whole body poised, ready to fight or flee. "Now who's sneaking up?"

Carly froze at the foot of the stairs and told herself she wouldn't back up no matter how fierce Dan looked. "Sorry. The door up there was open because they needed paper and Gus told me you were in the archives so I thought it would be all right if I went through more microfilm."

Dan sorted through the tumble of words. "Go ahead. Is Winifred feeling better?"

"I guess so."

"Haven't you seen her today?"

"Yes. This morning." Carly hesitated. She wanted to talk to someone about Governor Quintrell's threat—promise, actually—but didn't know if Dan was the one.

Then there was the phone call. She didn't want to talk about that. Her stomach pitched even thinking about it.

"What's wrong?" Dan said, coming toward her quickly. "Another dead rat?"

"What? Oh. Um, no, not exactly." **A screaming phone call isn't a dead rat, is it?**

"How close to exactly was it?" he asked.

She grimaced. "Someone called in the middle of the night."

Dan went still. "And?"

"Breathing, screaming, sobbing, and an invitation to get out of town before I joined the chorus."

"Not good. Male or female?"

She shrugged. "Whispers and screams and sobs aren't real gender-specific."

"Why didn't you call me?"

"To whisper, sob, and scream?" Her smile was as pale as her skin. She didn't like remembering the screams. She really didn't like to think about what might have caused them.

"That room doesn't have a lock on it," he said grimly. "You should have called."

"I shoved a chair under the door."

He let out a breath. "Well, you aren't entirely naïve."

"Gee, thanks, but if getting used to threats and gory rats passes for sophistication in your circles, then I'll be as naïve as I can for as long as I can."

He smiled slightly and touched the strand of hair she was winding around her index finger. "Did you get the number of your admirer?"

She let go of her hair as if it had burned her. "Automatically recording an incoming number isn't on that phone's agenda. It doesn't even have numbers on it. Incoming calls only."

He shook his head. "Keep your cell phone handy."

"I always do." Her hand crept back up to the strand of hair and started winding it again.

"What else happened?"

She blinked. "Am I that transparent?"

Dan didn't want a conversation about how he arrived at conclusions when other people were still wondering what hit them, so he just waited.

"Can you think of any reason Governor Quintrell wouldn't want a family history published?" Carly asked after a few moments.

Dan laughed without humor. "Oh, yeah. I can think of a few beauts."

"Are we talking statute of limitations here, legal issues?"

"Best estimate? Yes."

"The Senator?"

"His life was a scandalmonger's dream, but that's old news. He's dead."

"That's what I was wondering," she admitted. "You can't, uh, slander or libel a dead man, can you? Even a public figure?"

"Nope. Especially a public figure."

"What about a living public figure?"

"That's a lot trickier."

"I was afraid of that. Well, **damn**."

Dan waited for Carly to tell him what was wrong. Instead, she stopped twisting the strand of hair, went to the microfilm files, selected a roll, and walked to the reader. As much as he enjoyed watching the sway of her denim-clad hips beneath the hem of her Chimayo jacket, he'd rather she kept talking.

He knew trouble was coming down on one Carolina May. He just didn't know what or where or when.

And sometime during his long, restless night, he'd realized that he wasn't going to let her face it alone. When it started raining shit, he'd be there to help her. He didn't like that fact, but he knew himself well enough to stop struggling and make the best of a situation he'd never asked for.

The temptation of finally doing some of the things with her that he'd stayed awake thinking about had helped make up his mind to aid her. Or at least sweetened the prospects quite a bit. Which meant a change of tactics was in order.

"So the governor told you to back off," Dan said.

Her head snapped up. "How did you know?"

"Your questions and body language, the combination of anger and worry in those beautiful, smoky gold eyes."

Carly wondered if her chin hit the desk or if it just felt like it. The words and the caressing tone of his voice shocked her as much as it made her heart beat faster. "Now I know how the stories about alien body-stealing start."

Dan smiled.

The contrast between harsh black beard stubble and the beauty of his unexpected grin squeezed her heart. He was his mother's son, with a smile that could light up winter.

"God, don't do that," Carly said huskily. "I'll drool and embarrass myself."

"Don't do what?"

"Smile. You have to know you're gorgeous when you smile."

The corners of his mouth curved up. "Nobody ever mentioned it before now."

She shook her head sharply, like she was throwing off cold water. Red stained her cheeks. She fell as much as lowered herself onto a chair. "Right. Pardon me while I sit down and take both feet out of my mouth."

Dan came over, sat on his heels in front of her, and said, "Need any help?"

She laughed despite her embarrassment.

He touched her flushed cheek with a tenderness that made her breath fill her throat.

"It's okay," he said. "I don't mind knowing that I'm attractive to you. In fact, I like it."

"Oh, come on," she said, looking at his jade green eyes and the dark thickness of his hair. Her hands itched from wanting to feel that hair between her fingers. As for his mouth . . . **no, don't go there.** "You have to be used to women tripping you and beating you to the floor."

He shook his head.

"Then you must have been living in a monastery," she said.

"You're going to make me blush."

"I'll sell tickets," she retorted.

He smiled again. "I like you, Carolina May." He brushed a kiss over her startled lips. "I like you a lot. Want to see if something comes of it?"

"You don't waste any time, do you?"

"No." His smile vanished. "I'm living on borrowed time."

She was too shocked to speak.

"We all are," he added. "Most people just don't notice." He took her hands in his. Her fingers were cold. He rubbed them lightly between his palms. "Tell me about Governor Quintrell."

The warmth of Dan's hands and the intensity in his eyes were another kind of caress. She'd been intrigued by him from the first glance. And it had been way too long since a man made her feel like a woman.

"The governor." Her voice was too husky. She cleared it. "He doesn't want anything in the family history that he doesn't approve of in writing."

Dan's musical whistle was as unexpected and alluring as his smile. "Slander, libel, and lawyers?"

"Yes. And I don't even know the difference between slander and libel."

"Slander is defaming through speech. Libel is defaming through writing or photos."

"Are you a lawyer?"

"Nope. Disappointed?"

She smiled slightly. "Relieved. The worst date I ever had was a lawyer. The second-worst, too. Do you think Governor Quintrell put that rat on my pillow and then made a threatening call when I didn't bolt?"

"The call, possibly. You can download all kinds of sound effects from the Net and play them back anywhere, anytime. But the rat . . ." Slowly Dan shook his head. "I don't think so. I'm not saying the governor isn't mean enough, but people notice him wherever he goes, even at home. He wouldn't risk getting caught with a dead rat in his pocket."

"He could have had somebody do it for him."

Dan thought about the bodyguards he'd seen in the kitchen. One of them certainly could have pulled a rat from a live trap, gutted the rat, and dropped it on Carly's pillow. Yet even as he thought about it, he shook his head.

"Not likely," Dan said.

"Why?"

"It would give the errand boy a hold on the governor."

She thought it over, then nodded. "Pragmatism, not ethics, is that what you're saying?"

"Politicians are a pragmatic lot. They have to be." Dan stood up, wincing slightly.

"Your leg," Carly said.

"Did the governor say anything else to you?"

"You know," she said, standing up, staying close to him, pushing his personal space the same way he'd pushed hers, "whatever there is between us won't go far if you keep ignoring simple questions."

For a moment his eyes were those of a stranger again. Then he muttered something under his breath, sighed, and said, "I did a lot of PT this morning."

"PT? Physical therapy?"

"Yes." It could also mean physical training, PT of a very specialized type. But he didn't want to explain that to the little historian who had innocence and female interest simmering in her eyes. "It makes the leg stronger and it hurts like a bitch."

"Which volcano were you climbing?"

"The wrong one. Carly, I want to help you."

She looked like she was going to pursue the subject of where and how he'd been injured. Then the corner of her mouth quirked in a half smile. "Help me, huh? Never heard it called that before."

He snickered and shook his head. "Damn, but you're getting to me. I thought nothing could, not anymore." Before she could ask what he meant, he kept talking. "What did the governor say to you?"

"That if I published anything without his permission, his lawyers would make my life a living hell."

Dan's eyebrows rose. "Just like that?"

"Yeah. He wasn't feeling warm and fuzzy when he said it. I've got it recorded, if it matters."

"It might. I'll listen to it while we have dinner."

"Tonight?" she asked.

"Sure. Unless you're doing something else?"

"Going through my notes over cheese and crackers doesn't count as something else."

"Did Winifred feed you breakfast or lunch?" he asked, remembering the day he'd met Carly, how hungry she'd been.

"I happen to like cheese and crackers. And peanuts and raisins."

"Sounds like e-rations. Compact and survives well without refrigeration. Easier, more reliable, and more nourishing than snake."

"Were you a soldier?"

"I'm assuming from your presence here in the archives that you're not going to back away from Winifred's history."

Carly took the change of subject without missing a beat. Around Dan, mental flexibility was required. "I signed a contract. I'll honor it unless and until Miss Winifred tells me to stop."

He laughed curtly. "Don't hold your breath on that one."

"I won't. What is it between the governor and Winifred anyway?"

"I don't know."

"I'm easy. I'll settle for gossip."

"I still can't help. Lucia might be able to." Or his mother, if he could get her to talk about the past. "Maids overhear a lot. People are so accustomed to them coming and going that no one notices."

He took her arm and led her toward the stairs.

"Alma sure won't be helping me," Carly said as cold air poured over her.

"Why?"

"She disliked me on sight."

"Odd."

The courtyard was bare but for patches of snow in the shade. Last summer's weeds lay brown and flattened on the wet ground. The sun had been hard at work on the snow, but another storm was on its way. Dan opened the back door to the newspaper office.

"Maybe Alma resents the extra work," Carly said, leading the way down the hall. "Not that there's been that much. Everything I get in that household I have to do myself."

"What does Winifred say about that?"

"I haven't told her. She has enough grief just taking care of her sister." Carly shook her head at the thought of that sad, wasted body kept alive only by Winifred's determination.

As Dan opened the front door of the newspaper

office, he filed the maid's surliness along with the other facts he'd been accumulating since the moment he'd found himself standing on a ridge watching his great-grandfather being buried and not knowing why he'd walked three miles to do it.

He hadn't wanted to get involved in life again. To feel rather than to think. Somehow Carly hadn't given him a choice. He didn't know if that was good or bad, but he knew it was real.

Her little SUV was parked half a block down, in one of the narrow alleys that crisscrossed Taos. He took her hand and headed down the block.

"You're sure you won't back off?" Dan asked.

"Yes."

He weighed her response. He didn't sense any hesitation or weakness. "Too bad there's only one bed in your room. Unless you'd rather stay at my place?"

She stopped and stared at him. "Aren't you taking a lot for granted?"

"No. You are." He tugged at her hand, leading her toward the alley.

"What do you mean?"

"You're assuming that a dead rat and a threatening phone call are the worst you'll have to face." He watched understanding change her expression from anger to pallor. "Your place or mine?"

"Why are you doing this?" Carly asked.

"Doing what?"

"Helping me."

"You were the only real color at the Senator's funeral. Life is precious, Carolina May. You take it for granted. I don't."

She didn't know what to say, so she followed Dan in silence, wondering how his hand could be so warm and hers so cold.

Abruptly, he stopped walking and said something really unpleasant beneath his breath.

Carly followed his glance. Her car was sitting oddly, like it had been parked on a stairway.

At first she thought someone had let the air out of the tires. Then she realized that three out of four tires had been slashed. Shreds and chunks of tread were scattered around like pieces of black flesh. Red spray paint was smeared over the windshield. When she looked in through the open door, bloodred paint pooled all too realistically on the front seat.

The driver's seat.

She swallowed past the sudden dryness of her mouth. "Your place. If you still want me."

# 19

THE SHERIFF'S TEMPORARY OFFICE WAS A LOT newer than the tourist part of Taos. Most of the double-wide mobile home set down in a vacant lot was given over to various county functions, civil and criminal. The sheriff's desk had been wedged into a corner. Office furniture of all ages was crammed everywhere in the room. There wasn't any space left for partitions that would have offered at least the illusion of privacy.

Carly grimaced. "You're sure we need the sheriff? How about the city police? They must have better quarters."

"The sheriff has more territory."

"My car is inside the city limits."

"The rat was in the county. So was the governor's threat. So was the phone call. I'd rather start with the sheriff and let him coordinate. Besides, the police chief is his cousin by marriage. What one knows, so does the other."

"Just what I need," Carly muttered. "A general announcement that some nutcase is harassing me."

"Maybe when word gets out that you went to the cops, the asshole will think before he gets cute again."

"Don't malign anal orifices. At least they have a useful function."

A smile flickered over Dan's mouth.

The aisles between desks were so narrow that Carly had to turn sideways in places just to get through. The radio dispatcher's voice and the answering deputies or police officers made a background noise that was like the sound of a file gnawing through metal. There were three microphones and only one woman to handle them.

"... **scene with victim. We'll need a chopper to get him down the mountain before ...**"

The radio dispatcher took rapid notes while at the same time speaking into another microphone about a drunk and disorderly at a different location. A third call came in.

"... **request backup on milepost ...**"

In the distance came the sound of a siren, either fire or ambulance or local police. Maybe all three.

"Busy day," Carly said.

"They all are when you're understaffed," Dan said.

Sheriff Mike Montoya was solidly built with just enough gray hair and gut to put him well into middle age. The wide leather belt circling his waist held everything—flashlight, handcuffs, keys, a big sidearm, plus other items Carly couldn't identify. If the set of the sheriff's jaw meant anything, he had the temperament of a chained pit bull.

There were empty chairs at the desk closest to him, the one that had name plaques for three different deputies.

"No wonder he looks mean," Carly said under her breath to Dan. "Even though he's the only one left to deal with the public, he still can't cough without contaminating someone's coffee."

"Yeah. I've seen more spacious prison cells."

"Really?"

He ignored her and went closer to the man at the desk. "Sheriff Montoya? The lady at the door told us to come right in, because you're the only one left to take a report."

Montoya grunted and said, "Been a long time, Duran." His voice said it hadn't been long enough.

"This is Carolina May," was all Dan said.

"You the woman Winifred Simmons called in?" Montoya asked Carly.

She nodded.

In the background the radio kept spitting out partial phrases as deputies and dispatcher spoke in clipped words to each other. Carly shut out the other sounds and focused on the sheriff.

"What happened?" Montoya asked her.

"I parked my car in an alley—legally, by the way—and when I came back, someone had slashed three tires and smeared red paint around the inside."

The sheriff said something under his breath in Spanish that wouldn't have been approved language in English. **"Hijo de la chingada."**

Carly felt like answering the sheriff's gutter Spanish with some of her own, but didn't. The man obviously had enough on his plate without a smart-mouthed bilingual Anglo civilian adding to his troubles.

Besides, there were some currents running between Dan and Montoya that she didn't understand. Until she did, she'd be a polite, cooperative seat cover.

"Within city limits?" the sheriff asked.

"Yes."

"You need to see a city cop."

Carly gave Dan a look.

"It's part of a pattern of harassment that began at the Quintrell ranch, which is county territory," Dan said. "So let's save everybody double paperwork, handle it as a county matter, and you can tell the Taos police chief over beers tonight."

Montoya gave Dan a hard look. Then the sheriff

stood up, went to the empty desk, and began rummaging through drawers until he found the correct form. He returned to his own desk and gestured at the empty chairs where deputies sat when they weren't on patrol.

"Sit down," he said.

Carly and Dan chose chairs, knocked knees and elbows, and waited. They answered questions patiently while the sheriff filled in the blank spaces on the form. When he was finished, he glanced up at them.

"What happened at the ranch?" he asked.

Carly told herself the sheriff was tired rather than bored or indifferent. Not that she blamed him for being less than excited. The staccato words coming out of the dispatcher's radios made it clear that the sheriff had a lot more important things to cope with than an ugly prank.

"Monday night," Dan said, "somebody left a freshly gutted rat on her pillow at the Senator's guesthouse."

The sheriff narrowed his dark eyes at Dan and said roughly, "I don't remember reading a report about it."

"I blew it off," Carly said, drawing the sheriff's attention away from Dan. "Figured it was just some kid having fun with the lady outsider. But after the, um, phone call and—"

"What phone call?" the sheriff asked.

"The one at the ranch that played her a symphony of screams and sobs and told her if she didn't leave town, she'd be next."

"Bottom drawer, blue file," Montoya said flatly, looking at Dan. "I need more forms."

Dan pulled open the drawer, found the file, and pulled out fresh forms.

Without a word the sheriff took them, filled in the personal information from the first form, and began asking questions. When he was finished writing, he pushed back and reached automatically for a package of cigarettes. Then he remembered the no-smoking edict and hissed out some more Spanish.

"Who knew you were coming to town?" Montoya asked Carly.

"I assume the entire household did," she said.

"Not much help. Who was there at the time the rat wandered in and died on your bed?"

"It didn't wander anywhere," Dan said. "It was gutted on her pillow. It was still warm and its neck wasn't broken, which means the rat had recently come from a live trap."

The sheriff gave Dan a look. "You were the first one in the room, right?"

"Yes."

"Was she with you?"

"No."

"Then you could have done it."

"Excuse me, Sheriff," Carly said before Dan spoke. "I'd have noticed if he had a foot-long live rat in his pocket while we walked to my room. Ditto for a foot-long dead rat."

Despite the neutrality in Carly's voice, the sheriff's mouth flattened.

"In any case, why would Dan care if Miss Winifred hired me?" she continued.

"He might not, but his mother sure would."

"Why?" Carly asked.

"She and the Senator were close."

"Bullshit," Dan said calmly. "He threw Liza out before she had Mom."

"So I hear." The sheriff dropped the forms onto a mound of papers on the next desk. His body language said that the reports would be ignored. "Anything else?" he asked.

**How about you kiss my ass?**

But Dan didn't say it aloud. He had better ways to spend time than having a dissing contest with the sheriff of Taos County.

# 20

"WHAT ABOUT JIM SNEAD?" MELISSA ASKED, resting her hip casually against Josh's desk. "Do you want to keep him on?"

Josh looked at the employment log, hesitated, and shrugged. "Keep him. He doesn't cost much and he's a hell of a shot."

"Blaine?" she continued.

"I didn't know Jim's twin was on the payroll."

"Not full-time. Just whenever we need an extra hand for odd jobs or running ranch errands in town. He's had a tough life. We help out when we can. You don't remember it because you almost never came here, but he pretty much grew up on the ranch. We all did. It was a lot of fun." Melissa smiled, remembering tagging along with the twins for raids on orchards. "Anyway, Blaine can be handy for the small stuff."

Josh frowned and weighed the political consequences of hiring a felon. On the plus side, it polished his liberal image. On the negative side, it polished his liberal image.

New Mexico's voters were a divided lot.

The sound of a helicopter flying up the valley reverberated through the air.

Impatiently Josh waved his hand. "As long as Blaine doesn't show up drunk or loaded, hire him. Otherwise, send him away."

"Of course." Melissa made a note in the margin of the employee log. "What about the maids and the cook?"

Windows rattled lightly as the chopper set down.

"You take care of adding or subtracting people and hours," he said. "That's what the Senator hired you for—running the place. As long as I keep the ranch, I'll defer to your judgment. What's the point of having good people if you don't trust them?"

Melissa smiled. "Thank you, sir. Do you need to see Pete again?"

"Has he found out anything about those charities?"

"He's working on it."

"Good. As soon as he has anything, I want it. Even using Anne's family money, I need every bit of cash I can get my hands on for my campaign."

"Yes, Governor."

Josh stood up and strode out of the room with the vigor of a man half his age. Quintrell blood might throw some wild cards, but the survivors tended to live long and healthy lives. He walked quickly through hallways and rooms without noticing their wealth and tasteful furnishings. Unlike the governor's Santa Fe mansion, which was a showcase for the finest in New Mexican art and artisans, the Quintrell ranch home reflected a cosmopolitan lifestyle not bounded by any local artistic tradition.

He knocked on the door to Sylvia's suite and entered without waiting. Not for the first time, he thought that walking into the room was like turning back the clock. The youngest piece of furniture in the suite was thirty years old. Most pieces were sixty or older, much older. Only the medical equipment was recent.

As usual, Winifred was in the chair beside her sister's bed, holding her sister's limp hand. Sylvia's eyes were open, black, and empty, looking toward the door and focusing on nothing. Slowly, slowly, her head turned to the window and the outside pool's dance and shimmer.

"We're leaving now," Josh said to Winifred.

She just looked at him.

"Be careful what you let your historian print," he reminded her.

"Good-bye, Governor. Ask Melissa to— Oh, there she is."

"I was just coming to check on you," Melissa said. "Would you like tea and cookies?"

"Yes. And some of that soup we had for lunch, if there's any more."

Without a word Josh turned and left.

Winifred's black eyes tracked every step he took until he was out of sight. When the sound of his footsteps faded into the lazy **whap whap whap** of the idling helicopter blades, she switched her fierce glance to Melissa.

"What is he going to do?" Winifred asked bluntly.

"Nothing yet."

Winifred let out a rasping breath. "He's smarter than I thought."

"Don't count on it staying that way."

"You think he's going to sell everything?"

Melissa nodded.

"Over my dead body," Winifred said, coughing.

Melissa looked at the slack outline on the bed. **Or hers.**

But Melissa didn't say it aloud.

# 21

AS CARLY CLIMBED DOWN THE STEPS OF THE sheriff's temporary quarters, the high-mountain sunlight cut like a knife across her eyes. She stumbled slightly and caught herself, ignoring Dan's hand held out to steady her.

He stopped on the sidewalk, pulled his cell phone out of a jacket pocket, and called a local garage to pick up Carly's car.

She kept walking, not even looking over her shoulder to see if he was following.

Dan finished the call in record time. His long strides closed the distance between himself and Carly before a block had gone by.

"You planning on telling me why you're mad?" he asked.

"You know why."

"Probably, but I'd rather not guess."

"Why didn't you tell me you were related to the Senator?" she said curtly. "You knew I was researching the—"

"Winifred hired you to do a Castillo history," Dan cut in. "I don't see how my mother fits into that."

"She's part Castillo, that's how."

"Winifred doesn't see it that way. She's only interested in past Castillos, not present ones."

Carly wanted to argue but couldn't. He was right. Not once had Winifred showed any interest at all in the governor or his son, even though Castillo blood ran in them as surely as did Quintrell.

"And you're only interested in the present," Carly said.

Dan shrugged and nudged her toward his truck. "The present is where things happen. Like getting your SUV hauled to a garage for new shoes and a bath in paint remover."

"That's such a load of crap."

He opened the truck door. "You don't want your SUV fixed?"

She climbed in and ignored the change in topic. As soon as he started the truck, she said, "You're way too smart to believe that the present just invented itself without any help from the past."

"And you're way too smart to believe that the past is more important than the possibilities of today."

Dan steered the truck down a block, turned onto a side street, and drove toward his little rental.

Carly said something under her breath and leaned

back into the seat, feeling twice her age. "Don't tell me you thought I wouldn't care about who your mother is."

"She's my mother and John's wife and a good woman who has helped a lot of kids become worthwhile adults. That's who she is. Period."

He slowed for an ancient pickup truck that was hauling a load of willow poles. Blue-black smoke poured from the truck's exhaust as it turned a corner and headed off at a right angle. The truck's load shifted and shivered beneath the twine holding it in place. The peeled willow poles were between five and six feet tall and one to two inches thick. People in the valley had been using similar poles for fencing for a thousand years.

"The fact that my maternal grandmother was a psychopathic liar and an addict who turned tricks for a fix doesn't mean squat today," Dan added. "Not to me and not to anybody else in town who matters."

He accelerated down the street.

Carly bit the inside of her lip. It was one thing to think of Liza Quintrell as a wild child; it was quite another thing to think of her as a member of Dan's family, his grandmother, the mother of his mother.

**An addict who turned tricks for a fix.**

"I'm sorry," she said.

"Why? It was long ago, far away, and besides, the bitch is dead."

"Whew. Did you know your grandmother?"

"No. Before I was born, she was murdered by a nutcase wired on angel dust. Mom left home when she was fourteen. She married Dad when she was sixteen. I came along real quick after that."

"Why did she leave?"

"It must have seemed better than staying with what her mother had become."

"Did the Senator help your mother?"

Dan shrugged. "Not that I know of."

Carly waited.

"My mother hates the Senator so much she won't allow his name to be spoken in her house," Dan said finally. "Dad thinks it's because of the way her mother was treated, the hypocrisy of a womanizing son of a bitch getting his dick in a knot because his daughter does the nasty with any man who can get it up. Or maybe it was the fact that the Senator couldn't find room for his fourteen-year-old grand-daughter on a ranch the size of Delaware." Dan shrugged. It didn't make much sense to him; but then, he'd never had to live his mother's life. "Whatever. Mom doesn't talk about her mother or the Senator or her childhood as the daughter of a psychopath, an addict, and a whore."

Carly blew out a breath and wondered how a fourteen-year-old had supported herself until she married at sixteen; then Carly decided not to ask. She'd had enough of tiptoeing through the minefield of Dan's family.

For now, anyway.

Dan turned onto a little side street that dead-ended in a pasture fence made of peeled willow poles held close together by wires. Unlike the poles on the slow truck, these were weathered gray, crooked, no two alike. There was no garage for the truck, not even a lean-to.

Without waiting for Dan, Carly climbed out of the vehicle, shouldered her big purse, and looked around curiously. The cloudless sky was huge. The closest houses were several large pastures away. Snow covered the fields in shady places and melted on the dirt streets. Right now the wind was a gentle sigh sliding down the rugged mountains, but her experience with the Rocky Mountains told her that during storms the wind would be wild, powerful. Except for some ruined outbuildings that were relics of past farming days, Dan's little house faced the wind and mountains alone.

Then Carly realized the house wasn't really alone. The cottonwood that spread thick bare branches over the house and a lot of nearby pasture was company of sorts. The sort she liked.

Though the tree couldn't talk, it had seen centuries of history pass with the seasons. It was deeply rooted in the past, growing in the present, and its strong arms reached toward the future spring.

Ignoring the snow and slush under her boots, she walked toward the tree, put her bare hands on its rough, deeply seamed bark, and closed her eyes. When she opened them again, Dan was standing close to her, hair dark against the sky, watching her with eyes the color of the future spring.

She laughed self-consciously. "Did I mention that I like trees?"

"All of them? Or just the special ones, like this one?"

"You feel it, too?"

"It's why I rented the house, leaky roof, bad plumbing, and all. I felt something here. Calm, maybe. I don't know. I just know that being around the old cottonwood tree made me feel . . . better."

She tried to think of another man she knew who would have sensed the different life of the tree so clearly, much less admitted it aloud. With a sigh she let her anger at him slide away.

"Not mad anymore?" he asked.

She jumped. "You read me way too well."

He smiled, lifted the heavy purse from her shoulder, and headed for the front door. "C'mon. My chili isn't as good as Mom's, but it will separate your stomach from your backbone."

"I'm going to ask questions," Carly warned.

"That's how I know you're breathing."

"Are you going to answer them?"

"I don't know." He put the key in the lock, slid the heavy deadbolt aside, and pulled on the old wrought-iron handle.

"You spend a lot of your time not knowing," she said.

"It's one of my specialties."

He put his hand between her shoulder blades and nudged her into the living area. The furnishings were minimal and obviously worn. There was a small, rump-sprung sofa whose threadbare upholstery was mostly covered by a Navajo blanket that looked as old as the little adobe house. Nearby there was a homemade side chair built of twisted wood and covered by another old blanket. Metal floor lamps whose finish was either corroded or worn away completely stood out like weary flagpoles.

Her eyes took in the tiny corner fireplace, a card table, and two plastic lawn chairs. Nearly bald cowhides had been thrown on the warped wooden floor. More old, worn-shiny blankets hung on the walls. The colors weren't faded so much as they were from a time before intense commercial dyes, when weavers made their own subtle colors from local plants. There was enough clutter to make everything cozy.

The windows were wired for security.

So was the front door.

Dan watched Carly's face as she looked around the modest room. He waited for her to ask questions.

"For a man who's not interested in the past, you sure surround yourself with it," she said.

"The condos in town are too noisy. Besides, this was furnished."

The look she gave him said that she wasn't buying what he was selling.

He put her purse on the sofa. "Give me a minute before I show you the rest of it."

Curious, she watched while he opened a door at the back of the room, opposite the tiny kitchen. The room beyond was nothing like the front room. Newspapers, magazines, journals, and what looked like computer printouts or abstracts were stacked on every surface, including the floor. There was a wall of electronic equipment that could have come off a spaceship. The bed was new, neatly made except for stacks of papers on the blankets, and oversize. It covered two-thirds of the room.

Dan went through his bedroom quickly, grabbing printouts here and there, stacking them, and putting them in a dresser drawer. He shut down computers, turned off some other machines she couldn't identify, picked up one of them, and sat on his heels close to a long metal box the size of a foot-locker. It was the silvery color of spun aluminum or titanium and had a digital lock with two keypads, one numbered and one with a fingerprint reader as well as numbers.

Even though Dan's back was to her, she could tell he used both pads to unlock the box. When the lid opened, the metal itself was almost as thick as her finger. It would take more than a hacker to get into that box without the combination. It would take a welding torch. Or a bomb.

She wondered what Dan had that needed such high-tech protection, but she didn't ask. Why bother? He wouldn't answer.

He locked the case and stood.

"Ready for visitors?" she asked.

"Close enough. The bathroom is opposite the bed. There's no door, because there's no room to open or close one. When you want to use the facil-ities, just close the bedroom door. And don't fiddle with the electronics, please. You can't get anything on that wall to work without passwords and such."

"And if I asked you why you need such elaborate electronics on 'vacation,' you would say . . . ?"

"I'm a game freak."

She rolled her eyes. "You mentioned something

about **two** beds. Unless there's one hidden in the refrigerator, we're one bed short."

He reached under the big bed and pulled out something that looked like a deflated Zodiac. He plugged it into the wall, hit a button, and what sounded like a vacuum cleaner started forcing air into the mattress. One minute later, a twin-size mattress teetered on top of all the papers stacked on the bigger bed.

"After I fold up the card table and stack the chairs in the kitchen, this fits in the corner by the fireplace," Dan said. "Warmest bed in the house."

She looked over her shoulder at the living area, measured the space, and said, "Works for me."

"No, it works for **me**."

She turned back so fast her hair bounced. "Don't be ridiculous, you're way too big for that mattress."

"I've slept on worse."

Carly thought of his occasional hesitations, a slight favoring of his left leg. The last thing he needed was to sleep on the floor, no matter what kind of inflated mattress was underneath him.

"Let me put it this way," she said. "I sleep on the inflatable or I get a hotel room."

"Aren't you worried about rats on the floor?"

She wasn't buying that, either. "I'll make sure you empty your pockets before I go to bed."

He just shook his head.

"Speaking of which," she said, "what does the sheriff have against you?"

"I was a teenager when he was a deputy."

"So? A lot of people were teenagers twenty years ago."

"Some Sandoval boys jumped me. They ended up hurt. I didn't."

"Some? How many?"

"Not enough to get the job done." Dan pulled a fist-size plug on the mattress and began deflating it to get it out of the way.

"What did the deputy do to them?"

"It was their word against mine. Deputy Montoya was dating a Sandoval girl at the time. Ended up marrying her."

"Well, that just sucks."

He shrugged. "It's a small town. I didn't belong to any of the factions—Anglo, hispano, or Native American. I was a smart-mouthed pain in the butt."

She watched while Dan deftly rolled the mattress, forcing air out the big valve with every motion of his strong hands.

"Okay, you and Montoya have a history," she said. "That's no reason for him to accuse you of putting a gutted rat on my pillow."

"Look at it from his point of view. If I didn't do

it, someone at the governor's household did. Montoya won't win any prizes making headlines at the governor's expense."

"I still say it sucks."

"It's just the way it is." He bent and shoved the deflated mattress back beneath the bed.

"So I'm guessing your personal motto is 'Life's unfair, get over it.'"

"Good guess." He stood and looked at her, enjoying the rich color of her hair against the white-washed adobe walls. "You ready for some chili?"

"I'm ready to go kick Montoya right in his fat badge."

Dan hooked his arm around Carly's neck and pulled her close. "Can I watch?"

"Don't you want to help me?"

"I'd never get between you and Montoya's fat badge."

Before she could grumble any more about the sheriff, she found herself at the card table eating a bowl of chili con carne with tortillas on the side. A bottle of Mexican beer appeared at her elbow. She grabbed the beer, poured green sauce over the chili, and dived in.

Dan sat, dumped sauce on his own bowl of chili, and finished it before she was halfway through hers. He refilled his bowl and cleaned it again while she was mopping up the bottom of her bowl with a tor-

tilla. Then he settled back to enjoy the last swallows
of his beer.

"You don't ever need to call your chili second-
best," she said, leaning back with a satisfied sigh.

"Is this where I tell you Mom gave me the
recipe?"

"That's what I figured." Carly sipped a little more
beer. "When did you figure out that the Senator's
daughter was your grandmother?"

His eyelids lowered slightly. "I always knew. Just
like everyone else in the town."

"Including the Sandovals who jumped you?"

Dan shrugged.

"Does Winifred know?" Carly asked.

"She never said anything one way or the other."

"Did you ask?"

"No."

"Why not? You obviously like her."

Dan spun the clear beer bottle between his hands.
"I didn't care. I still don't."

"She's your blood relative."

"We're hardly close enough to be shirttail
cousins."

"But—"

He kept on talking. "Winifred's sister's legally
disowned daughter is my mother's mother," he said
sardonically. "Yippee-do. Talk about a close rela-

tive. I'll have to be sure and turn up at the family barbecue."

"What about your grandfather?"

"Which one?"

"Is John related to the Quintrells or the Castillos?"

"No. He's from Idaho."

"Right." Carly glanced at Dan. He looked bored and irritated in equal parts, but at least he was answering her questions. "Who is your maternal grandfather?"

"I don't know. My grandmother never married anyone."

"What about on your mother's birth certificate? Who was listed as father?"

"No one."

Carly drank a swallow of beer. "What does local gossip say?"

Dan's eyes narrowed to green slits. "That she was a junkie and a slut who started screwing around at thirteen and got knocked up when she was fifteen."

Carly winced but kept on asking questions. She told herself that she needed to know about the people of the area before she could do justice to Winifred's family history. And she knew she was lying to herself. Sure, local history would be helpful, but it was a need to know Dan's personal history that was driving her.

"No particular boyfriend?" she asked.

"Three of the Sandoval brothers. If you believe what the boys yelled at me before they jumped me, she liked more than one at a time. Or maybe she was too whacked out to care how many climbed on."

Carly swallowed hard. "Why would young boys know about something that happened to your grandmother?"

"The smaller the town, the longer the memory." When Carly started to ask another question, Dan cut her off. "My turn. Tell me about your parents."

She looked at the line of foam sliding down the inside of the beer bottle. When people asked about her family, she usually said something meaningless and changed the subject. But she couldn't. Not now. Dan wasn't just anyone, and he hadn't liked talking about his family any more than she was eager to talk about her lack of family. If she was going to see where their mutual attraction led, she'd have to do some sharing of her own.

"I don't know anything about my biological parents," she said after a moment. "The couple who adopted me, Glenn and Martha May, were fifty-five and forty-eight when I came into their lives."

Dan's eyes narrowed again. "How old were you?"

"I think I was taken immediately from my birth mother. My parents never said."

"And you never asked?"

"Oh, I asked. They said it didn't matter, I was way too young to know what was going on at the time, my home was with them, they loved me." She shrugged. "The usual things adopted children hear when the adoptive parents don't want to talk about it."

"Was it a formal adoption, through a licensed agency?"

"No. That's why the records stayed sealed even after I turned twenty-one."

Dan nodded. From what he'd seen of Carly, she wouldn't have taken her parents' reluctance about details as the final word. She would have pursued it on her own. And she had.

"Blank wall?" he asked.

"Completely." She grimaced. "Don't get me wrong. My curiosity about my biological parents wasn't a slam at Martha and Glenn. They loved me as much as any parents could."

"How about you? Did you love them?"

Carly looked surprised. "Of course. They were kind, careful to introduce me to a wide range of experiences, and committed to my education. As I got older, they taught me about the genealogies that were their life's work."

"But it was the past that compelled them, not the present or the future."

"You're quick. It took me years to figure that out. They were fascinated by ancestors, by the past.

Both Glenn and Martha taught at the university—European history and Latin. They were a well-matched couple."

Dan thought about a much younger Carly, bright and curious and energetic, raised by a couple old enough to be her grandparents, people whose life work was the past. "Any siblings?"

"No." She smiled wryly. "I think I was enough of a handful. They didn't need more."

He clicked the beer bottle lightly against his chili bowl. "Did they ever say why they adopted you? Had they always wanted kids?"

"They never said, but . . ." Carly sure had wondered more than once. She ripped off a bit of tortilla and nibbled. "Martha was the last of her family in the U.S., an only child raised by only children. It was the same for Glenn. No siblings, no aunts or uncles, no cousins closer than fourth or fifth. Nothing but a genealogy narrowing down to one name."

"Onlys raising onlys."

She nodded. "It was one of the many things they had in common. But Glenn and Martha couldn't have even one child. So one day they got me, and here we are."

"Were they pleased that you loved the past as much as they did?"

Carly nibbled some more. She wasn't hungry. She

just needed something to do with her hands besides twist a strand of hair around her finger. "I think so. We never talked about it in those terms."

"So what did you talk about, the rise and fall of the Roman Empire?"

She laughed. "We talked about genealogical sources, how to trace female ancestors versus male ancestors, history at the time of their grandparents and the seventh generation in the past. That sort of thing." She leaned toward him eagerly. "I loved that part the best, figuring out what people wore and ate in fifteenth-century England or Italy or Spain. I loved thinking about the consequences to ordinary people of the violent infusions of Viking and Dane blood and culture into a local population, of the Crusades, of the plagues and famines, of the adventurers and colonists and the ones who stayed home, of how the new generations of a family changed and forgot each other, of how much fun it is to find an American's fourth cousin in County Clare, then listen to them when they finally get together and share family photos and memories that bridge time and the ocean."

"Connection," he said.

"Exactly. So many people take it for granted or don't even care that they're an entry on a much larger genealogical chart," she said, spreading her arms, "a chart that could span centuries and countries and weave together the whole of—" She stopped abruptly as her right hand smacked against the wall and sent a piece of tortilla flying.

Dan captured her left hand before it collided with his nose. He laced his fingers through hers and held her hand against his thigh. Safer that way. Felt good, too.

"Sorry," she said, flushing as she bent to pick up the piece of tortilla with her free hand. "I get a little carried away when I talk about my work."

"I like your enthusiasm." He had felt the same way about his work. Once. When he'd quit the State Department and joined St. Kilda Consulting's affiliation of loose cannons, he'd been enthusiastic again. Then the **narcotraficantes** who wanted him dead had opened fire in a crowd. Three schoolchildren and a nun had died. He'd survived. He wondered if God was happy with the body count. Dan sure wasn't. "How did Winifred find you?"

"She always has the TV on in the background when she's with Sylvia. One of the yak-yak shows was interviewing me about a family history I'd just published. She was curious enough to call the show. I sent her a clipping from a recent newspaper article, along with the book I'd published for the family I'd just finished working with."

"You do it all yourself, even the publication?"

"Sure. Computers make it easy and the result can look as good as anything you buy in the store. But if my clients want more than, say, two hundred books, I job it out to a printer."

Dan looked at the fingers interlaced with his. "No ring."

"No husband. No fiancé."

"Boyfriend?"

She tilted her head and looked at him. "No. How about you?"

"No husbands or boyfriends."

"That's a relief. What about women?"

"I like them."

"Well enough to have one of your very own?"

"Not so far," he said.

The corners of her mouth curved up slightly. She decided to give him some of his own conversational switches right back. "What do you think Sheriff Montoya will do?"

"File and forget."

She laughed. "What would it take to catch you off-balance?"

**Dying children and a few slugs from a Kalashnikov.** But saying that would start a conversation he didn't want to have.

"Did Winifred ever say how the rest of the family felt about the history she'd commissioned?" Dan asked.

"No. But I figured out real quick that not every-one was on board with the idea."

"The rat on your pillow?"

"Even before that."

His fingers tightened on hers. "What happened?"

"Nothing huge. When I got there, my room wasn't ready, and when it was ready, it wasn't exactly what I'd call the best room in either house. Alma was outright rude to me. Or maybe I'm just being oversensitive. The Senator's death caught everyone by surprise." She waved her free hand. "Whatever, only Winifred seemed glad to see me."

"Anyone else give you a hard time?"

"The governor's son is a jerk, but I don't think it's anything personal. Just his natural style."

"What about Anne Quintrell?" As Dan spoke, he absently ran his thumb up and down Carly's index finger.

"I was introduced to her after the funeral." The feel of Dan's thumb rubbing her skin sent a shiver of sensation over Carly. She swallowed and ignored it. "Anne Quintrell was polite. So was the governor. So was the rest of the staff, except for Alma. Maybe she was having a bad hair week."

Dan closed his eyes and began arranging and rear-ranging facts, possibilities, scenarios. While he thought fast, his thumb moved slowly back and forth, back and forth on Carly's finger. The lazy rhythm worked its way into her blood, scattering her thoughts.

"If you're trying to distract me, you're succeeding," she said after a minute.

"What?"

She tugged at her hand. "This."

Dan looked at their interlaced fingers. "Too tight?"

She slid her own thumb up and down his, stroking lazily. In the instant before he lowered his eyelids, she saw a flare of desire.

"See what I mean?" she said. "It's distracting."

"That's one word for it." After another slow stroke, he released her hand. "If Montoya tied you to a chair and grilled you like a lamb chop, what would you tell him about me?"

She didn't bother to hide her surprise. "I don't know enough to be worth grilling."

Dan knew he should leave it that way.

And he knew he wasn't going to.

# 22

LUCIA HEARD THE RUMBLE OF HER HUSBAND'S BIG Ford Expedition, the slam of car doors, and the front door of her own house opening. Armando called to her in Spanish.

"English, my heart," she said, running out of the kitchen to meet him. "Otherwise the children will be left behind in school and you will be stuck with Anglos for lawyers and accountants."

Armando laughed and lifted Lucia in a big hug, enjoying the trim warmth of her against his sturdy body. Although he and his wife didn't agree on his career, they had real affection for one another. He'd had many women and would have many more. Only Lucia was his wife, the mother of his children.

One of Armando's bodyguards appeared at the front door. This man was slender, dressed in black, and carrying a slim black briefcase. Silently Armando gestured for him to enter.

"Come with me," Armando said to his wife.

Puzzled, Lucia followed her husband out of the

house to the big black vehicle parked in the front yard a few feet from the front door.

"I can't leave the children," she said.

"You can hear them from here."

At another silent gesture from Armando, the bodyguard opened his briefcase, took out a hand-held electronic sweeper, and went to work.

Armando closed the front door and turned to Lucia. "You had visitors last night. Were you with them the whole time?"

"I made coffee. I went to the bedroom to get photos."

He hissed through his teeth.

Shivering from more than the cold outside, Lucia waited for Armando to say something. He just rubbed her arms to warm them and stood with the air of a man waiting for something.

A few minutes later the bodyguard came out of the house. "**Es** okay," he said to Armando, mixing languages into a common border slang.

Armando nodded and led his wife back into the warmth of the house.

"**Los niños,** how are they doing?" Armando asked, closing the door behind him.

Lucia forced herself to act like everything was normal, because for Armando it was.

"They are at the top of their classes, even with

this awful flu," she said. "Your brother and father will be very pleased." She looked at her husband's pale brown eyes and black hair. Threads of gray were showing in the thick natural waves. The life he'd chosen was a brutal one. It showed in the deep lines of his face. "Are you hungry?"

"For your posole and carne asada, always." The response came easily, in spite of the hangover that made Armando's head feel like the soccer ball in a World Cup match.

His cell phone rang. He pulled it out of his back pocket, read the incoming caller ID, and shooed his wife into the kitchen. When she couldn't overhear anything, he answered the call.

"**Bueno.**" He listened, started to answer in Spanish, and thought of the kids in the back room. To them, English was still a second, often difficult language. Much safer to use it right now than Spanish. "Listen to me, Chuy," he said in a low voice. "You will cross the border at the usual spot at the usual time. All is in place. Mano is at the drop house in Las Trampas. When he okays the load, the money is wired to Aruba. Your jefe is told when it's done. Savvy?"

Chuy understood.

Armando punched a button to end the call.

Immediately the cell phone rang again.

He looked at the incoming number, swore under his breath, and dodged the call. The cell phone was necessary for his business, but it was worse than a nagging wife. He set the signal to vibrate and shoved the unit into his back pocket. Now that he'd talked to Chuy, he didn't have anything urgent to worry about until tonight, when the load would arrive.

Armando went to see the children, treating his nephews as warmly as his own kids. All of them were pale, tired, and cranky. He took temperatures the old-fashioned way, cheek to cheek. Joking, teasing out smiles, he straightened blankets and let each child discover the sweets he'd hidden in various pockets.

Lucia stood in the doorway, watching, smiling despite her fear each time Armando came home. It had been years since violence last exploded in the Sandoval smuggling trade, but Lucia would never forget the sight of Armando's cousin and best friend bleeding on the floor of Armando's house, dying with sixteen slugs in him. The miracle was that none of the children had been hit by the hail of bullets coming from the front yard.

After that Lucia had moved into a separate house and had taken a job to support herself and their young child. To this day the sound of gunfire turned her stomach. She couldn't make Armando change jobs, she wouldn't divorce him, and she feared that someday he would be murdered in her house in front of the horrified eyes of his own children.

Armando kissed and tickled the smallest child, a girl with her father's eyes and her mother's luminous skin. Then he stood, stretched wearily, and told himself he had to cut back on the homemade pulque and cocaine. The hangovers he'd thrown off with ease twenty years ago now hunted him throughout the day. Right now he should be sleeping at his luxurious condo in Taos, getting ready for the dangerous time when the heroin arrived and had to be repackaged for his distributors.

But first he had to know what Dan Duran had been doing in his wife's home on Monday night.

He followed Lucia into the kitchen, saw the icy beer and hot soup waiting for him, and hoped his stomach was up to the job. He sat and ate a few tentative bites, then more eagerly. Even the beer tasted good. Maybe it was food rather than youth he needed. When his soup bowl was empty he turned to the carne asada. He ate the way he did everything, with speed and no subtlety.

"More?" Lucia asked.

He shook his head.

She sat down next to him with a cup of coffee for herself and a smile for him.

Armando ignored the cell phone vibrating against his butt. "Tell me who was here last night."

"Dan Duran and Ms. May."

"The old curandera's historian?"

Lucia nodded, not at all surprised that Armando knew who Carly was, much less that she'd been in the house. Armando's business required that strangers were investigated instantly and family watched as a matter of course.

Armando drank the last of his beer and wiped his mouth carelessly on his hand before he remembered where he was. He grabbed the faded cloth napkin next to his bowl and scrubbed his hand and lips. Once he'd been impatient with Lucia's efforts to improve his manners and English. Now he knew she was right; if he ever wanted a better, less violent life for his children, they had to be raised to fit in with a culture that was larger than the ancient hispano way of life.

"What did Duran want?" Armando asked.

"It wasn't him, it was Carly who had all the questions," Lucia said.

Armando's face tightened. "About me?"

"No, no, no!" Lucia said instantly. "About the old times, when the Senator was young and Sylvia still laughed and danced with her husband. About the yearly barbecues and the babies."

Armando wasn't convinced. "And Duran, what did he ask?"

"Nothing. He nearly fell asleep on the couch. He was keeping a pretty lady company, that's all."

Armando grunted. "What did they want to know about the governor?"

"Listen to me." Lucia leaned forward and touched her husband's face, ensuring his attention. She didn't want any trouble for Dan or Carly, who had only been doing as Miss Winifred asked. "I talked about nothing more recent than Liza." As always, Lucia crossed herself when she mentioned the Senator's tragic daughter.

"What else did Duran say to you? Think hard, **mi esposa**."

She clenched her hands together and tried not to scream at her husband's bloodsucking career, a way of life that demanded he trust no one, even his wife.

"I think he . . . yes, he asked where Eduardo's wife is."

"Why?"

"Because I'm raising Eduardo's nephews."

"How did he know that?"

"Everyone in the pueblo knows and his mother teaches there. It's not a secret."

Armando's eyes narrowed. It was true, but it wasn't the only possible truth. "What did you tell him?"

"What you told me to say if anyone asks. She is in Mexico with the girls."

"What did he say to that?"

"Nothing."

"He didn't ask more questions about her?"

"No," Lucia said firmly.

Armando drummed his fingers on the worn wood table. "What else did he ask about?"

"Nothing. I talked with Carly and then they left."

Lucia wasn't about to mention the money Dan had given to her. Armando would be furious that she took money from Miss Winifred when his wife wouldn't accept money from her own husband.

She couldn't. To Lucia, every dollar he made dripped violence. She couldn't change her husband or the nature of his business, but she could refuse to benefit from it.

Armando relaxed. **"Bueno."**

The phone vibrated against his butt again. He pulled the unit out, checked the window, and knew he had to leave. He turned to his wife.

"Every time Duran is close to you or your car or your home, you call me." Armando grabbed her chin in his hand. "I mean it, Lucia. Every damn time."

She didn't doubt it. "I will call you. But what could he do? He's still recovering from a climbing accident."

Armando's smile reminded Lucia of everything she hated about the drug business.

"A climbing accident?" he asked, then laughed.

He was still laughing when he got in the Expedition and slammed the door behind him.

Lucia stood in the doorway, shivering, knowing that Armando had had something to do with Dan's injury.

# 23

MELISSA OPENED THE FRONT DOOR. "HELLO, DAN, Carly." Though she hadn't expected either one, she smiled and stepped back to clear the doorway. "Come in. How's your mother, Dan? Lucia keeps talking about the miracle she's working with her tutoring."

"Mom is like you, always busy, always beautiful."

Melissa's smile broadened. "You be sure to give her a hug from me when you see her. And that handsome father of yours, too."

"I'll do that."

The housekeeper turned to Carly. "Winifred said something about your car needing work and you would be staying in town . . . ?"

"How did she know?" Carly asked before she could think better of it.

Melissa tried not to laugh. "Blaine was in town running errands for the ranch. He heard about your car getting trashed from the mechanic who heard about it from the tow truck driver. Living in a small town takes getting used to." Then she shook her head and said irritably, "It's that snowboarding riffraff. They take designer drugs and then they do whatever they want and think the townsfolk shouldn't get upset because they're spending so much money here. I'll bet the sheriff said as much, didn't he?"

It took Carly a moment to sort out the syntax and realize that Melissa was giving out the standard full-time resident's complaint about the high-living tourists who brought money and irritation to the town in equal measure.

"The sheriff didn't mention anything about snowboarding," Carly said.

"Well, I hope your insurance covers the damage. Cars are so expensive, and we can't do without them, no matter how little we earn." She shook her head. "I hope you won't have to delay your work with Winifred over this. She's not getting any younger."

"Dan offered himself as a taxi service while my car is being fixed," Carly said. "I'm just here to pick up my stuff."

"But what about the history project?"

"This won't put me behind at all," Carly assured the housekeeper. "I'll stay in town so Dan won't have to make the drive out here several times a day. Instead of interviews, which Winifred shouldn't be giving until her cough gets better, I'll concentrate on newspaper archives and scanning in the photos and documents she has already provided."

"Documents?" Melissa frowned. "Winifred didn't mention anything like that to me. What kind of documents? Some papers are certainly too important to be removed from the house without Governor Quintrell's permission."

And both women knew that permission wouldn't happen.

"I'm talking about simple family documents," Carly said. "Marriage and birth and death certificates, diplomas, old letters, memorabilia such as wedding invitations and special-occasion greeting cards, report cards, a child's first drawing, whatever the family thought important enough to add to the 'box in the attic.' Or boxes, in Winifred's case. Sylvia apparently was quite the collector before her stroke."

"Oh. Well, I suppose that's okay." But Melissa was still frowning. "I should probably make a record of whatever you take with you."

"Let's ask Winifred," Dan said, easing Carly past the housekeeper. "They're her documents, after all. Please tell her that we're on the way to see her."

Melissa stood for a moment, undecided. Then she went to the intercom that connected Sylvia's suite to the rest of the house.

Dan didn't wait for Melissa's permission. He simply led Carly through the hallway that ended in Sylvia's suite.

"Melissa wasn't real thrilled, was she?" Carly said.

"From what I hear, Governor Quintrell isn't as easy a man to work for as the Senator was. Melissa is probably reporting daily to her new boss. Everyone will be nervous until they're sure their jobs are secure."

"And housekeepers tend to think they run everything—or should."

"In Melissa's case, it's pretty close to the truth," Dan said. "She got the job from her mother. I think one of her grandmothers worked for the Senator, too. But then, so have most of the old families in the valley, one way or another."

As Dan and Carly approached the closed entrance to Sylvia's suite, both of them started shedding everything they could and still be reasonably decent. Dan stopped at the black T-shirt he wore beneath his wool shirt and jacket. Carly wasn't that lucky. She'd come back to pick up her equipment and some clothes. She really hadn't expected to see Winifred tonight, so she was wearing a knitted silk body shirt under a heavy pullover sweater, plus coat. She thought about leaving the sweater on, but knew she wasn't going to. She'd been through enough for one day.

From the corner of his eye, Dan watched her struggle out of the heavy forest-green sweater. When she finally managed to yank it over her head, he forgot to breathe. Something that was thin, midnight blue, and fit like skin itself covered her from shoulders to wrists, and neck to waistline and beyond.

He'd wondered about her breasts and if she wore a bra. He didn't wonder anymore. Her breasts were just right for a man's hands and there wasn't a bra in sight. If there had been, the dark blue material was so tight he'd have been able to tell if the bra fastened in front or in back.

He wondered if the top was stretchy enough to be pulled up over her hips or if it had snaps at the crotch.

"Something wrong?" Carly asked, watching him watch her. "Technically this isn't underwear, if that's what is bothering you. It's workout gear."

"Workout." He smiled slowly.

"Yes." She looked sideways at him. "And it's no tighter than your T-shirt."

"Um," was all he said.

His pants weren't going to fit right if he kept looking at her nipples pushing against the sleek fabric. He raised his hand and knocked on the door when what he really wanted to do was find out how Carly's body shirt stayed in place.

Instead of calling out, Winifred opened the door herself. "You all right?" she asked Carly gruffly. "Melissa told me about your car."

"Other than being angry, I'm fine."

Winifred looked at Dan as if for confirmation.

"She's a lot tougher than she looks," he said.

"She better be. The Senator's son is a hard one." Winifred gestured curtly. "Get on in here. Can't have Sylvia's room getting cold. Glad you brought your man with you," she added to Carly. "I have a lot of stuff for you to take out of here."

Before Carly could object that Dan wasn't hers, she saw the cartons, bags, and boxes stacked against the wall.

"Photos," Winifred said, following her glance. "Documents, all the stuff you said you wanted. Even my mother's wedding dress."

"I didn't mean that I had to take everything with me right now," Carly said. "I can just take a box or two at a time and—"

"Here's a list of local women who might have been the Senator's lovers," Winifred interrupted curtly. "As for the boxes, take all you can and then come back for the rest. The stuff is no good to me unless it gets into the book you're going to write. There aren't any more Castillos in my line to give it to."

"What about the governor?" Carly asked.

"He's a Quintrell."

Carly looked at Dan.

He was watching the old woman intently, adding up facts and hunches, and not liking the bottom line. A distinct chill blew across his nape.

**Danger.**

He'd felt the same way when he walked out of a hotel in Colombia—and right into an ambush. He'd survived, but only because he'd worn body armor and carried a Desert Eagle. He was firing before the attackers figured out to aim for his legs. The 10 mm Eagle was like carrying a sawed-off elephant gun in his pocket—great stopping power if you were a good shot.

He'd been good enough to survive. Not good enough to take out the men before the children screamed and fell.

"If you need help," Dan said, "you call me or Dad. Anytime, day or night, Miss Winifred. Anytime at all."

Winifred waved off the suggestion with a motion that shifted the heavy Indian bracelet she always wore at her wrist. "You just keep the rats off Carly's pillow and I'll do fine."

"How did you find out about the rat?" Carly asked, startled.

"Alma's sister-in-law works for the sheriff," Winifred said. "She about hurt herself laughing over the rat."

"What a sweetheart," Carly muttered.

If Winifred heard, she didn't show it. She just went to the corner adobe hearth and added two more chunks of piñon to the already fierce fire. "With the Senator dead, things are going to change. His son isn't a patient man. I want my history book in one month, not three. You get it done, and get it done right, and I'll give you twice as much as we agreed on."

Carly looked into the old woman's blazing black eyes and wondered again just how sane Miss Winifred was. "I'll do everything I can."

"If you need to hire some work done, I'll pay for it," Winifred said.

Dan put his hand on Carly's arm. "I'm lazing around doing nothing. I'll help her just to keep from getting bored."

"Then start hauling boxes," Winifred said.

"Melissa was worried that some of the documents you have might be so valuable that Governor Quintrell would have to approve their removal," Carly said.

"Sometimes Melissa is as full of crap as a Christmas goose."

Carly blinked. "So I guess it's not a problem."

"Not for me," Winifred said. "What's mine is mine and to hell with the Senator's son."

"Okay, then I guess I should pack the things I'll need in the next few days," Carly said.

Reluctantly she started to leave. She really hoped that there wouldn't be any more gory surprises on her pillow, but she was afraid there would be.

"I'll come with you," Dan said. "Wait while I load this stuff into the truck."

"You don't have to go with me."

"Yes I do."

Carly smiled, hoping she didn't look as relieved as she felt. She wasn't a helpless little flower, but the sly violence of the dead rat, the paint-drenched car, and the threatening phone call made her feel angry and sick and more frightened than she wanted to admit. She'd much rather deal with Alma's brand of in-your-face bitchiness.

Dan made quick work of the cartons, boxes, bags, and ancient leather suitcase Winifred had gathered. Carly picked up the shirt, sweater, and jackets that she and Dan had shed.

"I'll call you as soon as the car is fixed," she said to Winifred.

"You do that. And put that man of yours to work. He has the best mind of the lot."

Carly didn't ask which "lot" Winifred meant. She just let herself out of the overheated room with a sigh of relief and went to catch up with Dan.

Together they pulled on warm clothes, got in the truck, and drove it around to the guesthouse.

"Thanks for doing this," Carly said when Dan parked close to her room. "I know I shouldn't let that dead rat bother me, but . . ." She sighed. "It does."

"Don't worry about it. You're not used to ugly little games."

"Can people get used to this?"

"Oh, yeah." **And a lot worse.**

But talking about it wouldn't make her feel better, so he shut up and climbed out of the truck. Together they walked quickly through the cold night to the old house. The wide front door stuck as it always did, the gallery was chilly and dark, and there was a light burning in Carly's room.

"Did you—"

"No," she cut in, her voice low.

"Same shit, different day," he muttered.

"The door is wide open this time, does that count?"

He pushed her down next to the antique sideboard. "Stay here."

"Déjà vu all over again," she grumbled, but she didn't get up and follow him.

Dan walked quietly toward the open door. There wasn't any noise from the room. He crouched and took a swift look inside.

The bed was neatly turned down.

Not a dead rat in sight.

No living ones either.

Just to be sure, Dan went through the room and then the small bathroom next door, which served the other guest rooms as well. Clean towels neatly folded. Clean glass in the holder.

He went back to the hall. "It's okay."

Despite the assurance, Carly hesitated just an instant before she looked at her neat room. "Well, somebody lit a fire under somebody's butt."

"What do you mean?"

"Turn-down service on the sheets. My pajamas neatly folded at the foot of the bed. Everything but a piece of chocolate on the pillow."

"The towels in the bathroom looked fresh. Place smelled like disinfectant, too."

Carly lifted her eyebrows. "Gee, and I have to leave all this belated luxury."

"Life's a bitch." Dan went to the tall cupboard that served as a closet. "Where's your suitcase?"

"Under the bed, along with my other stuff."

He bent and pulled out a suitcase and several other pieces of luggage, including some specialized aluminum cases of the kind made for carrying cameras or guns. Given what he knew about Carly, Dan was betting on cameras.

"Dan?"

The quality of her voice brought him to his feet in

a single motion. She was standing at the foot of the bed, staring at some boxes that had been pushed into a corner of the small room.

"What's wrong?" he asked.

Carly went to the boxes and looked again. No mistake. The boxes had all been closed wrong.

"I left them lined up along the bed," she said. "Now, even if a really helpful maid put them along the wall out of my way, what was the maid doing pawing through the contents?"

"How can you tell?"

"I get a lot of boxes of stuff in my line of work," Carly said. "The first thing I learned was to mark the boxes so that I know what's inside without having to look. With cardboard cartons I mark one flap on the top and two sides. I close the box so that the inventory flap is on top."

He looked at the top box. The overlapping flaps were bare of any writing.

"Wonder what's missing. Or added," Carly said bitterly.

He caught her hand before she could touch the box. "Let me do it."

But instead of opening the box, he pulled off his jacket, crouched on his heels, and studied the two-foot-square carton.

"What are you looking for?" she asked.

"Wires."

"Wires," she repeated. Then she understood. Her breath came in raggedly. "You don't really think anyone would rig my files to explode?"

"Paranoia is just part of my job description."

Carly swallowed hard. "What job is that?"

"I'm on vacation."

Dan reached into his back pocket and pulled out a folding knife. A flick of his thumb opened up a wicked blade. He didn't really expect anything lethal in the box, but he didn't want to die with a surprised look on his face. Gently, patiently, he slit each flap where it joined the box until nothing visibly attached the flaps to the box. The flaps shifted and slid to the floor.

Nothing on top but papers.

"How does it look?" he asked.

She cleared her throat. "Normal."

"About as full as it was the last time you closed it?"

"I guess so. I don't stuff the boxes. It creases everything."

"Okay." He casually riffled through the papers inside. No wires. No rats. Not even a mouse turd. "Looks good. Check it out for anything obviously missing."

Carly crouched next to him and flipped through the box. Notebooks, genealogical forms, manila envelopes of photos or documents labeled as to approximate decade and/or family relationship.

There wasn't anything missing, but something wasn't right.

"Someone has been through this," she said.

"You sure?" he asked without looking up from his study of the remaining boxes.

"Yes. I'm totally anal when it comes to my work," she said. "Genealogy and family history are built on small facts. If you don't organize, organize, **organize** every single little piece of information you find, you'll drive yourself crazy looking for proof of something that you've already researched and nailed down—and then put the document in the wrong place. But in this box, an envelope holding documents is mixed up with the photo envelopes. The decades are out of order on the photo envelopes. It's not a big thing," she added, rearranging envelopes as she spoke, "but it's real."

"Anything missing?"

"No."

"Check these out."

She looked up. The other cartons were open. She was pleased to see that the flaps were still attached to the boxes. She started going through the contents quickly.

"Same thing on all of these," she said after a few minutes. "Nothing missing. Everything not quite in order. Wonder what they were looking for. Or maybe they were just nosy."

Dan stacked the three cartons on one another and picked them up as a unit. "I'll put these in the truck." Then he saw the look on her face. "What?"

"I was thinking of breaking into a chorus of how nice it is to have a man around the house. I usually lift those suckers one at a time."

"I'm too lazy to make that many trips. Get the door for me, will you?"

Carly grabbed a camera case and a briefcase and trotted after him, opening doors as needed. They repeated the process until she had everything she needed but her suitcase. Dan picked it up and headed for the door.

"Wait," she said. "I forgot my pajamas."

He smiled slowly. "Don't feel you have to wear any on my account."

"Ha ha." She grabbed the pajamas from the bedspread and then recoiled with a gasp.

Instantly Dan was between her and the bed.

No rat.

No gore.

Just a note made from letters cut out of newspaper headlines:

## DONT COME
## BACK

# 24

THE GOVERNOR'S MANSION HAD BEEN DESIGNED TO invite visitors to be comfortable and learn about New Mexico's distinctive art and artists. The national TV personality pacing the parlor and waiting to talk to the governor wasn't gracious, comfortable, or artistic. She was, however, distinctive. Jeanette Dykstra had a huge national following for her television show **Behind the Scenes,** a combination of gossip, speculation, ambush interviews, and "news" of the sort that gave journalism a bad name.

Anne Quintrell set her teeth delicately, pasted on a smile, and walked toward the small-screen bitch queen. Dykstra looked older off-screen, harder, almost skeletal. It was the tyranny of TV's added twenty pounds, which resulted in a constant diet for people who made their living in front of a camera.

Anne understood the skinny edict. What she didn't understand was why women with brown eyes and olive skin thought they looked good as a bleached-crispy blonde.

"Ms. Dykstra, I hope I haven't kept you waiting," Anne said. "My secretary didn't mention an evening appointment."

"Call me Jeanette." The reporter smiled, showing perfect teeth and no warmth. "Obviously there's been a mistake. My appointment was with the governor."

Anne's smile didn't falter. "I'm so sorry. Someone must have forgotten to notify you. The governor cleared his calendar after his father's sudden death."

"Sudden?" Dykstra's dark eyebrows pinched together.

"Death is always sudden, even when it's expected."

Dykstra looked at the immaculately dressed governor's wife; no ambush photo op would ever find a hair out of place on her. And there wasn't any hint of gossip about a bad marriage or girls on the side. Or boys. Nothing but Ken and Barbie Quintrell smiling out at the world. Dykstra looked around the parlor, noting the colorful, carefully stenciled designs on the dark beams, the beige overstuffed furniture that somehow managed not to be casual, and the expected southwestern art. Nothing juicy here, either.

The silence grew.

"I'm sure the governor will be glad to reschedule," Anne lied. "He has great admiration for your work."

"That so?" Dykstra made a sound that was close to a snort. "Then the rumors must be true."

"What rumors?"

"That Josh Quintrell is running for president."

"My husband is governor of New Mexico, and is honored to be trusted by the people with such an important responsibility."

"That's what they all say. Then they throw their hat into the presidential ring and never look back." Dykstra's brown eyes narrowed. "Your husband has some real handicaps in a presidential race."

"Since he's not—"

The other woman kept talking. "His son is a boozy screwup who goes through women faster than a ten-million-dollar athlete. The governor keeps his poor ill mother shut away from the world. His dear, recently departed father was a womanizer the likes of which we haven't seen since the heyday of the Kennedys. If anybody looks, I'll bet there are bastards galore out there with the Senator's blood in them. Your husband's family is the stuff of soap operas."

Anne kept her pleasant expression in place. She'd had a lot of practice smiling through her teeth at the gossips, groupies, and guttersnipes who pursued high-profile politicians. "My husband is a compassionate, intelligent, public-minded man who has done a great deal for the citizens of New Mexico."

"And zip for his family. Half the voters in America are women. They have a right to know what kind of man is asking for their vote. I'm sure the governor would like to have an on-camera half-hour interview at the ranch with **Behind the Scenes,** exploring the tragedy of his personal life contrasted with the success of his professional life."

"That's very generous of you," Anne said neutrally. "I'll tell the governor of your offer."

"You do that." Dykstra readjusted the strap of her leather briefcase. "And while you're at it, tell him that without his cooperation, **Behind the Scenes** will air a segment on his family life just in time for the major primaries. Some of the topics I'll cover will include his mother's doctors, people who remember his tragically murdered drug addict/slut sister, rumored illegal sources of campaign contributions, and any of the Senator's bastards we find between now and then. If the governor prefers to cooperate with us, we'd concentrate on him rather than his sister, father, bastards, and tainted money." She smiled thinly. "When he thinks about it, I'm sure the governor will want to put his own words before the people."

The man who was a cross between a butler and a bodyguard appeared in the doorway as though summoned. Or perhaps he'd merely been eavesdropping and decided to step in. Dykstra didn't know and didn't care. She'd gotten her message across.

"Please give Ms. Dykstra a card for the governor's appointment secretary," Anne said to the man. She turned to the TV journalist and held out her hand. "A pleasure meeting you. If I can help you in any way, don't hesitate to call."

Anne kept her game face on until the bodyguard showed Dykstra out. Then she turned and walked quickly toward the governor's home office. She knocked lightly and pushed the door open without waiting for an invitation.

"Josh, we've got a problem."

# 25

DAN GLANCED AROUND HIS RENTAL HOUSE. IT looked like a photographic archive after a tornado. Piles of pictures were everywhere—table, chairs, bed, dresser, leaning against the wall, and all over the floor.

"Okay," Carly said. She peeled off her slightly dusty cotton gloves and pulled on a clean pair. "Normally I'd go over all these in detail with Winifred first, but she wasn't interested in any photo that had anyone except a Castillo in it."

Winifred's illness, which had severely limited the interviews, was bad enough. But her stubborn determination to ignore the Quintrells, Sandovals, and everyone else not a Castillo was making Carly's work a lot harder than it had to be. No matter what Winifred's prejudice dictated, the families were all deeply intertwined. Leaving out such important connections would gut the family history.

**You get what you get and you don't throw a fit,** Carly reminded herself.

She didn't think that digging up a list of the Senator's bastards made up for otherwise ignoring the Quintrells. Especially as the list of his lovers was as long as her arm. When the Senator hadn't been in Santa Fe or Washington, D.C., he must have been shagging everything female in Taos County. It gave Carly a whole new slant on the disease called satyriasis.

"Let's see what we have," she said.

"A disaster, that's what." Dan gestured to the papers everywhere. "I'll have to rig hammocks for us to sleep in."

She grinned. "You rig them, I'll fill them with photos."

"You would, too."

"You bet. This is the messiest part of the job, and in some ways the most important."

He shook his head, but he was almost smiling. He'd enjoyed watching Carly's concentration as she went through envelope after envelope of Winifred's photos and decided on a probable date for each image. The much smaller group of Sandoval photos had been set out on the card table.

When he wasn't enjoying the view, he was running the names on Winifred's list through his memory bank and that of the newspaper. Trying to take the times the Senator—at whatever age—had been home to diddle the locals and matching those times against the online birth registry nine or ten months later was like a logic problem.

He enjoyed it.

"We'll start with the daguerreotypes," she said. "Unless I see something that doesn't fit, I'll assume that the dags are no earlier than 1840 and probably no later than 1860."

"Why?"

"Daguerre patented the process of photography on metal in 1840. By 1860, ambrotypes and tintypes largely replaced the daguerreotype."

"I've never heard of an ambrotype."

"Most people haven't. They were produced on glass instead of metal. They were easy to look at. You didn't have to tilt the glass this way and that to see the image, the way you do with a dag. See?"

She held out a daguerreotype to Dan on her palm. He had to tip her hand in various directions before light met the metal at an angle that revealed the image. Even then, it wasn't easy to see.

"It shifts," he said.

"From a negative to positive image," she agreed. "That's how you know it's a daguerreotype instead of a tintype." She put the image back in its place. "Ambrotypes were a lot easier to produce than dags. No long exposures with the sitter's head held immobile in a contraption that must have come from the Spanish Inquisition. Dags were expensive.

Ambrotypes were cheaper. Not cheap, mind you. No new technology ever is. Ambrotypes were really popular in the mid-1850s."

"Then someone developed a better technology?"

"Better, cheaper, and a whole lot quicker. Tintypes."

Dan looked at the various images scattered across his house. So many ways to take pictures, so many things to mount the images on to preserve them. "So tintypes are photographs on tin?"

"No. Iron. Originally they were called ferrotypes or melainotypes, a salute to the iron backing. Then they got the name tintypes because tin shears were used to cut up the photographic plate into halves, quarters, sixths, ninths, even as small as one-inch square. There wasn't another really significant advance in photography after that until the 1880s, when flexible film and Kodak cameras made everyone his own historian."

"I'd swear some of those paper photographs are older than 1880," Dan said, looking at the bed.

She followed his glance. "Absolutely. The paper print process was developed at the same time as daguerreotypes. But paper didn't become really popular until people figured out how to make multiple images. Prints. Then you had people making visiting cards and cabinet cards and stereographs. Unfortunately, everyone collected cards of the rich and famous and bought stereographs for the fun of it. Stuff you have in your family history box might have no more actual relationship to your family than I have to a postcard of Queen Elizabeth."

Dan started to ask another question.

"But right now," Carly said firmly, "I want to concentrate on describing Winifred's dags for my file."

She opened her computer to the file that held photographic forms for the Castillo project. Then she hesitated and looked up at Dan before she handed over the computer.

"You don't have to do this, you know," she said. "It's really boring."

"Groundwork often is," he said, taking the computer, "but without it you don't have anything except hot air."

She let out a long breath. "Not many people understand that."

"See?" He settled cross-legged on the floor near her. "Just one more thing we have in common."

Carly looked at his innocent expression and crystal green eyes. "You're laughing at me."

"No, at me. I'm going to spend the next few hours working my ass off with a pretty lady instead of being all smooth and seductive and getting her in bed."

"Can I have that in writing?"

His smile was as real as it was slow. "No."

She felt like fanning herself but didn't want to encourage him. He was way too sexy as it was. **Why did my hormones decide to wake up now? Is it my biological clock running amok?**

She wanted to believe that. She really did.

And she was afraid the truth was that Dan pushed her female buttons just by being alive. Handsome she could shrug off. Intelligent with a wicked sense of humor slid right past her defenses.

**I'm in trouble.** Then she smiled. **About time, too.**

"What?" he asked, seeing her smile.

"Ready to type?"

He started to pursue the source of that secret feminine smile, then decided against it. He didn't want to crowd her.

At least not too much.

Yet.

"Sure," he said.

"Winifred Simmons y Castillo File. First image. Daguerreotype, half plate, frame is wood with embossed leather, hook-and-eye clasp, no photographer name or studio embossed on the velvet backing. Standing woman, dark hair, probably a riding hat. Costume simple, low waist, long, full skirt, slightly fuller sleeves on the forearms, large decorative buttons down the front, possibly a type of gathering or bustle behind, fabric is medium to dark with dark accents, backdrop is painted columns and drapery . . ."

As Carly continued describing the contents of the photo, she took several views of it with her digital camera, which was connected by cable to the computer Dan was typing on.

"Hey, you're fast," she said, watching him.

"Only for some things. For others, I'm slow and thorough."

She opened her mouth, closed it, and told herself that she was imagining a double meaning. Then she saw the curving line of his mouth and knew that anything she was imagining, he was, too.

And she couldn't even call him on it without putting both feet in her mouth.

"Right," she muttered. "Date assigned to first image is tentatively mid-1840s, based on the case and the costume."

Dan started to ask a question, then didn't. They would be up all night if he let his own curiosity off the leash. Even so, it was hard not to ask. Expertise of any kind fascinated him.

And he could have sworn some of those images looked familiar. It couldn't have been family photographs from his own past, because his mother didn't have any that were older than her children.

Carly downloaded the digital images of the daguerreotype into the appropriate part of the e-form Dan had just finished filling in. "Second image. Daguerreotype, half plate, wood case, embossed leather, rose motif. Standing woman, not the same person as in first image, appears old enough to be the mother of the first, same style of costume . . ."

Dan called up another blank form, typed quickly, and thought about how different this was from his usual reports, which were a combination of political rumor and innuendo, facts and body counts, educated insights and outright hunches, players and police and the poor sons of bitches caught in between. Those were the people he felt sorry for, wanted to help, and all too often had been able to do little more than bury the dead and pray for the living.

Maybe Carly had a point. If you investigated the past instead of the present, at least the blood was already dry.

Together Dan and Carly quickly described and catalogued six daguerreotypes. When they came to the seventh, Dan felt like a hunter that had just spotted dinner.

"I know that one," he said, pointing to an image of a bride and groom. "I've seen it before."

"Where?" Carly demanded. "Winifred ignored it when I asked questions."

"Newspaper archives. I can't remember if it was

a drawing or a photograph of the original daguerreotype. But that's the first Andrew Jackson Quintrell and his bride, Isobel Quintrell y Castillo. Only after her marriage, she was careful to use an Anglicized version of her name—Isobel Castillo Quintrell. So the daguerreotype was taken in 1865, New Mexico Territory, the year of their marriage. Probably taken in Santa Fe, but I can't be sure. The article might name the photographer, or daguerreotypist, or whatever they were called, and will certainly give a date for the marriage."

Carly grinned and planted a smacking kiss on Dan's cheek. "Fantastic! Has anyone ever told you you're a genius?"

"Kiss me again and you can call me anything you want."

"Oh, the temptation."

"The kiss or the name-calling?"

"Yes."

He pulled her close with startling speed, kissed her lazily, thoroughly, and released her with a slow smile. "Let the name-calling begin."

Carly couldn't catch her breath, much less use it to yell at the man who had just showed her that when it came to kissing, she had a few things left to learn. The thought was dizzying.

"No comment?" he asked.

"Does 'Whew' count?"

His hand snaked around her nape. "Want to go for 'Wow'?"

Her body said yes.

Her mind said not yet.

Dan read her well. He released her with a slow caress along her jawline. "What comes after the daguerreotypes?"

"The what?" Abruptly she looked away so that she wouldn't get lost in the hothouse green of his eyes. "Ambrotypes." She let out a long breath. "You're a very disturbing man."

"Thank you."

"It wasn't a compliment."

"Sure it was. When you're concentrating, it would take dynamite to break through. Therefore, I'm dynamite."

She laughed almost helplessly. Then she just laughed. It had been a long time since she'd enjoyed a man as much as Daniel Duran. In truth, it had been forever.

"If I'm going to earn Winifred's bonus for finishing early, I have to stay focused," Carly said. The slow trailing of her fingertips down his stubble-rough cheek said focus wasn't easy right now. "Help me out, okay?"

He nodded, brushed a kiss over her fingertips, and turned back to the computer. "Ambrotypes."

She sighed. "Right. Ambrotypes." Very gently

she picked up the first one in her cotton-clad fingers. "Eighth image. Size, quarter plate. Case is probably mid-1850s. The collodion is very badly damaged and curling away from the glass in fragments. I doubt that restoration is possible. In any case, Winifred doesn't want to pay for it. The best I can do is photograph the ruined image and play with it digitally."

Dan typed while Carly photographed and mourned the ambrotypes that hadn't survived the passage of time. Sometimes cheaper and faster wasn't good in the long run; daguerreotypes survived intact while ambrotypes were reduced to little more than black flakes and glass.

"How long were ambrotypes popular?" he asked when she paused.

"Less than a decade, thank God. Tintypes are a lot more durable." She shook her head. "It's almost not worth the hard drive space, but you never know. Some bright tech type might eventually figure out a way to resurrect the images."

When Carly reached for the first tintype, she glanced sideways at Dan. From the way he was acting, the kiss had never happened. Even as she told herself that she couldn't complain, that he was doing exactly what she'd asked, she looked at his mouth. Soft and hungry over hers, hard to forget, impossible not to want again.

"You're distracting me," Dan said without turning from the computer.

"Work on your concentration."

He snickered.

"Image twenty-one," she said briskly. "Tintype, half plate, brown tint, very probably Isobel Quintrell or a close relative based on the line of the chin, the space between the eyes, and the cheekbones. This woman is in full mourning clothes holding what appears to be a stillborn baby wrapped in baptismal white."

Dan's fingers paused over the computer keyboard. "You're joking."

"No."

He glanced up at her in disbelief.

"It's true," Carly said. "Women often were photographed with their dead children and the image sent to distant family members as a kind of memorial for the dead child. With multiple camera lenses, multiple photos could be taken at the same time, so you could send out as many memorial photos as you had the money and patience for."

He raised his dark eyebrows. "A lot of cultures make offerings to the dead, but this is a new one to me."

"The nineteenth century had a much greater understanding of the inevitability of death and the importance of death rituals than we do in the twenty-first. They lived a lot closer to the bone then."

"So some of the men in those photos who look like death masks probably were?"

"Dead?"

"Yes."

She nodded and began photographing the tintype, talking as she worked. "Mortuary photos or funerary photos or whatever you call them had quite a vogue. They were a way to unite families separated by miles that couldn't be covered any faster than a horse could gallop or a ship could sail."

He glanced sideways at Carly. She was wearing jeans and one of his old sweatshirts, no makeup, barefoot, clean white cotton gloves on her hands, wielding a high-tech camera, and talking matter-of-factly about the great American taboo—death.

"Not that they didn't pretty up death," she added. "The family corpses were washed and dressed in their finest for the photographers. The only time death was taken head-on was with posthumous photos of criminals. Then the bodies were just propped up so that the camera could record the bullet holes and the faces. Proof of death, as it were. Much easier than hauling a corpse all over the West to claim a Dead or Alive reward." She put her fists into the small of her back and stretched. "Same for hangings. Photo cards of executed outlaws were real moneymakers for some photographers."

Subtly Dan shifted in his chair, easing his healing leg into a new position.

Carly saw the motion. "Maybe we should take a break."

"I've got another two hours before I get restless."

"But your leg—"

"Is fine." He held his hands over the keyboard. "What's the next image?"

She swallowed her objections and picked up the next tintype, describing the presentation case, background, and other pertinent aids to dating. "Same woman, different mourning dress, different baptismal wrap for the child, who looks to be perhaps two months old. Dress is very flat down the front, cinched severely at the waist, and has a short train. Probably late 1870s."

Dan typed in the description of the mortuary image. The next three tintypes were the same— only the style of the mourning clothes and the age of the dead child changed.

"Okay, that takes care of the deceased," Carly muttered, taking a final photo. "On to the kids that made it."

"Six dead children, none of them old enough to

crawl. It's a wonder that she survived," Dan said. "You're sure they're all the same woman?"

"The black rosary dangling from her hands looks the same in each image. When I enhance it digitally, I'll be certain."

The next three tintypes were of living children, two girls and a boy. Even as a baby, the stamp of the first Andrew Jackson Quintrell came down in the son's pale, brilliant eyes. His mother was in the shape of his jaw and the tiny ears.

"If you're right and the woman is Isobel," Dan said, "then the boy is A. J. Quintrell Junior. His sisters are . . ." He frowned and rummaged in his mind through old research, the kind that had made his mother so angry she didn't speak to him for a week. "María and Elena, I think. Their birth would have been announced in the newspaper. Ditto for their death."

"Do you remember any details? Winifred only talked about these," Carly said, pointing to a swath of tintypes on the bed that looked very similar to the ones they had just recorded.

He shook his head. "Mom never talked about her immediate parents, much less her great-greats."

Carly made a frustrated sound. "No matter what Winifred wants to believe, this is part of her family, too."

"She's paying the bills."

"Still, I don't like doing a half-assed job."

He gave her a slow sideways look. "I'm so glad to hear that."

"Stop that."

"Stop what?"

"Acting innocent and throwing out double meanings for me to trip over."

"You trip and I'll beat you to the floor."

She tried not to laugh. She laughed anyway. "Focus, Dan. Focus."

"I am."

"Don't focus on **that**."

"What?"

"Sex."

"I'm a man, honey. That's like asking me not to breathe."

What he didn't say was that it was good to feel like a man again, instead of a bloodstained wraith raging at what couldn't be changed. But if he mentioned that, his curious Carolina May would have a thousand questions, none of which he could answer.

Carly saw the change in Dan's expression, dark again rather than amused, and wondered what he was thinking about. Not sex. She would have bet on it.

With a stifled sigh, she picked up a tintype from the group Winifred had agreed to talk about, and started describing it. When she was finished, she added the information she'd received from Winifred. "The date is January third, 1870. Juana Castillo married a third cousin, Mateo Cortéz de Castillo." Carly picked up another tintype, described it, and said, "Two years later she died in childbirth. This image is of her dead." Carly picked up the next tintype, described it, and said, "María, daughter of Juana. Mateo Cortéz de Castillo remarried two years after his wife's death. All trace of him in the Castillo family history stops as of his remarriage. His descendants didn't count, even if they were half siblings to María."

"Clannish lot," Dan said.

"To put it mildly. From what I've gathered, Winifred and her mother didn't think much of Mateo. He's the one who pretty much lost the farm to the Anglos. That's why he married off his barely fourteen-year-old daughter María to Hale Simmons."

Dan whistled. "Fourteen? Even in the bad old days, that's a little young."

"Hale was at least forty. The odd thing is that they didn't have any kids for almost twenty-five years. Then Sylvia María was born in 1916."

"So Sylvia's daddy is over sixty-five before he starts fathering kids with the same woman he's been living with for a quarter century?" Dan asked skeptically. "Sounds like María finally jumped the fence to look for sperm donors."

"You want to suggest that to Winifred?"

"Why not? She's the one who's hell-bent on detailing the maternal family history. Does she think she's descended from a long line of Mother Teresas?"

"Um, right. I'll ask her, but it probably won't matter to her anyway. Simmons isn't a Castillo."

"You have a point. So Winifred was born right after her sister?"

"If you think ten years is right away, yes."

He did some fast addition. "Menopause baby?"

"It happens. That's why there's a name for it."

"New boyfriend? Hale was likely too old to get it up, much less shoot anything but blanks."

"I'll be sure to ask Winifred," Carly said dryly. "But there were some stillbirths along the way, so I'm guessing the boyfriend was a steady one."

"If you want to be sure, find Hale's grave, get some DNA, and see if me or my mother could be related to him."

Carly thought quickly. "It's been a long time since Hale died."

"You'd be amazed at what the labs can do."

"I wonder if Winifred would pay for the tests."

"Forget her. I'll pay."

Carly stared at Dan. "Why?"

"Because if Winifred realizes that she can't control the results of her family history, she'll probably decide not to do it at all."

Carly put her hands on her hips and faced him. "Oh, gee, thanks. Forget about digging up Hale. Nice to know you want me out of work."

Dan stood before she could back up even half a step.

"What I want," he said, his face very close to hers, "is to keep you from being the one screaming into a microphone."

# 26

DAN STRETCHED HIS LEFT LEG AND KNEADED
muscles that wanted to knot up. Walking and
running he could do well enough, but sitting at a
computer for hours at a time was guaranteed to
make his leg ache. He glanced over the summary of
his report and hit the send button, letting people in
D.C. know that Colombia was going to hell in a
handbasket. Again. Maybe Colombia's staggering
government could pull the country out of the mire
created by drug money and illegal armies. Maybe
the World Bank could pump in enough legal money
to keep things afloat for a while.

But nothing would replace the middle-class pro-
fessionals and the upper class whose wealth and tal-
ents were hemorrhaging out of the country at a
chilling rate.

**Greed, the engine of the global train wreck.**

He hoped his report made a difference in the
speed of U.S. and world reaction to Colombia's rapidly developing crisis. Nobody needed another

failed state. Nobody benefited from it but the crooks at the top, the ones that rode the body politic right into the ground, murdering the competition and grabbing money with both hands as long as the ride lasted.

Thinking about it didn't make Dan's leg feel any better.

**So think about Gus's kids smiling and laughing. Soon they'll be over the flu and running around, bursting with health and intelligence, well fed, well loved, well educated, and ready to take on the world.**

**Fuck the politicians.**

**It's the kids that keep me trying to salvage something from the train wreck.**

Quietly, efficiently, Dan shut down the computer, disconnected the box that automatically encrypted outgoing material and decoded incoming messages, and stored the machine in its titanium nest.

There was no sound from beyond the closed bedroom door, where Carly slept. At least Dan hoped she was sleeping. Thinking about her lying awake and alone in the living room would keep him awake and restless.

**Don't forget the bone.**

**How could I? The evidence is right there in front of me.**

Two dogs barked in the darkness, from the direction of the Rincon house. The barks rose in savagery and then shut off at a shout.

Dan waited, listening for whatever had set off the dogs. He didn't hear anything but the settling of piñon logs in the fireplace beyond the bedroom. Wind sighed over the roof and cried in the cottonwood's massive branches. Moments later the dogs started barking again, drawing another irate shout from their owner.

**Something is upwind of the house. The dogs bark every time the wind blows.**

Suddenly glass shattered in the living room and something thumped to the floor. Alarms went off everywhere.

Dan was on his feet and in the living room before the missile stopped skidding across the wood floor. He saw instantly that it was an adobe brick, not a gasoline or pipe bomb. An envelope was tied to the brick.

Ignoring it, he went to the alarm panel in the living room and shut off the noise.

The neighbor's dogs were going nuts.

"What's going on?" Carly's voice was hoarse with adrenaline and being yanked out of deep sleep.

"Don't get up. I mean it, Carolina May. Stay put."

She didn't move, held in place more by the quality of his voice than his words.

He crossed back to his bedroom, knelt by the titanium case, and quickly went through the locks. This time he didn't pull out a decoder.

The Desert Eagle didn't shine with chrome. It was matte finish, dark, and all business. The weight of the weapon told Dan what he already knew—it was loaded. With automatic motions he released the safety and held the gun down along his leg. Quickly, silent but for the faint crunch of glass beneath his shoes, he went back across the living room and stood to the side of the broken window.

Moonlight poured into the living room through the torn curtains. He stared out at the front of the property. Nothing moved except a black shape speeding away down the road.

Someone was running without lights.

"Dan?" Carly's voice was a whisper.

"Not yet." His voice was low, pitched to reach only her. "I think he's gone, but I want to be sure. Don't move from your bed until I get back."

"But why should you be the one to . . ." Her voice died as she spotted the gun held against his leg. "Oh."

He tossed his cell phone to her. "Call 911. My house is in the county's jurisdiction."

She grabbed the phone out of the air and began punching in numbers. "You're really going to have to tell me about your job," she muttered.

He went out the kitchen door without saying anything. The night was bright and clean and icy. The faint smell of a badly tuned gasoline engine lingered on the air.

If Dan had thought he was the target, he would have taken a long, careful time going around the house and narrow lean-to. But Carly was the target and he wanted to wrap his fingers around someone's neck. He went through the motions of a search with a speed that would have appalled his Special Ops trainers. But then, as he'd told them every day of training, he was a scholar, not a soldier, and there was no way they could turn him into a lean, mean killing machine.

All Dan found was a blurred set of tracks going from the road to the frozen front yard and back again. The combination of half-melted and then refrozen snow and mud didn't offer much in the way of information. The person hadn't been a giant or a midget, and hadn't worn spike heels or anything that left a distinct impression.

He put the gun on safety and jammed it into his jeans at the small of his back. It wasn't comfortable that way, but it wouldn't wander.

"It's okay, Carly," he called out. "But stay in bed

anyway. There's glass all over and it's damned cold."

He went to the lean-to, found some old fence posts, and brought them into the house.

Carly watched in silence while he nailed the posts over the broken window. He wielded the hammer like a man with vengeance on his mind. The butt of the big handgun showed against his shirt.

Moonlight glittered through broken glass and vertical posts.

"Looks like a jail," Carly said.

He smiled rather grimly. "It won't do anything for the warmth, but it will keep out visitors. I'll get some plywood in the morning." He really looked at her for the first time. She was pale in the moonlight, almost ghostly. She was holding what looked like a greeting card. Her hand trembled. "You okay, honey?"

"Sure. Why wouldn't I be? People throw bricks through my windows all the time. And leave dead rats, and trash my car, and scream at me over the phone, and . . ." She swallowed hard, trying to remove the adrenaline huskiness from her voice. "Outright death threats are still new. They'll take some getting used to."

He crunched through the glass and sat on his heels beside the inflatable mattress. Silently he took the card from her hand. It was a standard greeting card, available in any store. The front said: I'VE BEEN MEANING TO TELL YOU . . .

He opened the card. The action triggered the tiny recorder that was part of the card. A voice whispered, **"Get her out of town before she dies."**

# 27

MELISSA COVERED HER FACE WHILE THE HELICOPter settled onto the small pad and shut down. She didn't step forward until the rotors stopped turning and the air settled down.

"Governor, what an unexpected pleasure," Melissa said. Her expression asked what was wrong. She raised her hand, signaling to one of the ranch employees. "Jim just brought the mail in from Taos. He'll take care of your luggage."

Josh rubbed his face wearily. He and Anne had spent a long night hashing out the least politically destructive way to handle the Jeanette Dykstra situation. He hadn't planned to move this quickly after the Senator's death, but he didn't have any choice now.

"Thanks, Jim," Josh said, shaking the man's hand. "How's the hunting?"

"Real slow. The drought has cut way back on the predators."

"Good news. I could use some."

"Yeah, you look kinda like you been rode hard and put away wet."

Josh almost laughed. "Good thing you're a hell of a shot. You'd never make it in politics."

"That's the Lord's truth." Jim scooped up the single duffel the chopper pilot unloaded. "Traveling light."

"Yes."

Josh's tone didn't invite conversation, but he knew Jim wouldn't be insulted. The wolfer's job kept him away from people most of the time. If Jim didn't like being solitary, he would have found other work.

Biting her lip, feeling fear clench her stomach, Melissa followed the governor to the main house.

"Is the doctor finished with Sylvia?" Josh asked.

She glanced at her watch and then at the driveway. The doctor's Mercedes was still parked to the side, dusty from the ride in.

"He'll be through soon," she said. "As you requested, I told him to wait for you."

Josh grunted. As soon as they were inside, he headed for Sylvia's suite. When he got there, he walked in without knocking.

Winifred glanced up, frowned, and then turned to Sylvia again, rubbing in more smelly goo. Though no one could tell it, Winifred was impatient for everyone to leave. In the mail Jim had brought there was a package from a DNA testing group. She wanted to get the samples mailed as quickly as possible.

And as quietly.

Dr. Sands removed his stethoscope, draped it over his neck, and straightened up from his exam of his patient.

"Well?" Winifred asked the doctor.

"She's slipping. It's fairly slow, but it's sure. Pulse is shallow and rapid, same for breathing, dry skin, barely any flesh."

"You said that last week."

"I meant it then. I mean it now. It's a miracle she's still alive. I should send that stinking cream you use to a lab for analysis."

For a moment, Winifred closed her eyes. She knew more than the doctor how close her sister was to death. Only Winifred's all-day, every-day care kept her alive. **Damn that womanizing son of a bitch to the deepest circle of hell. And damn his son, too.** She opened her eyes and gave Josh a bleak look.

He said, "I think it's time to admit Sylvia to a care facility."

Whatever Winifred had been expecting, it wasn't that. "No!"

"Yes." Josh's voice was like he was, calm and immovable, a man used to being heard.

The doctor busied himself putting away the blood pressure cuff and other gear.

"I've kept her alive for years," Winifred said.

"We're grateful. Unfortunately, you've traded your health for hers. Most nights you spend sleeping in a chair next to her. Now, even five feet away from you, I can hear the difficulty you have breathing." Josh looked at the doctor, who nodded.

"I'll check Miss Winifred before I leave," Dr. Sands said.

"It's nothing," she said. "My lungs just got cold when I went out for more firewood, that's all."

The doctor looked at her and frowned. "If you don't take care of yourself, you'll have pneumonia. Sounds like you're more than halfway there right now."

"In any case, we can't have you close to Sylvia when you're ill," Josh said. "She's too fragile. Dr. Sands, I want you to arrange medical transport for Sylvia to Oasis Nursing Home in Santa Fe as soon as possible. Surely within the next few days."

"I'll—" began the doctor.

"No, I won't allow it!" Winifred cut in fiercely. The force of her statement was spoiled when she went into a fit of coughing.

Dr. Sands listened to her and shook his head. "Do you still have the oxygen apparatus the Senator used?"

Josh turned and looked toward the hallway, where Melissa waited in case she was needed.

"Yes," Melissa said. "I kept it to have on hand in case Sylvia's breathing deteriorated any more."

"Bring the equipment, please," the doctor said. "I'll set it up in Miss Winifred's room after I've listened to her lungs." He looked at Winifred. "Come with me to your room, unless you would prefer to be examined right here."

"I don't want to be examined at all."

"Until Dr. Sands declares you to be free of any communicable disease," Josh said evenly, "I can't allow you near your sister."

Winifred went very still. Then she walked slowly to Josh. Though he was tall, she was nearly at eye level with him. She looked at him for a long, tense moment.

"Melissa's right," Winifred said in a low voice. "You're going to clear us out and sell the ranch."

"I kept the ranch going for the Senator. He's dead. We can't afford the losses any longer."

"You mean you'd rather spend your money in the city. This is **Sylvia's** ranch."

"And I'm her guardian. If I feel my mother's best interests would be served by living in a city with first-class medical care, then I'll sell the ranch and use the money to ease whatever of her life remains."

"You say that like you've been rehearsing it for the cameras," Winifred said bitterly.

He didn't bother to answer.

She looked at his blue eyes, so like the Senator, so determined, so cold. She coughed once and couldn't stop. And then she knew it was all slipping away, the plans and the hopes, the victory and the just vengeance of Castillo against Quintrell.

The room began to spin slowly, going gray.

"I'll see you in hell," she said hoarsely.

Josh didn't doubt it.

# 28

THE HOUSE PHONE RANG, WAKING DAN FROM A restless sleep. By the time the bored sheriff's deputy had left with another report to be ignored, it was almost dawn. Even so, Dan hadn't been able to fall asleep immediately. Knowing that Carly was in the next room made it way too easy for him to think of finding out just how warm she was beneath her clothes, of how she would taste and feel tangled up with him, of heat and pressure and release.

He'd tried to tell himself she'd feel safer with him, but he'd never been very good at lying to himself. She needed safety and sleep, not sex. That was all she'd asked of him. Safety.

**Hell.**

Then, somewhere in his sleep, he'd begun dreaming of Black Hawks dropping down out of the sky, death blazing from every weapon. He woke up sweating, heard the fading sound of a helicopter flying over Taos Valley, and finally managed to get back to sleep.

The only good news was that the size of his morning woody announced that he was fully healthy again.

The reason for his health gave a muffled shriek when her bare feet hit the icy floor in the main room.

"Watch out for glass," he yelled. "I might have missed some."

"I thought that sparkly stuff was ice," she retorted.

The phone kept ringing. He reached for it and sent a stack of photographs sliding.

"Damnation," he said roughly, catching the photos and putting the receiver to his ear at the same time.

"Is that any way to greet your brother?" Gus Salvador asked.

"What time is it?"

"The sun's up."

"So am I. So what?" He looked at his watch and saw that it was almost eleven. He'd slept more than he thought. "Is everything okay?"

"If by everything you mean my wife, children, and parents, yes."

"Then why did you wake me up?"

"Thought you'd like to know the latest on the Quintrell family."

Dan sat up, not noticing the cold air of the room on his skin. "What." It was a demand, not a question.

"Winifred has walking pneumonia. Sylvia is going to be moved to a facility in Santa Fe. The Quintrell ranch is for sale."

Dan shook his head like he'd been slapped. "You sure?"

"As sure as I can be without talking to the governor, and I'll be doing that at two o'clock. He agreed to an interview before he flies back to Santa Fe this afternoon."

"How's Winifred doing?"

"All I've heard is that she's on antibiotics, fluids, oxygen, and bed rest, but she still gets up and checks on Sylvia every few hours."

"When does the ranch go on the block?"

"The governor is having papers prepared in town right now. That's how I heard."

"Anything else?"

"I'll let you know."

"What about Mom?" Dan said. "Are you going to tell her or wait for the town gossips to spring it on her?"

There was a long pause.

"Gus," Dan said, sighing. Then, "I'll take care of it."

"Thanks. I don't want to be on her shit list for mentioning the forbidden name."

"But you don't mind being on mine?" Dan retorted.

"What are brothers for? Besides, you know you love the kids and they love you. You won't stay mad at me long."

"Blackmail."

"Yeah, ain't it grand?" Laughing, Gus disconnected.

Dan replaced the receiver and looked at the doorway. Carly was standing there wearing his favorite old sweatshirt, the faded black one with the sleeves ripped off. If she was wearing anything else, it didn't show.

"What happened?" Carly asked. "I can't believe I slept this late."

**You have really amazing legs,** Dan wanted to say. **And toes just made for nibbling. Knees and thighs, too. And . . .**

"Dan?"

He shook himself out of his sexual fantasy. The problem with getting a sex drive back was keeping it under control. Not since his raging-hormone teen years had he been this quick off the mark.

And this hard.

"That was Gus." Dan pulled a blanket over his lap and hoped it concealed everything it should. "Winifred's got pneumonia, Sylvia will be transferred to Santa Fe, and the governor is selling the ranch."

Carly let out air with a whoosh. "When did all this happen?"

"Probably this morning. That's when I heard a helicopter heading toward the ranch."

"But . . ." She spread her hands, feeling sad for no reason except the end of someone else's family tradition. "The ranch has been in the Castillo-Quintrell families for **centuries**."

"The governor is a city man. He doesn't have any emotional connection to the ranch."

"He was raised there," she protested.

Dan shook his head. "When he was seven, he was shipped out to the first in a long string of military schools, the kind that never close for holidays. If he spent two weeks total on the ranch from that day to the present, I'd be surprised. It was his older brother, A.J. IV, who was being groomed for the succession. He was the one who spent time with his father and the people of New Mexico."

"What happened to make Josh the favored son?"

"Vietnam. His older brother died."

Carly rubbed her chilly arms. "The things Winifred didn't think worth mentioning about the Quintrell family are boggling."

"You just said why. Quintrell, not Castillo."

"Oh, that's bull. These days they're pretty much the same family."

"Not to her. Winifred tells her own story in her own way."

"Well, I haven't had much time with her. She might have been planning to tell me more about her sister's family. Still . . ." Carly shook her head. "To think of all that struggle, all that wealth, all those lives and deaths, all the history; and it all comes down to a useless piece of protein like A. J. Quintrell V."

Dan lifted his eyebrow. "I've never met him."

"Be grateful."

"What do you have against him?"

"He thinks women are one endless roll of toilet paper created solely to wipe his butt."

"Sounds like his granddaddy."

"Why is it that the worst breed true and the best die young?"

"You figure that out and you'll be the next TV guru."

The wind blew hard, as it had on and off all night. The adobe part of the house didn't tremble with the weight of the shifting wind, but the broken window let in a lot of cold air. Carly rubbed her arms again.

"Is it okay if I start a fire in the hearth?" she asked.

"The woodpile is outside."

"Is that a yes or a no?"

"The temperature dropped again. It's freezing

out there. I'll get the wood while you put water on to boil for coffee."

Her eyes gleamed and she sighed. "Coffee. What are you waiting for?"

"You to leave so I can get dressed. Or," he said, reaching for the blankets covering his lap, "you can stick around and we'll warm up the old-fashioned way."

"Bundling?" she asked, all but fanning her eyelashes.

The blankets started rising.

Carly turned her back and ran for the kitchen, grinning every step of the way. It was fun to tease Dan, to watch the grim lines of his face shift into a smile. She didn't know what he'd done before he came back to Taos, but she knew it hadn't been easy.

And he was way too comfortable with a gun.

By the time she put together coffee, heated tortillas, and scrambled eggs, the fire was snapping and dancing over chunks of frozen piñon. The heat was on, too, but its surly electric fire didn't make a dent in the cold, wind-driven air rushing through from the living room. She shivered, handed Dan his coffee and breakfast, and went to stand beside the fire.

"Tell me again why you rented this place," she muttered.

"The cottonwood tree." Then, "I thought you loved history."

"I hate getting up to a cold floor."

"That's okay. You made up for whining by cooking breakfast along with the coffee."

"I didn't whine."

"You shrieked."

She waved her hand. "Different thing entirely."

"Then you whimpered until your feet went numb."

"Your point is?"

He smiled at her. "Damned if I know."

She gave him an eye-roll and smiled into her coffee. Even with icy feet, it was fun to wake up with Dan nearby. The fact that she'd spent a lot of restless time last night wishing **nearby** had been a lot closer was her problem. She'd been sending out I-don't-think-I'm-ready signals, and he'd respected them. The fact that he didn't push, shove, crowd, demand, nag, or sulk told her more than a night of wild jungle sex with him could have.

And the thought of that kind of sex with Dan stopped her breath.

"When are you leaving?" he asked.

"Leaving? You want me to go to a motel?"

"No, I want you to go home, where it's safe."

"The deputy and I had this conversation last night. That's when I pointed out his office wasn't exactly sweating over my safety so why should I?"

Dan looked at her stubborn expression and knew

he wasn't going to have any better luck than the deputy.

"Besides," Carly added, "when you think about it, it's been all show and no go."

"Sound and fury signifying nothing?"

"Exactly. No harm, no foul." She forced a casual shrug. "Anyway, running was never my best sport."

"What could I say to make you change your mind?"

She thought about it. "Nothing. But if you want to get away from the fallout zone, I completely understand. I'll pay for replacing the window and—"

"Are you trying to make me mad?" Dan cut in.

She looked at his face, swallowed too much hot coffee, and winced. "No. I'm trying not to back you in a corner. This is my problem, not yours."

"Bullshit."

"Well, that's an adult argument."

"Were we arguing?"

"Dan, you don't have to do this. You don't know me and—"

"You **are** trying to piss me off." He leaned over, pulled her close, kissed her cross-eyed, and lifted his head. "It won't work, Carolina May. I know everything I need to about you, except how good we'll be together in bed. Sooner or later, I'll know that, too." He smiled at her, his mother's smile, the one that could light up winter.

"You're sure?" she asked.

"Very."

"Not about the sex. The rest of it."

"Yes."

She blew out a long breath. "Okay. But if you get hurt because of me, I'm going to wring your neck."

"Sounds kinky."

"You're such a **guy**." Carly pushed back from the table and looked away before she grabbed him and did interesting things to his body. "I'm going to work on the stereographs."

Dan's expression said he'd rather she worked on him. "I printed out the list of things you wanted from the archives," he said, pouring himself more coffee.

"Thanks. Leave them by my purse and—"

"No," he cut in easily, "we'll do it together, after I call my mother. But I thought we described the stereographs last night, or was I hallucinating from lack of sleep?"

"We did everything but try to date by the type of card itself. Shape, color, that sort of thing. If that agrees with the costume and the guesses someone wrote on the back of the stereographs, then we can be reasonably certain we have the correct date."

Dan glanced at his watch. His mother should be home now, unless she had extra tutoring. "You want to shower first, second, or conservatively?"

"Conservatively?"

"Together." His green eyes gleamed at her.

"Doesn't sound conservative to me."

"When it comes to saving water, it is."

"Go take a liberal shower."

He laughed and walked to the bedroom. She listened to the intimate, intriguing sounds of Dan showering and told herself she was doing the right thing staying dry. She wasn't sure she believed it, but she was certain that sex with him wouldn't be casual.

That was what was holding her back.

She didn't know if she was ready for something that could break her heart.

With a sigh Carly pulled on white cotton gloves and reached for the stack of stereographs on Dan's bedside table. Although photo albums had been available since the 1880s, apparently no one in the Quintrell family had caught on to the idea until the 1910s. After that there were several albums. Sometime in the 1940s, someone in the family had made one or several attempts to identify the people in the ancestral collection.

At the back of her mind she heard the shower turn off, then the low murmur of Dan's voice talking to someone.

She dragged her attention back to the stereographs. Nothing had improved. Whoever had been trying to do the family history had relied as much on guesswork as fact, leaving a tangle for Carly to sort out along with the cramped yet flowing handwriting of the mysterious wannabe historian.

"You're frowning."

Startled, she looked up. Dan was standing in the doorway of the bedroom, freshly shaved, shirtless, barefoot. The fact that he was decently covered by old jeans didn't keep her pulse from skipping, then jumping into double time. While she stared, he pulled on a T-shirt that was as faded as the jeans. As the last of the tempting male landscape vanished, she swallowed hard and tried to ignore the humming in her blood, in her body.

"Bad family historians are worse than none," she said huskily.

He looked at the stack of card photos in her hands. "Our elusive spider woman, she of the shaky script?"

"I can live with the handwriting. It's the foolish dates that get to me."

"Go shower," he said. "It's nice and warm."

And she was hot.

Carly set aside the cards and turned a tablet on the small cardboard table so he could see it. "These are rough categories for dating stereographs. Use tissue to hold them while you sort. I won't be long."

Dan nodded absently. He was already reading the

neat printing on the tablet. Forcing himself to concentrate. Telling himself he couldn't hear her strip off his sweatshirt. He'd sunk pretty low when he envied a sweatshirt that was old enough to vote.

Blindly he yanked up the covers over the mattress where she'd slept. Then he reached for a nearby box of tissues, pulled out one, and picked up the first card.

**If my friends could see me now, they'd bust something laughing. Mint-colored tissues. Is this any way to run a special op?**

He looked at his hands, hard and scarred from training, and the dainty green tissue sticking to the ridge of callus on his right palm.

And he laughed. Just threw back his head and howled like a lunatic until he could barely breathe. Finally he took a shaky breath, swiped his sleeve over his eyes, and began sorting faded stereographs from a time before humanity split atoms, walked on the moon, and died in the bloody, anonymous mire of special operations.

"Okay," he said to himself, "the three-inch-by-seven-inch are likely earlier. The four-by-sevens are later."

Despite being hampered by tissue, he quickly dealt the cards into two piles based on size. He checked the tablet and sorted by the type of corner—rounded or square. Then he sorted within each category for the color of the card the individ-ual image was mounted on.

By the time Carly tiptoed out of the bedroom wrapped in a big towel and grabbed fresh clothes from her suitcase, Dan had filled the first sheet of tablet paper with notes. When she came out of the bedroom again, she was dressed in slacks and a sweater, and boots that could handle snow. Her hair was a damp riot of coils swept back and up and held in place by a barrette carved from driftwood. She looked at the many small piles of cards.

"I'll say it again," she said. "You're fast."

He smiled slightly and resisted temptation. Barely. "The spider lady and your list of what was used at which time don't agree real often. She thinks the stuff is a lot older than it is. Or younger. Have you ever considered using transparent sleeves for all this?"

"Not until I'm more certain of dates. It's a pain to have to arrange and rearrange a page of sleeves. In any case, I'm waiting for an order of individual sleeves in various sizes."

"Run out?"

"Lost in transit. Gotta love airplanes and baggage carousels."

"MATS isn't any better."

"Mats?"

"Military airline," he said absently, placing the last card.

"So you're in the military?"

Dan looked up sharply. "What gave you that idea?"

"MATS."

"Well, I'm not." **Not exactly. But they sure trained me to within an inch of my life.** "Civilian all the way."

She tilted her head, felt a trickle of water run from her hair down her spine, and decided to dig out her hair dryer after all.

And hit him with it.

**Civilian all the way, my ass.**

"It's true," he said, as though she'd spoken aloud. "Never mustered in and never mustered out. Wrong temperament. Too bookish."

"Stop reading my mind."

"Don't need to. Your expression says it all."

"Bookish?" she asked in disbelief.

He took the change of subject without a pause. "Yeah. I got distracted before I finished my Ph.D. or you'd be calling me doctor."

At first she thought he was joking. Then she looked at his careful listing of the different cards, remembered his ability to concentrate and absorb odd facts, and knew that he wasn't teasing her.

"Doctor, huh? Okay, you surprised me," Carly said. "What did it take to distract you?"

"I don't remember."

"I don't believe it."

"Smart as well as sexy. Damn, I've got it good. What do I do with the cards that are round all the way rather than just at the corners?"

"Divide them into black, gray, or buckskin."

He sorted quickly.

She sat down beside him, booted up her computer, and began recording tentative dates based on the type of stock used to mount various images.

It wasn't until later, much later, that Carly realized he had steered the conversation away from his past.

Again.

# 29

JEANETTE DYKSTRA'S LIPS MOVED BUT NO SOUND came from the TV screen. Celebrity images flashed, promoting her next show. The picture cut to an improbably sparkling toilet and a dancing toilet brush that threw glittering stuff everywhere.

Winifred ignored the TV until all the commercials and station promos were finished. Only then did she pick up the remote control from her bedside table and take off the mute.

A man in a blue shirt, multicolored tie, and gray-blue suit leaned earnestly toward the camera. His eyes were the same pale color as his shirt. The size of his ears gave him away as a man approaching seventy, but his hair was pure blond and his cheeks didn't sag. His hand had more wrinkles than his entire face. He held the obligatory yellow tablet and blunt pencil in camera view, suggesting that he'd had actually been out doing some old-fashioned reporting a few minutes ago instead of being powdered and primped for the camera.

"Good evening. In five minutes we will interrupt our normal programming to bring you breaking news from the governor's mansion, where it's rumored that Governor Quintrell will announce his candidacy for president of the United States."

Winifred's hand clenched around the remote control. Despite the pallor of illness, color burned high on her cheekbones. She'd been busy today, taking swabs of Sylvia's cheek and her own, packing them for mailing, pushing Blaine Snead until he drove the package to town and returned with her mailing receipt. Small things, really, but everything took so much energy now.

She watched without moving while the usual scenes of international war, famine, and shouting heads marched in tightly edited procession across the TV. Politicians and pundits mouthed ten-second sound bites.

"He wouldn't dare," she said hoarsely.

Yet she knew he would.

He'd dared a lot more and he'd won. The Senator's death had changed many things, but it wouldn't change that. Josh Quintrell was as clever and ruthless as anyone the Senator ever spawned.

Tears of rage and regret shimmered in Winifred's eyes. Even when Josh appeared on the screen, she didn't blink the tears away. She didn't have to. She knew what Josh looked like. The Senator's eyes and arrogance and meanness. None of Sylvia's sweetness. None of her kindness. Nothing of her at all. Just the Senator, a man who had raped his own daughter at thirteen, sending her careening down the road to hell, taking Sylvia with her. One daughter lost to polio. One daughter lost to the drunken lecher who couldn't keep his hands off any female, even blood kin.

And that was just the beginning of his sins.

Long after Josh vanished from the TV in a flurry of applause and American flags, Winifred lay staring at the screen. There was a lot to do, and none of it good.

But it would be done.

Ignoring the dizziness that had begun to plague her, she sat up and put her feet on the floor. The cool tile beneath her feet helped to focus her. She stood slowly, waiting for her heart to settle.

She had the strength to do what must be done. She wouldn't accept anything less.

All the years of hate would be repaid.

After several minutes of forcing herself to breathe steadily, evenly, Winifred felt stronger. She took a wrapped syringe and a small clay bottle from her bedside drawer. Slowly, using the backs of chairs and then the doorframe, she worked her way to Sylvia's room.

Her sister was facing the window, watching the

pool or the silvery moonlight or perhaps nothing at all. For the first time Winifred saw Sylvia as she really was, a husk of the past, a transparent mockery of life, a spirit chained when it should be free, a creature kept alive for a vengeance that never came.

"Never enough time to live," Winifred said to her sister. "Always time to die. Forgive me, **querida**."

Whether the forgiveness was for the past or the present, Winifred didn't say and Sylvia didn't care. With trembling fingers, Winifred opened the syringe she'd brought from her bedroom, took the stopper out of the small clay bottle, and filled the syringe. She closed her eyes, crossed herself, and injected the fluid into the IV that dripped slowly down to Sylvia's wasted vein.

When the syringe was empty, Winifred went to the fireplace, added several more chunks of wood, and sat in her familiar chair next to the bed. Gently she took Sylvia's hand and held it, cool and frail, between her own. Together the two sisters looked out the window.

Moonlight shifted and slid across the land, ghostly and beautiful and untouchable. Sylvia's breathing slowed, then slowed even more, until it sighed out one last time and she became like the moonlight, beyond the reach of man.

Only then did Winifred stand. She threw the little pot into the fireplace with enough force to shatter the clay and heaped more wood on top. With the fire blazing behind her, she went to her own room, buried the hypodermic in a pot of lemongrass, washed her hands, and went to bed.

She fell asleep certain that she would see the Senator's son in hell.

# 30

MELISSA MADE HER FINAL ROUNDS OF THE HOUSE, checking that outer doors and windows were secure, ovens and lights were turned off, and nothing was out of place if the governor made a surprise visit. In many ways, it was her favorite part of the workday. Everything was quiet and clean, a silent tribute to her efficiency.

A strip of light still showed at the base of the door to the Sisters' Suite. Melissa hesitated, then knocked lightly.

"Winifred? Can I get you anything?"

There wasn't any answer.

Again Melissa hesitated. "Winifred?"

Silence.

Melissa pushed open the door, saw Winifred sleeping, and walked softly over to the bed. Dr. Sands had been quite forceful about having Winifred checked every few hours. Melissa bent down and listened to Winifred's breathing, glancing at her watch as she did. After a minute she straightened and frowned. The antibiotic hadn't made much progress against the pneumonia. The old woman's breathing was strained, with a distinct rattle. Melissa adjusted the oxygen tube with the skill of the nurse trainee she had been until she decided she'd rather clean houses than bedpans.

Quietly she turned off the bedside light. A series of night-lights glowed to life, pointing the way to Sylvia's bed in the other half of the suite. Melissa followed the lights, looked into the sickroom, and saw what she had for years—a hot fire casting flickering shadows over a lump beneath the covers. From the height of the flames, Winifred had been up and checking on her sister sometime in the past half hour.

A glance told Melissa that there was plenty of wood to get through the night. She turned and quietly went back through Winifred's part of the suite. The door closed with the click of a well-oiled lock. Just one more of Melissa's many jobs.

She walked swiftly toward the quarters she and Pete had made into an apartment for themselves. Once the apartment had been a second, separate guesthouse, complete with kitchenette, for the Senator's private use. Or abuse. Melissa had heard the housemaids talking about the sex toys and such that the Senator's "guests" left behind. When he'd become bedridden, he insisted on moving into the library, where he could see everyone coming and going.

She hurried through the cold breezeway connecting the guesthouse to the main house. The clear night had frozen everything again, leaving little daggers of ice on the muddy path. She opened the door quickly and then locked it behind her with a sigh. Off duty.

Finally.

"Pete?"

"In the den," he answered.

Melissa kicked out of her boots, found a pair of slippers, and padded quietly toward the den. Pete sat in front of a foldout desk. He'd stacked papers and files on every surface.

"What's up?" she asked.

"Josh is jumping up and down for the charity report."

Uneasiness shot through her. "It's only been a few days."

"Yeah. He makes the Senator look like the saint of patience. Josh is hell to work for. But I'm hoping to be so valuable that he'll make me his accountant, like the Senator did."

"Don't bet on it. I heard Anne asking Josh if you were up to the task."

Pete went still. "What did he say?"

"He saw me and said something about how he trusted you."

Pete swore.

Melissa started pacing. Everything had been so certain for so many years and now . . . now it was unraveling faster with every hour. "Damn that priest anyway. Everything was so perfect."

Pete looked surprised and then shook his head. "That was then. This is now. And now, in my spare time, Josh needs an updated P and L statement on the ranch for the realtor. Plus all the water patents, land grants, rights-of-way, easements, a new survey, septic inspection, well inspection, the whole tortilla. That's the stuff I'm sorting out now."

**Josh is hell to work for.**

"He's a real smart shark," Pete said with as much admiration as unhappiness. "Makes me realize how good we had it with the Senator. **Sic transit gloria** and all that."

"I think we should quit," Melissa said. "Really quit. All the way. Stop talking about the Caribbean and Brazil and **go** there." She laced her fingers together and then forced them apart. "Let's take our retirement and live a little before we're too old to enjoy it."

Pete pushed back from his desk and looked at his

wife. The lines of tension between her eyebrows and around her mouth added years to her age.

"We're some distance from our retirement goal," he said. "A few more years should do it."

"That's what you said years ago."

"Then the economy slowed and our investments tanked. We're just getting back to where we were."

"It's coming apart," she said tightly. "All our dreams."

He pushed back from the desk and went to hug her. "Hey, darling. We'll be fine. Ranches like this can take years to sell." **Or they can sell overnight to one of the vultures that had begun circling with news of the Senator's declining health.** "Plus Josh is bound to give you a good severance package. Me, too, if it comes to that. He can't afford to look stingy or exploitive of the common man. Can you hang in long enough to get fired when the ranch sells?"

She looked at him for a long moment, knew he was right, and sighed. "Sure. What's a few more months or years? But if he fires you before that, then what?"

Pete laughed. "Then we'll be on the next plane to warm waters, cool breezes, and stiff drinks."

**For as long as it lasts.**

But neither one of them said that aloud. They really needed a few more years to make up for some bad choices in the stock market.

They really needed Josh Quintrell.

And whether he knew it or not, he needed them.

# 31

A BLEARY-EYED DR. SANDS CONFIRMED WHAT everyone already knew: Sylvia Castillo Quintrell had died in her sleep. He went to the telephone and called Governor Quintrell on his private line.

"What?" The word was a growl.

"Governor Quintrell, this is Dr. Sands. I'm sorry to tell you that your mother has passed away."

At the other end of the line, there was silence, a woman's voice asking a question, and then Josh said, "Thank you for calling. Do you need anything from me immediately?"

"No. Miss Winifred has a list of Sylvia's wishes. She'll be cremated and her ashes scattered over the ranch. Given that she has been ill for so many years, I've recommended against an autopsy. There's no point in distressing the family any more than death already has. It's a miracle she lived as long as she did."

"I appreciate that. I have nightmares about the sleaze media ghouls drooling over autopsy photos. How is Winifred doing?"

"Not well," Dr. Sands said. "She wasn't strong before this. Pneumonia in a woman her age is very dangerous, but she refuses to go to a hospital."

"Sylvia was all she had to live for."

"Yes. I'm sorry to be so blunt, but you should be prepared. It's quite probable that Miss Winifred's life span can be measured in days. A few weeks at the outside. She's not responding well to the antibiotic. I'll switch to another, of course, but in patients her age, pneumonia often is the body's way of saying it's tired of struggling with life."

"You think she's given up?"

"Finding her sister dead was very hard on her."

There was a long silence.

Finally Josh said, "I'll check my schedule, but I don't think I'll be able to get up to the ranch today. I'm booked for three meals a day in New Hampshire for the next six days. But if I could combine seeing Winifred with a memorial service for Sylvia . . . yes, that would be possible. A red-eye both ways. There will be a memorial for Sylvia Quintrell within forty-eight hours."

Dr. Sands was impressed with Josh's ability to juggle personal and private demands when awakened from a dead sleep at 4:00 A.M. "In addition to my condolences, Governor, please accept my congratulations. I believe you'll make a fine president."

"Thank you. I'll send you an invitation for my next fund-raiser."

Laughing, Dr. Sands hung up the phone and made arrangements to have Sylvia's body taken to a crematorium.

# 32

"WHAT DO WE HAVE SO FAR?" CARLY ASKED, LOOKing at her checklist.

Dan shifted on the uncomfortable wooden chair that was the best the newspaper archive offered. He was bleary-eyed from old photos and computer monitors, and frustrated by his relentless physical awareness of Carly. Yesterday's hours and hours of solid, boring groundwork on Winifred's project should have taken the edge off his need.

It hadn't. It was there today, up close and personal. If Carly felt the same way, she wasn't sharing the information.

Swearing silently, he tapped out a few more commands on the keyboard and hoped she would catch up with him soon. Never had the wait for someone to discover what was obvious to him seemed so long.

While Dan worked, Carly unrolled a sheet of paper that was twenty inches long and ten wide. Penciled notes went down the left margin. A faint grid divided the sheet into six long sections. The top center of the sheet was labeled CASTILLO SIS-TERS, GENERATION 6. From there, each horizontal section was labeled 5, 4, 3, 2, 1, separating genera-tions of the family.

"Marriage date for Isobel Castillo and the first Andrew Jackson Quintrell is March 11, 1865," Dan said. "Isobel was born in 1850, probably before March 11, because her age is given as fifteen for the marriage. Quintrell was thirty, according to his Civil War record. Johnny Reb, by the way."

Carly wrote quickly, connecting married couples and keeping track of special dates along the margin for each generation. It wasn't the approved method for creating a genealogy, but it worked for her. Later she would transfer everything onto ready-made forms.

"Still want me to concentrate on the female Castillos?" Dan asked.

"For now. I'll go through the list of possible ille-gitimate offspring later. I can't believe there are eleven of them."

"All maybes," he reminded her.

"The Senator was a swine."

"Swine are fertile." Dan looked at the computer screen. "Isobel's sister Juana married Mateo on June 3, 1870, at the ripe old age of seventeen. Mateo's age isn't listed. Neither is his family history."

"Surprise, surprise," Carly muttered. "If Juana

wasn't Isobel's sister, I doubt that the marriage would have made the newspaper at all."

"Welcome to the wonderful world of society sections." Dan hit another key. "Juana died in childbirth in September of 1872. The baby, María, survived. In May of 1887, María married Hale Simmons. She died of cancer after a long illness on August third, 1966. Since a surviving husband isn't mentioned, I assume old Hale kicked the bucket before then. Nothing in the archives about a funeral, though."

Carly worked quickly, neatly, filling in blanks with a mechanical pencil, the better to erase it later if/when new information appeared.

"After an improbable gap of almost thirty years, María gave birth to—"

"Improbable? Is that what the archive says?" Carly cut in.

"No. It's plain old common sense."

Smiling, Carly put a question mark in the margin and said, "Go on."

"Sylvia María Simmons y Castillo, no exact birth date. All we have is 1916."

"That's okay. I have lots of sources I haven't tried yet. We'll stick with the archives and Winifred's stuff for now and fill in gaps later."

"Eighteen years after Sylvia's birth, in a totally fab June wedding complete with white roses and just **yards** of satin—"

Carly snickered at Dan's warbling tone and kept writing.

"She married Andrew Jackson Quintrell III. Do I get to mention the Quintrells now?"

"Hard to avoid them."

"Let's see . . . A.J. Three's grandmother was Isobel and his great-aunt was Juana, right?"

Carly nodded and looked up. "Why?"

"I'm trying to figure something out. Sylvia's grandmother was Juana and her great-aunt was Isobel, right?"

"Right. So?"

"So they were cousins, of a sort."

"Not close enough to upset the civil or religious authorities. From what you translated on the death certificate Winifred gave me, Isobel and Juana were only half sisters and might even have been simply cousins. You'd have to be a genealogist to even care about the degree of blood relationship in their offspring. Besides, consolidating the land came first. Ask the royal families of Europe. They raised cousin-marrying to a high art."

Dan stared at the screen a moment longer, trying to figure the exact degree of kinship between offspring of half sisters or cousins twice removed. Or was it three times? He shrugged. If Carly decided it mattered, he'd strain his brain over the answer. Better yet, he'd let Carly strain hers.

"I've got the wedding date for A.J. Three, universally known as the Senator, and Sylvia María Simmons y Castillo," Carly said. "And the four children's birth dates, plus three death dates for the kids."

"Plus the Senator's death date. Wonder whatever happened to his sisters? He had three of them, right?"

Carly checked her notes. "Three, all older. I'm saving them for later. Winifred only—"

"Wants Castillo history," Dan cut in. "Got it. On to Generation Three, children of the Senator and Sylvia. Whoa. There's a lot of stuff. Once the Senator became a senator, he couldn't take a dump without the paper doing a two-page spread."

"Now there's a visual I could live without."

Shaking her head, Carly went back to sorting the Sandoval photos on one of the long tables. She'd been so obsessed with recording Winifred's material that she hadn't done anything else. Now it was time to see if she could fill in some gaps. While many of the photos weren't dated, a lot of them had writing on the back. She arranged them in rough order, oldest to newest.

"Holler when you find something worth recording," Carly said. "I've got all the birth dates for the kids, but I'm really short on photos of Josh. Older brother Andrew got all the camera time. I'm hoping something will turn up in the Sandoval family photos at the yearly barbecue."

"Don't hold your breath. From all that's been left **out** of the newspaper, Josh must have been a hell-raiser from the time he could walk."

"Too bad there wasn't more than one newspaper. I'd like to see more of the Spanish and Native American side of the local history."

Dan winced at the thought of what more newspapers would have meant in terms of archiving. Even with his nifty, mostly homemade program, the process still took time.

"The white-bread approach wears thin in the sixties," he said. "There's more ink for the hispano politicos, and more hispano politicos in areas that have a big Anglo population."

"Thus all the yearly barbecues," Carly said, lining up the photos. "Taking the pulse of the hispano voters over a rack of ribs and a keg of beer."

"It worked. Without support from the hispano communities, the Senator wouldn't have made it, and neither would his son. Josh Quintrell is the first Anglo governor New Mexico has had in years. It was a close race. Without the Sandovals he couldn't have made it."

"The same Sandovals that run drugs and hold cockfights?"

"Yeah."

"Are you saying that the governor is involved in the drug trade through the Sandovals?"

"If by involved you mean getting paid on a regular schedule, probably not. If you mean accepting political contributions and having a damn good idea where the funds came from and how they were laundered, yes."

"I haven't read anything like that in any newspaper."

From overhead came the slam of the side door, followed by the sound of footsteps and heavy rolls of paper being moved across the floor.

Dan glanced at the ceiling and then back at the computer. "You won't read about laundered political contributions in this newspaper, no matter how many rolls of paper Gus uses up." Dan shrugged. "Unless someone gets caught dirty with a bag of cash, of course, but it's not likely. The Quintrell family might be a lot of things that I don't like, but stupid isn't one of them."

"No wonder Winifred wants to distance herself from them."

"Winifred would have hated any family her sister married into." Dan typed rapidly, scanned the screen, and typed again. "Besides, the Castillos are a lot closer to the Sandovals by blood and choice. And it's not like the Quintrells are the first politicians on the planet to accept laundered money in political contributions. Hell, in the bad old days on the East Coast and in Chicago, the pols didn't care if the cash was laundered, just so it was plentiful and green."

"You have a sour view of politicians."

"Realistic," he corrected. "And don't forget bankers and lawyers. One runs the laundries and the other facilitates the process. Then they take the squeaky-clean cash and invest it in legitimate enterprises on behalf of the illegitimate. Welcome to the real world, honey, where nothing is the way it seems and everybody's hand is in somebody else's pocket."

Carly grimaced and kept looking at the backs of photos. Some were dated. Some had names.

One of the names was J. Quintrell.

She flipped the photo over, picked up a magnifying glass, and went hunting for the younger Josh. He'd been caught in the act of upending a bottle of beer over another boy's head. Both young men— teenagers, probably—were laughing and leaning drunkenly on each other. In the background, the Senator watched with a grim line to his mouth. Next to the Senator was another young man, but this one stood straight and tall.

"I have a feeling Josh went back to boarding school right after this," she said.

Dan got up and walked over to Carly. He bent

over the table near her, close enough to smell the
light spice of her shampoo. He told himself that he
hadn't left the computer just to inhale her unique
scent, it was just a very nice side benefit. Like
breathing.

"Good catch," he said. "If there's another newspaper photo of Josh before he came back from Vietnam, I haven't been able to find it, not even in the
fifties and sixties stuff I scanned in a few years ago
when I was home for three months."

"Months? How'd you manage that much time
off?"

"Leave of absence," Dan said, staring at the rawboned young Josh. "Just like now."

"But you're not in the military."

"No. Just clumsy." He looked at the date on the
photo and then went back to his computer.

"Clumsy," she said under her breath. "Yeah.
Right. I've seen professional athletes who are less
coordinated. Must have been one mean volcano you
climbed."

He ignored her and set up a search for the name
Quintrell, starting with one week on either side of
the date on the photo. Then he skimmed through
the articles he'd recalled, clicking from one highlighted Quintrell name to the next. The Senator was
most often mentioned, with A.J. IV getting some
ink for having graduated from college and then vol-

unteering for the army. He was posted to Fort Benning, Georgia, for ranger training.

**Poor bastard. Wonder if he knew what he was getting into?**

"What was that?" Carly asked.

Dan realized he'd spoken his thoughts aloud. Not good. He was getting entirely too comfortable around Ms. Carolina May.

"A.J. IV was a ranger," Dan said.

"Ranger? Are we talking National Park Service and Smoky the Bear?"

For a few seconds Dan wondered what it would be like to live in a world where the first association with the word **ranger** was a cartoon figure. "Special Ops."

"Ops? Operations?"

"Yeah. The balls-out warriors."

"Another visual I could have lived without," she said. "Did he make it, or was he a wannabe?"

"A.J. IV made the grade and the Senator didn't have a damn thing to do with it. The old man was furious that his son didn't take the cushy admin job in the Pentagon that was all laid out for him."

"What article did you find?" Carly took the photo over to where Dan was and began reading the computer screen over his shoulder. "Where does it say that?"

"Between the lines."

She read aloud the section he pointed to on the screen. " 'The Senator, while naturally disappointed that his son passed up an opening at the Pentagon as a public information officer, is very proud that Andrew Jackson Quintrell IV has been accepted into the elite Army Rangers.' So what are you talking about? It says the Senator was proud."

"You didn't know him. Anyone who crossed the old man paid in blood. Lots of it. I'd love to have heard that father-son screaming match, but it happened before I was born. I'm betting that A.J. told the Senator to go crap in his mess kit. And I'm betting that's why Josh was invited home from his first year of college abroad, just for the barbecue. It would be the Senator's way of telling his first son that there was another heir in the pipeline."

Carly studied the photo again with the magnifying glass. "So the handsome dude with the rebar up his butt is A.J. IV?"

He looked where she pointed. "Handsome, huh?"

"Hey, they can't all be tall, dark, and oozing sex like you."

Dan wanted very much to bite the tender lobe of her ear but didn't. If he did that, the next thing he'd do was stick his tongue in her mouth and pretty soon after that they would be rocking and rolling on top of the heavy wooden table.

**And how would this be bad?**

"He sure looks more than three years older than Josh," she said.

"Ranger training is hell."

"Been there, done that?" she asked.

"I know some of them."

"The, um, balls-out warriors?"

"Yeah." In addition to being trained by them, he'd debriefed a lot of special forces types, but that was just one more on the long list of things he wasn't supposed to talk about, because the men weren't supposed to have been in the places Dan had been. And vice versa.

He watched Carly looking at the photo and tried not to think about how good it would feel to have her mouth all over him.

"Why are you frowning?" he asked after a few moments. Anything to get her talking instead of him fantasizing about stripping her naked and diving in.

"I'm trying to see the future Governor Quintrell in that rawboned baboon pouring beer over his primate buddy. The eyes are right but the chin looks off. Must be the stubble. He's got quite a crop of it. Josh's eyeteeth are just like the Senator's—that slight overlap that is more a sexy come-on than a flaw. He must have had them straightened later."

"Or else had his mouth redone entirely when he hit forty," Dan said. "A lot of politicians do. In

America, bad teeth are equated with poverty and moral turpitude." He took the magnifying glass and studied the photo. "You've got a good eye, Carolina May. That chin isn't as impressive as Josh's is today. Gotta love implants and plastic surgeons."

"At least he let his hair go gray. A lot of them don't."

"Them?"

"Anyone, man or woman, who spends time in front of cameras."

"Gray is distinguished, haven't you heard?" Dan said, smiling slightly.

"Tell that to an anchorman who has someone thirty years younger leaving footprints up his spine. You, of course, would be exempt."

He glanced at her. "I would?"

"Yes. You're going to be like your mother, dark except for one extraordinary silver streak over your left temple."

"I already have the streak."

"If five hairs make up a streak, sure."

"I have more than that."

She pretended to count the gray hairs above his left temple and gasped. "Omigod. Seven! You're definitely headed for the downhill slide into Viagra-land."

Dan was tempted to stand up and show Carly just how wrong she was about the sex pill but didn't.

People were still moving around the storage area above them. At any moment a reporter could come down to the basement to research past newspaper articles. Dan didn't want Carly embarrassed or inhibited when they made love, biting her lip when she wanted to groan or scream.

Overhead, someone dragged the tarp aside, lifted the door, and called down. "Dan? You in there?"

**Go away, Gus.** "C'mon down, Gus."

"How long have you been down there?"

**Too long. Not long enough.** "Since breakfast. Why?" Dan said.

"Then you haven't heard the news."

"What news?"

Gus appeared on the bottom step. "Sylvia Quintrell finally died."

# 33

GOVERNOR JOSH QUINTRELL SHIFTED ON THE METAL folding chair. His expression was engaged, interested. Behind the façade, he devoutly wished he was anywhere but in a gently shabby hall full of veterans of foreign wars trying to digest the indigestible, and reminiscing about wars nobody else gave a damn about anymore. Josh would use his service record and purple hearts to reassure voters, especially veterans, but did he talk about it every chance he had? Hell, no. He'd rather dye his hair pink and wear a tutu. Ninety-seven percent of the people in the dining hall hadn't been shot at, hadn't been tortured, hadn't killed; the three percent who had didn't want to talk about it.

The chicken salad lunch was truly incredible. They should pass out medals for eating it.

**I'm going to get a doggie bag for my campaign manager,** Josh thought as he clapped mightily for a speech that had left most of the hall comatose. **Why should he miss all the fun he signed me up for?**

His cell phone vibrated against his waist. He glanced at the call window, saw that it didn't list a number, and went to the message function. No voice message, just text. He punched in commands and wondered what had been so urgent that it had to break in to his campaign time.

Words scrolled across the tiny window: THE SENATOR HAD SECRETS WORTH KILLING TO KEEP. STOP INVESTIGATING CHARITIES.

Josh thought about it.

He thought about it some more. As the second speaker was talking about **our brave boys overseas** he decided to stop investigating charities on the ranch end.

Then he'd light a fire under the New York accountant's ass and wait to see what crawled out from under the rocks.

# 34

THANKS TO BAD WEATHER IN NEW HAMPSHIRE, THE governor's plane had been late landing in Santa Fe. Sylvia Quintrell's memorial service would be delayed until the governor's helicopter arrived.

Carly didn't mind. Over Dan's protests, she'd driven out early in her newly cleaned and shod SUV, eager to interview Winifred on various subjects, including the possibility of the Senator's illegal offspring. Dan had followed her in his own truck. The extra hour delay before the memorial service had given Carly more time to talk with Winifred—and to prepare herself for another poet-mangling effort by the good minister, who was hovering in the hallway near Winifred's suite like a car salesman looking for a live customer. Dr. Sands hovered with him. He hadn't wanted Winifred to exert herself talking.

Winifred had told him to get out.

Silently Dan handed Carly another photograph for Winifred to look at. The box of plastic sleeves and forms that the airline had misplaced had been waiting at the ranch when he and Carly arrived for the service. While she talked with Winifred, he put various photos and documents between sheets of the clear protective plastic.

Winifred coughed. The sound was husky and dry, shallow, like her breathing. Dan had heard unhealthy noises like that in places where war or plain governmental incompetence kept antibiotics from reaching hospitals and villages. He wasn't a medic, but he really didn't like the sound of her breathing. He knew pneumonia was most dangerous when the chest was tight, not when the lungs loosened.

"Are you sure you should be talking, Miss Winifred?" he asked gently.

She ignored him and peered through reading glasses at the photograph Carly was holding out. Normally Winifred wouldn't have needed—or admitted that she needed—glasses, but she was too tired to struggle tonight.

"Andrew," she said. "Grammar school."

Carly filled in a label, peeled it from its backing, and stuck it to the plastic sleeve. Dan handed Winifred another sleeved photo.

"Victoria. After Pearl Harbor. She was seven."

Carly entered the data and labeled the photo.

"Victoria. On D-Day. Polio. Killed her before— she was ten."

"You need to rest," Carly said quickly.

"I need—to die," Winifred said.

Grimly Carly sorted through the pictures she'd selected for positive ID by Winifred. She'd hoped to find some of Josh and Liza after they were ten, but so far she'd come up empty. All the school and professional photos were of Andrew and Victoria. Family snapshots had stopped after Victoria died. The closest thing to group photos Carly had found after 1944 were the yearly political barbecues. Often as not, neither Sylvia nor the children attended—or if they did, there weren't any photographs to prove it.

The Quintrells weren't what Carly would call a close family. No surprise there.

When the photographs ran out, there was a list of names. "These are the Senator's possible children," Carly said in a low voice. "That is, these children were born to women within ten months of a probable liaison with the Senator. None of the birth certificates list the Senator as a father. Often they list another man, but you asked me to ignore that, correct?"

Winifred nodded curtly and took the list. Eleven names stretching over a period of sixty years, but most of them were clustered around the years before the Senator became a senator.

Jesús Mendoza. María Elena Sandoval. Manuel

Velásquez. Randal Mullins. Sharon Miller. Christopher Smith. Raúl Sandoval. Maryanne Black. Seguro Sánchez. David McCall. Suzanne Fields.

All or none of them could be the Senator's. Four of them were dead. Two of them were grandmothers or great-grandmothers. Not one of them had claimed to be the Senator's offspring.

The name Winifred had expected, hoped, feared, wasn't there.

She handed the list back to Carly. "Keep digging. There were more kids born than are on this list."

Carly started to object but thought better of it.

"Why didn't Sylvia divorce the Senator?" Carly asked as she put the list away.

"Catholic. And keeping the land. For Andrew."

"Then Andrew died and she had a stroke."

"No," Winifred managed. "Tried to—kill the Senator. Fought him. Survived. Brain didn't."

Carly and Dan both went still. There was nothing, not even a hint of a whisper, in the family record or in the doctor's report after Sylvia's so-called stroke.

"My God," Carly said. "How did you—"

"Find out?" Winifred cut in.

"Yes."

"He told me—to let her die. And why."

"But you didn't," Carly said.

The line of Winifred's mouth was too savage to be

called a smile. "He drove her—to it. Castillo land. **Always.**"

"Of course," Carly said gently, trying to soothe the increasingly agitated older woman. "The Senator is dead and the land will go to Sylvia's son, a Castillo as well as a Quintrell."

Winifred's face darkened as she coughed harshly, uselessly, gasping for air.

Dr. Sands rushed into the suite. "No more talking, Miss Winifred. I mean it." He bent over and replaced the oxygen mask she'd pulled off an hour ago. "If I have to, I'll transport you to a hospital against your will. The governor agreed with me. If necessary, we'll call a judge and have you declared incompetent."

Winifred gave the doctor a burning look and fought to control her breathing.

Carly started to gather up photos and documents, only to discover that Dan already had. Together they quickly walked out of the room, leaving Winifred and the doctor to their clashing wills.

"I should have asked her about the old Spanish documents first," Carly said.

"Other people read old Spanish. Winifred is the only one left alive who remembers the Quintrell family during the last half of the twentieth century."

"What about the governor? He's alive."

"He probably knows less about what his family was like than you do. Josh Quintrell didn't even come home for Christmases."

"So Sylvia tried to kill the Senator," Carly said. "I wonder what triggered it?"

"Maybe she found out he was fathering bastards when he damn well knew how to prevent it. We'll check the birth dates around that time. All of the birth dates, not just the probable ones."

The **whap whap whap** of a helicopter's rotors announced that the governor might have missed all the holidays with his family, but he would make it to Sylvia's memorial service.

Carly wondered why.

"Why what?" Dan asked.

"Sorry, I didn't know I said it aloud."

Dan waited.

"Why does he bother coming here at all?" Carly said. "His parents sent him off to year-round boarding schools when he was seven and never looked back until his older brother died."

"Josh is the Senator's son through and through," Dan said.

"What does that mean?"

"He's political to his core. The last thing a politician would do is miss his mother's funeral."

"Gee, you have a cheery view of human nature," Carly said.

"What does cheer have to do with it?"

"Nothing."

"Bingo," Dan said, smiling grimly.

He set down the cartons of supplies and photos before he gestured for her to precede him into the next room, the place where Sylvia had spent so much of her life. Winifred had wanted the memorial service to be here. No one had argued.

Maybe no one had cared. Certainly the guests hadn't eaten much of the food that had been put out, despite the attractive presentation of canapés and glass coffee cups and saucers, and crystal wine goblets. There was a striking geometric design made by very small cups with no handles, like Turkish espresso cups, set out on an antique silver tray. Apparently the cups were meant for later in the ceremony, because two red ribbons in the form of a cross were laid protectively over them. The rich satin of the ribbon contrasted with the unglazed, undecorated clay cups and the nearby small, unglazed clay pitcher. The plain clay looked quite at home next to the array of santos glaring down at the table from nearby walls.

Carly glanced away from the primitive, and somehow primal, carvings of saints. There was something about the obviously hand-carved santos that made her uneasy in the same way that much Mayan art made her uneasy.

A fire burned cheerfully in the corner hearth, as if to counter the dark oppression of the santos.

Melissa, Pete, Alma, and Lucia were already sitting in four of the folding chairs that had been set up in the back of the room. Three other chairs were set up near the quietly burning hearth. Carly assumed those seats were for the family, so she headed toward Melissa and the ever-sullen Alma. Lucia nodded and smiled toward Carly. Feeling like a second thumb, Carly smiled back and sat in an empty chair. Dan sat next to her. If he felt out of place it didn't show in his expression.

A few moments later, Dr. Sands wheeled Winifred past the folding chairs to the front of the room. He set the brakes of her wheelchair, checked the oxygen flow, and walked briskly to the back of the room. Without a word to anyone, he sat near Dan.

Governor Quintrell came into the room, shook hands and exchanged pleasantries with everyone except Carly and Dan. Whatever the governor said to Pete surprised him.

"You're sure, Governor?" Pete asked.

"Absolutely. I decided that you're right, that now isn't a good time to think about cutting back on charitable contributions. I want you to concentrate exclusively on getting the ranch books in shape for the sale."

"Do you have someone interested already?" Pete asked.

"Several parties. It's not often a ranch this size comes on the market. Everyone from developers to conservation outfits are lined up waving money at me. Tell Melissa to start packing up the small stuff in the house and sending the contents to Santa Fe."

With that, the governor chose the chair that was closest to Winifred and sat down, ignoring the other empty chairs. He glanced at the minister and nodded abruptly.

The minister walked to the fireplace and faced the room. "We are gathered together here today to commemorate the valiant spirit of . . ."

After listening for thirty seconds, Carly decided that the minister hadn't had enough time to pillage dead poets for Sylvia, or perhaps only the Senator's death required such resonant language. Today the minister had come down solidly in the dead center of the mundane.

With a small sigh Carly began memorizing the feel of the room so that she could record it in the history she would write. Someone had brought in fresh pine boughs and placed them on a linen-covered table. The boughs were arranged around the tray of ten, no eleven, cups. The santos gave color to the table and peered from unlikely parts of the room.

The bright colors and dark features of the santos reinforced the crude vigor of the statues.

But the longer Carly sat there, the less she liked the look of the primitive saint figures. Something Dan had said about Penitentes lashing themselves through the stations of the cross came back to her. She wondered if the Castillo side of the family worshiped at the small roadside altars she had caught glimpses of as she drove through rural New Mexico, if the Castillos relished the darkness that surrounded the santos like ghostly cloaks.

Dan felt the slight shiver that went through Carly and followed her glance. The grim santos watching from the hearth and the walls and the table were considered collectibles by many and outright art by a few. Whoever had gathered or created these figures had been drawn to the horror and pain of the martyrdom that had preceded sainthood. Less grotesque than gargoyles, more raw than the usual Crucifixion portrayals, the santos haunted the room, describing pain and treachery and death far better than the minister's bland words.

Deliberately Dan laced his fingers through Carly's and squeezed lightly, silently telling her that he was there. She gave him a quick glance and squeezed back. She didn't know why the santos made her uneasy, she only knew they did.

Finally the minister closed his Bible and went to the governor, and then to Winifred, saying something too soft to be overheard.

"Just a few more minutes," Dan murmured against Carly's hair.

She nodded.

After a few fumbles, Winifred released the brake on her wheelchair and turned it to face the room. She nodded once.

Alma stood and hurried forward to remove the ribbons and pick up the tray of small cups.

Carly saw that the cups were filled to the top with something too thick to be coffee but just as dark. There were nine cups now, not eleven. They were laid out in the design of a diamond. She guessed that the missing cups had to do with the two missing Quintrells, but she couldn't be sure. In any case, this part of the ceremony certainly felt more pagan than modern Christian.

"We Castillos have a tradition to ensure the passage of the soul to God." Winifred paused, drew from the oxygen mask, and continued. "It began a thousand years ago as a stirrup cup for the dead." Another breath. "But now it is a large shot glass. The modern tongue finds the ancient brew bitter." Another breath. Her voice strengthened into something close to a command. "Yet still we drink it. As we drink, we pray for the dead. Every drop drunk, every prayer prayed, helps my beloved sister. Every drop not drunk makes the devil smile."

Alma offered one tip of the diamond to Winifred. She took the cup, drained it, turned it upside down to show that it was empty, and put the cup back on the tray in its place. Then she folded her hands in prayer. Alma went to the governor and gestured toward the next row of the diamond. He looked warily at the small cups, then followed Winifred's actions and took one. The taste must have been terrible, because he visibly fought not to spit it back out. Grimacing, he swallowed, upended the cup, and put it facedown in its place on the tray.

Alma worked her way through the small group, following the pattern decreed by Sylvia's closest kin, handing out cups and waiting for them to be emptied and put upside down to re-create the diamond. Carly braced herself for her own turn.

"Don't taste it," Dan said very quietly in her ear. "Just throw it to the back of your throat and swallow."

"Have you done this before?"

"No, but I've sat around some strange campfires."

And then Alma was in front of them. There were three untouched cups left, forming a triangle. Out of old habit, Dan reached across the bottom of the triangle and chose his own cup rather than take what was handed out. Alma started to object that the diamond was supposed to be taken in order, following the governor's choice.

It was too late. Dan had already tossed back the contents, turned the cup upside down to show that it was empty, replaced it, and closed his eyes.

Alma looked at Winifred, who had coached her in the correct ritual. The old curandera's eyes were still closed. Melissa, who had repeated Winifred's coaching, was still struggling with the bitter brew and hadn't noticed anything amiss. With a sigh of relief that the breach of ritual hadn't been noticed, Alma offered the tray to Carly.

Two cups left.

**Pretend it's a raw oyster,** Carly told herself. **If you can swallow a mouthful of cold snot, you can do this.**

Carly took the next to last cup and managed to get the contents down without choking.

Alma took the final cup, drained it, shuddered violently, and sat down again.

The room was so quiet Carly was certain everyone could hear her tongue scraping against her teeth as she tried to get rid of the taste. **Thank God stirrup cups went out of vogue.** She couldn't have managed a second swallow.

The sound of the helicopter revving up signaled

an end to the gathering, at least as far as the governor was concerned. He shook hands all around—even Carly and Dan this time—and left.

The two of them went to Winifred, saw that she was still praying for her sister, and waited.

They waited for a long time. When the old woman finally raised her head, Dr. Sands and the minister had already gone. Only the household staff remained.

The tears in Winifred's eyes made Carly understand how futile words were. Yet they had to be said anyway, heard anyway, while everyone knew that words couldn't describe the emptiness death left behind.

"I'm sorry," Carly said gently.

Winifred nodded. "Tomorrow."

Carly understood that Winifred didn't want to talk now. Carly hadn't expected her to.

"I'll walk you to your car," Dan said to Carly.

He didn't say anything until they were out of the suite. He bent, picked up the cartons of photos they'd left outside Sylvia's room, and faced Carly.

"I don't want you staying here alone," he said.

She didn't answer for the simple reason that she wasn't wild about the idea herself. "Nobody knew my car was fixed until I showed up here, so . . ." She shrugged.

"So nobody had enough lead time to get fancy with rats and paint, is that it?"

She nodded.

"Bullshit," he said.

"Hey, you checked my room out and found nothing."

"That was almost two hours ago."

"Everyone was here for the service. Anyway, I already told Melissa that I was going to drive back to town tonight. I don't feel right about staying here when the household has had so much sorrow."

Dan knew Carly was right. He also knew he didn't want to leave her alone, even just to drive her little SUV down the mountain. The part of his mind that kept adding up things was heading toward a bottom line that he couldn't read yet but already knew he didn't like.

With a muttered curse, he followed her toward the outside door.

"You know what I'd like?" Carly asked after a minute.

"A toothbrush?"

"There isn't one big enough." She grimaced and swallowed while something acid tried to crawl back up her throat. Whatever the potion had been, her stomach wasn't thrilled with it.

"I've got water in the truck," he said. "As soon as

we're out of sight you can gargle and spit as much as you want."

"You're a mind reader. I've always liked that about you."

"I'll remind you of that."

He walked with her into the icy air. As they headed for her SUV, the governor's helicopter leaped up, pivoted around an invisible center, and gathered speed down the valley.

Carly looked around the ranchland. Houses might be built and abandoned. Cattle might be born and grow and be sold. The valley would be grazed or plowed or left fallow, and the mountains would watch over all of it, unchanging. The land survived. Man didn't. For all the power the Senator and his wife had wielded while alive, in death little remained but the ranch.

For the first time Carly began to understand Winifred's obsession with Castillo land.

"What?" Dan asked.

"Just thinking."

He waited.

"Nothing is left of Winifred's family and their ambitions but the land," Carly said as they walked toward her SUV. "The ranch is as close to immortality as the Castillos will ever get, and Governor Quintrell has put it up for sale."

Dan nodded, started to say something, then

thought better of it. Carly didn't need to know what he already did. Immortality was worth killing for.

"Come home with me," he said abruptly. "Leave your SUV here. I'll bring you back in the morning. I don't want you to be alone."

She started to object, then saw the shadows and urgency in his eyes. Without a word she turned and started walking toward his truck.

# 35

THEY HADN'T BEEN ON THE ROAD VERY LONG, BUT Carly knew she'd throw up if Dan's truck hit one more icy rut. Frantically she lowered the window on the passenger side. They were on the winding part of the ranch road, where it dropped out of the valley to snake along the far side of Castillo Ridge. There was nothing below the vehicle but darkness and nothing above but stars.

Dan watched her closely. He knew how she was feeling. His stomach wasn't happy with whatever herbal concoction had been in those cups. He was feeling nauseated and light-headed. If it got any worse, he would pull over and get it all out of his system.

"Dan?" Carly's voice was ragged. The world spun crazily. Despite the rush of icy air over her face, her stomach heaved. **"Stop."**

Dan slammed on the brakes without asking why. He didn't have to. She was pale and sweating, her head wobbling unsteadily.

Carly managed to get her seat belt off but couldn't wrap her fingers around the door handle. He dragged her across the center console and out his door. She pushed him away, fell to her hands and knees on the ground, and threw up again and again. Finally she tried to stand. Her knees wouldn't cooperate.

"Easy, honey," Dan said, biting back his own nausea and light-headedness, wanting to help her. Then training kicked in.

**Throw up, fool. You've been poisoned.**

He went down in the snow next to her and vomited repeatedly, ridding himself of Sylvia's goodbye potion. His head spun but his stomach felt better immediately. He scrubbed out his mouth with a handful of snow, spit, and waited.

No more nausea.

Carly wasn't so lucky. She was retching again, swaying even though she was on her hands and knees. He steadied her, held her head, and did everything he could think of to help her throw off whatever had been in the small cup.

Opium or heroin was his bet. Part of his training had required taking various drugs so that he would know his own limits—or know what was happening if somebody had slipped something into his coffee. When he was finished with that part of his training, he'd wondered why people spent good money to screw up their brain and body.

Finally Carly stopped vomiting.

"Better?" he asked her gently.

She tried to talk. Couldn't. The world was turning around her. She tried to focus, but her eyes wouldn't work. She tried to hold on to Dan but her fingers wouldn't work. All her body wanted to do was sleep, right now, forever.

Dan's heart stopped when Carly went slack in his arms. He carried her to the truck, propped her up against the hood, and took her pulse.

Weak, slower than it should be.

Same for her breathing.

**Shit.**

Her head thunked against his chest. He grabbed her chin, lifted one of her eyelids, and saw a pinpoint pupil. He opened her mouth. Despite the recent vomiting, her tongue was dry. The color of her lips was tending toward blue rather than pink. She had all the signs of an opium overdose.

No point in making her throw up; there was nothing left in her stomach. Mother Nature's way of taking care of unwanted cargo. Traditional medical care was too far away and he was damned if he'd let anyone at the ranch house touch Carly.

Someone there had poisoned both of them.

But Dan was much bigger, more able to tolerate

the drug without succumbing. Carly wasn't. It had hit her like a falling building.

She was going under.

Fear slammed through Dan in a wave of adrenaline that made him forget his own light-headedness, his own slowed reactions. He pulled Carly away from the truck, clamped his arm around her, and tried to walk and shake her awake at the same time. He had to keep her moving until her system could cope with whatever drug she hadn't already vomited.

She hung from his arm, sliding away.

"Carly!"

Her head lolled.

He grabbed her hair with his free hand, brought her face up to his, and shouted, "Carly! You have to wake up and move. **Do it now.**"

Her eyelids flickered. Her head jerked unsteadily. "Dan?"

"I'm here, Carly. Somebody gave you an opiate. You threw up most of it." **I hope.** "Now you have to stay awake until your breathing is better. Walk, honey. I'll be with you every step of the way."

She heard someone talking to her at a distance. A long way away. A dream. After some effort she identified the voice as Dan's. No matter how many times she told him to go away, he wouldn't stop shouting at her so that she could sleep.

Finally, slowly, her legs started to get the rhythm of walking. She couldn't wholly support herself, but she at least could keep her feet under her some of the time.

"That's it, Carly. Good. Good. Much better. Hang on to me, honey. We're winning."

Slowly she became aware of her feet, icy, and her body, heavier than wet sand. She didn't see how she stood up. Then she realized she wasn't standing, not really. Dan was supporting her and at the same time forcing her to put one foot in front of the other.

"Walk, love," he said, rubbing his cheek on her hair. "Just walk. I'll take care of the balancing act for both of us. It's helping clear my head, too."

Carly opened her eyes and understood that it wasn't a dream. Dan was frog-marching her up one side of the frozen road and down the other. The truck jerked by her. No, the truck wasn't lurching. She was. But with every step, every heartbeat, every breath, she felt more in control.

"When I catch the fucking coward who did this to you," Dan continued, "I'm going to do the entire Colombian dance on him—necktie, cock and balls, the whole tortilla."

She licked dry lips with a tongue only slightly less dry. "Sounds painful."

Abruptly Dan stopped. "Carly?"

"I think so."

He swept her up in a hug that told her how worried he'd been. His face was buried against her neck and he held her with the strength of desperation. His skin was clammy against hers.

"What . . ." She swallowed against the dryness of her throat.

"Someone dropped an opiate in our toast-the-dead cup. I threw it up before it could really take hold. You were more susceptible, but you threw up enough to keep from going under."

"An opiate? You mean like heroin?"

"Yes."

She swallowed again. A bit of moisture was finally returning. Her head was only spinning some of the time. She felt like she'd been beaten with a sock full of sand. The taste in her mouth would have gagged a skunk.

"You're saying people pay to feel like that?" she asked in disbelief.

He grinned slightly. "Most people don't take enough to get sick. They just get woozy and nod off."

"I'm never getting close to that dog crap again."

"You didn't exactly volunteer this time."

She leaned against him. "I still feel fuzzy."

"Yeah, I know what you mean." He took her pulse and listened to her breathing. "You'll do fine."

"Because of you."

Dan had been trying not to think about that. If Carly had been alone when the narcotic hit, she could have driven off the road and died when her vehicle hit something hundreds of feet below. Even if she had realized something was wrong and managed to stop on the road and get out to be sick, she wouldn't have been able to climb back in her SUV afterward. She would have passed out and frozen to death before anyone even noticed she was gone.

She sighed and leaned harder on him. "Sorry to be such a wimp."

"Wimp?" He lifted his head and looked at her. "You don't get it, do you?"

She just looked at him.

"You could have died," he said harshly. "Overdose. Driving off a cliff. Passing out and freezing to death. Take your pick. That's what somebody dished out to you when they filled your cup with drugs."

"Maybe my stomach just didn't like—"

"Bullshit, honey," he cut in angrily. "Just plain bullshit. I know what opiates are like, what they do to me. We were drugged."

The white plumes of his breath looked like smoke.

"I don't live in a world where people try to kill me," she said faintly. She still felt woozy, and beneath that she was plain scared. At least adrenaline was useful; it began to clear the fog from her brain. "People might frighten me and try to make me go away, but they don't try to kill me. Besides, anybody could have picked up the cup I did. You could have."

"I should have, but I jumped the queue. I got Alma's dose."

Carly blinked. "Huh?"

He started to explain how he'd taken the point of the remaining triangle rather than a cup from the base of the triangle. "Never mind. You're still not up to par. Think you can sit in the truck and not fall asleep or do you want to walk some more?"

"Keep scaring me. Adrenaline helps me focus."

"Adrenaline." He smiled, lowered his head, and bit her neck with exquisite care. His hand roamed down her back to her buttocks, flexed, squeezed, caressed, rubbed her against him.

Her breath came in with a strangled sound. Her heart raced. Her breathing deepened.

"How am I doing in the adrenaline department?" he asked after a few moments.

"Overload." She wrapped her arms around his neck and shivered. "Pure overload. Do it some more."

"Time to get back in the truck. You're cold."

She laughed. "A little wobbly around the edges, but not cold."

"You shivered."

"It wasn't from cold."

Dan's eyelids went to half-mast and he took a deep breath. "Right. Into the truck with you."

She nuzzled against his neck. "You sure?"

"We'll see how frisky you feel after the emergency room."

"What emergency room?"

"The one I'm taking you to as soon as we get to town."

"Wrong."

He opened the truck door on the passenger side, lifted her in, and fastened her seat belt.

"If I had too much wine and threw up," she said, "would you take me to a hospital?"

Without a word he shut her door and walked around the front of the truck.

"Well," she said when he climbed in and slammed the door, "would you?"

"Not unless you passed out," he said reluctantly.

"Ha. You went to college. How many of your buddies threw up, passed out, and woke up the next day with a hangover the size of Australia?"

"A few."

"How many did you take to the ER?" she asked.

Dan started the truck.

"That's what I thought," Carly said. "Besides,

what would you tell the doctor, that I ate the wrong brownie and things went south?"

"You're thinking of hash or pot, not an opiate."

"The point is the same. You go to the doctors, they find traces of heroin or whatever, and I get to explain to the sheriff how it got there. Imagine how he'll react when I say, 'Gee, it must have been that farewell cup for Sylvia. You know those Quintrells—notorious dopers every one of them.' He'll have me locked up in a hot second. Then I won't be able to work on the Quintrell-Castillo history, which seems to be the whole point, doesn't it?"

Dan felt like banging something against the steering wheel—her head, his head, both.

She was right, but he didn't have to like it.

Without a word he drove the truck down the road, watching for lights in the mirror. Nothing but darkness. As soon as the road allowed, he pulled off and backed into the cover of the forest. When he was satisfied that he would be able to see the road but nobody could see him, he turned off the truck. Darkness slammed down around them.

Carly sat straighter and looked out the windows. "What's the attraction—submarine races?"

Smiling, he shook his head. "You're well on your way back to sassy."

"Thanks to you." She tried not to yawn. "Other

than feeling more than a little buzzed, I'm fine. Do you have any more water?"

He reached under the seat and pulled out a fresh bottle. "Let me know if it makes you sick."

"You're such a Pollyanna."

"It's a gift." Dan sat and watched his passenger from the corner of his eye. The rest of his attention was on the road.

After a bit of a struggle, Carly managed to open the water. She took a mouthful, let it dissolve the foul flavor in her mouth, and spat it out the open window. The third time she did it, her mouth tasted more like her own. She sipped and swallowed tentatively. Another sip. Another.

"You doing okay?" he asked.

"So far. It's not like having too much booze in my blood. Drinking water doesn't make me feel worse."

He waited.

After a final sip she capped the water. "Let's see how that settles."

"Good idea." With that, Dan gave his full attention to the road. After five minutes, he glanced over at Carly again. "Doing okay?"

"I'm still fuzzy. But not like before. I can stay awake."

He took her pulse. Slow, but nothing to worry about. She was just really, really relaxed. He turned the ignition key so that he could run up the passenger window.

"Here," he said. "Sleep if you want to. It's safe now."

"You mean you aren't going to jump me?"

"This minute? No."

"Well, damn. Then why are we freezing our butts off out here?"

"Humor me."

"But—"

"Do you really want to know?" he asked.

"Yes."

"I'm waiting to see who comes along."

"I figured that out. But why?"

"Somebody might be curious about how well the dope worked. Or to finish the job if you're still . . ." He shrugged.

**Alive.**

Neither said it.

Both thought it.

# 36

WINIFRED IGNORED THE SLUGGISHNESS OF HER body and mind, strength lost to a drug, strength she couldn't afford to lose.

**Who was it?**

**Who drugged us?**

**Why?**

The questions battered her mind as much as illness battered her body.

**Everybody could have. Once the doctor brought me into the room, my back was to the bottle holding the farewell toast. Or it could have been put in the empty cups.**

**Anyone. Anyone at all.**

With a sharp movement of her head, she tossed back the stimulant she'd mixed for herself as soon as she'd understood what had happened. While the false strength hummed through her blood, she put away the old questions and asked another one.

**Who couldn't have drugged us?**

That was the person she would trust to mail the envelopes.

With steady rhythm and unsteady hands, she wheeled herself through the house's wide hallways to the Senator's office. She didn't see the paintings and sculpture, the expensive knickknacks from another time; she thought only about the members of the household, the people who had access to her herbs and those who didn't.

Nothing changed. It still could have been anyone. She would have to see to the copying and mailing herself.

She opened the door to the office and nudged her wheelchair through. Across the room, the old-fashioned clock ticked between photos of the Senator smiling into the camera, his eyes on the main chance and his hands ever ready to grab a female butt.

**I should have killed him years ago.**

But she hadn't. She'd been afraid of his son, a fear that proved wise.

She wheeled over to the desk. Everything she needed was there, from copier to computer to supplies. Melissa kept the office as if the Senator was still alive, still able to dictate letters and watch them typed. Outgoing material—bills and checks and orders for supplies—lay bundled on the polished wood tray at the edge of the old desk, just as mail always had at the ranch.

Winifred turned on the copier and went to work,

reproducing the old document she'd taken from a locked box hidden in her room. When she was finished copying, she shut off the machine and turned to the desk. The wheelchair made reaching everything awkward, but she had no choice.

The side drawer stuck, then finally gave with a creak when she kept tugging. Deliberately she counted out three envelopes crisp with the Quintrell ranch logo and began addressing them. Into each envelope she put a copy of the old document. She hesitated, then put the receipt for the DNA samples that she'd sent into the envelope destined for Carolina May. She also put the original document in that envelope, folding the brittle paper ruthlessly.

With deliberate motions that belied the frantic beating of Winifred's heart, she sealed the envelopes and put stamps on each. Then she carefully mixed the three envelopes in with the ranch's normal outgoing mail, bundled everything up again, and set it neatly on the tray. Whoever took them in to town tomorrow morning—the Snead boys or Alma or Lucia—wouldn't notice the extra mail.

Winifred hesitated, but finally couldn't resist. She wanted the Senator's son to know. She wanted him to understand that she'd won. Grimly she dialed the governor's cell number. The governor answered after four rings.

"What is it, Pete?" Josh asked. "More problems with the books?"

"It's not Pete," Winifred said. "But you have more problems than balancing the ranch books."

"Winifred? Is something wrong?"

"No, something's right." She coughed but managed to get her breath. "Finally it will be right."

"Look, it's late. I have a speech to edit, a plane to catch in four hours, and I'm still sick from whatever—"

"Oh, it's late all right," she interrupted. "Late for you and the Senator's plans. I fixed him, and you." She wanted to laugh but was afraid it would dissolve into coughing.

At the other end of the line, Josh pinched the bridge of his nose, shook himself like a dog coming out of water, and wondered what in hell was going on. Had the old woman finally cracked?

**Just what I need right now—a certifiably nutty aunt.**

"Winifred," he said curtly, "you're not making sense. Put Melissa on the line and—"

"Sylvia's great-grandmother, Isobel's mother, was **una bruja**," Winifred said, ignoring Josh's attempt to talk. "She knew the Senator couldn't be trusted with the land. She made him sign a document agreeing that—"

"Isobel? Isobel who?" Josh said impatiently. "What's this all about?"

"Castillo," Winifred hissed. "It's about the marriage between Castillo and Quintrell."

"That was a long time ago, long before the Senator was even born. How could anyone trust or not trust a man who wouldn't be born for forty years?"

Winifred took a shallow, careful breath. She had to focus so that the governor would understand.

So that he would know she'd won.

"They signed a marriage agreement," Winifred said. "Sylvia and the second Quintrell. One of the things they agreed was that only children with Sylvia Castillo's blood in them could inherit the land. **Her** children, not his."

"And your point would be?" Josh asked sarcastically. "Sylvia and the Senator had kids, and only one survived. That would be me. I inherited the ranch, and this whole conversation is nuts."

"Can you prove it?" Winifred asked, her voice hoarse and triumphant. "Can you prove Sylvia Castillo Quintrell is your mother?"

"Of course I—"

"No you can't," Winifred said, her voice trembling with victory and rage and illness. "You're no more a Castillo than I'm a Quintrell."

"You're crazy. Don't make me prove it and lock you up. You don't want to spend whatever time you have left wearing a hug-me jacket in a padded room. And that's just what will happen if you keep flogging this nonsense."

The governor hung up before Winifred could say another word.

**You're crazy. Don't make me prove it and lock you up.**

"You can threaten me and brush me off like a fly," Winifred said to the dead phone, "but not Jeanette Dykstra."

The thought made Winifred smile, then laugh, then cough until she was dizzy. Leaving the office was harder than entering had been. She was feeling age and sin and illness like a thousand cuts bleeding her strength away, even the raging strength of hatred. Death was coming to her in the body of a raven soaring on the wind. She didn't know when it would come, but she was certain it was soon.

If the pneumonia didn't kill her, the Senator's son would.

# 37

CARLY AWOKE WITH THE FIRST LIGHT SLIPPING PAST the curtains into Dan's bedroom. She felt a moment of disorientation at the warm weight along her left side and over her waist. Then she remembered what had happened the night before.

Part of her still didn't believe someone wanted her dead.

Most of her did.

None of her liked it.

"You awake, honey?" Dan asked very softly.

His breath stirred her hair.

"Yes," she said.

"How do you feel?"

"Like myself. Mostly."

His arm tightened around her waist, pulling her closer. He made a low sound as her rear fit against his crotch. "What's not like you?"

"I'm scared," she said.

He stilled. "Of me?"

She looked over her shoulder and deliberately moved her hips against his erection. "No."

"Good. I'd let you go if I had to, but . . ." He let out a long breath. "I want you, Carly."

"So that's not a giant pickle in your pocket?" she asked wryly.

"I'm not wearing any pockets. No clothes, either."

"Funny thing. Neither am I."

"That was your idea," he said.

"It was?"

"Yeah. You decided you had to have a bath. At three A.M. You spent the next thirty minutes in the shower. Used up all the hot water and still didn't get out until you were shivering." He nuzzled against her nape. "Then you started for your bed wearing only a wet towel."

"Something must have happened on the way. This is your bed, not mine."

"You were cold and headed barefoot for a room that probably still has pieces of glass on the floor somewhere. Couldn't have that happen, could we?"

Carly smiled. She hadn't wanted to sleep alone but hadn't been up to being anyone's sex kitten, not even Dan's. He hadn't pushed her. He'd just wrapped her up in a dry towel, put her in his bed, curled up around her to keep her warm . . . and she'd fallen asleep. Sometime during the night, she'd lost the towel.

"Once we were in bed," Dan said, tasting her

warm neck, "I didn't want you to feel under-dressed, so I took off my clothes."

She murmured, savoring the feel of Dan's body pressed against hers. She liked the faint roughness of his hair rubbing over her skin. She liked the smell of him.

She couldn't wait to taste him.

The thought startled her. She'd never thought of herself as a particularly sensual person. She liked men, enjoyed the physical differences between the sexes, and had never found a man she couldn't do without. But Dan sparked a hot kind of curiosity in her. She wanted to know what it would be like to have sex with him, what **she** would be like in his arms, if the heat pooling in her body would finally find release.

"Now I remember," she said lazily. "The hot water ran out and I was cold and then this electric blanket warmed me up."

"Electric blanket? Have I just been insulted?"

"It was a really superior electric blanket."

He nipped her shoulder.

"Hey, at that point I still was a cheeseburger short of a Happy Meal," she pointed out. "I just assumed anything that warm had to plug into a wall socket."

She felt as much as heard Dan's laughter.

"So that's why you wouldn't kiss me," he said.

"You didn't want a mouthful of flannel and wires."

"No, I just tasted too bad to share. Even those industrial-strength mints you bought for me weren't enough to get rid of the taste in my mouth." She grimaced. "I vaguely remember stuffing a mint under my tongue just before I fell asleep. Which explains it."

"Okay, you lost me. Which explains what?"

She licked her lips and swallowed. Everything was in working order, including her salivary glands. "I don't usually wake up tasting like a peppermint factory."

"Really?" He tipped her chin up and kissed her slowly, sampling the flavor. "Spearmint, actually. My favorite."

"You sure?"

He kissed her again, loving the feel of tongue against tongue and his woody snug against her naked hips. "Oh, yeah. I'm sure."

"Not peppermint?" She watched him, her smoky golden eyes alive with teasing and something more, something hot.

"Maybe I should taste again," he said.

Carly turned to face him fully. "Maybe you should."

He caught his breath at the feel of her breasts moving against him, her nipples hard and hungry.

"You sure?" he asked, repeating her question.

"Very sure. But I'm not taking anything, so we'll have to be creative until we get to a drugstore."

"Creative." His smile was like his kiss, slow and hot. "We'll try that, too, but I bought condoms after the first time I saw you."

She blinked. "I must have looked real easy."

"You were fire and I was cold all the way to my core. I needed you so much I couldn't breathe. I still do."

The look in his eyes and the catch in his voice sent heat through her in a liquid wave, preparing her body. She'd never been wanted the way Dan wanted her. Blindly she reached out to him, understanding in that moment that she needed him in the same way, no questions, no hesitation, just a certainty that burned through a lifetime of doubts.

"I want you so much I don't know what to do first," she admitted raggedly.

His eyelids lowered in a sensual reflex that was as uncontrollable as the increased heart rate sending blood beating through his veins.

"Come here," he said, rolling over on his back, taking her with him. "This way I know I won't rush you."

She gave a shaky laugh as she fought off bedding to straddle him. "You aren't rushing me, you're driving me crazy."

He groaned at the sleek feel of her sliding over him. "You're making it hard for me to slow down."

"Did I ask you to?"

"I want it to be good for you." His hands cupped her breasts and his thumbs rubbed over the tips. "I want it to be the best you ever had."

He caught her hard nipples in his fingers and squeezed with sensual precision.

Twin spears of pleasure shot through her, going from her breasts to her thighs, making her breath and her body come apart. She felt liquid heat bathing her, spilling over to him. Suddenly his fingers were opening her, tracing over her hot folds, moving inside her, sending pleasure spiraling until she couldn't think, couldn't see, couldn't breathe, could only need and need and **need.**

And then it stopped.

"No!" she said.

"Easy, darling, let me get this damn thing on."

Her eyes opened, dazed and hungry. She saw him toss away a foil wrapper and sheathe himself with an impatient motion of his hand. Her breath filled her throat. She'd forgotten what a big man he was.

Way too big.

"Too late to be scared now," he said, teasing her with his fingers, positioning himself at her entrance. "You're wet enough to take me. Slide down, Carolina May. Trust your body. Trust us."

It was impossible not to, for her body was once again on fire, rings of pleasure radiating up, shaking her. He felt the lush heat of her response, felt her widen her thighs to take him, felt the hot satin inside her pressing around him, and gritted his teeth against coming right there. He wanted to be all the way in before he came, as deep as possible. He wanted to feel her orgasm squeeze him from tip to base. He wanted it all with her, everything he'd ever imagined, every way, every—

The wild shuddering of her release tore away his breath and his control. He held her deep and hard, pumping into her until there was nothing left but a kind of dazed satisfaction that turned his body to sand. The way she lay slumped against him told him that she felt the same way.

"Carly?"

"Wow."

"Whew," he said, smiling.

"No, wow."

"You're wowing. I'm whewing with relief."

Her laughter was a ripple of her body around his. She lifted her head, swiped hair out of her eyes, and kissed him almost shyly. Red stained her cheeks.

"What?" he asked, touching her face.

"**Cosmo** articles don't cover this moment."

Dark eyebrows rose. "Really? There's something

about sex that hasn't been headlined in a woman's magazine?"

"Yeah."

"What?"

She shook her head and glanced down, sending her hair flying again.

"C'mon." He lifted her chin gently. "I'm dying here."

"How do you say thanks for the best sex of your life?" she mumbled, looking at his mouth rather than his eyes.

His smile made her warm all over again.

"That's easy," he said against her lips. "Thanks for the best sex of my life."

"Not you, me."

"Both of us."

She banged her forehead lightly against his chest. "One of us isn't making sense."

"Do that some more, honey. I like the way it feels."

"I could tell. Do you have another condom or is it time to be creative?"

"Hell of an idea," he said, pulling her mouth down to his.

The phone rang.

He ignored it.

It kept ringing.

Blindly he felt at the bedside for the receiver, picked it up. "What," he snarled.

"Just wanted to make sure you got home okay," Gus said. "Two of the guests at the memorial service ended up in Urgent Care. Something in the food apparently. It was touch-and-go for Winifred just because she was already weak, but she's stable now. The governor was dog sick, but he recovered and is on his way back to the campaign trail."

Carly could hear Gus's voice. She separated from Dan and lay along his side. He tilted the phone so she could hear both ends of the conversation.

"Anyone else?" Dan asked.

"Alma and Melissa both were sick. Alma was the worst, really woozy, but Winifred gave her something before she started getting nauseated herself."

"What about the minister?"

"He was a little queasy but didn't hurl. Same for Pete. Lucia said she threw up once and that was it. No one else on the ranch was sick, even the Sandoval women who prepared the food and drink. Same for the Snead brothers, who were snitching samples."

Shivering, Carly drew blankets up over herself and Dan. He pulled her back into place along his side, tucking her head against his neck.

"Carly and I were sick, but we're fine now," Dan said. "Are they testing the drink we toasted Sylvia with?"

"Nothing was left of it."

"Not even a drop?"

"The container is gone. So are the cups. One of the maids saw Winifred smashing everything and throwing it in the fireplace to burn. She said it was part of the ritual. But that's not for the general public," Gus cautioned.

Dan looked at Carly. She nodded; she wasn't going to spread the news around.

"What did Sheriff Montoya say?" Dan asked.

"For the record?"

"Fuck the record."

"Right," Gus said without a pause. "Montoya said that the old curandera must have screwed up her potion, added something that was an emetic, and made folks sick."

"That's how he's treating it? Accidental poisoning?"

"Poison was never mentioned. Bad food, according to the report. Maybe even flu."

"Off the record," Dan said.

Carly looked at the grim line of Dan's mouth as he waited for Gus to speak.

"Agreed," Gus said unhappily.

"I don't know what hit the others, but Carly and I were fed a hefty dose of opiate."

Gus whistled softly. "You okay?"

"I had enough body mass to dilute the dose. Carly

didn't. If she'd been alone, she would have nodded off and frozen to death. Somebody was expecting her to be alone."

She felt the tension that didn't show in Dan's voice. Coolness slid over her skin. She didn't like remembering how close she had come to waking up dead.

"What?" Gus said. "How can you be sure? Wait. Forget I said that. You're like Mom, always knowing things. Shit, brother. **Shit.** Why would anyone want to hurt Ms. May?"

"Somebody doesn't want the Senator's family history researched and put into print. Things have happened to her since she arrived. Threats and vandalism."

"Are you talking about Governor Quintrell being the one behind it?" Gus asked cautiously.

Carly was curious about that herself.

"He's number one on my list," Dan said. "But there has to be someone else working with him."

"Why?"

"He didn't have a chance to slip anything into whatever Winifred prepared," Dan said.

"You're sure? From what the doctor said, it was a near thing for Winifred. If she's dead, the history won't get done."

"The governor never came near the stuff except to drink some. In any case, Carly has made it real

clear that she's going to finish the history, no matter what."

She nodded vigorously.

"She can't finish it if she's dead," Gus pointed out.

Dan made a rough sound.

"What can I do?" Gus asked.

"Find out everyone who was born in this county
three years on either side of Sylvia's stroke." Then,
remembering his work with the photos, Dan added,
"Stillbirths and miscarriages, too."

Gus didn't say anything.

Dan looked at Carly and saw the same question in
her eyes that must have been eating at Gus.

"Mind telling me why?" Gus asked finally.

"I don't know."

"You don't know? Then how—"

"Call it a hunch, okay?" Dan interrupted.

"A hunch. Hell, bro. You and that silver forelock
are going to make me crazy. You sure you're all
right?"

Dan brushed a kiss over Carly's lips. "Never better."

"Then tell Mom. She knows where you were.
Everyone knows there was something wrong with
the food. She'll be worried and she's too stubborn
to call you and ask. I'll let you know when I have the
names."

"Thanks. And, Gus?"

"Yeah?"

"Don't tell anyone what you're doing for me. **Anyone.**"

"You're saying you don't trust anyone, including family?"

Dan waited.

"Okay," Gus said. "Call me Zipped Lips."

The phone went dead.

"Why the births?" Carly asked when Dan hung up.

"Something sent Sylvia over the edge. Given the Senator's track record, I'm thinking it was one of his women. Question is why? And who? When we know that, maybe we'll know who wants you seriously inconvenienced, as in dead."

She winced. "You really think I should leave, don't you."

"Yes," Dan said instantly.

"No harm, no foul, just let the son of a bitch have his way?" she asked in a climbing voice.

"I didn't say that."

"Sure as sunrise the sheriff won't do anything about it. Or are you going to tell him?"

"Waste of time."

"You're going to do it all yourself," she accused. "Just shove the little woman in a closet and go bare-handed after some murderous dickhead."

"Talk about images you could live without."

She refused to be sidetracked. "Well?"

"I won't be bare-handed."

She remembered him standing by a window with a weapon held down along his leg. Her breath came out with a hoarse sound.

"I don't want you to get hurt over something that has nothing to do with you," she said.

"Everything is connected, Carolina May. Especially you and me."

"Then stop trying to get rid of me."

"I'm trying to keep you safe."

"And I'm trying to keep **you** safe."

He opened his mouth. Closed it. Shook his head. "I'm not believing this conversation."

"Then don't have it."

He laughed almost helplessly.

"What?" she asked.

"I'm picturing the reaction of my . . . friends if they could hear this." Dan's mouth turned up in a bemused curve. "Would it help you to know I've been trained in various kinds of self-defense, I'm fluent in five languages, and I've lived in failed and failing states for ten out of the last twelve years?"

"I'm happy for you, even though it sounds like you have a sucky, dangerous job."

"Sometimes. Mostly not."

"Maybe I should rescue you." She smiled.

"You're missing the point," he said.

"The point is I'm staying."

He looked at her smoky gold eyes and knew he wasn't going to win this argument.

"If you stay, there are going to be some ground rules," he said.

"There's no if about it. I'm staying. Wait," she said, sensing he was going to argue some more. "Let me finish. I'm not crazy or naïve. I know how close I came to dying last night. But if I run off, whoever is behind this isn't going to just go back to playing with himself. Winifred is in danger right now. Anyone who asks the wrong questions is in danger. I can't just shrug and say, 'Not my problem,' and walk away. It's like you said. Everything is connected. I can't live with being the weak link that made someone else's life fall apart."

Dan couldn't argue with Carly. He felt the same way. It was one of the reasons he'd kept on doing a sucky, sometimes dangerous job.

"Okay," he said.

She blinked. "That's it? No argument? Just okay?"

"Keep it in mind when you start objecting to commonsense advice."

"You don't advise, you order."

He just looked at her.

She blew out a breath. "Okay."

Smiling, Dan kissed her quickly and shot out of bed before he changed his mind.

Or she did.

# 38

DAN PARKED IN FRONT OF HIS PARENTS' HOUSE, next to the old car they had last seen in front of Lucia Sandoval's house.

"I won't be long," Dan said to Carly. "Wait here. I'll leave the engine running so you keep warm."

She gave him a sideways look. "Are you trying to get rid of me?"

"I'm offering you a chance to avoid what might be an ugly family wrangle."

"About?"

"Opiates."

She reached for the handle and opened the door.

He cursed under his breath, got out, and held the little gate open for her. As she walked by, he took her arm and stopped her. "Whatever you hear doesn't go into Winifred's damned history without my mother's permission."

"I don't think your mother will give it."

"She has a right to her privacy. So does Lucia, whose only mistake was to fall in love with the wrong man."

Carly looked into Dan's eyes, shadowed and green and determined. "I'll respect their privacy."

"Thank you." He shifted almost angrily, releasing her. "I don't like doing this."

"Asking me to censor a family history?"

"That, too."

Dan knocked on the door and called out. His father's voice called back.

"Great," Dan muttered. "That will put a real gloss on this clusterhug."

"Clusterhug. Is that a word?"

"It is in my mother's house."

Carly bit her lip against a smile. The idea of a man like Dan tiptoeing around his mother appealed to her. "Gotcha."

The door opened. John grinned when he saw them. "Answered prayers. Your mother and Lucia are in the greenhouse talking about woman things."

"Carly is your answer," Dan said, gesturing her into the house. "I need to talk to Mom."

John's smile vanished. "It better not be about your great-grandfather."

"It isn't." **This time.**

"Fresh coffee in the kitchen," John said to Carly. "You want some, Dan?"

"No thanks. This will be short and sweet." **I hope.**

Dan went through the kitchen to the attached

greenhouse. The temperature was about that of the kitchen. The humidity was higher.

"Hi, Mom," he said, hugging her briefly. "Lucia. How are the kids?"

"Healthy and in school," she said, rolling her eyes in relief. "Your mother's medicines are such a help."

"They can be." Dan's smile vanished as he looked at his mother. "Or they can hurt."

Diana drew in a sharp, shocked breath.

"Who supplies you and Winifred with opiates for your medicines?" he asked. "Armando?"

Lucia made a small sound.

"What do you know of opiates?" Diana asked.

"A lot more than you want to hear." He glanced at Lucia. "Isn't that right?"

She flushed and looked away.

"Armando told you, didn't he?" Dan pressed.

She nodded slightly.

"What?" Diana asked. "What are you talking about?"

"Part of my work includes tracking black money," Dan said evenly. "Illegal money. The kind Armando Sandoval and his kin make buttloads of smuggling Mexican brown or Colombian cocaine, depending on which branch of the family he's working with on a load."

Diana shrugged. Everyone knew what Armando did. "So?"

"So when I got too close, his Colombian kin put out a contract on me." Absently Dan rubbed his left leg. "The story about a climbing accident was just that, a story."

This time Diana wasn't the only one who made a shocked sound. Carly had been standing in the doorway, listening. Her eyes were wide and horrified.

Lucia crossed herself and looked at the floor in shame. **"Lo siento."**

He knew she was sorry, just as he knew she loved her husband anyway. She had walled herself off from reality until she was able to see Armando only as her man and the father of her children.

"It has nothing to do with you," Dan said, touching Lucia briefly. "But it has everything to do with my question."

"Why?" John asked coolly. "Have you come to arrest your mother on drug charges?"

"You know better."

"Then why do you care? She doesn't use enough opiates to make a blip on anybody's radar."

"I've been assuming that Carly was the target of the drugging at Sylvia's memorial service," Dan said. "But it could have been me. Armando could have figured this would be a good, clean shot at finishing the contract."

Lucia put her hands over her ears and shook her head. "No! He said nothing about that. He just laughed when I said you were hurt climbing. I hear that laugh before. I know it has to do with . . . business."

Dan looked at his mother. The darkness in her eyes made him wish he hadn't opened his mouth. "You and Winifred share the same source for opiates."

"Yes," Diana said. "Alma."

"She certainly would have had the opportunity," Carly said from the doorway. "But she was sick, too, wasn't she?"

"**Sí.** Yes," Lucia said.

"I never ask where Alma gets her medicines," Diana said. "Ultimately, I suppose it is Armando."

"Medicines." Dan's lips turned down. "Hell of a name for it."

"The way I use opiates is medicine, just as it was before Anglo laws changed what was legal and what wasn't, but didn't change poverty and disease. **Los curanderos** exist because there is a need. We use what we have always used, the gifts of the land, poppy and peyote, morning glory and mushroom." Diana's dark eyes glittered with anger and impatience. "No Anglo law will change that."

It was an old argument, one that wasn't going anywhere new, especially as Dan didn't really disagree.

"The point is that someone put an overdose of opiates in the cups we all drank at the memorial service," Dan said.

Diana's hand went to her throat. "But I heard it was the food."

"No, it was an attempt to murder Carly or, maybe, me. Since no one has notified me about a new death threat, I have to assume Carly was the target. At least, until Armando tells me otherwise." Dan looked at Lucia. "Call him. Tell him to meet me at the Pico de Gallo in Las Trampas in half an hour."

# 39

"WHY CAN'T I COME WITH YOU?" CARLY ASKED. "Why should Gus have to run down and check on me every few minutes?"

"Every half hour."

"Whatever. You know what I mean. And I'm not talking about the archive babysitting rules."

Dan looked at the woman standing in the middle of the crowded basement. Cold air filtered down the stairway through the gaps in the cellar door that was also part of the basement's roof. His leg felt like something was gnawing on it.

He ignored everything but Carly. "The man I'm going to see is an international **narcotraficante**. I don't even want you in the same country with him, much less the same room. He's good for five murders on both sides of the border that we know of, and that doesn't include the poor illegals who died in the desert carrying forty-kilo backpacks of Mexican brown over the border in the middle of the desert. All those men wanted was a chance at a better life. What they got was death."

Her chin came up. "I read the newspapers and watch TV. I know what happens."

"But it doesn't happen to **you.** I want to keep it that way. I'll be back before lunch. If you aren't here, you'd better be in the office with Gus or with my parents."

"Is that advice or an order?" she asked through clenched teeth.

"Whatever works."

When she would have argued, he distracted her by sticking his tongue in her mouth and kissing her until she softened and returned the favor. And the flavor. Slowly, reluctantly, he lifted his head.

"Be here for me, Carolina May."

"You're not playing fair."

"I'm not playing at all."

"Like I said . . ." She closed her eyes for an instant. "Okay, okay. You win."

"No, **we** win."

She watched him walk up the stairs and out into the overcast, snow-threatening day. The scars she had seen and touched on his leg this morning were red, barely healed; she knew they must hurt. Yet he refused to let it slow him down.

In or out of bed.

**Don't go there,** Carly told herself quickly. The man was way too distracting and she had a lot of work to do if she hoped to have a rough draft of

Winifred's history in the next few weeks. Even if Dan came through with a bridge program to transfer material from microfilm to scanner to her computer, she would still be working sixteen-hour days to meet Winifred's new deadline.

Mentally bracing herself, Carly went to the microfilm files. Somewhere in all those metal boxes was the answer to old questions and two very new ones.

Who was trying to kill her?

And why?

# 40

SNOW LAY SPARSELY ALONG THE NARROW ROAD. The housing was a combination of cement block on the newer buildings and ragged, cracked adobe on the older ones. Both new and old buildings had tin roofs. House trailers of all ages and conditions hunched beside the uncertain protection of sagging wooden barns and outbuildings. Fences were made of willow posts and old boxspring mattress frames and discarded tires. Chickens and lop-eared mutts scratched out a living side by side in the cold mud.

Occasional bursts of prosperity showed in houses covered by bright paint or brighter murals. Dan had parked near one of them. The long two-story building's ancient adobe bricks were hidden beneath a painting that combined the artistic traditions of Mexico's muralists with the flowing graffiti of barrio gangs. The result was darkly colorful and oddly menacing, a blunt statement that strangers weren't welcome.

Dan had ignored it. The combination beer bar and taqueria was open, but as soon as he'd said he was Dan Duran and had come to talk to Armando Sandoval, everyone except the barkeep/cook had packed up and gone somewhere else. Dan wasn't surprised. He took his beer to a newly vacated table and waited. The room smelled of Mexican cigarettes, beer, fresh tortillas, and roasted peppers. The tables were like the men who had sat around them—dark, sturdy, and scuffed by use.

Methodically Dan began emptying his pockets onto the table. As he'd left everything but keys and some money locked in the truck, it didn't take long. He toed off his boots, set them on the table, and took a sip of beer. It tasted like South America, thick and rich, earthy.

Somewhere in the back of the building a door slammed. A minute later two men younger than Dan strode into the room. The first man was slim and dressed in black but for a belt with a solid gold buckle. There was a heavy diamond-studded gold cross hanging around his neck. The gun he carried was steel with silver and gold inlays. The briefcase was the same supple black leather as his jacket and pants. The second man wore jeans rather than leather pants. His gun was all steel and fully automatic. The blind muzzle followed Dan's heart.

The barkeep went into the kitchen. He didn't come back.

Without a word Dan stood up, held his arms out from his sides, widened his stance, and waited to be searched.

The first man looked at the stuff on the table approvingly. "Señor Sandoval, he said you would understand."

The second man stepped to the side where he'd be able to keep Dan under his gun without getting in the way.

Dan watched with interest as the first man pulled a lightweight, very sensitive metal detector from the case. Cutting-edge and very expensive.

**Not a low-tech operation. No surprise there.**

Sandoval might use human mules for his heroin and pistol-whip people he didn't like, but when it came to conducting business he protected himself with the best technology money could buy.

The man put the metal detector back, pulled out another piece of equipment, and all but combed Dan's hair and clothes with it down to and including shoving it inside his underwear.

**Wish I'd had this model in Colombia,** Dan thought wryly. **Bet I'd have found the bug before they used it to track me down. Then those kids wouldn't have been killed.**

But he wouldn't think about that. He needed to stay calm, businesslike, in control.

The bug detector went back into the case.

The final test was as old-fashioned as pistol-whipping—a thorough, slyly sexual pat-down that the slim man enjoyed more than Dan did. Dan knew the search was meant to be intimidating and humiliating. It failed. He'd been through a lot worse.

**"Bueno,"** the man said, taking Dan's boots and walking out of the room.

Dan watched his boots disappear. "Careful with those. I just got them broken in."

"Sit," said the second man, the one whose gun muzzle kept staring at Dan's heart.

Dan scooped his keys and change off the table and sat.

And sat.

No impatience showed on Dan's face or in his posture. He leaned back, crossed his arms over his chest, and did a good imitation of falling asleep.

Just one more part of the game.

Armando must have had better things to do than watch his caller sleep. After fifteen minutes he put an end to the nap by walking into the room. The gun in his shoulder holster was obvious enough. The gun in his boot less so.

Dan spotted them both. He didn't react. He wasn't here for a fight and he doubted Armando was, either. The **narcotraficante** was simply doing the machismo dance so as not to lose respect with his men.

He hadn't liked being told to meet Dan.

Dan knew it, just as he knew that the pat-down by **un pato** had been Armando's revenge.

"I am busy," Armando said. "What do you want?"

The bluntness surprised Dan. He'd been expecting a lot of fencing, a lot of posturing. Armando must have a load coming or going right now.

**Not my problem,** Dan reminded himself. **Not this time. This time my only problem is keeping Carolina May alive.**

"I'm on medical leave," Dan said. "In other words, I'm not in New Mexico for any other than personal reasons. Personal, not professional. **Tú comprendes?**"

Armando's thick black eyebrows rose at the use of the intimate address rather than the more formal Spanish.

**"Sí."** And his tone said that he wasn't buying it, not completely.

"Did you tell Alma to put opiates in Sylvia's death toast?" Dan asked.

Armando didn't even try to hide his surprise. Of all the questions he'd expected Dan to ask, obviously this wasn't even close. He looked at Dan and shook his head. "No."

Dan believed him. "Do you know who did?"

Armando shrugged. He didn't know and he didn't care. "Señorita Winifred is old. The old people make errors—mistakes. Even **las brujas.**"

Dan studied the other man. There was no nervousness, no shifting of feet or licking of lips, no unconscious gestures with his hands, no looking away. Either he was an uncommonly good liar or he was telling what he believed to be the truth.

**"Bueno,"** Dan said. "Do you have any professional or personal interest in Ms. Carolina May?"

Armando frowned. "I no like her and Lucia." He lifted his shoulders slightly in a shrug. "But is a small thing, like a fly buzzing."

A corner of Dan's mouth turned up. "Are your Colombian cousins still trying to kill me?"

"In Colombia, maybe, but not here. Here I am **el jefe.** I say killing well-connected Anglos is bad for business."

"Yeah. You'd be up to your lips in jalapeños real quick."

**"Sí.** New Mexico is not Colombia."

**Yet.**

And Dan was doing everything he could to keep it that way.

# 41

CARLY STRETCHED, THEN BENT OVER THE MICRO-film reader and went back to work on the articles about the death of Isobel Castillo Quintrell in 1880, when she was only thirty. Reading between the lines, Isobel had been worn out by marrying at fifteen, then bearing three live children, plus ten premature or stillborn babies in the next fifteen years.

"They had methods of birth control then," Carly murmured into her recorder. "It must have been obvious what all the pregnancies were costing her. Why didn't . . . cancel that. She was a deeply religious Catholic wife."

Carly read quickly, skimming for the facts she would need to re-create the funeral in print. " 'Predeceased by only sister, Juana de Castillo y Castillo, tragically lost during the birth of her first child in 1872.' Editorial comment: the Castillo sisters had a hard time with labor and pregnancy; maybe their parents married one too many cousins. Or maybe they married and started getting pregnant too early. Interesting. Wonder if there are any studies about the correlation between very young brides and wives dying very young."

Her eyes searched the text, looking for names of people attending the funeral. There weren't any unfamiliar names, so she went to the next item on her list and read, talking occasionally into her recorder. For the Castillo book, she would include reproductions of newspaper articles and images; she was already compiling a list for Dan to transfer. What she needed now was some sense of how close the children of the Castillo sisters had been.

After two hours of reading, it was clear that major events—funerals, marriages, baptisms, Quincean-eras—were shared by first cousins. The generation after that there was more separation. They gathered for some funerals, but little else. The Quintrells became the backbone of the emergent gringo po-litical system. The Castillo/Simmons/Sandovals stayed a fixture within the hispano community, making up a secondary, nearly parallel government. Instead of taxes, there was tribute. Instead of cat-tle, there was smuggling. Instead of English, there was Spanish and/or Indian languages.

And through both cultures ran the same blood, the same genes, the same hopes and disappoint-ments and joys.

A feeling of excitement fizzed in Carly. She forgot the careful list she'd made and simply enjoyed the tapestry of family and New Mexico history that was condensing in her mind. This was what she loved about her job, the moment when the chaos of facts and questions stopped whirling around and settled into a pattern of family generations played out against a timeless land and a constantly changing culture. This was what she wanted to give to future generations of Quintrells and Castillos, an under-standing that each person was part of a chain stretching back across the centuries and reaching out to the coming centuries. This was—

The bang of the cellar door startled Carly out of her thoughts.

"You're back early," she said without looking up from the reader. "Or is it Gus come to babysit me again?"

"Keep guessing."

Carly spun around and saw Sheriff Montoya standing six feet away.

He didn't look happy to be there.

She felt the same.

"Good morning," she said coolly. "Or is it after-noon?"

"Doesn't much matter. I understand you had some trouble out at the Quintrell ranch yesterday."

**Well, that's certainly blunt.** "Trouble?" She

shrugged. "Something didn't agree with me. I was sick."

"What about your Siamese twin, Duran?"

"He threw up, too." She didn't say any more. She didn't like the feeling of being grilled like a criminal about something she hadn't asked for and nearly hadn't survived.

The sheriff took off his hat and smacked it against his thigh. Snow sifted to the floor.

"Why didn't you tell me?" he asked curtly.

"Since when do citizens report hurling to the local cops?"

"You can't be as stupid as you sound, Ms. May."

"Oh, you'd be surprised," Dan said from the stairway. "There's a big dose of stupid going around Taos right now."

Montoya stiffened, then turned around to confront Dan. "You must have caught a double dose of it. What the hell were you doing with Armando Sandoval?"

Dan whistled softly. "Quite the grapevine you have, Sheriff. Or did Armando tell you all by himself?"

The sheriff didn't answer.

Dan hadn't expected him to.

"Well?" the sheriff asked.

For the first time in years, Dan wished he had federal credentials again. A gold FBI shield was something the sheriff could understand. But all Dan had these days was a business card that read ST. KILDA CONSULTING. Below that was a toll-free telephone number.

All things considered, Dan doubted that the sheriff was knowledgeable enough about the real world to be impressed by the card.

"Nobody told me you were working on my turf," the sheriff said. "It purely pisses me off how arrogant you federal boys can be."

**Federal boys?** Carly's eyebrows went up and her mouth stayed shut.

"Nobody told you because I'm not working for the Feds anymore," Dan said.

"Then why were you talking to Sandoval?"

"Why do you care?"

"Listen here—"

"No," Dan cut in. "You listen. Until Armando Sandoval is proved in court to be a **narcotraficante** and a murderer, he's a citizen in good standing. What we have to say to each other is none of your business."

The sheriff wanted to argue, but he had the losing side and he knew it. "You ever think I might be able to help?"

"Not after the first round of complaints we filed and you forgot," Carly said behind him.

A dull red showed on the sheriff's cheekbones

beneath his toast brown skin. "I have enough problems with rich tourists," he muttered, not taking his eyes from Dan. "I don't need whining from a homeboy who sticks his nose in the wrong places and gets smacked for it."

"Carly isn't a homeboy. She didn't deserve what happened to her."

Sheriff Montoya looked over his shoulder at her. "Sounds like somebody wants you to leave."

"Sounds like," she drawled. "Too bad this is a free country. I don't feel like leaving."

The sheriff's dark eyes narrowed. "Ms. May, most times I'm lucky to have one deputy for every hundred square miles. That's how free this country is."

"Is that a threat?" she asked.

"It's a fact. That's why I don't have any patience with troublemakers, and there's trouble written all over both of you."

"What? Armando Sandoval isn't trouble?" Carly asked in disbelief.

"Armando Sandoval is the devil the sheriff knows," Dan said. "If it wasn't for Armando, there would be **narcotraficantes** killing each other until the next **jefe chingon** rose to the top of the cesspool and peace returned. With Armando in place, the sheriff knows there won't be any Taos County voters caught in the crossfire of a drug war, which means the citizens are happy, which means the sheriff is real likely to hang on to his job. It's win-win-win, except for the occasional outsider getting ground up between the gears of politics as usual."

Carly grimaced, certain that she was the "occasional outsider" who was caught in the meat grinder.

"You're a lot smarter than you used to be," the sheriff said calmly to Dan.

Dan waited.

"Now show me how smart," the sheriff said. "Take the little lady and go on a nice long vacation in the Bahamas."

"Wait just a—" Carly began.

"I don't have enough deputies to protect you if you stay here," the sheriff said, pinning her with a black glance. "By the time I get to the bottom of the rats and slashed tires and bad food, you could be badly hurt. Or dead."

# 42

CARLY PUSHED AGAINST THE PLYWOOD, HOLDING IT in place while Dan hammered nails in. The result was ugly, but kept the wind out of the little house. And right now, the wind was blowing hard enough to bring tears to her eyes.

"I still think—" Dan began.

"No," she cut in loudly. "Not unless you have something new to say."

"Shit."

"That's not new."

He said something in Portuguese.

"Same word, different language," Carly said.

He drove the rest of the nails in silence, letting the crack of steel on steel express his frustration. The longer he thought about Carly's position, the less he liked it. He didn't need a sixth sense to know that the whole situation was spiraling out of control.

**How can anything so sweet and soft-looking be so bloody stubborn?**

Carly winced as the final hammer blow drove the nail in so far the hammer left a dent in the plywood. "Feel better now?"

He shot her a jade green glance. Then the corner of his mouth turned up. "Yeah."

She let out a long breath of relief and smiled at him. "Thank you."

"For what?"

"Not hammering on me until I gave up."

"Would it have worked?"

Her smile faded. "I'm scared, Dan."

He tucked the hammer into the back of his jeans and pulled her close. "That's the first intelligent thing you've said in hours." Before she could argue, he kissed her until she forgot everything, even fear. Slowly he lifted his mouth and leaned his forehead against hers. "We'll get through this. There might be some mutual yelling from time to time, but I respect your courage too much to want to hammer it out of you. Okay?"

His eyes were a vivid green blur to her, whether from her tears or being so close she couldn't focus, she didn't know and didn't care. "Okay. But I don't feel real brave right now. I keep thinking about being alone on that ranch road, no one to pull me back and make me walk and . . ."

"I keep thinking about it, too. I don't want to lose

you, Carolina May. I spent too long wondering if I'd ever find someone like you."

Her stomach growled as she kissed him. "You see what you do to me," she said.

"Starve you?"

"Make me feel safe enough to be hungry."

He smiled slowly and took her hand. "C'mon. I've got chili left. I'll heat it while you check out more of those so-called might-be senatorial offspring."

He opened the front door and nudged Carly into the relative warmth of the house.

"The problem is that a lot of those offspring are dead," Carly said, frowning, "others have moved away, and all I have to go on is community speculation. The only way to be certain if they're the Senator's is DNA testing, and for that to be effective, we have to have a DNA profile of the Senator first. Short of exhuming him, there's no way to get a sample for testing. Unless he froze his sperm for the ages, or something like that."

"I'm sure if he had, it would have been front-page news in town." The door closed behind Dan, shutting out the wind. "As for exhumation to take a tissue sample, I don't see that happening short of a court order, and I don't see us getting a court order."

"Not unless the governor agrees, and I figure that will be about the time they hold the Summer

Olympics in Siberia. Josh Quintrell really doesn't like Winifred's project."

"Ya think?" Dan asked sardonically. He lit a match, turned on a burner on the stove, and started heating chili.

"So why keep on pursuing the maybe offspring?" Carly asked. "It's a waste of time. We can't prove anything more than rumor and innuendo, and that's not the sort of thing I feel happy about putting in a family history."

"Why pursue the offspring? Because Winifred told you to and she's paying the bills?"

Carly smiled wryly. "Okay. But it doesn't get us any closer to why somebody wants me to leave."

"If we assume that someone doesn't want the history done—"

"Good assumption."

"—then getting the history done will get us closer to whoever is behind scaring you," Dan finished.

**It will also get Carly the hell out of Taos.**

But he kept that to himself because she didn't want to hear it.

Carly's expression said that she wasn't impressed with her assignment. With a shrug, she got a three-ring binder from one of her boxes in the living room and sat at the little card table that served as a dining table.

"Okay," she said, flipping the binder open. "Here's

what I have so far. Let me know if any of the names tickle your fancy. Jesús Mendoza—son of Carlota Mendoza, a maid at the Quintrell ranch—went into the army, went to war, got decorated, married a San Diego woman, had four kids, died fifteen years ago. None of the kids have any connection to Taos or the Quintrells that I've been able to discover."

Dan wrapped some tortillas in tinfoil and tucked them in the oven.

"María Elena Sandoval, daughter of one of the many Sandovals running through New Mexico in general and the Quintrell ranch in particular. Cousin lovers every one of them."

He snickered.

"María Elena Sandoval finally married a gringo and moved to Colorado. Two children. No particular contact with New Mexico. She's dead, the children have married and had children of their own. One lives in Florida. One in California."

Dan tested the chili, stirred, and listened to the litany of people who were either old as dirt or already dead. Some hadn't left children. Most had. None of their names made him pause.

"Randal Mullins. His mother was Susan Mullins, who worked at the ranch."

Dan frowned and stirred chili. "Mullins. Susan's son."

Carly checked. "Yes."

"I've run across his name before. Isn't he on the Senator's monument to the local dead in Vietnam?"

Carly flipped to the back of the binder, where she had printouts of important documents. The newspaper article that had listed the dead soldiers was one of them. She ran her finger down the column of names.

"Good catch," she said after a moment. "Randal Mullins. Died in 1968. Four years after the Senator's first son died. Wonder if they knew each other?"

"It's possible," Dan said slowly. "A lot of guys made it a point to get to know other soldiers who were from their own home areas. Made them feel less lonely. But since Mullins and A.J. are both dead, having them know each other won't do us much good."

"Do you suppose the governor knew about Mullins, a man who was possibly his half brother?"

"Doubt it. The governor didn't spend much time here as a kid, so he wouldn't have heard the gossip. I think he was in Vietnam when Mullins died. I'll have to check."

Carly sighed. "Right. Anyway, Randal never married, so we can't ask his children what they remember, if anything, of their father's childhood or their grandmother's likelihood of having a Quintrell child."

"Randal could have had children without a marriage license."

"Bastards having bastards," she muttered.

He smiled slightly.

She made a mark by Randal's name. "How would we go about chasing his offspring?"

"He had a half sister, Betty. Mom went to school with her."

"Your mother mentioned her?"

"Fat chance." Dan spooned chili into a bowl. "There's a photo somewhere in the newspaper archive of two pretty grammar school kids dancing around a Maypole. Mom was one of the kids. Betty was another."

"Is Betty or her mother still alive?"

"Susan Mullins was killed along with my grandmother in 1968. Another sex worker was killed at the same time. Some guy wired on angel dust."

"So Susan knew your grandmother?"

Dan shrugged. "They worked the same alleys, if that's what you mean."

Carly winced. "What about Betty?"

"She died twenty years ago, after her husband divorced her. Suicide. She worked at the Quintrell ranch until the booze and downers got to her. I think you have the article about it on your computer or in the printouts."

"I do?"

"Under the single or double hits for the name Quintrell. How hot do you like your chili?"

"Are we talking temperature or spice?" she asked, flipping through a list of articles she'd printed out.

"Temp," he said.

"Anything above freezing."

He smiled, dished a bowl of chili for her, stuck a spoon in, and set everything in front of her on the card table. "Tortillas?"

"Please," she said absently, reaching for her computer. She booted it up and began to eat while the machine tested all systems, reassuring the silicon brain that everything was in working order.

Dan sat down kitty-corner from her, uncovered the tortillas, and flopped one over her bowl of chili. She rolled the tortilla, scooped chili, and kept on eating, waiting for her computer to be fully functional. Then she did a search of the Quintrell database for an article that mentioned the Quintrell name along with the name Betty.

"Was Mullins Betty's last name?" Carly asked.

"No. It was something common. Smith or Jones or Johnson, something like that."

"How do you know all this stuff? And don't tell

me you grew up here. A lot of people did and they don't know squat about the local begats."

Dan chewed, swallowed chili, and swallowed again. "I was an odd kid. People interested me. Not just in the here and now, but what they were when they were young, and their parents, and grandparents." He shrugged. "Maybe it came from not knowing who my grandfather was. Maybe I was just nosy. I spent a lot of time checking out old school yearbooks, working in the newspaper archives, trying to computerize everything so all I had to do was hit a button and watch the patterns emerge."

"Patterns?"

"Who was named, who wasn't, who stood next to the Quintrells in the photos, who didn't, who went to weddings and funerals and baptisms and political rallies." He shrugged. "All kinds of things. Like I said. Nosy."

"Or curious about all the things your mother refused to talk about."

"That too."

"So what did you learn?"

"More about local marriages, births, divorces, and drunks than I should have," he said dryly. "Mom saw me drawing up these elaborate relationship charts featuring people on the Quintrell ranch and their cross-connections with the local community—it was for my senior high school project. Man, did the caca fly. She got furious and said that the past was dead and buried and should stay that way."

Carly's spoon stopped halfway to her mouth. "Did you argue with her?"

"No, I asked her if it was true that the Senator was my great-grandfather."

Carly swallowed hard. "What did she say?"

"She told me if I ever mentioned that name again in her home, I could start packing."

"Yikers."

"Yeah. So I shifted the topic of my senior project to protecting newspaper archives through specially designed computer programs. Then I started applying to every out-of-state college that might have me. I'd had a gutful of this place."

"Where'd you end up?" Carly asked.

"Georgetown. Did I mention I was a geek with high grades who swam a mean backstroke and won various shooting contests? Georgetown gave me a full scholarship."

"Athletic?"

"Nope. They wanted my brain, not my body."

She smiled to herself. "They didn't know what they were missing."

His thumb skimmed her jawline. "Neither did I. Wait, it was Smith."

"What?"

"Betty Smith, then she married someone—Shilling or Shafter or something like that. Melissa is their kid."

"Melissa Moore?"

He nodded and took a big bite of tortilla.

"So Melissa could tell us about her mother who was half sister to Randy Mullins who might have been the Senator's bastard?" Carly asked.

Dan swallowed tortilla. "Maybe. If she knows anything and wants to talk."

"I'm sure Winifred will help with that."

"If she's well enough to care. What about the rest of those names, the maybe-bastards?"

"I hate that label."

"What?"

"Bastard. Like it's the kid's fault."

"The only bastards I care about are self-made." He tugged at a stray piece of her hair, the one she kept twisting around her finger when she was fretting. "Illegitimate child takes too long to say and love child is the kind of lie that turns my stomach. My mother wasn't any man's **love** child."

The edge to Dan's voice reminded Carly that small towns had long memories and short forgiveness of personal choices. Diana had suffered for being born outside of marriage. Diana's son accepted that, but he didn't have to like it.

Carly turned back to her list of names of children perhaps conceived and certainly forgotten by Andrew Jackson Quintrell III, known to most as the Senator and to his sister-in-law as a philandering son of a bitch. The more Carly knew about him, the more she agreed with Winifred.

"Sharon Miller," Carly said.

Dan shook his head. "No bells on that one."

"She was the daughter of the Senator's social secretary, born two years after he retired to Taos in 1977."

"What happened to her?"

"Her mother took her and left Taos when she was a year old. No contact with the Quintrells after that, at least not that I've found in the records. Next one is Christopher Smith. Son of the replacement social secretary. She was married, by the way, so it's likely the baby belonged to the husband, not the hound dog. It lasted six years."

"The marriage?"

"The job with the Senator."

Dan spooned a second helping of chili into his bowl and wondered how many more children the fornicating old goat had sired.

# 43

THE WINTER SUN WAS GONE FROM THE SKY, LEAV-ing only the faintest tinge of yellow-green along the western horizon. Light glowed in great sheets of glassy gold along the front of the ranch house. The wind was fingernails of ice scraping over every-thing, lifting the recent dry snow into swirls and eddies.

"Brrrr," Carly said as soon as she opened the door of Dan's truck. "There's a reason I don't ski."

"Watch the path to the door," he said. "Nothing has been salted or sanded."

"Maybe they don't want visitors."

"More likely they're just easing back now that the governor's gone. Besides, the place is for sale. Once that sign went up, everyone working here had at least one foot out the door."

Squinting against the wind, Carly watched the last bit of color drain from the sky. Then she turned toward the buildings, seeing the Spanish influence in the old and high-tech modern in the new. They didn't clash; they were simply from different cultures and times.

"Centuries of tradition and he's just walking away from it," she said sadly.

"The governor?"

"Yes."

"He was never really a part of the ranch, or the family, for that matter," Dan said. "That was reserved for the heir apparent, Andrew Jackson Quintrell IV. All Josh got was a long string of military boarding schools."

"Still . . ."

Dan put his arm around her waist and tucked her under his arm, shielding her from as much of the wind as he could. "Not everyone loves the past, Carolina May."

She sighed and leaned her shoulder against him for a moment. "Would you have walked away from this?"

"In a heartbeat. Let the governor sell it to someone who loves the land, loves the wildness and the silence and the wind."

She looked up at him. Against the radiant twilight, the planes of his face were drawn in shades of black. Only his eyes were alive, vivid. "It sounds like you love it."

"The land, yes. The people?" Dan shrugged and

started down the path, keeping her close to his side in case she slipped. "Most of the people can go to hell."

It was the lack of heat in his voice that told Carly he meant every word. "Don't you have any good memories of here?"

"Sure."

"Then why do you hate it so?"

"I don't hate it. I just don't like people who are more cruel than survival requires."

"Like the Senator?"

"He's one," Dan agreed. "Then there are the people who ragged on my mother for being the daughter of the town whore."

"And on you for being your mother's son."

"That stopped after I beat the crap out of some Sandovals."

She winced. "And you're still paying for it."

"Like I said—the smaller the town, the longer the memory. Too bad the people around here aren't as big as the land. But they aren't."

"Some of them are."

"Damned few. Not that the people here are worse than people anywhere else," he added. "They're simply no better than they have to be. And sometimes, well, sometimes that's just not good enough to get the job done."

He rapped on the front door.

A moment later, Melissa opened the door. Clearly she'd been waiting for them since she'd seen headlights coming up the long driveway. "Hello, Dan, Carly. Winifred said you'd be visiting. Something about wanting to talk to people, take pictures, and get the feeling of the ranch outdoors at night?"

"That's right," Carly said.

It had been as good an excuse as any she could think of to search the family graveyard and find out if the Senator's wild child had been buried there.

Melissa shrugged like the whole thing sounded like nonsense to her but it really wasn't her business. "Both of you are looking much better than I expected after talking to the sheriff."

Carly made a noncommittal sound and studied the other woman, trying to see Melissa as the granddaughter of the Senator. Fair hair artfully frosted to hide any gray. Eyes the right size and tilt to be Quintrell, but the wrong color. Long legs like the governor, long fingers. Like Dan.

**Okay, stop right there,** Carly told herself fiercely. **Fingers are either long or short, fat or thin. That's four categories for all of humanity, which means a twenty-five percent chance that otherwise unrelated folks will have long fingers.**

"We heard you were ill, too," Dan said.

"That will teach me to eat canapés," she said, patting a round hip. "I didn't need the calories anyway."

"So the sheriff still thinks it was the food?" Carly asked.

"That's what he said."

Before Carly could say anything more, Dan's arm tightened around her waist. She glanced at him. A slight negative motion of his head told her that he didn't want to upset Melissa.

Yet.

Carly smiled and said nothing. She agreed with Dan that an amiable Melissa was more useful than an irritated one.

"Come in, come in," Melissa said. "It's cold out there. Sometimes I wonder if winter will ever end."

A voice called from the back of the house.

"It's Dan Duran and Carly May," Melissa called out. "They're here to see Winifred."

Carly and Dan didn't look at each other. They'd clearly asked to see Melissa, too.

"That's my husband, Pete," Melissa explained. "The governor has him working overtime on the books. From what Josh said at Sylvia's wake, there's already considerable interest in the ranch."

Carly saw that Melissa's smile didn't go beyond her lips. Obviously the housekeeper was worried about the future, both for herself and her husband. She had reason to be.

**One foot out the door.** Whether they liked it or not.

"I'm sorry to hear that," Carly said. "It's sad to end a long tradition."

Melissa nodded tightly.

"I understand your mother and grandmother both worked on the ranch," Carly said.

"Yes."

"Do you have time now to talk about that with me?" Carly said. "Your family has been and is an integral part of the Quintrell family history. Your viewpoint would be invaluable."

Melissa's mouth turned down. "The governor made it very clear that no one was to talk with you about the Quintrell family. I'm sorry."

"So am I," Carly said.

Dan looked at Melissa and asked, "How long does the gag order last? Until the ranch is sold?"

Melissa stiffened. "Governor Quintrell didn't say."

"And he's the one writing your references," Dan said. "Got it." He looked at Carly. "Let's see how Winifred is doing."

"Wait," Melissa said, touching Carly's arm.

Carly looked at the older woman curiously. "Yes?"

"Winifred." Melissa sighed. "She isn't . . . well."

"We know," Carly said. "We won't stay long."

Melissa's fingers tightened on Carly's arm. "No, you don't understand. I think . . ." Her voice died. "I think," she whispered, "that Winifred is losing her mind."

"Why?" Dan's voice was rougher than he meant it to be. "What makes you think that?" he asked more gently.

Melissa frowned. "Losing Sylvia, and the pneumonia, and the food poisoning, and the ranch being sold, well, I just think Winifred's losing her grip."

Carly looked at Dan. He was watching Melissa with an intensity that both women found uncomfortable.

"What happened?" Carly asked, patting the fingers that were clamped around her arm.

Slowly Melissa's grip lightened. "She's always hated the Senator, but lately, it's like some kind of obsession. She burns with this wild energy whenever his name comes up. It's crazy. And now she's been talking wild, saying that the ranch is hers, not the governor's, because she's the last living Castillo and the ranch can only be inherited by someone with Castillo blood."

Dan's eyebrows lifted. "What's the basis of her belief?"

"That's just it," Melissa said in a rising voice. "There's no reason at all. It's just crazy. The governor is Sylvia and the Senator's son. He has Castillo blood in him through his mother, but Winifred hates the Senator so much she can't stand to see his son inherit, so she's insisting that the ranch belongs to her." Melissa let out a harsh breath. "I'm afraid she's losing her hold on reality."

Uneasily Carly remembered the times she'd seen Winifred's fervor and wondered about the woman's sanity. Carly glanced at Dan. He was looking past Melissa. His expression said he was thinking hard.

"I'll take you to her," Melissa said with a bright, unhappy smile. "Just don't tire her too much, and don't believe everything she says. Maybe she'll be better in a few days. Here, let me have your coats. Would you like some coffee or tea and cookies?"

"Not for me," Carly said instantly. She wasn't interested in eating or drinking anything at the Quintrell house that she hadn't personally prepared.

"None for me, either," Dan said. He helped Carly out of her coat and shrugged out of his jacket. "We had a late lunch."

Because they knew they wouldn't be eating at the Quintrell ranch if they could avoid it.

Carly and Dan followed their jackets and Melissa's tight butt down the long arcade that led to Winifred's suite.

Melissa tapped lightly on the door. "Winifred? Do you feel up to visitors?"

"Yes."

The single word was hoarse, almost urgent.

Melissa opened the door, then followed Dan and

Carly inside. Winifred was in the recliner she liked better than Sylvia's hospital bed. The heavy steel cylinder of an oxygen tank stood by the chair. She adjusted the clear plastic tube so that she could talk more easily.

"Remember to save your strength," Melissa cautioned.

Winifred made a disgusted sound.

With another brittle smile, Melissa left to hang up the coats.

"Have you found any more names?" Winifred asked.

"Do you mean possible children of the Senator's?" Carly asked.

The old woman nodded curtly.

The door to the hallway didn't close after Melissa. Dan noted it and said nothing.

"No new names," Carly said.

Winifred shook her head. "Then why are you here?"

"We hoped to talk to Melissa about her mother and grandmother."

"It didn't take you long," Winifred said.

"The governor issued a gag order," Dan said. "Since he's the one who will be writing recommendations for Melissa and her husband . . ." Dan shrugged. "How about you, Miss Winifred? Are you under the governor's gag order?"

Her dry laugh ended in a cough. "He wouldn't dare. Why do you care about Melissa's family?"

Without looking away from Winifred, Carly checked that her recorder was on. "Susan Mullins worked for the Quintrell household and had a baby out of wedlock in 1941," Carly said. "The boy, Randal Mullins, had no father listed on the birth certificate."

"The Senator's bastard," Winifred said.

"Are you sure?" Carly asked.

"There wasn't a skirt within reach that he didn't lift. It was a point of honor with him. He even made a grab for me after Sylvia's so-called stroke. I told him I'd poison him if he touched me again. He believed me."

Dan just shook his head. "The man was clinical."

"The man was evil," Winifred said.

Carly tried to head off the savage anger she saw in Winifred's eyes by changing the subject. "When Susan married Doug Smith, they had a daughter, Betty Smith."

"Melissa's mother," Winifred said after a moment. "Beautiful woman, but she was as loose as her mother. I've always wondered if Melissa was the Senator's child."

"Melissa is his granddaughter, not his daughter," Carly said.

Winifred's eyes changed, opaque as stone, black

as her thoughts. "The womanizing son of a bitch wouldn't have cared either way."

"What do you say to that, Melissa?" Dan asked, turning toward the partially open door. "Is the Senator your father or grandfather—or both?"

At first there was silence. Then the door to the hallway opened wider and Melissa walked through, their coats still over her arm.

"He might be my grandfather," Melissa said evenly. "My father is Mel Schaffer."

"Might be your grandfather?" Carly asked. "Don't you know?"

Melissa shrugged. "My grandmother wasn't very reliable. She took too many drugs, drank too much. A lot of what she said wasn't true."

"Sounds like my own grandmother," Dan said.

"Liza," Melissa said. "I heard about her."

"A lot of people did," Dan said.

"Whatever," Melissa said, turning to Winifred. "Suggesting that the Senator could be my father is not only sick, it's the kind of wild accusation that will cause you a lot of trouble. The Senator would have laughed it off, but his son won't."

Winifred's eyes narrowed. She didn't say a word.

Melissa's hand went to the older woman's shoulder. "I'm sorry. I shouldn't have snapped, but I worry about you. The governor could make life . . . very difficult."

"I won't be around here long enough to worry about it," Winifred said. "And neither will you."

Melissa's mouth thinned.

Dan said to Winifred, "What do you remember about Randal Mullins?"

"He died in Vietnam."

"Did he have any children?" Though he was asking Winifred, he was looking at Melissa. The way her eyelids flickered told him that she knew the answer.

"Not that I know of," Winifred said. "He never married."

"Turn off the recorder, Carly," Dan said.

She looked at him, then hit the pause button.

He stared at Melissa.

Silence grew.

"Oh, all right," Melissa said finally. "But if you tell the governor I told you, I'll deny it."

"We won't tell Josh Quintrell the time of day," Dan said.

Melissa let out a long breath. "Randy Mullins was my uncle, or half uncle. Whatever." She made an impatient gesture. Her words came out clipped, rapid, like she was getting through something distasteful as fast as she could. "He hated my father, Mel, and started running away when he was eleven. Most of the time Randy went to live with Angus Snead up in the high pastures or in his winter quarters on the ranch. Laurie was the old man's daughter, seven years younger than Randy. Randy spent most of his time with Old Man Snead. Laurie was pretty much raised by her aunt after her mother walked out. Angus Snead pretty much raised Randy."

Carly held her breath and hoped that her recorder had done its usual wake-up trick five seconds after being told to pause. She had a feeling Melissa wasn't going to go through the story twice.

"Anyway, just before Randy shipped out to Nam, he went on a tear-down-the-town drunk. Angus was sick, so Laurie drove down to pick Randy up from jail. About nine months later she gave birth to twins."

"Jim and Blaine Snead," Dan said. "Your cousins. And likely the Senator's grandsons."

"Maybe, maybe not," Melissa said, shrugging. "He never treated them any different from anyone else."

"Including you?" Dan asked.

"I was a woman. Of course he treated me different from the Snead boys. I was real, real careful never to be alone in the house with him when he was at the ranch. Winifred helped a lot." Melissa smiled at the older woman. "She told me to watch out and I did."

Carly's mouth turned down. The more she heard about the Senator, the less she liked him.

"Even after his heart trouble when he was in his seventies?" Dan asked. "Didn't that slow him down? It sure ended his career as a politician."

"He was plenty spry until a few years ago," Winifred said. "But after he turned eighty he wasn't strong enough to wrestle an unwilling woman down to the floor anymore."

"Winifred . . ." Melissa looked unhappy. "No rape was ever proved. It was whispers, that's all. With a man like the Senator, there was always gossip."

Carly looked at Dan, who shrugged and said, "Just one more thing that didn't make the local paper."

"Do the Sneads know who their grandfather is?" Dan asked.

"Nobody **knows**," Melissa said, gripping the coats hard against her body.

"Do they **think** they know?" Carly asked.

"Why?" Melissa said.

"She's curious," Dan said easily, but his eyes were hard, intent.

"Oh, hell, I'm sure someone told them." Melissa hugged the coats to her. "Gossip goes around quicker than truth."

"Is that why the governor is so touchy?" Carly asked Melissa. "He's heard the gossip and doesn't want the truth known?"

"What truth?" Melissa asked impatiently. "There's precious little of it in gossip."

"You know the old saying about smoke and fire," Carly said.

Melissa just shook her head. "The Senator is dead. Let it all die with him. Would it do the Sneads any good to have all the old gossip and lies raked up? They're grown men and don't give a damn who their grandfather might or might not be." She glared at Carly. "Anyway, a wolfer and a felon have no business being in a Quintrell family history."

"Castillo," Winifred said harshly. "This is a **Castillo** history and the Senator's bastards have no part of it."

"Then why did you want me to—" Carly began, but Winifred talked right over her.

"That's what the—" A spasm of coughing shook Winifred, then another and another.

"You'd better go," Melissa said, looking worried. She shoved the coats at Dan.

He took the coats but made no move to leave. He didn't want to. He had a feeling Winifred was weaker than she wanted people to know.

"Shouldn't you call the doctor?" he asked Melissa.

"He was here today," Melissa said as she replaced the nasal feed on Winifred's oxygen. "There's nothing more he can do except take Winifred to the hospital, and she refuses to go. Unless the governor goes to court and has her declared incompetent to handle her own affairs, there's nothing anyone can do. Besides, if Winifred wants to stay here as long as possible, who are we to interfere?"

Winifred kept coughing. Her face was ruddy from effort.

Carly took her coat from Dan and headed for the hallway. The sound of Winifred's dry, racking cough followed them to the front door. The door opened and then shut behind them, leaving them in the wind-haunted cold of night.

Neither said anything.

Both wondered what Winifred had been trying to tell them.

# 44

THE NIGHTSCOPE MAKES IT EASY. GOOD THING. THE **cold is taking the feeling out of my hands, and the wind . . .**

The wind was always a rifleman's enemy.

The sniper watched through the scope as Carly and Dan left the house. They got into his truck, but instead of heading toward the road leading back to Taos, the truck turned toward the outbuildings.

**Now what?**

The headlights would blow out the nightscope, so the sniper tracked them with binoculars. They drove past the barn and out the pasture road to the graveyard.

**Well, damn. I had my spot all picked out and they're going in the other direction.**

Cold, stiff, cursing silently, the sniper watched the truck pull up to the Quintrell family graveyard. As soon as the lights went off, he switched back to watching his target through the nightscope mounted on his rifle barrel. It was more for practice than anything else. The graveyard was just under a mile from the main house, but that wasn't the real problem.

The eight-foot-tall wrought-iron fence made shooting really dicey.

The angle wasn't great enough for him to shoot over the fence unless the target stood tall and straight away from the fence instead of bent over grubbing around the gravestones on perimeter, right next to the fence. The gravestones themselves were another shooting hazard. Not to mention the trees that had been planted on or near some graves.

The faint sound of voices lifted on the fitful wind. A flashlight turned on below.

The sniper went back to night-vision binoculars.

**Finish whatever you came for, get on the road, and circle back around the other side of the ridge to get to the highway.**

He ached with cold. It was time to get it done and move on.

**Come on, come on, hurry up. Make it any harder on me and I'll kill both of you.**

# 45

CARLY SMACKED HER HANDS TOGETHER. EVEN IN-side lined gloves, her fingers were getting cold.

"I can't figure out any rhyme or reason for the placement of graves," Dan said.

"Usually, the closer to the founder's grave, the higher the rank," Carly said. "But Liza's grave isn't with her brother's or her sister's."

Dan dusted snow off the last headstone. "Nope. This one is a memorial stone to a Quintrell who died in the Civil War."

"Really?" Carly came over, took a digital photo, and shoved the camera back in her pocket. "Samuel Quintrell. Wonder if he was a brother or a father or an uncle or—"

"Doesn't matter," Dan cut in. "Winifred only wants—"

"Castillos," Carly finished in disgust.

"Let's try the lower half of the graveyard."

Carly looked toward the section of the graveyard reserved for ranch workers. "Are you saying that some of the employees had higher 'rank' than the Senator's daughter?"

"If we're talking about my grandmother, yes," Dan said as he walked the length of the ghostly white fence. "I'm guessing that Liza was lucky to be buried here at all. Probably wouldn't have been, but the Quintrells didn't want to make any fuss that would attract more attention to Liza's sorry life."

Carly moved the flashlight over the modest gravestones that paralleled the fence. "These are all Isobel's cousins or retainers or whatever."

"Same difference. Back then, the whole family—distant cousins, in-laws of cousins, in-laws of in-laws—followed the money. Isobel had it and Andrew Quintrell made it grow. Once the Senator got into politics and increased his connection to the Sandovals through Sylvia, he kept the money growing."

"You're so cynical."

"It's my middle name."

"Really?" she asked.

"It's better than Warden."

"Warden?"

"My middle name."

Bright as moonlight, Carly's laughter floated up into the darkness until the wind caught it and swept it away.

After poking around the fence, Dan knelt near it and rubbed wind-driven snow off a headstone. The grave that had been set apart from even the distant family who worked on the ranch.

"Here we go." His voice was matter-of-fact. He could have been talking about the weather. "Elizabeth Isobel Quintrell, 1936 to 1968."

"Thirty-two years old," Carly said. "What a waste."

"She must have liked her life well enough."

"How can you say that?"

"She didn't do anything to change it."

Carly looked at the silver and darkness of the grave. "Maybe she couldn't."

"Such a tender soul." Gently he touched Carly's face with a cold gloved fingertip. "She never tried, Carolina May. Not even once."

"She didn't deserve to be murdered."

"No one does, but it happens just the same. You want a picture of this headstone?"

Carly knelt and waited for the autofocus to wake up and get its job done. Light flashed once. She viewed the image, approved it, and turned the camera off again.

"Do you suppose Susan Mullins was buried here? She was a longtime employee, after all."

"And her daughter was probably the Senator's bastard."

"That, too."

Dan and Carly continued down the fence, searching for depressions in the snow cover that would indicate earth sagging into a grave when the coffin gave way to a combination of time and water. Other than an occasional Sandoval and two Sneads, Dan and Carly didn't find any names they recognized.

The wind flexed, stretched, ran cold between the white metal bars of the fence.

Carly stood and looked at the moon-silvered ridgeline that loomed a few hundred yards away.

"What were you doing up there?" she asked. "It was you, wasn't it, the day the Senator was buried?"

Dan followed her glance to Castillo Ridge. "Me, my dad, and one of the Sneads. Jim probably. Blaine isn't that good on the stalk."

"I don't understand."

"Dad and I parked off the highway and climbed up the back side of the ridge. There's an old trail there. Hunters use it a lot. So does their prey. Anyway, Dad and I watched the whole thing from up there. Neither of us noticed anyone, but when we started walking out, I saw where there were some tracks. Someone else had been up on the ridge with a dog, watching the burial."

"And you think it was Jim Snead?"

"He's the only one I know of who can get close to

me without giving himself away. I have good senses."

"Is that why you keep looking up toward the ridge?" she asked. "You think he's up there now?"

"I've felt watched a few times since we left the house. Then it goes away. Probably just the wind making branches move."

"Or Jim Snead looking down from the ridge?"

"Maybe," Dan said.

"Why?"

"I don't know."

And as soon as Dan had Carly in a warm, safe place, he was going to climb the ridge and backtrack, assuming the wind and shifting snow didn't cover everything before he got back here from Taos.

If he was alone, he'd have climbed that ridge the first time his neck started itching. But he wasn't alone.

"Can the ridge be climbed from this side?" Carly asked.

"Sure."

"Is it hard?"

"Not if you have good boots."

"Let's go."

"What?" Dan said, not believing what he was hearing.

"I want to climb the ridge and look out over the

valley and see the ranch in moonlight and darkness, the way it must have looked a hundred years ago."

He listened to his inner senses, found nothing that was worth arguing over, and gave in. "I'll break trail."

# 46

**THEY'RE COMING RIGHT TOWARD ME.**

Quickly the sniper thought about shooting angles and avenues of escape. He should go to ground and wait for them to drive around the back of the ridge. That was the plan.

That plan hadn't called for freezing his ass off while the two of them photographed graves and took a midnight hike up Castillo Ridge. If he had to wait much longer, he'd be too cold to shoot straight. Then somebody could die instead of just bleeding a lot all over the snow.

It wasn't that he minded the killing itself; like everything else, it got easier with practice. But a fatality was always investigated more thoroughly than a simple "accidental" shooting.

They were still coming toward him. Any closer and he'd have to use his eye rather than the scope. As it was, he couldn't see more than one or two square inches of the target at a time.

Finally Carly and Dan veered away, following the

informal trail horses and cattle used in the summer when they were turned loose to graze.

The sniper began to breathe a little more easily as the targets got farther away. When he realized they were going to climb all the way to the top of the ridge a few hundred yards from him, he sighted in and recalculated the angles.

Then he smiled. If they stood and admired the view, it'd be a piece of cake.

Confident again, the sniper held position except for his eyes. He looked away from his prey, barely tracking them with his peripheral vision. Animals, even civilized ones like people, often sensed a direct stare.

And from what he'd learned about Dan Duran, that boy was barely housebroken, much less civilized.

# 47

CARLY FOLLOWED DAN ALONG A TRAIL ONLY HE could see. Wind followed them, pushing and pulling and distracting. She shivered, then ached. And she remembered Dan's leg.

"Okay," she said. "This is far enough. I can—"

"My leg's fine."

"Tell me again that you're not a mind reader."

"I'm not a mind reader."

"Why do I so not believe you?" she muttered.

"I haven't a clue. And stop rolling your eyes."

"How did you know?"

"I heard them."

She snickered and slogged along behind him.

Dan heard, and smiled. He was following the trail as much by instinct as by eye. Animals weren't stupid. They took the easy way, around boulders and clumps of small trees, twisting and turning, slowly gaining altitude. People were mostly too impatient to be smart. They just plowed straight up a slope like there was a stopwatch on them.

In places the going was easy. The land was nearly

bare of snow, swept by the wind of all but a compact crust of snow. That same wind filled the hollows and creases with the kind of icy powder that drew people from all over the world to the high ski slopes near Taos. In the skiing scheme of things, this side of Castillo Ridge was a nonstarter. It was too windswept for snow really to accumulate anywhere but in ravines, and too rocky in the narrow ravines for safe skiing. The other side of the ridge had thicker snow because it was somewhat sheltered from the prevailing wind by the ridge itself. Rocks were mostly buried in snow. Piñons and cedar grew to real size, and true pines had a foothold on the dry land.

Dan wondered if the trail he and his father had beaten through two feet of snow almost a week ago was still visible or if it had been buried by new snow.

Just before Dan skylined himself on the uneven ridge, he stopped and searched the moonlight and darkness for any change, any movement, anything that could explain his occasional, uneasy sense of being watched. Like now. Someone was watching him.

**You're paranoid.**

**You say that like it's a bad thing.**

"What caused that?" Carly asked.

"What?"

"That grim little smile."

"I was talking to myself," he said.

"About what?"

"Paranoia."

"Was this a general or a particular conversation?"

"Particular."

She waited.

He didn't say anything more.

"Sometimes getting you to talk is like pulling hen's teeth," she said.

"Hens don't have teeth."

"That's what makes them hard to pull. What form did this paranoia take?"

"Sometimes I feel like I'm being watched," he said calmly.

Carly's breath came out in a long plume. "Me, too. Usually it's in an old house. So I'm paranoid, too?"

He laughed softly and finished the last few yards up to the ridge, pulling her along behind him. "You're something else."

"And that something is paranoid?"

"No, Carolina May. That something is—"

Suddenly Dan staggered back and away from her, yanking her with him as he went down the far side of the ridge.

The sound of rifle fire cracked like edgy thunder down the valley.

A snow-buried ravine broke Dan's fall. He hit bottom hard enough to make his head spin.

"Dan? Dan!"

Carly skidded to her knees and started clawing snow away from his face. Some of the snow looked black and shiny.

Dan's eyes opened and he groaned. "Bastard missed."

"It doesn't look like it from here," she said tightly. "You're bleeding."

"And you aren't. He missed."

"You're hurt. Let me help you up."

When she started to stand, Dan pulled her down into the uncertain shelter of the ravine and put his lips against her ear. There was snow in her hair, and her scarf was more off than on her head.

"Quiet," Dan murmured, finally starting to think past the ringing in his ears. "He might be coming back to finish the job. I sure hope so."

Only then did Carly see that Dan had eased off a glove and drawn a gun. She hadn't even known he was armed. She shivered with more than the cold, though the cold was bad enough to make her shake. It felt like a vampire drawing warmth and life out of her.

**You asked for it,** she told herself. **You could have quit the job and you didn't. Dan paid the price. Now suck it up and deal.**

She would rather have run screaming into the night, but refused to leave Dan behind. Since he wasn't going to leave voluntarily and was too big to carry, she was stuck lying in the snow watching him bleed and knowing the bullet had been meant for her.

Carly bit the inside of her mouth, hard, then harder, until the urge to scream died to a whimper she couldn't stifle. Her mouth tasted of salt and fear.

"It's okay, honey," Dan murmured against her ear.

She turned her head to him and breathed, "Bullshit."

His grin flashed white against the bloody shadows of his face.

Dan and Carly lay quietly while blood from a scalp wound ran down his face into the snow. She packed snow against his head, hoping to reduce the bleeding. It helped, but not enough.

Very slowly, he wiped blood away from his eyes with his free hand. Nothing moved on the ridgeline thirty feet above. No sound came from footsteps crunching through snow toward them.

Cold bit into him, numbing him until he knew it would be more dangerous to stay than to move. Neither of them were dressed to spend a night in the snow and freezing wind.

And despite the constantly renewed snow on his forehead, it felt like he'd been hit by a white-hot hammer. When it really thawed out, he would be screaming. Thank God Carly would be there to drive him out.

"Make me some snowballs," he murmured to Carly.

"What?"

"Snowballs."

She wondered if getting shot made someone crazy, but she carefully began scooping up snow and packing it into hard, rather eccentric balls. When she uncovered some small rocks, she included them in the mix.

Dan waited, thinking about where he had been when he was hit, where he'd fallen, where the shot probably had come from.

**On the ridgeline, where it bends back toward the valley. Probably that group of boulders to the right. Maybe the trees farther on. Eight hundred feet. A thousand at most. Easy enough shot with a nightscope.**

Impossible without one.

Cold clenched Dan's body. Without special gear—at the very least a survival blanket—a man had to keep moving to stay alive. That wind was a killer.

"Here," Carly whispered. "Some of them have rocks in the center."

"Sweet," he murmured, smiling thinly. "Give them to me first."

He felt something cold and hard nudge his left hand. He wasn't very accurate throwing left-handed, but that didn't matter. He just wanted to see how jumpy the sniper was.

In a single motion Dan rose to his knees, fired the snowball in the direction he would have taken if he planned to retreat over the ridge toward the ranch, and dropped back flat in the ravine.

No shot, no narrow thunder, no motion at all.

Silence.

Wind.

More silence.

Something hammering in his head and the feel of Carly shivering uncontrollably against him.

Time to go.

"Follow me," Dan said.

"What if he starts shooting again?"

**Then we're dead.**

But all he said was, "Let's go."

# 48

THE SNIPER TRACKED CARLY AND DAN THROUGH the nightscope, noting that Dan took advantage of every bit of shadow and rock and tree for cover. The sniper didn't get a single clean shot at either of them.

When he was certain they were on their way to the ranch house, he slipped down the back side of the ridge to collect his pay.

# 49

MOONLIGHT GLOWED IN FRAIL SPLENDOR AGAINST the wall of glass framing the Sangre de Cristo Mountains. The only light in the front of the house came from the Senator's office, and it was no more than a thin strip of yellow between the bottom of the door and the polished marble floor.

A shadow slipped down the hallway. Any sound of footsteps was muffled by Persian rugs as the shadow slid to the back of the house. There was a tiny glow beneath the big double doors leading to the suite. Silence, a faint brush of cloth against the wall, a murmur from the heavy hinges on one door giving way to steady pressure.

The shadow eased inside, leaving the door slightly ajar. A night-light from the bathroom cast a vague illumination that darkened everything not directly touched by light. Winifred lay in the recliner. Every few seconds the oxygen tube took on a faint, shifting glow, sensitive to the movement from the old woman's shallow breaths. Heavy blankets shrouded her body. While she slept, the oxygen tube had fallen away from her nose.

**Easy. They make it so easy for me.**

Gloved hands shifted the blankets, pulling them higher and then tucking them tightly around the old woman. Gently, relentlessly, blankets flattened down over Winifred's face.

Her nostrils flared, seeking oxygen, finding only cloth too dense to breathe through. Her mouth opened, dry as the pillow itself. Her head jerked. Nothing changed except her body's hunger for oxygen. It raged through her, twisting her. She tried to free her arms, to kick, but it was too late. All she could do was open her eyes and look into the face of her murderer.

Finally her motions stilled completely.

Gloved hands pulled blankets back as they had been. Fingers hesitated over the transparent flexible tube connected to the steel oxygen tank. Then the hand passed on, leaving the oxygen tube as it had been found, hissing faintly against Winifred's neck.

**That's two he owes me.**

The shadow withdrew, taking with it a woman's life.

# 50

PETE MOORE WOKE UP WITH A STIFF NECK AND drool marks on the spreadsheet he'd been reading when he fell asleep in the Senator's office. Groaning, he straightened and reached for the mug of coffee that was as cold as the room.

Now that the old bastard was dead, maybe he could sneak a microwave into the office; he really hated cold coffee. But it was better than no coffee at all. These days Melissa was too busy taking care of Winifred and packing up the house for sale to keep him in hot coffee.

He took a swig of the bitter brew, shuddered, and took another. The clock struck three. In the silence, the chimes were almost like distant church bells. The Senator had loved that sound.

Pete stared at the numbers on the spreadsheet he'd used as a pillow. The figures and their meanings were as blurred as his mind. It was time to give up and go to bed.

He turned off the office light as he went out. In the wide gallery/hallway, moonlight was bright enough to see by. Even if it hadn't been, he'd walked this way many times before at night while the household slept and Melissa waited in their small apartment watching television. The glassed-in walkway was as cold as the night. He walked quickly.

He opened the door to the apartment and hurried inside, shutting the door behind him. The flickering bluish light and vague colors of the TV screen lit the room. The laugh track of an old comedy show drowned out the lonely wind and silence of the night.

Melissa was on the sofa, snoring along with the laugh track. Pete bent down and shook her shoulder lightly.

"Time to go to bed," he said.

She woke up and yawned. "I'd better check on Winifred. Did you hear any more shooting?"

"No. Probably some fool tripped over his own feet with a loaded rifle."

Melissa shook her head. "Poachers shouldn't drink."

Pete grinned. "Maybe he killed himself rather than a cougar. But I'll go with you and make sure the outer doors are locked, just in case our poacher has a little winter larceny in mind."

"Jim Snead would track him down and skin him out like a coyote, and everyone around here with a rifle knows it."

Rubbing her eyes, yawning again, Melissa followed Pete back to the main house and to the suite of rooms at the end of the house. At every exterior door, she waited while he checked the lock. Finally he pushed open one of the double doors to the suite and went on through to check the outside entrance at the far end.

"What a smell," he said as he locked the outside door. "Has she become incontinent?"

"I hope not."

The night-light gleamed on the steel oxygen cylinder. Melissa walked quietly to the recliner, saw that the oxygen tube was displaced, and reached for it. Winifred's skin felt cool.

Too cool.

And the room was too quiet.

"Winifred?" Melissa asked in an odd voice.

Pete walked back quickly. "What is it? Is her fever worse?"

"I think she's dead."

With a muttered word, he bent over Winifred. No sound of breathing. No pulse in the lean wrist. No tension in the muscles.

And the smell.

"Call the doctor," Pete said. "I'll call the governor."

# 51

THE GRAY-BLUE CURTAINS SURROUNDING HOSPITAL beds in the emergency room gave an illusion of privacy, but the confusion of the ER surrounded them. Dan and Carly would have been long gone from there, but the sheriff had made it clear that he would be the one to interview them. Then he'd told them it could be at the ER or at the jail, their choice.

Carly had voted for the ER.

She was beginning to wonder if it had been the right choice. It had been a busy night. One facial numbness of unknown origin lay on the bed just beyond the left curtain, waiting for test results. In the other adjacent bed lay a slip and fall, which was headed for knee surgery just as soon as the doctor finished with an emergency appendectomy. Another slip and fall, broken wrist, was waiting for a second X-ray to make sure the cast was keeping the bones properly aligned. A screaming child with a high fever and a frantic mother were just beyond the curtains.

Then there was Dan, the gunshot wound. He had

a bandage over a short, nasty-looking furrow at his hairline. He'd been X-rayed and CAT-scanned, cleaned up and disinfected, and given pain pills, which he ignored. The doctor had also told him he was lucky to be alive, which Dan already knew.

Carly looked at the grim line of his mouth. "Are you sure you don't want the pain pills? I'm driving whether you take them or not."

"The stuff they hand out doesn't work on me any better than aspirin and a pat on the cheek," he said. "And yes, you're driving. If you hadn't been there to help me on that last part down to the truck and drive us out, I don't think I'd have made it."

"Then why didn't you ask for something that works?"

**Because I don't want to be half whacked if a sniper draws down on you again.**

But all he said was, "It doesn't hurt that much." Which was true. Once the burning and dizziness had worn off, the dull pain was easy to ignore. He'd been hurt a hell of a lot worse. "It's a scrape."

"From a bullet."

"Yeah, velocity does add a certain bite. Good thing I have a hard head."

She muttered under her breath and gave up trying to get him to take something stronger than aspirin.

Sheriff Mike Montoya's voice carried clearly through the background noise of the ER. "I'm looking for the gunshot wound."

"Curtain five," the nurse answered. "Don't take long. He's ambulatory and we need the bed."

A few seconds later, the curtain whipped aside and a sleepy, irritated sheriff glared at Dan.

"Nice to see you, too," Dan said. "I'd have been happy with the night duty officer."

"What the hell is going on?" the sheriff demanded.

"Why don't you shout?" Carly asked. "That way people won't have to strain to hear what's none of their business."

"You want privacy," the sheriff said, "we can go to the jail."

"No thanks," Dan said. "Whatever we say will be all over town anyway, just as soon as your clerk types up your report. Good old Doris has a mouth a lot bigger than her IQ."

"She's not the only one," Montoya retorted. He flipped open a notebook, took out a pen, and said, "What happened?"

Carly and Dan had already agreed that Dan would be the one to answer the sheriff's questions. She was exhausted, had never liked Montoya or his attitude, and was likely to let him know just how much. Then, Dan had assured her, what should have been a brief interview would take hours. Dan pretty much felt the same way about the sheriff, but had gotten over it a long time ago.

"Carly and I went out to see Winifred at about eight o'clock last night," Dan said. "Afterward, we decided to spend some time on the ranch outside, so Carly could get the feel of the place."

"Or the feel of something," Montoya said under his breath.

Dan's fingers curled around Carly's hand and squeezed gently, a reminder of their deal.

She gave the sheriff a smile that was all teeth.

"We spent some time in the graveyard, looking for gravestones and taking pictures," Dan said.

"How much time?"

Dan shrugged. "Half an hour, forty-five minutes. Long enough to get cold."

Montoya waited, pen poised.

"Carly wanted to climb to the top of the ridge—Castillo Ridge—to see the view from there," Dan said.

"In the dark?" The sheriff's voice was rich with disbelief.

"The moon was quite bright," Carly said, giving the man another double row of teeth.

Montoya grunted. "So you decided to go flounder in the snowdrifts. Then what?"

"We went up the windswept side of the ridge," Dan said. "It was an easy walk."

"Beautiful," Carly said softly, then remembered what had happened and shivered. "For a while."

Dan thought about mentioning that he'd sensed he was being watched several times. And then he thought about Montoya's reaction to a touchy-feely thing like **sensing**.

"As soon as we got to the top of the ridge," Dan said evenly, "I was spun around and knocked down the other side by a bullet. I managed to yank Carly with me so she wasn't skylined while the bastard took another shot at her."

"So you're assuming it wasn't an accident," Montoya said, giving Dan a black stare.

"Yeah," Dan drawled. "That's what I'm assuming. What with all the other attacks on Carly, it doesn't take a rocket scientist to figure out what the agenda was."

"Keep talking."

"Somebody wants Carly out of town," he said succinctly.

"Maybe. And maybe somebody was poaching cats or bears for the Chinese trade and bagged a human by mistake."

Dan felt Carly tense beneath his hand. He squeezed gently, hoping she'd keep her temper.

"It's possible, I suppose," Dan said, his voice neutral. "You have a lot of poaching up at the Quintrell ranch?"

"It happens," Montoya said. "What did you do after you took a header down the ridge?"

"We lay there and listened to see if the 'poacher' was going to finish what he'd started."

"What were you going to do, throw snowballs at him?" the sheriff asked.

"I'm licensed to carry. You know because you checked."

Montoya grunted. He didn't know what it was about Dan that had always pissed him off, but it sure did. "Yeah, yeah. Did the guy come after you or not?"

"No. I waited until it became more dangerous to stay than to go," Dan said.

"What does that mean?"

"We weren't dressed for a night in the snow."

The sheriff looked at Dan's calm face and unflinching eyes and sighed. Whatever else he could say about **la bruja**'s son, Dan wasn't a coward or a fool. It took **cojones** to lie out in the snow waiting for someone to put another bullet in you.

"Did he make another try for you?" Montoya asked, curious despite his prejudice.

"I gave him as little chance as possible, but no, there weren't any more shots."

"Well, that sounds like a poacher to me," Montoya said. "He made a mistake and ran like hell. What did folks at the ranch say?"

"We didn't stop. We drove right to town."

That surprised the sheriff. "No matter how you caught that bullet, it must have hurt like a bitch in heat. Why didn't you stay at the ranch until an EMT or a deputy could help you?"

"Most of the bad things that have happened to Carly have happened at the ranch," Dan said.

Montoya's eyes narrowed. "What's that supposed to mean?"

"Exactly what I said. Would you like me to repeat it?"

The sheriff thought about giving Dan an attitude adjustment, then decided it was more trouble than it was worth. Besides, the ER had gotten so quiet you could hear yourself breathe, which meant that everyone was eavesdropping.

"I got it the first time," Montoya said. "Anything else?"

Carly thought about where Dan had seen signs that a car had parked at the base of Castillo Ridge and someone had gone hiking up the hill. She waited for him to tell the sheriff.

"Not that I can think of," Dan said.

"If you remember anything else, call."

"Will do."

Carly watched the sheriff stuff the notebook in his hip pocket and stride through the ER. She leaned very close to Dan.

"Why didn't you tell him about the place where that car had parked?" she murmured against his ear.

He nuzzled against her neck and said softly, "Because I didn't want some clubfooted deputy messing up the sign before I get back there." He looked at his watch. "C'mon, if we hurry, we can get some sleep before dawn."

"Dawn?"

"Great time for tracking. Or backtracking."

"Dawn."

Carly closed her eyes, sighed, and wondered if she'd ever get a whole night's sleep again.

# 52

DAN PARKED HIS TRUCK JUST BEYOND THE PLACE where another vehicle had parked last night.

Carly shook herself awake and reached for the door handle. "I hope we don't need snowshoes. I haven't used them since I was a kid."

"You don't forget how. It's like—"

"Riding a bike," she finished. "And all strange white meat tastes like chicken."

Dan thought of some of the things he'd eaten. "Don't you believe it. Some of it tastes like what it is—disgusting. Stay here where it's warm while I check out the tire tracks."

"Disgusting? What was it?"

"Do you really want to know?"

She thought about it. "No."

"Good choice."

Dan got out, closed the truck door, and zipped up his parka. The sky was overcast and smelled of snow. The air felt almost warm after the stark, clear-sky iciness of last night. Swirls and veils of snow drifted out of the dawn. The air was hushed, the silence thick with falling snow.

As he'd feared, the vehicle had parked on top of the tracks left from the time when Dan and his father had hiked up the back side of Castillo Ridge to watch a funeral they hadn't been invited to. Though six inches of snow had fallen between the funeral and sunset last night, it was nearly impossible to find any pure tread marks. Obviously more than one car had used the turnout since the funeral. Tire tracks crisscrossed every which way.

He looked from the turnout to the ridge rising dark and silver with the dawn. As he'd expected, the "poacher" had used the trail that Dan and his father had already broken to the top of the ridge. Unfortunately, some sightseers and snow-sledders had done the same. The informal trail was trampled flat. Nothing to learn from it.

He went back to the truck.

"Well?" Carly asked.

"More than two vehicles have parked here the past week. More than two parties have gone up the ridge."

"Is that unusual?"

"Not really. The locals have been playing in the snow here for decades. When wind sweeps the snow off of other, more accessible places, there's always the back side of Castillo Ridge for an outing."

"So there's nothing we can find from tracks?"

"Pretty much. I'm going to take a look anyway. I might get lucky and come up with a bullet."

"Shouldn't we let the sheriff do that?"

"If he doesn't get out here in the next few hours, there won't be anything to see."

Carly got out of the car and felt the tender bite of snowflakes. Then she thought about the chance of an overworked, skeptical sheriff bucking a snowstorm for a look-around at the site of what he was sure was an accidental and therefore unsolvable shooting.

"No harm, no foul?" she asked sardonically.

"Yeah. If the bastard had killed me, then we might see some action. As it is . . ." Dan shrugged. "I can't say as I blame Montoya."

"I do."

Dan pulled her close, and melted the snowflakes on her lips with a kiss. "Have I mentioned how much I like you, Carolina May?"

"Same back," she said. Her eyes narrowed as she looked at the bandage on his forehead. **So close. So damn close. Why do we always think there's more time?** She kissed the rough, cool line of his jaw. "Next time, don't let me sleep in. Wake me up early enough to play."

He turned his head, caught her mouth beneath his, and gave her the kiss he'd wanted to give her before dawn. When he finally lifted his mouth, her cheeks were flushed and her eyes were smoky gold.

"It's a deal," he said. "And if I don't let go of you real soon, we're going to be rolling around in the snow."

Her eyelids went to half-mast. "Really?"

"Stop it," he said, letting go and stepping back from her. "You're supposed to be the sensible one."

"What? Since when?"

"Since I can't trust myself around you."

She licked her lips and laughed at the look on his face. "Okay, I'll be good. Really, really good."

"Starting when?"

"Right after I jump you."

Laughing, shaking his head, hands in his pockets so he wouldn't do anything stupid, Dan started off up the ridge.

"Wait," Carly called. "What about the snowshoes we borrowed from your folks?"

"We won't need them. This trail is pounded flat. Watch out for icy spots."

She didn't point out that she had on snow boots. She'd decided that watching out for others was built into Dan's bones. Giving unnecessary directions was the vice of his virtue of caring about others. She followed him up the bumpy trail and only slipped once.

Dan slipped more than that; his excuse was that

he was watching other things than the trail. He glanced back, saw that Carly was keeping up, and concentrated on his footing.

At the top of the ridge, the trail unraveled into sled runs, snow angels, and some marks that defied explanation. Dan turned left, toward the spot where he and his father had watched the Senator's family funeral. Very quickly the trail drew together again. From the look of it, no one but Dan and his father had walked there. Jim Snead— if it had been Jim—had taken a different route to the ridgeline.

"Wrong turn," Dan called to Carly.

She waited while he came back to her, passed her, and went in the opposite direction along the ridge-line. Again, tracks unraveled in all directions. Again, they came together in a single trail. Dan stopped and studied the blurred prints. It looked like the man had come and gone in the same tracks.

"Figures," Dan muttered.

"What?" Carly asked, coming up beside him.

"He didn't break trail twice."

Carly looked down at the valley where the Quintrell ranch lay all but hidden by falling snow. "Weren't we about over there?" she asked, pointing back to the left.

"Yes, but he didn't know that when he started out. He worked along the ridge this way."

"Somehow I think you know more about tracking than I learned in Girl Scouts."

"Somehow I think you're right." He touched her mouth with a snowy glove. "I hunted a lot as a boy, both with Dad and the Sneads."

"Why them?"

"They were the best hunters and stalkers in a hundred miles. At least they were until Blaine started seriously screwing with drugs and went to jail. He lost his edge real quick after that."

Carly hesitated, looking at the valley softened by swirling white veils. "Should I be worried that the snow is falling faster than it was when we parked?"

"Not yet."

"When?"

"About the time we're back in Taos." He touched her smile. "Try to stay in my footprints. It could get sloppy in the ravines and you're such a little thing I don't want to lose you."

Carly looked shocked, then threw back her head and laughed. "Little! I haven't been little since fourth grade."

"To me you're a fragile little flower."

She almost fell down laughing.

He winked at her and turned back to the man's trail. It was easy to follow. The man hadn't worn snowshoes, so he'd left holes in the snow that wouldn't fill up until the wind blew hard again.

From the look of the storm moving in, that wouldn't be long.

Carly was so busy leaping from footprint to footprint that she almost ran into Dan where he'd stopped by a thick, bushy piñon.

"What?" she asked.

"See how the trail has zigzagged? Almost like he was picking a blind."

"Like he was blind?" she repeated dubiously.

"Looking for one," Dan said. "A secure place to shoot from, a place where he wouldn't be seen."

"He's sounding more like a poacher."

"Or a sniper."

Dan's matter-of-fact tone made Carly wonder all over again exactly what he did for a living. She didn't think it was selling shoes.

"So what could he see from the places he looked at and decided against?" Carly asked.

"The road from the highway to the Quintrell ranch, among other things."

"You're scaring me."

"It's about time."

Dan followed the man's trail, walking swiftly, mindful of the increasing snowfall. There were several more blinds or observation posts that he'd abandoned. Then he'd found one he liked and settled in.

Without hesitating, Dan went down on his belly and sighted along an imaginary rifle barrel.

Carly watched and swallowed a rising feeling of dread.

"And?" she asked finally, when she couldn't bear to watch him shooting imaginary targets anymore.

"Whatever he was waiting for probably was on the road, but could have been on the ranch," Dan said. "He's got the high ground and a clear field of fire in both directions."

"Which means?"

"Nothing useful. The sheriff would be the first to point out that poachers love roads and ranch pastures because animals have to cross them to get from one place to another, and they make such easy targets without cover around them."

Dan stood, looked at the tracks, and began crisscrossing the area. A few minutes later he found what he was looking for. "He switched directions here. See where the tripod rested? Probably heard us talking and started tracking us through a nightscope."

"I don't like the sound of that."

"It gets better." Dan walked to the side of the trail, where it crossed over and blended into the windswept side of the ridge. "He shifted positions again here, and here. He knows something about the country—all right, he knows a hell of a lot about the country—because he knew where the animal trail we were on would top the ridge. So he picked his spot and waited for us."

"Cougars and bears don't talk. If he was a poacher, why would he stalk us?" Carly said through cold lips.

"The sheriff would say he was afraid of being found."

"What do you say?"

"He didn't come up here on the ridge to shoot us while we walked on the ranch, because he had no way of knowing we were going to do more than drive in and drive out."

"But you got shot."

Dan shrugged. "Maybe he got cold and tired of waiting and decided to take the best shot he had rather than the one he'd planned."

"Wouldn't a poacher have come prepared to lie in the snow all night? Or are we talking an amateur here?"

"Now you're thinking like the sheriff."

"Quick, get me a brain transplant."

Dan smiled despite the feeling in his gut that they weren't talking about an amateur poacher trying out a new scope.

"He couldn't have had much more than five minutes to find his new blind, sight in the scope, and wait for us to skyline ourselves. But this blind looks as 'lived in' as the first one. He spent more than a few minutes here."

"Waiting until it was safe to make a run for it?"

"Maybe." Dan started off along the holes the man had made once he left his blind. "Maybe not. He didn't head right down the hill."

"Where'd he go?"

Instead of answering, Dan walked swiftly along the tracks. "He went to check on his kill, but he waited until we were gone. See where his tracks come down on top of ours?"

"Why did he wait?"

Dan looked down at the muddled tracks and the dark splash where he'd lain and bled into the snow. The man knew what he was doing. He'd waited, shot, missed Carly, and waited some more.

And not shot again.

"Dan?"

"Maybe he came back to look for a bullet."

"In the dark?"

"It's possible. The truth is, I just don't know what happened here."

"And the sheriff doesn't care."

"Looks like."

"A real clusterhug," Carly muttered.

A grim kind of smile changed the lines of Dan's face. "That's one way of putting it."

# 53

"HERE ARE YOUR NUTCASES FOR THE DAY."
Jeanette Dykstra's assistant dropped a batch of mail
on the desk. Tom was a middle-aged former traffic
reporter who'd nearly crashed in a helicopter once
too often for his wife's comfort. His new job was to
get paper cuts opening Dykstra's mail and pointing
out the good stuff to her.

Dykstra looked up from the notes she'd been
making on an exposé of the bisexual lover of New
Mexico's youngest elected member of the House of
Representatives. The story had possibilities, but it
wasn't going to get her show promoted on the six
o'clock news. She needed that. Her ratings were flat.

"Anything juicy?" she asked without much hope.

"Anorexic pets of neurotic owners, how about
that?"

"Next."

"Another alien kidnapping."

"Jesus." Dykstra shook her head. "What do these
people think I am, a supermarket tabloid?"

"But this victim dropped a litter of little some-things nine months later."

Dykstra rolled her eyes.

"How about gambling?" Tom asked.

"Don't tell me, let me guess—Tuesdays at the Catholic church."

"Bingo," Tom said innocently.

She groaned.

He grinned. "The police chief is rumored to like little boys."

Dykstra's head tilted with her first sign of interest. "Proof?"

"He's a Cub Scout leader. And he buys candy from grade schoolers trying to go on trips."

"Funny," she said in disgust. "In your next life you'll be a comedian. And that life will begin real soon if you keep wasting my time."

"A fighting cock got loose in the barrio and raked a kid's face."

"Pictures?"

"If you hurry. It happened yesterday. The neighbor reported it. The kid's mother refused to press charges. Afraid of the dude that owns the cocks."

"Gee, I'm shocked," Dykstra said with a total lack of interest. She'd grown up in the barrios. She knew what it was like to be wary of neighbors who had enough money to buy fighting cocks, take bets, and carry guns.

From the mound of mail, Tom pulled an envelope with its contents fastened to the outside. "According to Ms. Mendoza—the one who wrote you—she's complained to the police numerous times about the presence and noise of fighting cocks. The cops thank her kindly and promise to drive by when nothing else is happening in the city."

"Even with a sad-faced kid, the day would have to be really slow before I lead with a barrio story. I did a scab picker about dogfighting three months ago. Didn't do shit for the ratings. Who the hell cares about chickens?" But while she said it, Dykstra made a note to see if the mother would agree to an interview before the kid's face healed.

Tits and tots, vets and pets. The grist of human interest stories hadn't changed in a hundred years.

"Is that it?" she asked.

Tom flipped through the pile. "A bowl of posole reveals the face of the Virgin of Guadalupe."

"You better be making that up."

He tossed her a letter and a photograph.

She glanced at the photo. "Okay, you aren't." She dropped the photo and letter in the trash. "When are these geeks going to figure out that I know about digitizing? Give me a computer and I could find the Last Supper in pond scum." She looked at her assistant. "You through torturing me yet?"

"Just about. Saving the good stuff for last." He

pulled an envelope out of the pile, waving the Quintrell ranch logo at his boss. "The governor's aunt is a nutcase."

Dykstra perked up. "That has possibilities. Has he been ignoring or abusing her, denying her treatment?"

"She didn't say."

"She who?"

Tom flapped the envelope and its contents. "The aunt."

Dykstra grabbed the papers and read quickly. The letter was quick and to the point. The photo-copied document was more difficult. It was written in old Spanish with an equally old English transla-tion at the bottom. Both versions were signed in the precise yet flowing script that centuries of nuns and schoolmistresses had drilled into students.

Miss Winifred Simmons y Castillo's handwriting was almost as dated, but the charge she made was very clear: in order to inherit the Quintrell ranch, Governor Josh Quintrell should have an mtDNA test to prove beyond any doubt that he is the descendant of Isobel Castillo.

Dykstra snorted. Obviously the aunt was a head case, but that didn't matter. The governor and pres-idential hopeful was **news.** With luck, this could be milked for a week, maybe even get featured on the evening news show. She'd have to set up an interview with the old bat, but first . . .

"You know anything about, uh, mtDNA?" Dykstra asked.

"Not a clue."

She handed back the letter. "Get busy. I want to do a brief promo on this at three o'clock."

# 54

WEARING A PAIR OF LEVI'S THAT HADN'T BEEN TAI-lored or ironed, Anne Quintrell met her husband at the door. There was no fanfare surrounding him, no town car and driver, no bodyguards. The vehicle in the driveway was one of the thousands of anonymous white rentals that infested airports. At Josh's request they were staying at a supporter's consciously rustic vacation house in Chimayo, rather than in the gubernatorial mansion. It was the only way he could dodge Dykstra.

Sometimes freedom of the press was a real pain in the ass.

As far as the public knew, the governor was still on the East Coast at a nonsectarian religious retreat to discuss the spiritual aspect of political office. Privately, Josh had thought it was a waste of time, but so was much of the public part of being a politician. When Pete had called, Josh had leaped at the reason for leaving, and everyone had agreed to keep it quiet so that he had time to grieve without the media ghouls hanging off every stoplight.

"I'm sorry," Anne said to her husband. She barely recognized him beneath the slouch hat and clothes that were better suited to a fishing trip than a public outing. White stubble covered his face from cheekbones to throat. He looked like he'd hitchhiked rather than flown in from his last fund-raiser. "I know there wasn't much love lost between you and your aunt, but it's still not easy."

Josh came inside so that Anne could close and lock the door behind him. He tossed his slouch hat aside, revealing his trademark thatch of silver hair. "I'm getting sick of bouncing back and forth for family funerals. In fact, I may be getting sick, period." He thought of the flat-out sprint for the presidency that awaited him. Eleven months of hell.

On the other hand, with a little luck, this time next year he'd be president of the United States of America. Not bad for a kid nobody had ever given a damn about.

"Did the Sorenson Foundation's lawyer reach you?" Anne asked, stepping inside so that he could follow.

"No. I had to change flights three times because of the weather. Unless somebody has my private cell number, I'm off the scope. I'd like it to stay that way. What did the lawyer want?"

She closed and locked the front door. "A discounted price on the ranch for public service."

"I'd like one of those myself, but I still have to pay for political ads the old-fashioned way—out of my own pocket."

"The old-fashioned way is out of some other guy's pocket," Anne said, smiling slightly. "Father always did it that way. Did you eat on the plane?"

"In coach?"

"I don't think I've ever flown coach."

"If you're lucky, they throw peanuts at you. Ten to a package, one package per customer."

Anne winced. "Do we have to do anything today or can you get some rest?"

Frowning, he set down his fat computer case and shrugged out of his coat. "I should see the lawyer about final arrangements for Winifred."

"Melissa is taking care of that."

"At least there won't be another nauseating toast to gag down." Josh rubbed his eyes and stretched his long frame. "I'm too old to be sleeping in a center seat in coach."

Anne shook her head. "Not too old. Too smart. But don't worry. When you're president, you'll have your own plane."

He grinned suddenly, looking more like forty than over sixty. "That's the spirit. Did you have a chance to get some food for this place or will I have to keep on these ratty hiking clothes, pull my hat low, and slink into the local market?"

"No need. I did my Holly Homemaker act earlier. You'd have fallen on the floor laughing at my baggy jeans and sweatshirt."

He snickered. "Thanks. I know you hate to go slumming, but it's a great way to stay under the media radar."

"I'm just terrified of meeting someone who recognizes me."

"That's the whole point. No one looks at ordinary people. Turn on the TV, will you? I want to catch the three o'clock local cable news. I told everyone to keep Winifred out of the news until I could get back, but you never know."

Anne picked up the controller, turned on the small TV in the kitchen, and hit the channel for the local cable news feed. "You want a beer and a sandwich?" she asked.

"I'll make it."

"A sandwich I can manage. If you want something hot, you'll have to do it yourself."

"I didn't marry you for your domestic skills," Josh said, looking at his watch and then at the TV.

"You knew I could afford a chef."

He smiled slightly. "And you knew I was on my way to the White House." Some things were more binding than love. Ambition was one of them. He and Anne understood the deal they'd made when they traded wedding rings.

On TV, some local siding salesman was giving his pitch.

Josh hit the mute button and lowered himself onto one of the two stools that made an informal dining area of the counter. He watched Anne work and thought that here was a family values photo op if ever there was one. About the only time Anne went willingly into a kitchen was to discuss the menu for an upcoming party.

The usual closely edited, high-energy shots of the cable news team flashed across the TV, a lead-in to their three o'clock promo of upcoming news events. Josh had often thought it was like a striptease—**Have you heard the sky is falling? News on the hour. Have you seen a crack in your sky? News on the hour. Did the sky fall near you? News on the hour.** By the time the story appeared, far more time had been spent hyping it than was devoted to actually covering it. It was the kind of ten-second-sensation mentality that had reduced political coverage to an exchange of slogans at six o'clock, with an occasional weekend recap of "news" for the people who lived under rocks on the far side of the moon.

**But each one of those rock dwellers has a vote,** Josh reminded himself.

His job was to get as many of those votes as he could and enjoy the benefits of power. The fact that

ALWAYS TIME TO DIE 477

political power was exercised in a way that would horrify the naïve didn't matter. It was the naïve who had the vote, the naïve who had to be courted, and the naïve who allowed national politicians to leave office richer than when they went in and "journalists" like Jeanette Dykstra to flourish. And speak of the devil . . .

Josh hit the mute button again, restoring sound.

A serious Dykstra looked straight into the camera and leaned forward to give out the physical cues that translated as: Listen up out there, this is hot! The fact that she did the same thing for a story about two celebrities wearing the same outfit to a party was all part of selling the news.

"Exclusively from **Behind the Scenes,** Governor Josh Quintrell's aunt Winifred Simmons y Castillo demands that her nephew have a blood test to prove that he is descended from Sylvia Castillo Quintrell. More as the story develops."

The camera cut away to another talking head selling another ten-second news promo.

Josh didn't listen.

"Did I hear your name?" Anne asked as she set a turkey sandwich in front of Josh.

Josh nodded. "Before Winifred died, she went crazy."

"What do you mean?"

"She wants me to prove I'm a Quintrell."

Anne stopped in the act of reaching inside the refrigerator for a beer. "Excuse me?"

"Like I said. She went nuts."

"Well, she's dead now, so it doesn't matter."

Josh thought of Dykstra's eager ferret eyes and wondered if it would be that easy.

His cell phone vibrated in his pocket. He pulled it out and saw the New York accountant's caller ID. He punched in and said, "Make it fast. I'm in a meeting and can't talk."

Anne looked at her husband. He gave her the kind of smile he always did when he was distracted.

"Okay," Josh said. "Thanks. Send me the bill."

"Who was that?"

"Nobody important." He yawned. "Forget the beer and make it a coffee. I have to go to the ranch."

"Right now? I thought Melissa had already arranged for Winifred's ashes to be scattered with Sylvia's."

"She did." Josh yawned again. "Still, I don't want that bitch Dykstra to think I didn't love my dear old auntie. At the same time, I'll give everyone their severance pay in person. And I should press some flesh in the hispano community."

"I won't wait up for you, then."

"Good idea." He rubbed his eyes. "If it gets too late, I'll stay in Taos. More snow is expected up there."

"Why not stay at the ranch?"

"Pete and Melissa usually go to town for dinner and a show on Saturdays and stay overnight for church on Sunday morning. There won't be anyone at the ranch to cook or see that a bed is ready for me."

"You shouldn't have told them the ranch was as good as sold. They don't care anymore."

"I couldn't just toss them out without warning. They've worked there for years."

Anne shrugged. "The Senator spoiled them. It's a job, not a sinecure. But he would never listen when I told him."

"Don't feel bad. The Senator never listened to anyone, including God."

# 55

CARLY WATCHED WITH GROWING EXCITEMENT AS archived data from the newspaper's computer flowed into hers. All but bouncing in place, she opened file after file and saw those glorious words. **Searchable documents.** It would save weeks of painstaking discovery and cross-referencing.

"Yes!" she said, slapping the table triumphantly.

Dan grinned and typed in some more commands. More files leaped from computer to computer.

"You doubted me?" he asked.

She rolled her eyes without looking away from the miraculously growing list of articles. "This time? Of course not. The first six tries that crashed, now that's different. I was afraid getting shot must have addled something."

"You expect perfection the first time?"

"Hey, you gave it to me the first time," she said absently, staring at her computer screen. "And the other times, too."

He grinned. "Are we talking about horizontal dancing?"

She replayed the conversation in her mind, fought a blush, then just gave up and swiped at him, taking care to stay well away from the bandage on his forehead. "You know better than to talk to me when I'm distracted."

"I'll keep it in mind."

She groaned, knowing him well enough to realize that she'd just given him another way to slide past her defenses. Like he needed any. All he had to do was get a certain look in his eye when he watched her and she was ready to jump in his lap and go treasure hunting.

"Knock knock," said Gus from the top of the stairway.

"Is that the opening line of a lame joke?" Dan asked.

"Nope, just a warning that you aren't alone."

Carly fought another blush. Gus had come in earlier today. She and Dan had been pretty much dressed, but the sexual heat had been enough to make the air smoke.

"Appreciate that," Dan said. "Hang on. I've got another two-month block of articles to set up."

Gus walked down the stairs and stopped by Carly's chair. Absently he tapped the envelope he held on the table.

"Told you he could do it," Gus said. "Bump on his head and all."

"You're right. Your brother's amazing. A nerd in wolf's clothing."

Gus smiled but it faded quickly. The image of his brother lying in the snow on Castillo Ridge had been a lousy way to start the day. The rest of the day had gone in the same direction. He looked at the envelope he'd carried in from his office.

"You hear from Winifred today?" Gus asked.

Caught by something in Gus's voice, Carly looked up from her computer screen. "No, why?"

"There's a rumor going through the hispano community."

Dan hit a key and faced his brother. "What kind of rumor?"

"That Winifred is dead."

Carly opened her mouth and shut it just as fast. Her hands clenched in her lap. "Surely someone would have told me."

"Would they?" Dan asked. He put his hand over her fists and rubbed gently. "No one wanted you here but Winifred."

"If they think I'll leave because she's ill or dead, they're going to be real disappointed."

Dan didn't bother to argue that Winifred's death would be a good excuse for Carly to go to a safer place. He was old enough to know which arguments would fly and which would die. She wasn't stupid.

She knew exactly what was at stake. Lying in a snowy ravine waiting to be shot had a real clarifying effect on thought processes.

"If she's dead, what caused it?" Dan asked.

"Pneumonia."

Carly bit the inside of her lip against a combination of anger and tears. Winifred wasn't an easy person, but she was a living encyclopedia of Castillo and Quintrell history. If she'd died, all the insights, the love, even the hatred—all the emotions and memories that made history more than a litany of names and dates—had died with her.

"She can't be dead," Carly said.

And she knew she could.

"She saw the raven flying," Dan said. **"Damn."**

"We can't be sure she's dead," Gus pointed out.

"Did you call the ranch?" Dan asked.

"Of course."

"And?"

"Melissa gave me a very polite runaround. The doctor was with Winifred, she couldn't be bothered, she'd get back to me."

"And she didn't," Dan said.

Gus shrugged. "Not yet. But maybe Carly can help."

"How?"

"This is addressed to you." Gus held out the

envelope he carried. "It looks like old-fashioned handwriting, it came from the Quintrell ranch, and I'm thinking—"

"Winifred," Dan cut in.

"Yeah," Gus said. "I guess she didn't know where Carly would be staying, so Winifred sent it care of me."

Carly looked at the postmark. Friday morning. Quickly she opened the letter. A receipt of some kind fluttered out. With a speed that made her blink, Dan snatched a corner of the paper before it had fallen more than a few inches.

" 'Genedyne Lab,' " he read. "Looks like a return receipt for some kind of tissue or blood samples."

"Why would Winifred mail her lab work receipt to Carly?" Gus asked.

Dan smiled slowly. It wasn't a nice smile.

Carly looked at him warily, reminded of the man who had been lying next to her in the snow, bleeding, waiting with a drawn weapon, hoping to meet whoever was stupid enough to approach them.

"It's one of the top genetic testing labs in the U.S.," Dan said. "Looks like Winifred mailed some samples to them."

"Why?" Carly asked.

"Good-bye, Gus," Dan said.

Gus looked hurt.

It would have been more effective if he hadn't

licked his lips at the thought of a hot story involving the single most newsworthy family in the state.

"If you stay, you promise not to write, hint, or pass by sign language anything you hear," Dan said. "If you want to keep Mom happy, you'll abide by not only the letter of what I've said but the spirit. Or I'll bust your balls and feed them to a coyote."

Gus gave a shout of laughter. "He's baaaack!"

"Who?" Carly asked.

"My real brother, the one who has been off somewhere sulking for three months. It took a rap on the head to wake him up."

"Men don't sulk, they brood," Dan said.

Carly snickered.

Dan pinned his brother with a level glance that said he was through playing. "Are you in or out?"

"Does this have something to do with the baby names I'm tracking down?"

Dan waited.

Gus sighed. "Yeah, yeah, my lips are sealed, my hands are tied, and I won't fart in code, okay?"

Carly laughed.

"I'm going to call the office," Dan said. "They'll be able to find out what Winifred sent to the lab."

"How can they—" Carly began.

"Finding out things is what they do," Dan said, "and they're good at it."

"They," Gus muttered. "I thought you weren't working for the Feds anymore."

"I'm not."

Dan took out his cell phone and wished he'd brought the satellite phone. But he hadn't. It was locked in the case with his encoder-decoder, gun, ammo, and a few other things he didn't want children of any age playing with. He punched in a number, listened, punched in another number, and left his name and callback number.

"Okay," he said. "What else is in Winifred's letter?"

Carly fished out what looked like an old legal document, unfolded it carefully, and shook her head. "She shouldn't have crammed this into a business envelope. There's damage."

"Maybe she was in a hurry," Dan said.

"What is it?" Gus asked, trying to get around Dan so that he could read over Carly's shoulder.

"Some kind of legal document," Carly said, scanning quickly. "Nineteen thirty-four. There's an English translation at the bottom. At least, I think it's a translation. My reading Spanish isn't up to a point-by-point comparison."

"May I?" Dan asked.

She leaned aside so that he could read.

"It's an accurate translation," he said after a minute.

"Of what?" Gus asked impatiently.

"Looks like a nuptial or prenuptial agreement between the Quintrell family and Sylvia Simmons y Castillo," Carly said, scanning the English version. "He agrees that in appreciation of their contribution of money and local support, he'll guarantee that only a child of Sylvia Quintrell's body can inherit the land, and thereafter only descendants of that child may inherit, world without end, amen. If anyone not of Castillo blood attempts to inherit—or in case of death before children or divorce—the land and all its buildings and livestock immediately revert to the Castillo family."

Gus looked surprised.

"From the look and feel of it," Carly said, "whoever made this document was working from an older template. If I had to guess, I'd say that template was the original Quintrell/Castillo marriage agreement in 1865. Maybe it's somewhere in all the stuff Winifred gave to me."

"Guess the Castillos didn't trust the Quintrells, then or now," Gus said.

"They were realists," Carly said, "and the reality was that women in the mid-1860s often died before their husbands, who then remarried and started another family. The Castillos were just trying to make sure that the children of a second Quintrell wife didn't inherit Castillo land."

"Then why the more recent agreement?" Gus asked, looking at the early twentieth-century document. "Women weren't dying in childbirth as often."

"The second prenuptial agreement is the Castillo family's estimate of the Senator's morals," Dan said dryly. "They were afraid he'd use the Castillo's influence with the hispano community to get elected, and then dump their lovely Sylvia for someone without Castillo blood."

"Okay. So why does that matter now?" Gus asked. "The Quintrell begats are a matter of many public records."

Carly put the old document on the table and removed another piece of paper. It was a holographic will leaving everything of Winifred's to Carly, plus the right to search for, copy, or otherwise gather anything from the ranch records that would be helpful to the family history. The will also stated that Carly was to have free run of the ranch as long as the ranch was owned by Castillo descendants. The document was dated last Tuesday.

"What is it?" Dan asked, looking at her.

Carly handed over the last paper. "Winifred must have felt worse than she let on. She made certain I would get her papers and access to the ranch if she died before the family history was finished."

"Smart woman," Dan said, reading quickly. "This will help if the governor tries to get everything back and quash the history. If nothing else, it will give us time to copy all the papers and photos."

Gus looked confused. "What are you talking about?"

"The governor didn't want any family history to be published until after the election in November," Dan said.

Carly took a final piece of paper from the envelope. Her eyes widened. "Looks like Melissa was right."

She passed the paper over to Dan.

"What do you mean?" Gus asked.

"Winifred finally lost it," Carly said. "She demanded that the governor prove he's a descendant of the Castillos."

Dan took the paper and read swiftly.

"It's in the public record," Gus said. "No problem."

"It was for Winifred," Dan said. "She's demanding a special test to prove the governor was a Castillo."

"What—bring back three golden apples from Olympus?" Gus asked.

"Nothing that mythic." Carly picked up the receipt and waved it. "She sent in saliva samples of her own and Sylvia's to Genedyne. That will give a comparison for the mtDNA."

"Translation please?" Gus asked.

"MtDNA is passed to children only from the mother," Carly said. "The father's mtDNA never makes it into the female's egg at conception. The mtDNA is carried in the part of the sperm's tail that falls off outside the egg."

"And?" Gus asked. "Help me here. I barely got through biology."

"Bottom line," Carly said, "is that any child of Sylvia Castillo Quintrell will carry her mtDNA, but only her female children will carry on the mtDNA to the next generation."

"So what? The governor has already inherited. What does Winifred think, that he was swapped in the nursery by passing aliens?"

"I think she wants to make as much trouble as possible for the governor," Carly said. "She was, um, real blunt on the subject of the Senator. Didn't like him a bit."

"If what she says is true, she had reason," Dan said.

"Because he liked women?" Gus asked.

"Because Sylvia tried to kill her husband and ended up a vegetable instead."

Gus stared at his brother. "You're joking."

"Nope." Dan stood up. "I'm going to talk to Mom."

"You're either meaner or braver than I am," Gus said.

"Getting shot does that to you." Dan dug his keys out of his pocket and handed them to Carly. "Here, you drive. I've got some people to call."

# 56

THE GOVERNOR'S PHONE VIBRATED AGAINST HIS thigh as he drove the winding winter road.

"Now what?" he muttered.

The caller ID said Mark Rubin.

Josh pulled over to the side of the road and answered. "Hello, Mark. I take it you saw Dykstra's latest?"

"The phone has been red hot since that show. Reporters clamoring for an interview with you, wanting a contact number for your aunt, wanting to interview everybody from grammar school friends to Vietnam buddies. What the hell is going on? When I asked you about possible land mines to be defused on the way to the presidency, you didn't say anything about your family."

"What's to say?" Josh asked wearily. "My aunt hated my father and transferred that hatred to me. End of story."

"Not this time. Everybody is saying if it's all kosher with your bloodlines, why not have the test? No big deal."

"You don't think it's demeaning for a presidential contender to jump through hoops when a fifth-rate gossip queen snaps her fingers?"

"Not getting a simple test gives her more ammo. Get in front of this story, Josh. Send in a sample. Spike that bitch's guns."

The governor smiled thinly. As always, his campaign manager's jugular instinct was on target. Josh fingered the thin, fresh scab on his neck. It galled him to give in to Dykstra.

But he would.

"Relax," Josh said. "I cut myself shaving this morning and mailed the bandage to Genedyne, just like my aunt wanted. I should have the results in a day or two."

"Do you want me to make an announcement?"

"To Dykstra?"

"Yeah," Rubin said.

"Not one word."

"But—"

"When the test results come in," Josh interrupted, "I'm going to make her eat them in front of a live camera."

Rubin was still laughing when Josh disconnected.

# 57

CARLY ONLY MADE TWO WRONG TURNS BEFORE SHE found her way to the Duran house. Dan hadn't been much help. He'd been on the phone nonstop. She shut off the engine and waited for him to finish his conversation. From what she'd been able to figure out listening to one side of the conversation, in this latest call Dan was talking with someone called Cheryl, a Genedyne technician who also had connections to St. Kilda Consulting.

"That's right," Dan said. "They were mailed Wednesday, arrived Thursday."

"No sign of anything in the computer," Cheryl said. "Could it have been a special order?"

"Check everything you have."

"Checking as we speak."

Dan covered the receiver and said to Carly, "It will be a minute."

She turned the engine back on to keep the truck warm. There wasn't enough snow coming down for a whiteout, but it was edging closer. Occasional gusts of wind buffeted the truck and made snow dance crazily.

"Do you have any of the lab kits we need to send in samples for testing?" Dan asked Carly.

"I had a dozen sent to Winifred. She only asked for ten, but I figured some extra couldn't hurt. And I sent a dozen to your house. They should be in today's mail."

"You're brilliant," he said, pulling her close for a fast kiss. "No, not you, Cheryl. What do you have?"

"A yen to be called brilliant," the tech shot back.

"You're brilliant," Dan said instantly.

"Two samples, one labeled Sylvia Castillo, one labeled Winifred Castillo, mtDNA only."

"Is there enough of each sample to do more tests?"

"Sonny, you'd be amazed how much I can do with how little. What do you want?"

Dan looked at Carly. "Y-DNA, mtDNA, and . . . ?" he asked, holding the phone out to Carly.

Carly took it and spoke quickly. "Go to at least twenty-five markers on the Y-DNA, and at a minimum, a maternal match and every other refinement you have for mtDNA, and I hope to God I can afford it."

"My treat," Dan said, taking back the phone. "Did you get that, Cheryl? Give the samples the works and bill everything to me. And don't let anyone know."

"Got it. How soon do you want it?"

"Somebody tried to kill me. How fast can you get it?"

Cheryl whistled. "Does Steele know?"

"No. It's personal."

"So is dying. I'll get back to you in twenty-four, max."

"Wait. I'll be sending more samples in. Same tests, same rush."

"Bring it on. We just got a dandy new machine that's so fast it scares me. Anything else?"

"No," he said.

"Then you're wasting my time and your money."

Dan didn't bother to say good-bye. Neither did Cheryl. He punched out and stared through the windshield.

"Something wrong?" Carly asked.

"Something else, you mean?" He took a long breath and adjusted the watch cap he wore to conceal the bandage on his hairline. "No, not yet. But it's coming."

Carly looked at the house, where lights glowed against the early twilight brought by snowfall.

"At least Dad isn't home," Dan said. "He's so protective of Mom that I have to fight him to get to her."

"Maybe we shouldn't—"

"Too late. This isn't a game anymore." Dan got

out and said through the open door, "But you don't have to come. It's not your problem."

**"What?"**

Carly shut off the engine, shot out of the truck, and hurried to catch up with Dan. She hit the small front porch at the same time he did. He put his arm around her as if he'd been doing it all his life, knocked, and opened the door.

"Company," he called out, pulling Carly in and shutting the door behind them. Knowing his mother, he headed straight for the kitchen. "I brought Carly."

"Come in," Diana said, hurrying into the kitchen from the greenhouse. Her dark eyes were stormy and her smile was enough to turn heads. "Have you eaten lunch?"

"We're not hungry, thanks," Dan said. "We had a late breakfast."

"You taught your son to make a mean chili," Carly added.

"He's a good cook, when he bothers." She looked warily at her son, then at Carly. "Should I ask why you're here?"

Before either could answer, Diana turned her back and went to the sink to wash her hands.

"Have you talked to Winifred today?" Dan asked.

Diana went still. "No. Is something wrong?"

"You tell me. You'd hear rumors before I would, especially from the hispano grapevine."

Diana gripped the edge of the sink. "Then it's true? She's dead?"

"No one has announced it."

An odd shiver went through Diana. She crossed herself and said, "It is done. It is finally done."

"Not yet," Carly said. "Someone shot Dan."

Diana whipped around, her shock clear.

"Guess the grapevine didn't have my name on it," Dan said, peeling off his hat.

Diana swayed and clenched her trembling hands together to keep from reaching for the son who watched her with distant eyes. "You are—all right?"

"As you can see, I'm fine. I have a hard head. The guy was trying for Carly. I just got in the way."

Diana's glance moved over Carly, taking in the protective way Dan stood close to the young woman.

"Stop asking questions," Diana said bluntly to Carly. "The violence will also stop."

"Do you know who's behind it?" Dan asked, his voice careful. Neutral.

Diana tilted her head back and fished in her pocket for a tissue. Even though she'd added another humidifier to the house, her nose was bleeding again.

Dan grabbed a clean tissue from a nearby box and pressed it into his mother's hand.

"Thank you," she said. "It will pass soon."

"My questions won't," Dan said evenly. "Do you know who is behind the violence?"

"No."

"Any guesses?"

"No."

"But you'd be happy if whoever it was succeeded, right?"

Dan's tone made Diana flinch. She looked automatically toward the back door, where John would come in as soon as he got back from buying a part for the old tractor.

"He isn't here," Dan said, trying to keep the anger out of his voice. "Even if he was, I'd keep on asking. If anything more happens to Carly, it will be over my dead body."

Dan handed his mother another tissue and took the soiled one.

There was silence for a long time. Then Diana sighed and stuffed the second tissue in her pocket. For now, the nosebleed was gone.

"I wouldn't ask you if I had any other choice," Dan said, shoving the first tissue into his jeans pocket. "I'm not a teenager anymore, curious about my grandparents and my mother's childhood. I'm a man who has been trained to evaluate threats and remove them when necessary. Please don't get in my way. I don't want to hurt you." His mouth settled into a grim line. "Carly is innocent of whatever happened in the past. It's the innocent who must be protected first. You taught me that, Mom."

Diana bowed her head. What Dan was saying was true. But there was another truth, and its ugliness made her stomach clench and cold sweat slick her body.

"Take her away from here," Diana said in a hoarse voice. "Far away. Don't come back until the last of the devil's spawn is dead."

"I won't go," Carly said gently. "I made a promise to Winifred. I keep my word. Do you know anything that would help me do my job?"

"I know evil exists."

Carly had no idea how to respond to that.

Diana looked at Carly, saw she didn't understand, and said to her, "You don't believe in evil, just in good. Evil knows its enemy. Good knows only itself. That is why the good die young." She looked at Dan again. "Take her away from here."

"Kidnapping is against the law." Dan pinned his mother with a bleak glance. "Do you know anything that could help us find out who's behind all this?"

"I haven't heard anything."

"Have you tried?" he asked.

She hesitated. "No."

"Try," he said. "Please. If we know which part of the Quintrell history is causing the problem, we'll have a handle on **who** as well. Your past can't be remade, but Carly's future can."

Diana closed her eyes and fought against the nausea turning in her throat, the memories of drunken men and a mother who never heard her own child's screams, a father who was more than that, hideously more.

"It's happening again," she whispered.

"What is?" Dan asked, his voice gentle. She looked so pale, so worn, her eyelids closed, quivering.

"Evil. Death that shouldn't have been. My mother, screaming and laughing, then just screaming."

Dan's breath caught. It was the first time he'd ever heard his mother mention her childhood. "Why was she screaming?" he asked softly.

"Because the dead walk among the living. I know this for truth. My mother's friend saw it. Susan. She told my mother and my mother told me."

Dan bit back a curse. His grandmother, the liar and addict, lost in her own twisted mind.

"My mother saw the ghost of another man," Diana said, opening her eyes. They were wide, staring, fixed on nothing. "A dead man walking, using the name of life."

The darkness in his mother's eyes made Dan want to hit something. He hated doing this to her.

"Two days later she was dead," Diana said in a raw voice.

"What other man did she see?" Carly asked gently.

"Cain."

Carly looked at Dan, who was watching his mother with sadness and pity combined.

"Is that what your mother said?" he asked.

"I remember. I remember the exact words. They live in my dreams. Nightmares." Diana spoke quickly now, the past a river whose dam was crumbling, a torrent seeking release. "She said, 'The dead walk and eat at my father's ranch. Cain lives and Abel is dead.' Then she started screaming and laughing and smashing everything she could reach, cutting herself on the glass, throwing knives and dishes and splashing blood everywhere, shrieking about a prodigal daughter finally getting even with God, and then she came at me with a knife and her hands were bloody and her eyes . . . **her eyes . . .**"

Diana's throat closed as she stared through the present into a past no child should ever have seen.

Dan caught his mother in a hug, trying to comfort her, hating himself and whatever had happened in his mother's past.

"I ran," Diana said starkly, tears spilling down her cheeks. "I knew she needed help but I didn't get help for her. I hated her and I hated the evil she sold me to, so I hid in the church and told no one." A shudder racked her body. "The next thing I remember, she was dead. I could have helped her but I hated her too much. I wanted her dead. She was evil and the evil came down to me. No matter how much good I do, I am as evil as my mother and her brother were, and my grandfather who addicted her and turned her into a whore who sold her own child."

Dan bent until his cheek was on his mother's hair. He held her, simply held her, hating the questions that had brought such pain.

And that was all they'd brought. Nothing in Diana's and his grandmother's half-crazed memories of the past could help the present.

"I've seen evil," Dan said, tipping up his mother's chin, kissing her cheek. "You aren't it. You're simply human. You were an abused, terrified child who grew up into a woman children run laughing to meet, knowing that they're safe with you. You're not evil at all. I love you and I'm very proud of you."

Diana's sad, bitter smile made tears burn in Carly's eyes.

"I have only one more thing to say, then we will never speak of this again," Diana said. "Ever."

Slowly Dan released Diana and looked down into the eyes of a woman who was both his mother and a woman he'd never known. "I can't promise that, because I'm certain you haven't told me all you could. Why?"

"The words would choke me," Diana said in a raw voice, "**and they would destroy you**. Take your woman away from here. Evil wants her, and evil always wins."

# 58

MELISSA WAS PACKING AN OVERNIGHT CASE WHEN
Pete called her.

"The governor's here," Pete said. He stood in the
doorway to their apartment in the big house.

"What are you talking about? No helicopter
would fly in this weather."

"He drove. I'll bet he has our pink slips."

Melissa's full mouth turned down. "We knew that
was coming when we were told to pack up the
house."

"How soon can we get our stuff out of here and
head for the land of perpetual sun?" Pete asked.
"I'm sick of this place."

"The furniture we own isn't worth moving," she
said. "Same for dishes and stuff. It'd be easier to
walk away and replace what we need at the other
end than fuss with an international move."

"A few days? More?" Pete pressed.

"What's the rush?"

"The governor isn't the Senator. I'm having a

hard time keeping my temper with him. It's time to move on, begin the rest of our life."

Melissa's dark eyes searched her husband's face and found only impatience.

"A week," she said. "We need at least that much lead time or the plane tickets will cost a fortune."

Pete nodded. "Okay. A week. Then we're gone. And if the books are a mess, the governor can just cope. I'm sick of this job and the ranch. Too many people dying."

"They were all as old as dirt." She shrugged. "What do you expect?"

The doorbell chimed.

"I'll get it," Pete said. "You finish packing for our time off in town. It's snowing pretty good. If we don't get out in the next hour, we might not get out at all."

Melissa hesitated, then followed Pete down the hall instead of staying and packing. She listened while the men exchanged meaningless words about the weather and how sad Winifred was dead yada yada yada.

The governor must have been as impatient as Pete. It didn't take but a few minutes to get to the bottom line: as of midnight, everyone at the ranch was terminated. As soon as they vacated the ranch, they'd receive three months' pay to ease the transition.

"I'm sorry," the governor said. "I know you've

given long and faithful work to the Quintrell family. There will be an extra six months' pay for you and Melissa. And of course I'll be happy to provide any references you need."

"I appreciate that," Pete said, managing a smile. "I'll tell the rest of the staff as they show up Monday, unless you'd rather do it?"

Josh closed his eyes briefly. "I should, but I don't have the time. I didn't have the time to come up here, but I just couldn't do this over the phone. Not with you two." He looked up, saw Melissa, and walked swiftly to her. "I'm very sorry, Melissa. I wish there was another way."

"It's all right," she said, her smile almost real. "There have been so many changes lately, this isn't exactly unexpected."

A few minutes later, Pete and Melissa watched the governor drive away. His generic white rental disappeared into the snow.

"He can't fire us, we quit," Melissa said, laughing without humor. "He just didn't know it."

"Good thing, too. You don't get severance pay when you quit." Pete smiled rather fiercely. "Rio de Janeiro, here we come."

# 59

THE PACKAGE FROM THE LAB WAS WAITING BY Dan's front door. Carly picked it up and held it while Dan unlocked the door, locked it again behind them, and reset the alarm system.

"Okay," she said. "Spit it out."

"What?"

"Whatever it is that's making you look like you want to hit something."

"I'm just kicking myself for being an idiot."

"Anything in particular?" she asked.

"Yeah. No matter how many times my nose was rubbed in it, I still acted like I was on vacation."

"You've been shot, had a brick heaved through your living room window, suffered a sneering sheriff, been drugged until you yakked up your toenails, and twice drew a gun with every intention of shooting someone. Which part of that qualifies as a vacation?"

Dan would have smiled if he hadn't been so disgusted with himself. "My job is to gather and analyze information and draw pretty damned accurate conclusions, but so far I haven't been real effective. Comes from being too close to the problem."

"I'm not sure I like being called a problem."

"Not just you, honey. The Quintrell mess. Mom knows a lot more than she's telling me."

"Do you think your father knows, too?"

Carly set her package down long enough to shake the snow off her coat and hang it by the front door. She toed off her snow boots and walked across the floor in thick wool socks. Dan did the same.

"If Dad does, he's never admitted it. But, no, I don't think he knows," Dan said. "He'd never have pushed Mom hard enough to make her talk."

"Who, besides your mother, might know?" Carly asked.

"That's just it. Her mother is dead. I don't know who Mom's father is and she says she doesn't know either." Dan shrugged. "The Senator might have known, but that's no help now."

"Ditto for Sylvia and Winifred."

"Jim Snead," Dan said.

"Who?"

"The wolfer. His family has been around the Quintrell ranch forever."

"So has Melissa's," Carly said. "But she won't talk about it. What about the Sandovals?"

"They'll talk only if the pertinent statutes have run out," Dan said. "Jim is probably our best bet."

"Doesn't he have a brother?"

"Blaine. If he's not too drunk or whacked out on something, he might talk to me. Or he might have the same problem with statutes that the Sandovals do. For sure he's on parole."

"Lovely."

Dan shrugged and started stacking kindling and piñon chunks in the little adobe hearth. "Welcome to rural America. Folks who think crime only happens in the cities have never lived anywhere else. People are people no matter where they call home."

Carly watched Dan strike a match. Smoke curled up, then tiny flames bit into fragrant wood. Soon light danced and glowed in the small hearth.

"I wish," she said, "that Winifred was alive and could give us permission to take a tissue sample from the Senator. And your grandmother."

"Why?"

"I've been thinking about Sylvia, about her going ballistic and attacking the Senator. Why would she suddenly just lose it? She already knew he had the fastest zipper in the West. Was there any scandal, local or otherwise, that hit about then?"

"That was '67, right?" he asked.

"Yes."

Mentally Dan flipped through the history he'd

once drawn of the Quintrells. "All that was going on was the hippie invasion in Taos, the Vietnam War, that sort of thing. No big divorces. No wife-swapping or getting caught with the gardener doing the nasty. No election or money-laundering scandals."

"That's not much help. I'm trying to put myself in Sylvia's shoes, how I'd feel if I was married to the biggest womanizer this side of Don Juan. What would it take to make me go crazy?"

Dan laughed softly.

"What?" she asked.

"If you'd been married to the Senator, the first time you found out about his women, he'd have awakened two balls shy of a reproductive package."

Carly looked surprised. "What makes you say that?"

"Anybody as passionate as you are in bed has a temper." He stood up and walked toward her. "I like that, Carolina May. Women with the personality of elevator music make me run for the nearest exit."

"You're not worried about your, um, package?"

"Honey, you can play with my package anytime you want."

"I walked right into that one," she said, laughing. She stood on tiptoe to kiss him, lingered, and made herself step back. "You're distracting me again."

He wanted to keep right on distracting her, but put his hands in his pockets instead. It was time—past time—for him to stop being on vacation and start using his brain. Standing close enough to breathe in Carly's warmth didn't quicken his thought processes one bit.

But it sure picked up his pulse.

"Okay," he said. "Sylvia was used to infidelity. Where does that leave us?"

Carly had a few thoughts on that subject. Several of them made her stomach clench. "Did she have a best friend? Someone she trusted who betrayed her with the Senator?"

"That's kind of a reach. Sylvia would have been just as likely to jump the friend as the Senator. It goes about fifty-fifty when you walk in and find them in bed."

"Fifty-fifty?"

"Yeah. Do you jump the spouse or the lover?"

Carly hesitated for a moment, then went on to the next possibility. "Okay. What about rape? If I found out my husband raped a woman, I don't know what I'd do. Taking a swing at him with a cast-iron frying pan would be a definite possibility."

Dan weighed the idea and nodded. "Good idea. Melissa might know. She's the one who brushed off Winifred's talk of rape."

"If Melissa knew, she wasn't eager to talk about it before."

"We didn't lean very hard before," he said.

"What do we have to lean with now?"

"Melissa can take her choice—talk to us and we won't talk to the governor, or don't talk to us and we'll talk to the governor and say she did."

Carly raised her eyebrows. "Remind me never to get between you and something you want." She took a deep breath. "Winifred said Sylvia tried to kill the Senator, right?"

"Yes."

"Okay." Carly took another breath. "The only thing I can think of that would make me want to actually kill my husband would be discovering that he'd had sex with our daughter."

Dan whistled tunelessly. "That would put me over the top," he agreed.

"It would also explain why your mother hates the Senator so much. She could be the child of incest."

Dan didn't like it. He certainly didn't want to believe it. But it explained so much. "My grandmother wasn't a saint, but why would she tell her daughter something like that, especially if it **was** true?"

"Why wouldn't she? She was a buzzed-up, drugged-out woman who hated life and the world because her father was a man with the sex drive of a goat and the morals of a maggot."

Dan stared into the fire, arranging and rearranging possibilities in light of what Carly had said. He didn't like the pattern that emerged, but he was too smart to ignore it.

Carly went to her computer, booted it up, and searched for references to Elizabeth, known as Liza, Quintrell. The photos came first. A young Liza on the Senator's knee. Liza being put up on a pony. Liza with a barrel racing ribbon from the local rodeo and a proud father standing by her stirrup.

"With his hand on her calf and lust in his eyes," Dan said from behind Carly.

"She can't be much older than thirteen."

"If gossip is correct, that's about the time she started going wild. Drugs, booze."

"That's also the last time the Senator and his daughter got together for a picture," Carly said. "Other people, other family, but not her."

"If what you think is true, Liza wouldn't want to be within a country mile of her father."

Carly divided the screen and called up the Senator's wedding. "I keep remembering one photo where he had his arm around his bride and—here it is. The look he's giving that other woman." She zoomed in on part of the photo, excerpted it, put it next to the photo of Liza and the Senator, and felt her stomach clench again. "I wish Sylvia had killed him."

Dan studied the two photos. Nothing had changed about the Senator's predatory look except the female it was directed at.

"When I think of how much my mother and grandmother endured because of him," Dan said finally, "I could kill him myself. There's only one problem."

"He's already dead?"

Despite the grim brackets around Dan's mouth, he smiled and tugged at the coil of hair Carly was winding around her finger. "That, too. But we're assuming that the secret—whatever it is—the one the governor is so worried about coming out, outlasted the Senator's death."

"Is there a statute on incestuous rape?" Carly asked bitterly.

"Sure. We have laws about when and where you can spit." Dan shrugged. "Even if we prove that the Senator had a child with his own daughter, I can't see it doing anything but getting a sympathy vote for Josh Quintrell. I doubt if the governor would get his dick in a twist over a fifty-year-old secret coming out. He would be publicly repelled, fund a committee to study and prevent the origins of incest and help the victims, and go to church to pray for the Senator's soul and that of his poor sister. None of the above would hurt him in the polls."

"So what you're saying is that no matter what crimes the Senator committed, legal responsibility for those crimes dies with him."

"Basically, yes. At least in terms of threatening Josh's political career at this point in time. There has to be something else that he's worried about."

"Worse than incest? That's a scary thought."

"Isn't it just." Dan frowned.

"Do you think Winifred knows—knew? Damn it, when will Melissa call us back about Winifred?"

"Whenever Josh gets here to spin everything for the media. Until then, my vote is with the hispano grapevine. Winifred is dead."

Carly closed her eyes. "I wonder if she knew?"

"The secret?"

"No. That she was going to die. It would explain why she mailed that letter to me."

"I wouldn't be surprised. Winifred was a woman out of her time. Maybe out of any time." Dan focused on the fire again. "If you wanted to prove incest fifty years after the fact, when both parties are dead and the living won't help, how would you do it?"

"Proof?"

"Genetic proof."

"I'd need a sample from the Senator. One from his daughter would be useful."

"But not vital?"

"Not at this point. The sample we really need is one from the supposed child of incest. If she shows the Senator's Y-DNA, then the Senator was her father. It's that simple."

" 'The child.' That would be my mother we need a sample from."

"Yes."

Dan pulled the bloody tissue from his pocket. "Would this work?"

# 60

A DOT OF BRIGHT RUBY LIGHT PUNCHED THROUGH the falling snow as the sniper sighted in his scope. The gallons of water he'd poured on the blind curve were invisible now, a sheet of black ice frozen beneath a dusting of snow. If ice didn't send their vehicle caroming out and down several hundred feet to level land below, then it would be up to close work to finish the job. On the whole, he'd much prefer an accident. Fewer questions that way.

Headlights glowed along the road from the ranch house. They bobbed and bounced but made good progress. Though the narrow road was technically on private land, the county managed to pass a blade over it often enough to keep ranch traffic moving. The headlights came on at surprising speed. Obviously the driver belonged to the part of the American population that believed four-wheel drive could handle anything weather could dish out.

Live and learn.

Or die.

The sniper waited, invisible on the ridge, white on white, patient.

The small truck bored through the late-afternoon gloom, eating up the road. Ruts made for a bouncy ride, but there were so many ruts they were bound to grab the tires from time to time.

The sniper was counting on it.

As the vehicle approached the deadly curve, the sniper's finger slowly, slowly took up slack on the trigger.

The front tires of the truck hit icy ruts and lunged toward the drop-off. The driver fought it and was on the verge of regaining control when a red dot gleamed on the inside of the right front tire and snow-muffled thunder cracked. The tire collapsed, headlights bobbed and lurched.

The truck slid wildly on ice, then shot off the road and somersaulted into the gloom below.

The sniper waited, watching snow fall.

And waited.

When he was certain no one had seen the accident, he strapped on snowshoes and took a round-about way down to the road and then on down the rest of the ridge to the wreck.

He found the man first. DOA, definitely. The fool hadn't worn a seat belt. The sniper continued on down to the wreck itself. The woman was still alive, dazed and bleeding, her face a mess against the shattered rime of glass that was all that remained of the passenger window. He sat on his heels, found her pulse, and sighed.

Not quite.

He took her chin in one hand, the side of her forehead in the other, and gently searched for just the right angle.

Her eyes opened, slowly focused on him in the gloom. **"You,"** she said weakly. "But I killed them both for you . . . the Senator and Winifred . . . to keep the secret."

"Always a good idea."

There was a single snapping sound.

The sniper stood and glided away on snowshoes into the concealing veils of snow.

# 61

DAN WASN'T HAPPY WITH CARLY COMING ALONG, but the idea of leaving her alone with his mother hadn't appealed, either. Besides, Carly was the one with permission to come and go at the ranch. What she would be doing wasn't, technically, breaking and entering. She still had the keys to the ranch house, plus she had a copy of Winifred's holographic will.

What Dan planned to do was a lot more dicey, legally speaking. So he wasn't telling Carly about that part. If it went from sugar to shit, he wanted her to be able to say she didn't have the faintest idea what he'd planned and was shocked, really shocked.

The only good news was that the snow came and went in squalls, rather than in endless veils that clung and buried everything. The ten inches they'd already had was quite enough. If the storm cleared later tonight as it was supposed to, the wind would begin to blow and powdery snow would blow with it. Dan wanted to be back in Taos before that happened.

Besides, if he entered one more picture into the computer, or filled out one more genealogical form, or thought any more about what his mother had said, he was going to go nucking futz.

There were two sides to his personality; the other side wanted some exercise.

There was only one bad patch of ice on the road, but since Dan was driving like every foot of the way was black ice and hugging the road cuts, he kept control of the truck without a problem. The fact that he had large, studded snow tires helped.

"Yikers," Carly muttered, bracing herself on the dashboard when the truck bucked.

"Yeah. We'll have to remember that one on the way out."

The windshield wipers moved sluggishly, compacting snow to the side of the rubber blades. The truck turned around the toe of Castillo Ridge and headed into the valley that held the Quintrell ranch. Gradually the snow squall thinned and vanished. The sky showed a few pale ribbons of blue and a glow where the sun was shrouded in clouds.

Except for security lights along the driveway and walkways, all of the ranch buildings were dark despite the gloomy day.

"Looks like Lucia was right," Carly said. "Sunday is everyone's day off."

Lucia had been very glad that Carly and Dan

didn't want to see her, so glad that she'd chattered on for several minutes before Dan could gracefully hang up.

Dan pulled up to the front of the house and turned off the engine. "Ready?"

"Even with Winifred's permission, I feel like a thief."

"That's why we're going to go right up to the front door, turn on all the lights, and in general behave like lords of the manor."

Carly got out with her digital camera, computer, and a box in case she found anything really interesting to take with her. Dan followed, carrying his own electronic equipment in a suitcase. She'd watched while he packed what looked to her like at least one hard drive, various cables and connections, a portable computer, a beefy camera, and some stuff she couldn't identify. All she knew for sure was that he'd spent fifteen minutes on the cell phone with some people from St. Kilda Consulting before they left Taos.

"You start in Winifred's room," Dan said.

"Then Sylvia's room, then the Senator's office," Carly said. "I remember. What are you going to be doing?"

"You didn't ask that question."

Carly thought about it, started to object, and thought about it again. "What question?"

She went to Winifred's room, flipping on every light she could reach along the way.

As soon as Carly disappeared, Dan pulled on exam gloves. Without turning on any lights, he walked quickly to the Senator's office, booted up the office computer, got past the laughable security in less than three minutes, and began copying the contents of the ranch's hard drive onto the one he'd brought with him.

While the computers were mating, he went through the desk with a competence that would have made Carly really nervous. Nothing caught his eye. No keys to files. No P.O. Box keys. Nothing but the usual paper clips and pens. The file folders were empty of everything except a few invitations to attend local groundbreakings. The most recent was nine months old.

With economical motions Dan examined the few books in the office. Decoration only. No papers slipped inside the pages, no pages dog-eared, nothing hidden beneath the endpapers. The closet held only supplies. The locked filing cabinet came unlocked in a few seconds and had neatly bound files with SCANNED IN stamped across them. Apparently the ranch records were fully computerized.

That would make his work a lot easier. Quicker, too.

Dan went back to the computers, saw that they

were still passing bytes from one to the other, and went to the end of the house where Melissa and Pete had their apartment. The glassed-in walkway was frigid. The locked door could have been opened by a monkey with a credit card. No office, just a master bedroom. The dresser drawers were stuffed with the usual things. Nothing had been taped underneath. Nothing surprising was between the mattresses or under the bed. The closet had clothes, shoes, boots, shoe boxes . . .

**Bingo.**

One of those shoe boxes was bound with a new rubber band. The box was worn at the corners and the lid was broken. Carefully Dan pulled out the box and took off the lid. There was a batch of post-cards, letters, and photos inside.

He laid everything out on the bed in the order it had come from the shoe box. Then he flipped on the lights and began photographing. The Nikon digital camera he used had a built-in wireless connection to his computer. The wireless was good for four hundred feet. The Senator's office was a lot closer than that. He photographed the front and back side of every item from the box.

As soon as he had the last image, he flipped everything over again, stacked it in the same order he'd found it inside the box, slipped the worn lid into place, snapped on the rubber band, and replaced the shoe box precisely as he'd found it. Each of his motions was quick, economical, and spoke of practice. A lot of it. What the Feds hadn't taught him, other members of St. Kilda Consulting had.

He turned off the lights and headed for the Senator's office again. The computers were finished. He disconnected his own, instructed the Senator's to forget it had ever been booted up, shut it down, and positioned the computer exactly within the faint rectangle of clean desktop where he'd found it.

The maids were getting careless about dusting. No surprise there. Nobody but Pete and Melissa lived here anymore.

As soon as Dan checked that the documents he'd photographed had been received by his computer, he packed everything into the suitcase and headed out for his truck. He swapped the suitcase for a tool belt with a battery-powered drill and a selection of twenty-four-inch bits which had been designed for drilling through everything from concrete to steel. There were several small containers from Genedyne Lab held like oversize bullets in the loops of the tool belt.

Dan grabbed the pick and shovel from the bed of the truck and headed for the Quintrell graveyard.

# 62

HUNCHED AGAINST WIND AND BLOWING SNOW, GUS knocked hard on the door of Dan's rental and simultaneously turned the doorknob. It was locked, even though his truck was out front. Gus shook his head. His brother was the only person he knew who locked his doors when he was home.

"Dan, it's Gus! I'm freezing my butt off out here!"

Thirty long, miserable seconds later, the front door opened. Carly peeked out, stepped aside, and slammed the door shut again one second after Gus got in the living room. Even so, Carly heard Dan swearing as various genealogical charts and papers went flying, courtesy of a frigid gust of wind.

"Sorry," Gus said. He gestured to the boarded-over window. "What happened?"

"Brick meets glass. Glass breaks," Dan said. "Snarky renter gets plywood and covers the hole."

"Somebody deliberately broke your window?"

"Yeah."

"What did the sheriff say?" Gus asked.

"You're kidding, right?" Carly said, disgusted. "I don't think we bothered him with that incident."

"We didn't," Dan said, "because there were others we did report and he didn't care. That's why she's living here rather than at the ranch."

"Dang, and here I was getting ready for nieces or—"

"Gus, shut up," Dan cut in.

Gus made muffled sounds like he was talking around a hand over his mouth.

Carly snickered.

Dan shot his brother a green glance that was halfway from amused to outright irritated.

"Okay, okay," Gus said. He turned to Carly. "When my older—much, **much** older—brother gets that look in his eyes, he's about to kick something. I don't want it to be me." He reached inside his snow jacket and pulled out a big envelope with the newspaper's logo on it. "This is a list of all the children in the area who were born within ten months of a visit from the Senator. The ones with an asterisk by the file name were born to women of the right age to attract the Senator."

"Puberty to menopause?" Carly asked.

"Near as I can tell, he didn't have many women who were over twenty-nine," Gus said. "Certainly none who looked it. The older he got, the younger he liked them, if you can believe gossip."

Carly thought of the picture of the middle-aged Senator with his hand on his thirteen-year-old daughter's leg. "Oh, I can believe it. What I can't believe is that nobody ever called him on it."

"Just one of the prerogatives of power," Dan said.

"Like leaving office richer than when you went in?" she retorted.

"Just like it." Dan opened the envelope, saw the CD he'd loaned his brother, plus a new CD. "How many names?"

"Didn't count," Gus said cheerfully. "Too many. We're a fertile bunch in Taos."

"You see Mom lately?" Dan asked.

"This morning."

"How's she doing?"

"She's pretty shocked about losing Pete and Melissa, but—"

"Losing?" Carly interrupted, startled. "Did the governor fire them?"

Gus looked from one to the other. "You don't know." It was a statement, not a question. "They were killed in a car accident yesterday on the way into town."

Carly just stared at him.

"Where?" Dan asked flatly.

"Do you know where the ranch road comes around the toe of Castillo Ridge and winds back along it on the way to the highway?"

Carly stopped breathing.

"I know it," Dan said. "What happened?"

"They must have been running late, because Pete was going along too fast. He hit ice, lost it, and went over the edge. They weren't found until early this morning. The Sneads were coming in with some emergency supplies for the line cabins, so if someone got lost they could survive until help came."

Dan nodded. It was a common, and decent, thing for ranchers to do.

"The Sneads saw light glowing under the snow at the bottom of the ridge, on the town side. It was headlights. They went down and found Melissa." Gus shook his head. "Took them a while to find Pete, about a hundred yards uphill from the truck. He must not have worn a seat belt. If the wind hadn't been blowing snow around, and Jim's dog hadn't had a good nose, no one would have found Pete until spring."

"What does the sheriff have to say about it?" Dan asked.

"There hasn't been a formal autopsy yet, but all the injuries look like what you'd expect from a nasty wreck. Why?"

Carly barely heard. All she could think of was the sniper on Castillo Ridge, able to fire toward the ranch or toward the far side of the ridge.

She looked at Dan.

He shook his head slightly. "Thanks for all your help, Gus. Now go back and spend time with your family. Give them all hugs for me, okay?"

"Here's my hat, what's my hurry, is that it?" Gus asked Dan.

"Yes. Don't call me, Gus. Don't be seen with me. And I'd stay clear of Mom, too. Just for a while."

"What's going on?" Gus demanded.

"I don't know. Until I do, stay away from me, and from her."

"What about Carly?" Gus asked.

"Same goes," she said in a low voice. "Stay away. Think of it as a temporary quarantine." **At least I hope it's temporary.**

"Please," Dan said to his brother. "Think of your kids."

"You're serious." Gus stared at his brother. "You're really serious."

"Yes."

"Does Mom know?"

"Don't ask her," Dan said. "Don't ask anyone. Don't trust anyone."

"Even—"

"Anyone," Dan said curtly.

Gus blew out a breath, turned, and stalked to the front door. "See you around, bro. And when I do, you'd better have an explanation for me. A good one."

The door closed behind him. Hard.

# 63

CARLY STARED AT THE FRONT DOOR, THEN AT DAN. "Are you thinking what I'm thinking?" she asked.

"That somebody could be getting away with murder around here?" he said.

"Isn't it the only statute that doesn't have any limitations?"

"Yes."

"But I'm having a tough time connecting the past with the present."

"So am I. There are too many people who hated the Senator, and too many good reasons for someone to kill him. Or . . ."

"What?"

"Blackmail him."

"Does that help us?"

"Just one more handful of pieces that don't fit anywhere. Why?"

Carly frowned. "When I get to this point in a genealogy, too many facts and no coherent pattern, I stop and take another approach, another way of looking at or getting to information."

Dan nodded. It was what he did, too. Sometimes it helped, sometimes it just confused the issue more. Either way, it was a new wall to beat against.

"What if we approach this a different way?" Carly asked slowly. "What if we assume that Winifred wasn't clinical on the subject of the Senator and the Senator's son? So we assume there was a rational aspect to her hatred."

Dan went still. "Go on."

"What if we also assume that your grandmother was more than a pathological liar and an addict? That maybe she knew what she was talking about, at least some of the time? Again, a possible rational basis for her actions."

His eyebrows lifted. "That's a stretch."

"Wait."

Carly went to the bedroom, returned with her recorder, and found what she wanted on the second try. Diana Duran's voice whispered into the room, followed by Dan's.

**"It's happening again."**

**"What is?"**

**"Evil. Death that shouldn't have been. My mother, screaming and laughing, then just screaming."**

**"Why was she screaming?"**

**"Because the dead walk among the living. I know this for truth. My mother's friend saw it.**

Susan. She told my mother and my mother told me. My mother saw the ghost of another man. A dead man walking, using the name of life. Two days later she was dead."

Then Carly's voice, gently questioning, **"What other man did she see?"**

"Cain."

After a moment, Dan's voice asked another question.

Diana's haunted voice answered. **"I remember. I remember the exact words. They live in my dreams. Nightmares. She said, 'The dead walk and eat at my father's ranch. Cain lives and Abel is dead.' "**

Carly stopped the recorder. "The Senator had two sons to speak of."

Dan looked at the envelope he still held. "And a lot he didn't speak of."

"Is it possible that Josh killed his older brother?"

Dan's eyes narrowed. He went to his computer, called up files, searched. "Not likely. The newspaper articles about the Senator's valiant sons in Vietnam make it clear that Josh wasn't there when the heir apparent was. In any case, there were witnesses to the older son's death. Viet Cong. He died saving the lives of his fellow rangers. If he'd survived, he'd have so many medals he'd have a hard time standing up straight."

"Okay. So Cain and Abel aren't an exact description." Carly paused. "But what if one of the bastards—"

"Somehow took the place of a legitimate son?" Dan cut in.

"Yes."

"How? When?"

She fiddled with a strand of her hair. "It would have to be after Sylvia had her stroke, or whatever happened to put her in a coma."

"Why?"

"No way Sylvia would let the Senator put one of his bastards in the family line of succession."

"I agree. Especially if she thought he was shagging their daughter."

Carly winced. "Not to put too fine a point on it."

"There's no nice way to talk about incest."

She let out a breath. "You're right. I just find the whole idea hateful."

"I'd be worried if you didn't." Dan kissed her gently, then released her, only to find she didn't let go.

"I'm sorry," she said. "I forgot for a moment that your mother . . ."

"Might be a child of incest?"

Carly nodded.

"That's no one's fault but the Senator's, and he's dead."

Dan led Carly back to the work area they'd set up. They were using the bed as a table, the card table as a computer center, and various cowhide chairs as storage units for files. The floor took the overflow.

"Okay," he said, feeling the excitement of the chase humming in his blood. Even if the ideas went nowhere, they went nowhere in new territory rather than trudging through the same old same old. "Following your assumptions, the switch had to take place no earlier than Sylvia's stroke."

"Unless the switch was what set her off so that she jumped the Senator," Carly said. "My point was simply that she wouldn't have sat still for it."

"Agreed."

Dan sat down in front of one of the three computers they were using—two were his and one was hers. He woke up his own, which had a much more flexible program for retrieving data than Carly's, and which now held everything about the Quintrell family that hers did. Plus the ranch records he hadn't told her about yet.

"At that time," Dan said slowly, "Josh would have been about twenty-seven. Anyone doing a switch with him would have to be close in age and build. Probably no more than five years on either side, and an inch either way in height. Also, that person would have to have 'died' when the switch was made. So I'm looking for a male senatorial bastard who was between six feet and six feet two inches in height, and between twenty-two and thirty-two years old, who died a few years on either side of 1967. Death certificates don't give height, so I'll do the age thing first."

He pulled out the CD Gus had left, fed it into the slot, and downloaded it. Very quickly he was querying his data pool.

"Vietnam," Dan said after a moment. "Has to be."

"Where he died?"

Dan nodded. "And where the switch was made. If there was a switch."

"If there wasn't, our assumption will fall apart pretty fast, won't it?"

"You'd be surprised," he said absently. "Assumption is the mother of all fuckups and has many children."

Carly watched the screen anxiously. "Remind me to steal this program from you."

"I'll modify it just for you. For a price."

She gave him a sideways glance, saw him watching her, and said, "It's a deal."

"You don't want to know what the price is?"

"If I can't afford it, I'll think of something. Or you will."

"You're distracting me," he said.

"Thank you."

"I'll be damned," he said, looking at his computer.
"Excuse me?"

"There are five candidates who fit the profile. Nine if you go the full five years on either side of twenty-seven years old."

Carly didn't know whether she was excited or dismayed. "That many?"

"Those are only the ones who died or disappeared and are reasonably close in height. A lot more than nine males were born in the area in the search years."

"They're all the Senator's?" she asked in a rising voice.

Dan laughed. "No. There's just nothing to prove they **aren't** his bastards."

"I feel better. I think. The Senator might yet give Genghis Khan a run for his money."

"What do you mean?"

"According to some genetic studies of Y-DNA in Asia, around eight percent of the population are direct patrilineal descendants of Genghis Khan," she said. "Compared to the average man, that's an astronomically successful rate of reproduction."

"What was his secret?"

"Rape and murder. Murder the men and boys, impregnate the women and girls, and move on. If the accounts passed down can be believed, he was, um, tireless on more than the battlefield."

Dan's eyebrows lifted. "The things I learn hanging around with a naïve genealogist."

"Naïve?"

"Beautiful. Did I mention beautiful?"

"Now I know that bullet caused brain damage."

Before Dan could retort, he felt the brush of her lips against his temple. Distracting. Very distracting.

"Candidates," he said out loud. "What other requirements would they need beyond dying or disappearing or—honey, if you keep breathing in my ear, you're going to be in my lap real quick, and I'm going to be in yours real deep."

Carly straightened and stepped back from temptation. "Candidates. Um, age, death. Got that." She blew out a breath. "What about height, eye color, that sort of thing?"

"Give me a minute."

She went to her own computer, booted up the family pictures and descriptions, and brooded over them. A.J. IV had black hair like the Senator and dark eyes like his mother. Josh had black hair and blue eyes, a complete senatorial copy. Liza had blond hair and dark eyes. The sister who had died of polio at nine had brown hair and blue eyes. Diana Duran had black hair and dark eyes. Dan had dark hair and the most amazing green eyes . . .

**Don't even start.**

Carly jerked her mind back to phenotypes. There

certainly was a variety to choose from. Everything from black hair and dark eyes to blond and blue-eyed. No help at all.

So she began thinking about why Pete and Melissa had to die. **Who benefited?**

Their children, probably, but they were grown and living out of state.

Carly's mind returned to the intriguing idea of an identity switch. Certainly the Senator must have known. Did he do it willingly, just to have his own genetic son inherit the land and the power, or did the impostor have something to hold over the Senator?

Something like incest?

Murder?

Not that Sylvia had died, but she certainly had been a victim of assault.

Carly pulled over a yellow pad and began thinking on paper. Who certainly knew about the incest. Who might have known. Who was still alive in the present that might threaten the governor—if indeed he was an impostor.

The Senator and Liza certainly knew. Given Liza's instability, she might have told or hinted to her best friend that her father had raped her. Probably more than one rape. She started going wild at thirteen but didn't have Diana until she was sixteen. Of course, it could have been one of Liza's boyfriends or tricks that impregnated her. As soon as Genedyne finished the test series, they would know if Diana had the Senator's Y-DNA. Until then, it was an assumption that fit the circumstances and memories of the living.

Carly circled the Senator's and Liza's names. Obviously Liza could have been blackmailing the Senator—probably was, one way or another—but Liza died a long time ago and Pete and Melissa had just died, so to connect them through blackmail was a stretch.

**Susan.**

Susan Mullins, grandmother of Melissa Moore. She'd died a long time ago, too.

With Liza.

Carly felt the sizzle of energy that came when she was working a promising genealogical trail.

If Susan knew, she could have told her daughter or her son—or even the Sneads, who might or might not be the Senator's grandsons.

**Wonder if they would agree to sending cheek swabs to Genedyne.**

If the daughter—what was her name, Letty, Kitty, Betty? That was it, Betty. If Betty knew, she could have told her own daughter, Melissa.

Carly drew lines of genetic connection and lines of circumstantial and geographic connection. Nothing impossible so far. Everything **could** have happened. That didn't prove everything **did** happen. That was why courts were iffy on the subject of circumstantial evidence.

She looked up and saw Dan watching her. "What?" she asked.

"Just enjoying watching another analytical mind at work."

"Fanciful is more like it, at least on my end." She wound a strand of hair around her finger and made a sound of disgust. "Well, it was fun while it lasted."

"What was?"

"It's too convoluted and loopy to explain."

"Trust me. I have a very convoluted and loopy mind."

Carly hesitated. "You're going to laugh."

"No. At this stage in the investigation, nothing is so far-fetched that it's laughable."

She looked at him and saw he meant it. "If you so much as smile, I'll bite you."

"Now you're tempting me."

Carly rolled her eyes but otherwise resisted the lure. "If there was an impostor, the Senator had to be in on it, right?"

Dan nodded. "The man wasn't exactly father of the year, but chances are that he'd know his own son."

"So there are two choices—the Senator agreed to go along or he was blackmailed."

"With what?"

"Incest."

"How would the impostor know about the incest?"

"Susan Mullins," Carly said. "She was Liza's friend—"

"Coworker," Dan said. "She turned tricks to pay for drugs."

"But she could have known."

"Agreed. In fact, it's likely. A background of incest isn't all that rare in the sex trade. It's one of the things prostitutes bond over."

"God," Carly said starkly. "What planet do those abusers come from?" Then she held her hand up, palm out. "Rhetorical question. Yes, I'm naïve. I don't want to think about that kind of sick, ugly . . ." She forced out air in a whoosh. "Sorry. Empathy can be a bitch."

"Can you think of this as parts of a puzzle rather than human beings who hurt and cried and hoped and lost?" he asked.

She went still. "You feel it, too, don't you?"

"I try not to."

"But you do."

"Yes. And all it does is get in the way of doing the job."

Carly took Dan's hand, held hard, and let go. "Puzzle. Right. Here we go. Where were we?"

"Susan Mullins reasonably could have had knowledge of the Senator's incestuous relationship with his daughter."

"Relationship? As in more than once or twice?"

"Incest, like rape, is about power rather than sex," Dan said neutrally. "As long as the child is within the age range of the predator's interest, the incest continues."

She didn't want to ask, but she couldn't help it. "Age range?"

"Abuse doesn't really have an age range. Abuse that has a sexual outlet is subject to the same peculiarities of preference as healthy sexual attraction. Some abusers are attracted only to prepubescent children. Some prefer infants."

Carly's skin crawled.

Dan's voice continued, relentlessly neutral. "Some abusers prefer the postpubescent child. The Senator seems to have been in the last category. Young, but not obscenely so. I believe thirteen is still considered a marriageable age in some states. In some countries, menstruation is the only division between a child and a woman. Between one week and the next, a girl becomes a sexually available woman."

**Pieces of a puzzle.** Carly forced herself to breathe. **Just pieces.**

"In other words," Dan said, "yes, the incest probably lasted until Liza left the house and possibly continued until she was thirty. So, yes, Susan could have had knowledge that would be useful to blackmail the Senator. Whether or not that happened . . ." Dan shrugged.

"If she did have knowledge, she could have told her daughter, Betty."

Dan nodded.

"Who could have told Melissa," Carly continued, "who could have decided to continue the blackmail."

"Only until the Senator died."

Carly nodded.

"Then why arrange an accident for Melissa?" Dan asked. "The only reason—other than bad luck—for the Moores to die is that someone **alive** had something important to lose if Melissa lived."

"If there was an impostor, and Melissa knew, couldn't she have blackmailed him—the Senator and/or impostor—over that?"

"Yes. So could her sort-of cousins, if they knew."

Carly blinked. "Sort-of cousins? Oh, the Sneads. I hadn't thought about them. Their father Randal Mullins could have known about the incest, and he could have passed the information on to his lover—"

"Folks were pretty clear on that point," Dan cut in. "Randal and Laurie Snead were a one-night stand, if they got it on at all."

Carly sighed. "So you don't think the Sneads are involved?"

"Jim Snead has my nomination as the sniper. He knows the land better than any man alive and is a dead shot at any distance under five hundred yards. I just haven't found a decent circumstantial thread to connect him to you."

"Me?" She sat up straight. **"Me?"**

"Jim or his brother empties live rattraps at the house."

Carly remembered the rat in her room. A rat, according to Dan, that had still been warm. Dead and gory all over her pillow, but still warm.

"Jim is the official Quintrell ranch predator control. He comes and goes from the place at will. He goes to town with the mail and brings back supplies. Sometimes Blaine does the errands. It depends on how straight Blaine is when he shows up wanting work."

"You're saying it was Jim Snead."

"No," Dan said, "I'm saying he has the skill and the opportunity. I just can't find a reason, and without a motive the rest is just so much circumstantial blue smoke and mirrors."

"Besides, there are the Sandovals," Carly said.

"You lost me."

"Given the number of Sandovals dodging in and

out of the Senator's life, and Liza's, it easily could have been a Sandoval who had knowledge of the incest and/or the substitute son, and therefore a reason to blackmail the Senator and/or the governor. God and the county sheriff know that some of the Sandovals have the means and mind-set required for crime." Carly muttered unhappy words under her breath. "The list of possible circumstantial suspects has just exploded. No wonder that kind of evidence is viewed with suspicion."

Dan closed his eyes and tried to do what he'd been trained to do. Find patterns.

Forget how close you are to the problem. Take your own advice.

**Pieces of the puzzle. That's all. Not people. Just pieces.**

But he kept remembering how it had felt to have Carly go dead limp against him, kept remembering the endless time marching up and down that frozen road, kept realizing how close Carly had come to dying.

# 64

"IT'S RUBIN," ANNE SAID, HOLDING JOSH'S CELL phone out to her husband. "He won't take no for an answer."

"I was expecting it," Josh said, taking the cell phone. "Hello, Mark."

"You sound like a frog."

"I told you I needed downtime. Now I've got a cold."

"Flu," Rubin corrected instantly. "Only plebes get colds."

"What couldn't wait until Wednesday?" Josh asked, then covered the phone and sneezed. "Sorry, what was that again?"

"Dykstra," Rubin said. "She's on the air every ten minutes pumping the blood test thing. The networks have picked it up. Even the **New York Times** is looking interested."

"Slow news week." He sneezed again.

"Yeah. So let's put our spin on this. I want you to do a sit-down with Jansen Worthy."

Josh looked surprised. "Going right to the top, aren't you? He's been anchoring a major news show longer than most people have been alive."

"It's called clout and credibility. He has enough of both to bury Dykstra. So go on his show and tell the voters about your personal and recent losses, that sort of thing."

"You want me to play the sympathy card."

"Hell, yes. You've lost a father, a mother, and a beloved aunt—"

Josh's sneeze sounded more like a laugh of disbelief.

"—and now this wannabe news bitch is doing the vulture thing with your life. Not satisfied with intruding on your grief, she's demanding that you prove what everybody already knows, and she's only doing it to hype up her flat ratings. She hasn't even waited for the test results to begin baying after you. Why? Because there won't be a story afterward. Now you know that elected officials are legitimate targets of interest to the media yada yada yada, but this is too much. If you can't make the interview good for a huge sympathy vote, you're no politician, and we both know you're a hell of a pol."

"How soon?"

"Tomorrow. Jansen is in Arizona on his ranch. He's agreed to fly with you to the ranch for an interview. The satellite relay stuff will be in place by noon."

"The ranch? Why not the governor's mansion?"

"Because this is personal," Rubin said patiently. "You're a grieving son, yada yada yada. Wear a dark sport jacket, plain cowboy boots, and jeans. Pale blue shirt, not western, just a shirt. When you're asked questions about your parents and aunt, pause a little, keep a stiff upper lip, and face the camera with manly emotional restraint. You know the drill. Any questions?"

"Just one."

"What?"

"I could have the blood results as soon as tomorrow. Is this charade really necessary?"

"I get you a freebie on the evening news with a powerful, sympathetic national institution, and you ask me if it's **necessary?**"

The governor sighed. "Sorry. Must be the fever."

"Take something for it. This is too important to blow. If you have the DNA results before the interview, give them to Jansen and let him shove them up Dykstra's ass. Then we can get on with something that matters, like winning votes."

Josh hung up and went to look for aspirin.

# 65

"HOW'S IT GOING?" CARLY ASKED DAN.

He didn't look up from either of the computers he had in front of him. "I'm getting there."

"Where's that?" She stood and stretched the kinks out of her back. She and Dan had been working for four hours already.

"To the end of the charity food chain."

"Is that supposed to mean something?"

"If it means what I think it does, somebody was hosing the Senator for about nine thousand a month since at least 1986. Eighteen thousand, really. Two separate payments, separate charities."

Carly pushed back from the most recent of the diagrams of people and circumstances and geography she was drawing. She felt like a spider on acid, spinning a crazed web.

"Why two separate payments? Why not one?" she asked.

"Federal law requires banks to report any transaction over ten thousand dollars. It's a way to slow down money laundering."

Carly started to ask another question.

"Gotcha," Dan said, his voice oozing satisfaction.

"What?" she asked, forgetting her own question.

"Two of the automatic monthly charitable contributions the Senator made were to a laundry. Nine thousand bucks in the charity accounts, but somehow the amount never gets recorded. The amount minus transfer fee goes on to an account in Aruba. No name. No number. No way of tracing who's getting fat. At least there's not supposed to be, but there always is. Otherwise no one could collect on the Aruba end."

She started to ask another question, stopped, and waited while Dan's fingers flew over the keyboard. There was no hesitation now. He was a hound on a hot scent, running flat out to overtake the prey. He typed in a final sequence of commands and sat back, waiting for the computer to run some names to ground.

"Looks like you've done that before," she said.

"That's what I do, chase black money. Charities are a particular favorite. It looks really tacky to investigate good intentions. Like asking your mother if she was a virgin when she got married."

Carly stayed with the part of the conversation that mattered to her. "Okay, you find black money. Then what happens?"

"Depends on what the client requested. Usually

there's a finder's fee, anywhere from twenty to forty percent of what's recovered."

"Recovered?"

"The ransom in a kidnap. Blackmail like this. Property stolen in such a way that the client has no recourse in law. Black money in a warlord's or **narcotraficante**'s account. That sort of thing."

"Is that legal?"

"Mostly."

"And when it isn't?"

"It isn't." Dan looked away from the line on the screen that showed how close the program was to being fully executed. "That a problem?"

"Um . . ."

He smiled. "I'm not talking civil penalties if I'm caught, Carolina May."

"You're talking 'climbing accidents'?" she asked.

"Yes."

She blew out a breath. "You go, um, climbing very often?"

"This was the first time since I quit working for Uncle Sam. Somebody else was supposed to make the physical connection, but her baby came a month early so I pinch-hit for her."

Carly opened her mouth. Closed it. "Does that happen often?"

"Early babies?"

"Pinch-hitting."

"No."

"Thank you, God."

Dan pulled her down onto his lap. "Does that mean you're not going to run screaming because I don't have a regular nine-to-five gig?"

She combed her fingers through his thick, dark hair. "Do I look like I'm running and screaming?"

His computer made an **I'm finished** sound.

Both of them looked at the screen.

"Who is this Pedro Moreno who has over two million bucks in a numbered account on Aruba?" Carly asked.

"Pete Moore. His real name, by the way. He just anglicized it to make life easier."

"Nine thousand a month?" Carly asked, remembering what Dan had said.

"Two payments of nine thousand each."

"That's not their wages, is it, Pete and Melissa?"

"According to the ranch records, Pete was paid three thousand a month and change. Melissa made about a thousand a month less."

"How do you know that?"

Dan shrugged. "Somehow the contents of the ranch computer ended up on my hard drive, and you never heard me say that."

"You're scary."

"Actually, a half-smart twelve-year-old could have hacked into the ranch computer. What's interesting is that at least one other charity fed 'contributions' into this same account. Minus three percent, of course."

"Three percent?"

"Transaction fee," Dan said dryly. "Once the amounts get into the high eight figures, the fee goes down. By the time you get to a billion, the transaction fee is usually one percent or even less."

She did the math and stared at him. "That's ten million dollars just to move money electronically from one place to the next," she said. "A little steep, don't you think?"

"Not if you have a dirty billion and get a clean nine hundred and ninety million back. Clean money that you're happy to pay taxes on and invest in legitimate enterprises because otherwise you'd have to hide all of it—in cash. At any given moment, there are trillions of black dollars zipping around the world, and every e-transaction takes a little bite of the overall pie."

"My head hurts."

"So think about what Pete Moore had on the Senator and/or the governor that would be worth eighteen thou a month to keep quiet."

"The governor, too?"

"According to the records, Josh had—and exercised—power of attorney for the Senator for the past four years. Unless the governor just let Pete do everything on the ranch bookkeeping, the governor had to know that about two hundred thousand bucks a year was going to questionable charities, so questionable that the Senator didn't even try to deduct them from his income tax payments."

"You're sure?"

"You want to see the tax returns?" Dan asked, his fingers poised over the keyboard.

"No. I don't even want to know you have them."

"Have what?"

"Ha ha." She twisted hair around her index finger. "So we're back where we started. Something that affected both father and son."

"At least we have a good reason for someone to kill Pete and Melissa. Blackmailers aren't real popular with their victims."

"But why kill the Moores now?" Carly asked. "Why not years ago, after Josh got the power of attorney? He must have known about the blackmail, or at least guessed that something was rotten in Denmark."

"Having power of attorney isn't the same as exercising it. He could have had a live-and-let-live attitude toward the Senator's expenses. It was, after all, the old man's money," Dan said. "Did you have any luck eliminating potential bastards who could have swapped places with the real Josh in Vietnam?"

"It sounds so bizarre when you say it right out. You only have to look at Josh to know he's the Senator's son."

"Yeah, but **which** son?"

"Too bad Melissa's dead. I'd ask her," Carly muttered.

"That reminds me," Dan said.

"What?"

"Somehow a file full of Melissa's family mementos found its way onto my hard drive."

"I can't hear a word you're saying. Print it out."

Smiling, Dan set up the printer, checked the paper, and went to work. As the computer spit out the first paper, Carly grabbed it and went to work.

"Both sides," Dan said.

"What?"

"I'm printing them the way I found them. A lot of the stuff had material on the back."

Carly nodded and went back to reading while the printer spit out paper at frightening speed.

Dan set up the last part of the file and turned to her. "What do you have?" he asked.

"A letter. The handwriting is . . . I'm getting used to it, okay?"

"What's the date?"

"November. Nineteen eighty-five." She flipped the paper over and saw the signature. "Betty Schaffer."

He connected the genealogical dots in his mind. "Susan Mullins's daughter by her husband, Doug Smith. Betty would have been closing in on forty when she wrote that. Wait, isn't that the year she killed herself?"

Carly didn't answer. She was concentrating on making sense of the jumbled, irregular handwriting.

Dan went to Carly's computer, searched old news files, and found the brief death notice in the obits. Betty Schaffer, née Smith, daughter of Susan Smith, née Mullins, had died on Christmas Eve, 1985. Recently divorced by husband. Reading between the lines, Betty had faced the family holiday with a load of booze, pills, and self-pity. Either she miscalculated the doses or she wanted out of her life. Whatever, she died. Survived by one daughter, Melissa Moore, née Schaffer. At the time of death, Betty had been living on welfare in a room on the wrong side of town. No religious services mentioned.

"Is that a suicide note?" Dan asked Carly.

"No. Betty's crowing to her daughter about the new 'source' she has. Fifteen thousand bucks. And there's more, a lot more. Betty is sending the key to Melissa for safekeeping."

Dan's eyebrows raised. He'd photographed the documents but he hadn't tried to read them. He had been in too much of a hurry to get out of the Moores' apartment before Carly caught him where he wasn't supposed to be.

"Do the blackmail payments go back that far?" Carly asked.

"Not quite. First one—at least in the account I cracked—was in '86. She died in '85. A few days after she put the bite on her 'source' for fifteen grand."

"Are you thinking what I'm thinking?" Carly asked.

"Blackmail can be a dangerous game. I'm betting she was helped into suicide. Backtracking Josh's whereabouts at the time is a job I'll leave for someone else."

Carly picked up the next sheet.

Dan leaned past her, grabbed the bottom half of the print pile, and started reading. When he was finished, he swapped for the sheets Carly was reading.

Other than a few disbelieving sounds from Carly, it was quiet.

Dan wasn't shocked. He'd spent quite a few years studying the underbelly of humanity. Without a word he started arranging the photos and documents in rough chronological order.

"I . . ." Carly cleared her throat. "Am I crazy or is there a vile kind of logic in these documents?"

"You're not crazy."

"Never again will I ask how people's lives get so screwed up." She blew out a breath and shook her head.

"Nobody starts out to end up the way they do."

"Just pieces of a puzzle, right?" she asked.

"Right. Let's begin with the piece called Susan Mullins," Dan said neutrally. He picked up one of the letters they had both read, but didn't look at it. "In 1941 Susan gave birth to Randal Mullins, called Randy, the Senator's bastard. The Senator had been shagging her, thinking she was of legal age. She wasn't. He dumped her when he found out, but kept her in drugs so she didn't care too much one way or the other."

"Lovely man."

"A real prince. Six years later she gets married. The guy is a drunk and an abuser. She sticks anyway. Her bastard by the Senator starts running away when he's seven, and usually ends up with Angus Snead." Dan paused, frowned. "Somehow, by the way Jim talked about the past, I always assumed Randy was his older cousin."

"Given the intimacy of the local gene pool, maybe he was. Wait a minute, let me refresh my memory." Carly flipped through the notebook she'd made and found the section marked Randal Mullins. "Randy grew up wild, hooky and sealed juvie record, hunting and trapping, poaching, public drunkenness, bar brawling, signed up for Vietnam, was a forward scout, several medals, killed in ambush in 1968."

"The same year that Josh Quintrell was injured," Dan said.

"Right. Over to you."

Dan looked back at the paper he was holding. "This is dated 1968. It's chaotic—obviously Susan was loaded when she wrote it—but the bottom line is that she truly believed she'd seen her son Randy in Taos."

"After he was dead?"

"Yes. What really knocked her sideways was when she approached him, looked him in the eyes, and started crying with happiness, he told her she was mistaken. Like she wouldn't recognize her own son. She started yelling and he just shook his head, said he was sorry for her loss, and walked away. It freaked her out."

"Understandable. And," Carly added, "it's likely that she shared her freaky experience with her good friend and fellow sex worker, Liza Quintrell, who apparently said something to her daughter, your mother."

"Likely, but not yet proved for a court of law."

"I know. Just one more strand of the circumstantial web."

Dan smiled. "You're spinning a beaut. Now we go

back and check the geography and make sure no one was out of town when we have them in town, and vice versa."

"I understood that. Does that make me certifiable?"

"No, what makes you certifiable is that you're enjoying this as much as I am, even though we both know that, rationally, there's a very good chance that a hype and booze hound might indeed mistake a blue-eyed half brother for a blue-eyed son who started making himself scarce when he was seven."

"I followed that, too. Now I'm worried." She smiled at him. "As long as I keep thinking of this as a game, it's fun. When I think of it as real . . ."

"Don't think of it that way," Dan said instantly. "Right now, it **is** a game. If we get to the point of going to the law, then it's not a game. We're not there yet. We might never be."

"A game. Right." She entered the date of the letter on the list she was keeping. There were other entries for the year. "That was the year Liza died. And Susan."

"No date on the letter itself?" Dan asked, leaning forward.

"No, just our assumption that she wrote the letter the same year Josh came back from Vietnam, where her son died. Maybe there's internal evidence in the letter itself." Frowning, Carly read the sprawling, jumbled lines again.

"Anything?"

"No. Wait. She mentions sneaking a picture of him the next day after he walked off."

Dan dived for the papers and went through them in a rush. "Baby pictures, kiddie pictures, teen pictures in front of various dead animals—really nice buck by the way—standard army photo, and one in town of a man feeding a parking meter."

Carly fished a magnifying glass out of her hip pocket and studied the image. "Same chin."

"What?"

"Same chin as Josh has. Same chin as the happy teenager standing next to the buck. I'd have to have more pictures to be certain—class books and such, but it looks like a younger Josh to me."

Dan flipped the piece of paper over. "August third, '68."

Carly swallowed. Hard. "She died two days later, Dan. So did Liza."

"And another sex worker. Collateral damage, no doubt." His voice was neutral but his eyes were bleak.

"What do you mean?" she asked.

"It's a military term for various things that get between you and your mission target."

Carly winced. "Things like people?"

"It happens." His eyes narrowed. The pattern was becoming clear, and it was uglier than most. "Where's the article on the triple murder?"

Wordlessly, she called up the article on the computer and turned the screen toward him.

"Crazed hippie, huh?" Dan said, reading through it again. "Slicing up whores in the name of God. I wonder if the three were killed together or if he killed them in various places and dragged them to the same scene."

"Does it matter?"

"Assume you're the impostor. Assume you were recognized. You kill that witness and anyone else the witness probably would have talked to. But you don't want it to appear planned, because that might make the cops curious, so you whack someone else and throw them into the mix."

Carly took a sharp breath.

"Then you find a big hippie who's too stoned to care, stuff some angel dust under his tongue, roll him around on the bodies, hand him the bloody knife, and disappear." From the tone of Dan's voice, he could have been reading out stops on a bus schedule. "By the time the PCP kicks in and the poor stoner races out into the night with the knife, he's way too far gone to be rational. Cops try to cuff him, he goes ballistic, cops pump seven bullets in him, and it's over. Too bad, how sad, shit happens. Case closed."

"This isn't feeling like a game anymore." Carly rubbed her arms where goose bumps had formed. "We're talking about a man who killed his own mother."

"Say the word and you're out of here."

She looked at Dan's level green eyes and knew he wanted her in a safe place. She wanted him there with her. "Will you go with me and leave this to the cops?"

"We don't have any proof that would make the cops want to take on the governor of New Mexico and a presidential contender. Everyone—everyone— who could prove anything is conveniently dead."

"Except Josh Quintrell. Or Randy. Or whoever the hell he is."

"Somehow, I don't see him lining up at the confessional," Dan said.

"So you're staying until we have something that will make the cops listen."

Dan nodded.

"So am I." She rubbed her arms again. "I don't like it, but I can't just blithely run off and leave a murderer sitting fat and happy. Especially one who's running for president."

Dan pulled her onto his lap and rubbed his cheek

against her hair. "That's one of the things I love about you, Carolina May, even though it can drive me crazy from time to time. You don't expect somebody with a badge and a gun to do all the work of civilizing the human beast."

"It's one of the things I love about you, too, even though I suspect it will drive me crazy from time to time." **Climbing accidents, for example.** "So what do we need to get the cops' attention?"

"Courtroom proof of the identity swap."

"MtDNA. That's why Winifred sicced Dykstra on the governor, to force him to be tested."

"Winifred didn't live at the ranch or even visit very often until after Sylvia had her accident. How would she know her nephew wasn't completely her nephew?"

Carly frowned. "Why else would she hate the governor so much? Why else would she have acted like the Castillo/Quintrell line ended with Sylvia? Why else was she working backward rather than forward with the Castillo family genealogical history?"

"I agree, but I don't see how we can prove it now. If Winifred could have proved it earlier, she would have. That's what matters. Proof. Courtroom variety."

"She didn't know about mtDNA until I came on the scene," Carly said unhappily.

"Don't go blaming yourself. You're the only innocent one around here."

Dan reached past Carly for more of the memento file. After a sigh, she picked up more papers. While both of them read, the fire crackled in the silence. When they were finished, she leaned back against his chest.

"I think summaries are more in your line of work than mine," she said.

"Betty Smith Schaffer died shortly after a blackmail attempt that might or might not have been successful," Dan said. "Her death was written off as suicide. She passed on the blackmail material to her daughter, Melissa, who had recently married an accountant who knew how to set up a laundry so the blackmail couldn't be traced back to them. They fleeced the Senator for almost twenty years to the tune of two hundred thousand a year, more or less."

"Nice retirement money."

"If you invest it wisely," Dan said dryly. "Interesting thing is, if this is the 'proof' of role-swapping Melissa had, it wouldn't have held up in court. Yet the Senator paid anyway."

"Because he didn't want Josh's identity to be questioned."

"What about military records?" Carly asked.

"If I'd been in the Senator's shoes, I'd have asked for all the military records of my brave Taos County boys, switched some pertinent dental, blood, and fingerprint records, and built a monument to the dead soldiers."

"Could the Senator get away with that?"

"Sure, as long as nobody looked at the records too closely. And why would they? People see what they expect to see. Nobody expected the Senator's son to be anything but what he said he was."

"A chip off the rotten old block."

Dan's smile wasn't pleasant. "Yeah. No wonder Mom was too frightened by the past to talk about it."

"Do you think she knows?"

"I—" He stopped abruptly and pulled the buzzing, vibrating cell phone out of his pocket. The caller was from Genedyne. "Duran here," he said into the phone. "What do you have for me?"

"Do you have a pen and paper," Cheryl said, "or do you trust your memory?"

"Both."

"All females share the same mtDNA, with a very minor variation in the fourth female. Perfectly normal. Nothing stays the same forever. And I went the whole nine yards on this one. The chance of these women not being from the same mtDNA line isn't worth mentioning. Probably within the same three- or four-generation group."

"Translation?" Dan asked, writing quickly on a tablet.

"Same grandmother or great-grandmother. As far as mtDNA goes, they could have been sisters. When you throw in the Y-DNA it turns out you have two sisters and two daughters."

Dan wrote quickly.

"The male sample you sent me has precisely the same Y-DNA as two of the female samples. Ergo, they're his daughter."

Dan's eyes narrowed. Not unexpected, but not nice. The Senator indeed had had a child with his daughter, and that child was Dan's mother.

"Got it," Dan said. "Is the second male sample done yet?"

"Just finished."

His pulse kicked. "And?"

"Definite match for mtDNA on mother's side and Y-DNA on father's side."

Dan couldn't believe what he'd just heard. "What? You're certain?"

"It's my job, sweetie. I'm certain. And considering the stature of the people involved, I'm **really** certain."

"Well, shit." He rubbed his eyes wearily. "Send me e-files of the tests on all subjects."

"Can I take a coffee break first? I've been working fourteen straight hours."

"Go ahead," Dan said. "And thanks."

He was talking to a dead phone. Cheryl had disconnected.

"You don't look happy," Carly said.

"I'm not. A bulldozer just drove through our beautiful circumstantial web and ripped it to atoms."

"What?"

"Josh Quintrell is Sylvia's son."

# 66

THE SOUND OF HELICOPTERS RATTLED THE SILENCE of the snowy pastures and penetrated through ancient adobe walls.

"World War III?" Carly asked sardonically.

Dan glanced away from his computer, where he was writing reports, and looked at her. She looked flat, exhausted, and altogether on the losing side of the war. He looked and felt the same way. **That will teach me to fall in love with a glittery chain of circumstantial evidence.**

"Probably the governor and the press corps heading for the ranch for the 'intimate' interview they've been promoting every fifteen minutes for the last four hours."

Carly grimaced. Dan's TV was small, but loud. She had heard every single word of every single promo for Jansen Worthy's exclusive interview with Governor Josh Quintrell at the home ranch, with hints of a breathtaking exclusive announcement, exclusively on this channel, exclusively for **you.**

"You're a masochist," she told Dan, gesturing at the TV.

"It helps to remind me of just how wrong circumstantial evidence can be. And it reinforces the roll of coincidence and randomness in everyday life." He shook his head. "Gotta admit, it's the first time my instinct for patterns has led me so far astray. Like to a whole different universe."

"I was with you every step of the way."

He smiled crookedly at her. "Best part of the trip."

His cell phone rang. He looked at the window and switched to message text.

**Open your e-mail, sweetie.**

"Anything interesting?"

"I'm guessing it's the Genedyne file of test results."

"Print them, okay?"

"Now who's the masochist?" he asked.

"Except for your mother's results, they're part of the history Winifred paid for."

Dan opened his e-mail and started printing stuff that looked like nothing he'd seen before. "If you can understand this, you can be a computer programmer."

"I'll leave that to you." She collected the tests results, labeled each with the name of the person.

Carly spread the charts out on the bed. The Senator and Josh shared the same Y-DNA to the limit of testing ability. He was the Senator's son. She pulled out the mtDNA for Sylvia and Josh, compared them, and sighed. A very slight variation in haplotype number, the kind of subtle, meaningless mutation that happened in the DNA of a germ cell.

"Well, damn," she muttered.

"Hoping Cheryl was wrong?" Dan asked.

"Yes."

"She wasn't."

Carly didn't bother to answer. She lined up Sylvia's and Winifred's results and checked the haplotype number. Exactly the same. The mutation in the mtDNA had occurred in Sylvia's germ cell and was passed to her son, where it stopped. Unless it was also passed on to her daughter, Liza . . .

After shifting papers quickly, Carly had Liza and Sylvia together. Their haplotype sequence was precisely the same.

"Okay," Carly muttered. "One got it and one didn't, which means the mutation was limited to one egg. So Diana won't have it."

Carly put the last chart in place and looked at it.

And looked again.

Then she started twisting a strand of hair around her finger.

"What is it?" Dan asked.

She shifted some of the sheets around without

answering. Then she picked up a yellow marking pen and began highlighting parts of each chart.

"Carly?"

"The haplotypes—"

"English, please," he cut in.

She looked up. "That's going to be tough. Like putting a computer program into English."

"Give it a try."

"Y-DNA, mtDNA, any DNA is just a series of sequences of compounds. The makeup and order of those compounds determines if you get a man, a woman, an elephant, or a guppy."

"Gotcha."

"Apparently there are a lot of nonsense sequences in germ cell DNA, sequences that don't appear to do anything to the final organism. Some of those nonsense sequences are called haplotypes. Every so often a mutation will occur when a sequence is being reproduced and you'll have two identical sequences where before you just had one. And if my genetics professor could hear me now, he'd be tearing out his hair with all the stuff I'm not mentioning."

"Keep skimming the surface," Dan said, smiling.

Carly blew out a frustrated breath. "The change in the sequence is passed along to the next generation. To way oversimplify, you have a haplotype 5 where you had a haplotype 4, that is, five repeats of a specific sequence instead of four, but nothing material changes in the organism that is born. It's a mutation that doesn't matter to anyone but geneticists. Still with me?"

"Just don't give me a pop quiz."

She narrowed her eyes. "Hey, you're the one who asked me to explain. I'm doing my best."

"I'm listening, Carolina May."

She looked at his intent, intensely green eyes and believed him. "The numbers going down the right-hand column on each page of the sheets are various mtDNA haplotype sequences. Winifred's and Sylvia's and Liza's are exactly the same through all haplotype sequences. The Senator's is very different, of course. He got his mtDNA from his own mother. Josh got his from Sylvia. See this number? Then this one?"

Dan leaned down to look at a highlighted number. "It's not the same."

"Right. All the other haplotype sequences are a dead match except for that one, which means there was a mutation in Sylvia's germ cell that was passed on to her son, Josh."

"What about Liza?"

"Nope. But your mother has the same mutation."

Dan looked at the sheets, absorbing the implications of the highlighted numbers. "Is that possible?"

"Anything's possible. But this one is about as

**probable** as two people having identical finger-prints."

"Not worth betting on."

"Not with my money."

"What do you need to sort this out?"

"I'd like to see if you have the same mutation."

"No problem." He punched up a familiar number on the cell phone. "Cheryl? Yeah, it all came through perfectly. Now we need mine for comparison." He winced at whatever she said. "Two pounds of really fine dark chocolate? A bottle of two-hundred-dollar champagne? Both. Right." He punched out.

"Bribery?" Carly asked, smiling.

"Grease makes the wheels go round."

"I'll get one of the test kits for you."

"No need." He went to his computer. "My genetic profile is already on record with the lab."

"Really? Why?"

"To make double-damn sure any remains that are found in some backwater are really mine."

"I don't like the sound of that."

"So far, so good. Gotta watch those climbing accidents, though." Dan's e-mail pinged. He opened the file and printed it. "Here you go. Without your highlighting it all looks like the same old same old to me."

Carly grabbed the paper and looked at it. And looked again. She checked the date on the file. It had been created three years ago.

"That's because it is," she said, frowning.

"What?"

"The same old same old." Carly put Dan's genetic profile down next to Josh's.

They were identical.

# EPILOGUE

CARLY SMILED AS SHE WORKED TO TRANSLATE A seventeenth-century Spanish document describing boundary markers on Castillo family common woodlands. Through a series of twists and turns that would have made Winifred grin, Diana Duran was now the legal owner of the Quintrell/Castillo lands, livestock, and buildings. At first Dan's mother had refused anything to do with the Senator's ranch. Then Dan had pointed out how much good would come if she turned the ranch into a safe place for children whose own homes were violent.

"Here it comes," Dan said.

Gus wandered in from Dan's kitchen, gnawing on a chicken wing. Garlic chicken, of course, and the house smelled like it.

Jansen Worthy's solemn face filled the TV screen at Dan's house. Slowly the camera pulled back. Behind him Governor Josh Quintrell, hands duly cuffed behind him, was being led by Taos County sheriff Mike Montoya to a waiting squad car. Whatever Jansen Worthy was saying was muted. Dan didn't need a media spinmeister to tell him what was happening.

Carly set aside the papers and sat next to Dan on the bed. Together they stared at the governor as he stopped to face the herd of reporters shoving microphones in his face. He stood tall, straight, and faced the camera directly. Wind ruffled his silver hair and his eyes were as clear and blue as high-country sky.

"It took two months of legal wrangling," Dan said, "but they finally got the perp walk."

"Told you they would," Gus said. He tossed the chicken bone in the trash and wiped his hand. "It's not often you arrest a sitting governor and presidential hopeful for assault with intent to kill—that would be on you, brother—impersonation of a rightful heir, and two counts of murder one."

"Murder?" Carly asked. "Which ones?"

"Melissa and Pete," Dan said. "I had a talk with Jim Snead as soon as I saw the identical gene results. We scouted Castillo Ridge, found where the sniper waited, where he went down to the wreck, finished off Melissa, and took a roundabout way to a car he'd left along the road. It was the same blind he used when he nailed me," Dan added. "When the ice wasn't enough to send the Moores' car over, he shot out a tire and the truck took a dive over the edge. The bullet took a bite out of the wheel rim as well. It's now Exhibit A for the prosecution."

Carly shivered. "If we hadn't gone for a walk in a graveyard, that could have been us at the bottom of the ravine and no one would have known."

Gus made a rough sound. "Don't tell Mom."

"Don't worry," Dan said.

"It doesn't seem real." Carly shook her head and stared at the man standing erect in front of the camera. He managed to look sad and confident at the same time, a man worn down by family deaths and a vindictive prosecutor. "He looks too . . . honest. A jury won't buy his guilt."

"They will when the medical examiner gives testimony that Melissa's broken neck wasn't due to the accident," Dan said.

Carly rubbed her eyes. "Then why does the governor look so confident?"

Dan lifted her onto his lap and tucked her head into its familiar niche under his chin. "He's got a great game face. But he's going to lose just the same."

The instant the governor opened his mouth to talk to the reporters, Dan turned on the sound.

**"I want to thank all the citizens who have written and called to tell me they are with me in my hour of trial."**

"I'm going to hurl," Carly said.

**"I'm sure that this foolish tangle of circum-stance and malice will come unraveled in a court of law."**

"Not a chance," Dan said. "No matter how good that murderer looks in a suit, he can't explain away the fact that his mtDNA and mine are different, and he sent mine to Genedyne under his name. He's no more the real Josh Quintrell than I am."

Gus smiled slightly. "I have to say, bro, your friends at the St. Kilda Society are ring-tailed terrors when it comes to digging up bodies."

"Mr. Steele takes a real hard line when someone shoots at one of his consulting team," Dan said with a certain grim satisfaction. "Especially when said shooter is being financed in large part by laundered Sandoval money. Steele hates **narcotraficantes**."

Gus straightened. "Now that's a story—"

"No," Dan cut in swiftly. "You have to live here. Settle for an inside exclusive on the governor's dual identity and murderous life. Let some East Coast hotshot break the story about the governor's laundered campaign money."

On-screen, the governor was tucked into the squad car by Sheriff Montoya. The way the sheriff closed the door said he didn't expect to be turning loose his prisoner anytime soon.

Dan turned off the TV. He'd seen all he had to. Randal Mullins, a.k.a. Josh Quintrell, was history.

"So what's the latest news you called me over to hear?" Gus asked.

"That's your cue," Dan said to Carly.

She reached behind him and pulled out a file that was as thick as Dan's thumb. Thicker, actually. The cover was stamped ST. KILDA CONSULTING. She riffled through the file rapidly.

Gus's eyes glazed over when he saw the stream of intricate color charts, graphs, numbers, and the like. "If I grovel, will you give me a summary?"

Dan snickered. "I said the same thing."

"You didn't grovel," she said.

"You didn't complain," Dan said.

She gave him a sidelong look and a very female smile.

Gus shuffled his feet.

"Okay," Carly said. "The year is 1968, the place is Vietnam. Randal Mullins is working as a forward scout aiding the outfit Josh Quintrell is in. There's an ambush. Everybody dies but Randal Mullins."

"According to the autopsy St. Kilda performed on the remains that were buried as Randal Mullins, the death wound was one shot to the back of the head from a rifle," Dan added. "Very close range. Execution style. The remains, by the way, have the Senator's Y-DNA and Sylvia's mtDNA. The dead man was the real Josh Quintrell."

"Are you saying that Randy killed Josh Quintrell in Vietnam?" Gus asked.

"Probably, but we can't prove it," Dan said. "All we can prove is that there was an ambush and a wounded man wearing Josh Quintrell's dog tags and suffering partial memory loss was the only survivor. A heavily mutilated corpse wearing Randy Mullins's dog tags was returned to the U.S. and buried in a Taos County graveyard."

Carly pulled a list of dates out of the file. "Senator Quintrell flew to the military hospital to see his wounded son, stayed overnight, and flew back to D.C. Two months later, Josh Quintrell came home to the ranch to recuperate. A few weeks after that, Susan Mullins sees her son in town. Her dead son, who claims he isn't her son at all. She tells her friend, Liza Quintrell, that Randy is calling himself Josh and pretends not to recognize his own mother. Two days later, three prostitutes are stabbed and mutilated by a hippie on angel dust."

Dan watched the car on the TV drive away and said, "A recent reevaluation of the crime scene records and autopsies indicates that the women were killed in different places and carried to the place where they were discovered. The hippie either tripped over them or was given the murder weapon and pushed into the scene. Either way, they were all together and the hippie took the fall for the deaths."

"Liza and Susan," Gus said.

Dan nodded.

"Do you realize," Gus said, "that if what we think is true, the man cold-bloodedly murdered his own mother along with two other women, and then dressed the scene so that it looked like they were all killed at once by some crazed hippie?"

"He also killed his half brother in Vietnam," Dan said. "But unless the governor confesses, we can't nail him for those deaths."

"Jesus, Joseph, and Mary," Gus said heavily, shaking his head. "It's hard to believe that someone you know . . ."

"It gets worse," Dan said.

Carly took his hand, squeezed it, and went on with the list. "Again, unless the governor confesses, we can't prove that he blackmailed the Senator into going along with the identity-swap scheme, but we think he did."

"Blackmail? With what?"

"The Senator had an incestuous relationship with Liza," Dan said neutrally.

Gus's jaw dropped. "Can you prove it?"

"Yes, but Mom will be the one to suffer."

"I don't see— Christ, you're not saying—"

"The Senator is Mom's genetic father," Dan

said. "Liza is her genetic mother. You do the math."

Gus pulled over a folding chair and sank into it.

"Once Randy was accepted as Josh, things quieted down for a time on the murder front," Carly said, reading from the list in front of her. "Then Betty Smith, Randy's half sister, ran out of money. Her husband had divorced her, she was turning tricks for small change, and decided to try a bit of blackmail."

"Over the father-daughter incest?" Gus asked.

"No," Dan said. "Her mother, Susan, had written down what happened when Randy/Josh claimed not to recognize her and mailed everything to her daughter. Betty sat on it for years, then got drunk enough or broke enough to make blackmail look easy."

"And?" Gus asked.

"She committed suicide a few days later," Carly said. "It could have been the Senator who did it. It could have been the governor. Both of them had a lot to lose. Or it could have been just suicide. We'll never know unless the governor feels chatty."

"Suicide, huh?" Gus said. "Convenient."

"Oh, yeah," Dan said. "Death has been a real convenient buddy to the governor. Again, nothing we can prove. What we can prove is that a few months later, the Senator began making contributions to a lot of charities. Two of those charities were a laundry. The proceeds ended up in a numbered account in Aruba that was traced to Pedro Moreno."

"So?"

"Pedro is Pete Moore," Carly said. "Melissa had an asset her mother didn't—she'd married an accountant who knew how to hide money. So when she inherited Betty's mementos, she waited a year and then took up where Betty left off."

"But the Moores were smart enough to make sure the Senator never knew who was hosing him," Dan added. "Somehow the governor found out, probably when he took over the ranch accounts after the Senator died." Dan shrugged. "I cracked the laundry and got Pete's name."

"How did you do that?" Gus asked.

"Do what?" Carly and Dan said at once.

Gus opened his mouth, closed it, and listened.

"I'm sure the governor has access to forensic accountants," Dan said, "so he could have found out who was blackmailing him. Again, not provable without the governor's confession. I'm not holding my breath for that one."

"The happy blackmail lasted until Pete and Melissa died in a car accident," Carly said.

"But it wasn't an accident," Gus said.

"No," Dan said. "Did I mention that Randy Mullins was a damn good sniper in Vietnam?"

"I have a headache," Gus said, rubbing the back of his neck.

"So did I," Dan said, touching the place where a bullet had trimmed his hairline a little too close. "That's how the governor got the blood he sent to Genedyne to prove he had Castillo mtDNA. He knocked me down with a bullet, waited for me to crawl off with Carly's help, and then he picked up a sample where I'd bled into the snow."

"I'll bet he wishes now that he'd killed you," Gus said.

Dan's smile was all teeth. "Yeah, I'll bet he does. But at the time it looked too risky. A little blood on the snow from a poacher is no biggie. A dead body requires a lot more police work."

"So how did you catch him?" Gus said.

Dan squeezed Carly's hand, silently asking her to let him be the one to pick out the truths and half-truths for his brother. "Carly spotted a slight difference in the mtDNA profile between Mom and Sylvia. That was the bomb that blew the governor's murderous game to smithereens."

"What was?" Gus asked impatiently.

"Genetically, the governor is carrying the same mtDNA as Melissa. Susan Mullins's mtDNA."

"So that's why you had her exhumed. Why didn't you have Liza exhumed at the same time? Was it Mom?"

"There wasn't any need to put her through it," Dan said, a half-truth if ever one had been spoken. What he didn't say was that he'd done some partial exhumations one frozen night in the Quintrell graveyard. "Given the nuptial agreement the Senator signed, his bastard child has no more legal right to the Quintrell ranch than your average Martian."

"How did Genedyne get a sample of the Senator? I sure can't see the governor agreeing to it."

"You'll have to ask St. Kilda Consulting," Dan said without a pause.

"Will they tell me?"

"Doubt it."

"Genes aside," Carly said quickly, not wanting Gus to look too closely at the genetic histories, "St. Kilda Consulting also uncovered numerous discrepancies in various military and school records relating to Randy and Josh, as well as campaign money from illegal sources for both the Senator and the governor, and some land swaps that benefited the Quintrells more than the citizens of New Mexico or the United States."

Gus's eyebrows climbed.

"Once you have a reason to go looking, you can find some incredible things in the records," Carly said.

"St. Kilda Consulting again," Gus said, looking at his brother like he hadn't seen him before. "I'd love to do a story on—"

"No," Dan cut in. "The people who matter already know. The rest watch the six o'clock news."

Gus looked at the file in Carly's hand. "I don't suppose I could take that with me?"

"Sorry," Dan said. "Background only. Deep background. But you'll find that Sheriff Montoya will be real cooperative. And if he isn't, let me know."

There was a knock on the front door.

"I'll get it," Gus said, winking at Dan with Carly on his lap. "You look too comfortable to disturb."

Dan tightened his arms around Carly. "You ready for this?" he whispered.

"For you, always."

"For Mom. I'm guessing it's her knocking at the door. She knows the report came in today."

"Do you want me to disappear?" Carly asked.

"Not unless you want to."

Carly kissed his jawline. "Only if you want me to."

He tipped her chin up and looked into her eyes. "Stay with me, Carolina May."

Before she could say anything, Diana and John walked into the bedroom. Diana looked worn yet somehow stronger. John looked like a man protecting his woman.

Dan stood up, taking Carly with him so that they could stand side by side. By tacit agreement, he hadn't mentioned the Senator's name or his scattered children in his mother's presence. Tonight, she had asked to see him.

To talk about the Senator.

"Where's Gus?" Dan asked.

"I told him to go home," John said. He looked at Carly.

"She's family," Dan said simply. "She stays with me."

Diana smiled, sad and beautiful. "So you know," she said to both Dan and Carly.

"Yes," Dan said. "Does Dad?"

Instead of answering, John looked searchingly at Dan. "Thank you."

"For what?" Dan asked.

"Still calling me Dad."

"Sperm donors make babies," Dan said, stepping forward to hug John hard. "Fathers raise them. That makes you my father in every way that matters."

"I should have told you," Diana said, tears running down her cheeks. "But I couldn't. John knew I was pregnant when we married, but he didn't know who the father was or any of the rest. I didn't know how to tell him. Or you. I felt . . . **unclean**."

"Hush," Dan said, scooping his mother up in a big hug. "Telling your son that his father, grandfather,

and great-grandfather were one and the same incestuous son of a bitch would be a hard thing to do."

Diana clung to Dan. "He—the Senator—"

"You don't have to tell me anything, ever," Dan
said fiercely. "It's enough to know that somebody as
good and clean and loving as you came out of the
hell that man created." He kissed her and set her
gently on her feet. "That's all that matters. The
person you are, not what he was."

"I was afraid that knowing, that if I told you, it
would destroy you," she said simply. "It almost
destroyed me." She looked up at John and smiled.
"John's love saved me."

"You saved yourself," John said, smiling. "You let
me love you." Then his smile faded. "I'm glad the
Senator is dead. I'd hate to spend the rest of my life
in jail for killing him."

Something savage flared in Dan's eyes. "You
wouldn't have had the chance."

Diana tugged at her husband's shirt. "Come, love.
It's time to leave them alone so that he can ask—
that is, it's time to go home."

"It is?" John asked, surprised. "But I thought you
wanted—"

"To go home," Diana interrupted firmly. She
kissed Dan, hugged Carly, and said to her son, "Let
me know right away."

Puzzled, Carly watched Diana hurry her husband

out of the house. When Dan closed the door behind his parents, she asked, "Was it something I said?"

Dan's smile reminded Carly of just how much Diana's son he was. "No, it's something I'm supposed to say. To you. My mother, the gentle, loving **bruja,** already knows what I'm going to ask you."

"About what?"

"Children. Marriage. I'd prefer marriage first, but I'm open to sexual bribery."

Carly stared at him with wide, smoky gold eyes. "I've always wanted it that way, too."

"Sexual bribery?"

She laughed and stepped into his open arms. "Marriage before children. But sexual bribery works," she added, nibbling along his chin. "As long as you're the one doing the bribing."

"You sure?"

"About your brand of bribery? Absolutely."

"No. About marriage." Though he was smiling at her, his eyes were serious, hungry, waiting.

"That, too," Carly said.

He kept waiting.

"That's a yes on my side," she said, touching the faint scar where he'd been shot. "What about your side?"

"Oh, yes."

His cell phone rang. He took it out and looked at the caller ID: St. Kilda Consulting.

Carly stopped tasting Dan's neck long enough to ask, "Who is it?"

"Wrong number," he said, tossing the phone across the room.

The phone kept ringing.

Neither of them noticed.